The pass

One

SEDUCTIVE
SHEIKH

OLIVIA GATES
FIONA McARTHUR
MEREDITH WEBBER

One Night with

COLLECTION

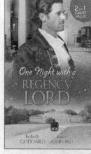

One Night with a REGENCY LORD

Isobel GODDARD
Janice ASHFORD

February 2015

One Night with Her BROODING BOSS

Susan STEPHENS
Cathy WILLIAMS
Red GARNIER

February 2015

One Night with a SEDUCTIVE SHEIKH

Olivia GATES
Fiona McARTHUR
Meredith WEBBER

February 2015

One Night with a TEMPTING PLAYBOY

Leanne BANKS
Alison ROBERTS
Marie FERRARELLA

February 2015

One Night with a GORGEOUS GREEK

Sarah MORGAN
Lucy MONROE
Chantelle SHAW

March 2015

One Night with a RED-HOT RANCHER

Diana PALMER
Charlene SANDS
Donna ALWARD

March 2015

One Night with a
SEDUCTIVE
SHEIKH

OLIVIA GATES
FIONA McARTHUR
MEREDITH WEBBER

MILLS
BOON

Published in Great Britain 2015
by Mills & Boon, an imprint of Harlequin (UK) Limited,
Eton House, 18-24 Paradise Road, Richmond, Surrey, TW9 1SR

ONE NIGHT WITH A SEDUCTIVE SHEIKH
© 2015 Harlequin Books S.A.

The Sheikh's Redemption © 2012 Olivia Gates
Falling for the Sheikh She Shouldn't © 2012 Fiona McArthur
The Sheikh and the Surrogate Mum © 2012 Meredith Webber

ISBN: 978-0-263-25365-8

012-0215

THE SHEIKH'S REDEMPTION

OLIVIA GATES

Olivia Gates has always pursued creative passions—singing and many handicrafts. She still does, but only one of her passions grew gratifying enough, consuming enough, to become an ongoing career—writing.

She is most fulfilled when she is creating worlds and conflicts for her characters, then exploring and untangling them bit by bit, sharing her protagonists' every heart-wrenching heartache and hope, their every heart-pounding doubt and trial, until she leads them to an indisputably earned and gloriously satisfying happy ending.

When she's not writing, she is a doctor, a wife to her own alpha male and a mother to one brilliant girl and one demanding Angora cat. Visit Olivia at www.oliviagates.com.

To my mum.
The most courageous, persevering and
accomplished woman I know.
Thank you for being you.

Prologue

Twenty-four years ago

The slap fell on Haidar's face, stinging it on fire.

Before he could gasp, another fell on his other cheek, harder, backhanded this time. A ring encrusted in precious stones dragged a ragged line of pain into his flesh.

Disoriented, he heard a crack of thunder as tears misted his sight. Admonishments boomed again as more slaps tossed Haidar's head from side to side. One finally shattered his balance, sent him crashing to his knees. Tears singed the fresh cut like a harsh antiseptic, mingling with the blood.

A tranquil voice broke over him. "Shed more tears, Haidar, and I'll have you thrown in the dungeon. For a week."

He swallowed, stared up at the person he loved most in life, incomprehension paralyzing him.

Why was she *doing* this?

His mother had never laid a hand on him. He'd never even gotten the knuckle raps or ear twists his twin, Jalal, drove her to reward his mischief with. He was her favorite. She told him so, showed him her esteem and preference in every way.

But there *had* been times lately when she'd been displeased with him, when he'd done nothing wrong. Actually, when he'd done something praiseworthy. It had bewildered him. Still, nothing could have prepared him for her out-of-the-blue, ice-cold fury just when he'd expected her to shower him with approval.

She stared down from her majestic height, looking as he'd always imagined a goddess of myth would, her eyes arctic. "Don't compound your stupidity with whimpering. Stand up and take your punishment like your twin always does—with dignity and courage."

Haidar almost blurted out that it was Jalal—*and* their cousin Rashid—who deserved the punishment. The "experiment" he'd warned them against and had refused to take part in had caused the fire that had consumed a whole chamber in the palace and ruined his and Jalal's tenth birthday party.

Being habitually wild and reckless, Jalal and Rashid had long depleted their second chances with their elders. Their punishment would have been severe. Being the one with a track record of caution and commitment, his reserve of leniency was intact. So he'd stepped forward as the accidental culprit.

Just when his confession had garnered what he'd expected from his and Jalal's father and Rashid's guardian—surprise followed by acceptance of his explanation and dismissal of the whole debacle—his mother had walked up to him.

Her eyes had told him she knew what had really happened, and why he'd stepped forward. He'd expected admiration to follow the shrewdness that made him feel she could read his slightest thought. What had followed were the slaps that hadn't stopped even when her husband, the king of Zohayd, had ordered her to cease.

Haidar rose and lifted a trembling hand to the sticky warmth oozing across his left cheekbone. She swatted it away.

OLIVIA GATES 9

"Now beg your twin's and cousin's forgiveness for being slow in coming clean about your thoughtless transgression, almost causing them to be punished in your stead."

Disbelief numbed him, chagrin seared his chest. It was one thing to take punishment for them, another to apologize *to* them, and in front of everyone present, relatives, servants… *girls!*

His mother clamped his face in a vicious grip, her long nails digging into his wound. *"Do it."*

She released him with a shove, made him stumble around to face Jalal and Rashid. They were staring at their feet, faces red, chests heaving.

"Jalal, Rashid, look at Haidar." His mother now spoke as Queen Sondoss of Zohayd, her voice clear and commanding, carrying to the whole ballroom. "Don't spare him the disgrace of groveling for your forgiveness in front of everyone."

Jalal's and Rashid's gazes wavered up to her before turning to him, apology and contrition blazing in their eyes.

His mother prodded him with a head whack. "Tell them you're sorry, that you'll *never* do anything like this again."

Burning with mortification, he looked into his twin's eyes, then into his distant cousin and best friend's, and repeated her words.

"I didn't do it!"

Haidar blurted the words out as his mother finished dressing his wound. Now that they were in the privacy of her chambers, he had to exonerate himself, if only in her eyes.

Her smile was filled with pride and love as she kissed the injury she'd inflicted. "I know." So he'd been right! "I know everything. Certainly about you and Jalal and that rascal Rashid."

His confusion deepened. "Then…*why?*"

She cupped his cheek tenderly. "It was a lesson, Haidar.

I wanted to show you that even your twin and best friend wouldn't say a word to spare you. Now you know that no one deserves your intervention or sacrifice. Now you know to trust no one. Most important, you know what humiliation feels like, and you'll always do anything you must to never suffer it again."

His head spun at her explanations, their implications.

He didn't want to believe her, but—she was always right. Was she about this, too?

She came down beside him, hugged him. "You're the only true part of me and I'll do anything so that you never get hurt, so that you become the man who will get everything you deserve. This world at your feet. Do you understand why I had to hurt you?"

Shaken by the new perspective she'd shown him, he nodded. Mainly because he wanted to get away, to think.

She stroked his hair and crooned, "That's my boy."

Eight years ago

"You're just like Mother."

Haidar flinched as if from a teeth-loosening slap.

Jalal was twisting the knife that had been embedded in his chest ever since they'd been old enough to realize what their mother was. What she was called. The Demon Queen.

To Haidar's heartache, no matter his personal feelings for her, he'd been forced to concede the title had been well earned.

While his mother possessed unearthly beauty and breathtaking intelligence and talents, she wielded her endowments like lethal weapons. She flaunted being *unpolluted* by the foolish weakness of benevolence. Instead of using her blessings to gain allies, she collected cowed servants and cohorts. And she relished making enemies, the first of which being her own husband.

If it weren't for her fierce love for her sons, or for him mainly and to a lesser degree, for Jalal, he would have doubted she was human at all.

But what had always tormented Haidar was that the older he got, the more he realized what a "true part" of her he was. He'd felt the taint of her temperament, the chronic disease of her traits spreading inside him. He'd lived in fear that they'd one day obliterate his decent and compassionate components.

It was ironic that Jalal had thrown that similarity in his face now, when he'd been feeling his mother's shadow recede, her legacy loosening its noose from around his thoughts and inclinations. Ever since he'd met Roxanne…

"I take it back." Jalal, the twin who resembled him the least of probably anyone in the world, shook his head in disgust. "You're worse than her. And *that* I didn't think was possible."

"You talk as if she's a monster."

They'd never spoken this openly about their mother. They'd been speaking less and less about anything at all.

Jalal shrugged, the movement nonchalant but eloquent with leashed force. A reminder that though they were similar in size and strength, Jalal was the…physical one.

"And I love her nonetheless. But that's the unreasoning affection a mother wrings from her child. You don't get the same leniency. Not on *this*. This is one instance where I cannot, *will* not, rationalize or forgive your heartlessness."

Unable to deal with his twin's disapproval any better than he ever had, he let the fury and suspicion that had brought him to this confrontation take over. "So this is your strategy? Like they say in Azmahar, 'Yell accusations lest your opponent beats you'?"

"It's you who are resorting to 'Hit and weep, preempt and cry foul.'"

Jalal's derision scraped his already raw nerves. "I never suspected you'd be such a sore loser when Roxanne chose me."

Jalal snorted, his eyes smoldering like black ice. "You mean when she was manipulated by you. *Conned* by you."

Haidar suppressed another spurt of indignation, the frost at his core resurfacing. "Can't find a more realistic excuse for trying to steal her from me? We both know I can get any woman I want without even trying, no manipulation involved."

"You couldn't have gotten Roxanne without it. She saw you for the ice-cold fish that you are that first night. It must have taken some Academy Award–winning acting to create the fictional character that she fell for."

Haidar had never resorted to violence, not even while growing up among an abundance of male-only relatives who relished rough…resolutions. He'd always suppressed his temper, used cold deliberation to outmaneuver them. Now he wanted to smash in Jalal's well-arranged face.

He gritted down on the urge. "The fact remains—she's *mine*."

"And you have been treating her like property. Worse, like a dirty secret, making her hide your intimacies from even her mother, forcing her to watch you flaunt the other women 'you have without even trying' in public. You told her they're decoys to draw suspicion away from her, right? It must be killing her, even if she believes your self-serving lies. I can't imagine what it would do to her if she knew you'd been playing her from the start, that she's just another source to feed your monstrous ego."

Haidar vibrated with a charge that seemed as if it would burst his every cell if it wasn't released. "And you know all about her supposed turmoil because you're her selfless confidant, right? And you want to take your so-called friendship from your squash dates into her bed. Well, hard luck. That's where I am. Constantly."

Jalal's snarl felt like an uppercut. "Very gentlemanly of you, to kiss and tell."

"No need for evasions since you know we're intimate. And still you try to take her away from me."

"You don't even want her," Jalal hissed. "You seduced her to beat me. She's just a pawn in another of your power games."

"You were the one who started *that* game, as you've conveniently forgotten."

"I forgot about that silly bet in five minutes. But you took it like you take everything, with obsessive competition. You went all out to entrap her."

"And you're out to save her from monstrous me? You're admitting you want her for yourself?"

Jalal's jaw hardened. "I won't let you use her anymore."

Rage blotched Haidar's vision. He wanted to pulverize Jalal's convictions. Arguments and defenses pummeled his mind. Then he opened his mouth and something from the repertoire of his lifelong rivalry with his closest yet furthest person came out.

A taunt. "How are you going to stop me?"

Jalal shot him a lethal glance. "I'll tell her everything."

His head almost burst.

Out of the rants clanging there, he snarled only "Good luck."

If he'd thought he'd seen antipathy in his twin's eyes before, he was wrong. *This* was the real thing. "Nothing good can come of this. You're not only like Mother—you inherited the worst of both sides of our families. You're manipulative and jealous, cold and controlling, and you have to win no matter the cost. It's time I exposed your true face to her."

Haidar's blood charred with the futility of watching this train wreck. "There's one hitch in that plan. If you do, it won't only be my face she won't want to see again, but yours, too."

"I'm okay with losing Roxanne, as long as you lose her, too."

The detonation of fury and frustration shattered his brakes. "If you tell her, Jalal, never show me *your* face again."

Bleakness spread in Jalal's eyes. "I'm okay with that, too."

A door closed, aborting the salvo of reckless bitterness he would have volleyed at his twin's intention.

Roxanne.

As she walked into the sitting room, his blood heated, his breath shortened. Her effect on him deepened with every exposure. Even when he *had* thought theirs would be a mutually satisfying liaison that would end when his fascination dissipated. Until her, he hadn't suspected himself capable of attaining such heights of emotion, plumbing such depths of passion.

She was fire made flesh, incandescent in beauty, tempestuous in spirit, consuming in power. And she was his.

He had to prove it, know it, once and for all.

The fear that she had feelings for Jalal had been compromising his sanity. His mother's passing comment about how Roxanne and Jalal shared so much had colored his view of their deepening closeness. But dread had taken root when he'd realized Roxanne had revealed the essence of her self to Jalal but not him. That had snapped his restraint, forced him to have this confrontation with both of them.

Jalal had made his position clear.

But it wouldn't matter, not if she chose *him*. As she had to.

He tried to get confirmation from the hunger that always ignited in her eyes at the sight of him. But for the second she spared him the touch of her focus, her eyes were blank. Then they swept to Jalal.

Haidar pounced on her, his fingers digging into her flesh, almost vicious in their urgency, his heart thundering. "Tell Jalal that he can't come between us no matter what he does or says. Tell him that you're mine."

Her face became a canvas of stupefaction. Then it set in hardness, her eyes becoming emerald icicles. She knocked his hands off as if they soiled her. "That's why you so impera-tively demanded I drop everything? How creepy can you get?"

It was his turn to gape. "Creepy? And this *is* imperative. I've sensed Jalal developing…misconceptions about you. I had to nip them in the bud."

Her eyes narrowed into lasers of anger and disgust. "I don't care what you 'sensed.' You don't get to summon me as if I'm one of your lackeys, and you can't trick me into a confronta-tion where you go all territorial on me and demand I parrot back what you say. You're the one who's under the miscon-ception that you have any claim to me."

His heart slowed to an excruciating thud, the pillars of his mind shuddering. "I have a claim. The one you gave me when you came to my bed, when you said you love me."

"You do remember *when* I said it, don't you?" When he'd been arousing her to insanity and driving her to shattering or-gasms. "But thanks for bringing things to a head. I'm going back to the States, and I was debating how to say goodbye. You men always take a woman walking away as a blow to your sexual ego, and it gets messy. I was worried that it would get extra messy with you, being the Prince of Two Kingdoms with an ego the size of both."

His shook his head, as if from too many blows. "Stop it."

She gave a careless shrug. "Sure, let's do stop it. You were the best candidate for the exotic fling I wanted to have while living here. But since I decided to move back to the States, I knew I had to end it with you. I have needs, as you know, and no matter how good in bed you are, I'm not about to wait until you drop by to satisfy them. I have to find a new regu-larly available stud. Or three. But a word of advice—don't pull that territorial crap on *your* new women. It's really off-putting. And it makes me unable to say goodbye with any goodwill. Now that I know what kind of power you imagined you had over me, I'm so turned off I don't want to ever see or hear from you again."

He watched her turn around, walk in measured steps out of the room.

In seconds the penthouse door closed with a muted thud, the very sound of rejection, of humiliation.

From the end of a collapsing tunnel he heard a macabre distortion of Jalal's voice. "What do you know? She has sharper instincts than I gave her credit for, took you only as seriously as you took her. Seems I shouldn't have worried about her."

He looked at Jalal through what felt like a stranger's eyes. "You should worry about yourself. If you ever show me your face again."

The twin he barely recognized now looked back at him with the same deadness. "Don't worry. I think it's time I detoxified my life of your presence."

Haidar stared into nothingness long after Jalal had disappeared. It wasn't supposed to happen this way.

Jalal should have told him he'd never trespass on the sanctity of his relationship with his woman. Roxanne should have denounced his doubts as ludicrous.

He should have had his twin back and his lover forever.

Those he'd thought closest to him shouldn't have walked away from him. But they had.

Trust no one.

His mother's words reverberated in his head. She'd been right.

He'd ignored her wisdom at a cost he might not survive.

Never again.

One

It wasn't every day a man was offered a throne.

When that man was Haidar, it should have been a matter of never.

But the people of Azmahar—at least, the clans that made up a good percentage of the kingdom's population—had offered just that.

They'd sent their best-spoken representatives to demand, cajole, *plead* for him to be their candidate in the race for the vacant throne of Azmahar. He'd thought they were kidding.

He'd kept his straightest face on to match their earnest efforts, pretending to accept, to brainstorm his campaign and the policy direction for a kingdom that was coming apart at the seams.

When he'd realized they were serious—*then* he'd gotten angry.

Were they out of their minds, offering him the throne of the kingdom that his closest maternal kin had almost destroyed, and his paternal ones had just dealt the killing blow? Who in

Azmahar would want him to set foot there again, let alone rule the damn place?

They'd insisted they represented those who saw him as the savior Azmahar needed.

One thing Haidar had never imagined himself as was a savior. It was a genetic impossibility.

How could he be a savior when he was demon spawn?

According to his estranged twin, he amalgamated the worst of his colorful gene pool in a new brand of bad. His recruiters had countered that he mixed the best of the lofty bloodlines running through his veins, would be Azmahar's perfect king.

"King Haidar ben Atef Aal Shalaan."

He tried the words out loud.

They sounded like a premium load of bull. Not only the "king" part. The names themselves sounded—*felt*—like lies. They no longer felt as if they indicated him. *Belonged* to him.

Had they ever?

He wasn't an Aal Shalaan, after all. Not a real one like his older brothers. Without the incontrovertible proof of their heritage stamped all over Jalal, he'd bet cries would have risen that *he* didn't belong to King Atef. From all evidence, he belonged, flesh, blood and spirit, to the Aal Munsoori family. To his mother. The Demon Queen.

The *ex*–Demon Queen.

Too bad he could never be ex–demon spawn.

His mother had besieged him from birth with her fear that her abhorred enemy, the Aal Shalaans, starting with her husband and his older sons, would taint him, the "true part" of her. She'd made sure they had no part of him. Starting with his name.

From the moment she'd laid eyes on her newborn sons, she'd seen that he was the one who was a replica of her, hadn't bothered thinking of a name for his twin. Their father had named Jalal, proclaiming him the "grandeur" of the Aal Shalaans.

Jalal was doing a bang-up job proving their father's ambitious claims right.

She'd named *him*. Haidar, the lion, one type of king. She'd been plotting to make him one that far back. When she'd known it was impossible. Through non-insurrectionist means, that was.

As a princess of Azmahar, she'd entered into the marriage of state with the king of Zohayd knowing her half-Azmaharian sons would not be in line to the throne. As per succession rules, only purely Zohaydan princes could play the game of thrones.

So she'd plotted, apparently from day one, to take Zohayd apart, then put it back together with herself in charge. She would have then been able to dictate new laws that would make her sons the only ones eligible for the throne, with him being first in line.

Two years after her conspiracy had been discovered and aborted, he still had moments when denial choked him up.

She could have caused a war. She would have, gladly, if it had gained her her objective.

She'd stolen the Pride of Zohayd jewels that conferred the right to rule the kingdom. She'd planned to give them to Prince Yusuf Aal Waaked, ruling prince of Ossaylan, so that he could dethrone her husband and claim the throne. Having only a daughter and being unable to sire another child, he would have named *her* sons his successors.

Haidar imagined she would have gone all black widow on Yusuf right after his sitting on the throne in the *joloos*, intimidated her brother—the newly abdicated king of Azmahar—into abdicating then, and put *him,* her firstborn by seven minutes, on the throne of a new superkingdom comprising Zohayd, Azmahar and Ossaylan.

She'd had such heartfelt convictions for such a heartlessly ambitious plan. When he'd pleaded with her to tell him where she'd hidden the jewels, to save Zohayd from chaos and herself from a traitor's fate, she'd calmly, *lovingly,* stated those convictions as facts.

After heavy initial damage, her plans were for the ultimate good. For who better than he to unite these kingdoms, lead them to a future of power and prosperity instead of the ruin they were heading for under the infirm hands of old fools and their deficient successors? He, the embodiment of the best of the Aal Munsooris? She was certain he'd one day surpass even her in everything.

He'd heard *that* before. According to Jalal, he already had.

But no matter what he'd thought her capable of, what she'd done had surpassed his worst predictions. And as usual, without obtaining his consent, let alone his approval, she'd executed her plans with seamless precision to force his "deserved greatness" on him. She'd been positive he'd come to appreciate what she'd done, embrace the role she'd tailored for him.

And she could have so easily succeeded.

Even Amjad, his oldest brother and now king of Zohayd, who suspected everything that moved, hadn't suspected her. As queen of Zohayd, she had seemed to have as much to lose as anyone if her husband was deposed. Ingenious.

He recognized that convoluted, long-term premeditation in his own mind and methods. But he consciously confined it to business, driving himself to the top of his tech-development and investment field in record-breaking time. His mother used her intricate intelligence with every breath.

"Please, fasten your seat belt, Your Highness."

He swept his gaze up to the flight attendant. He'd almost forgotten he was on board his private jet.

The beautiful brunette could have said, *Please, unfasten me,* for all the invitation in her eyes. She'd jump on the least measure of response in his attitude.

He regarded her with his signature impassiveness, which

had frozen hardened tycoons and brazen media people in their tracks.

Her color heightened. "We are landing."

He clicked his seat belt into place. "As I gathered."

She tried again. "Will you be needing anything?"

"La, Shokrun." He looked away, dismissing her.

Once she'd turned, he watched her undulate away, sighed.

He would order Khaleel to assign her a desk job. And to confine his immediate personnel to men, or women at least twenty years his senior.

He exhaled again, peered from his window at Durrat Al Sahel—the Pearl of the Coast—Azmahar's capital. From up here he had an eagle-eye view of the crisis he'd been called upon to wrestle with.

He'd thought he'd seen the worst of it in the oil spill off the coast. The ominous blackness tainting the emerald waters was terrible enough. But seeing the disorganization and deterioration even from this altitude was a candid demonstration of how deep the problem ran. How hard it would be to fix.

His heart tightened as the pilot started the final descent, bringing more details into sharper focus.

Azmahar. The other half of his heritage. Decaying.

What a crushing pity.

He hadn't thought he'd ever see this place again. The day Roxanne had walked out on him, he'd left Azmahar swearing he'd never return.

He wasn't only returning—he'd promised to consider the kingship candidacy. He'd made the proviso that his return would be unannounced, that he'd make his own covert investigations and reach a decision uninfluenced by more sales pitches or pleas.

He was still stunned he'd conceded that much. From all evidence, this was one catastrophic mistake in the making.

Life really had a way of giving a man reason to commit the unreasonable.

After his fatherland had rejected him, his motherland claimed to be desperate for his intervention. Investigating if he could be the one to offer it salvation was near irresistible.

He also had to admit, the idea of redeeming himself was too powerful a lure. No matter that logic separated him from his mother's treachery, the fact remained. Her actions *had* skewered into his very identity, which had already been compromised from birth by her influence. Her most outrageous transgression had tarnished his honor and image, no matter what his family said. Most of them, anyway.

Jalal had less favorable views. Of course.

Jalal. Another reason he was considering this.

His twin was another candidate for the throne, after all.

Then there was Rashid. His and Jalal's best friend turned bitterest rival. And yet another candidate.

Was it any wonder he was tempted?

Trouncing those two blowhards was an end unto itself.

So whether it was duty, redemption or rivalry that drove him, each reason was imperative on its own.

But none of them was the true catalyst that had him Azmahar-bound now.

Roxanne was.

She was back in Azmahar.

He took it as the fates nudging him to stop trying not to think of her. As he'd done for eight years. *Eight* years.

Way past high time he ended her occupation of his memories, her near monopoly of his bitterness. He had enough unfinishable business. He would lay the ghost of her share of it to rest.

He would damn well exorcise it.

"...repercussions and resolutions, Ms. Gleeson?"

Roxanne blinked at the distinguished, silver-haired man looking expectantly at her.

Sheikh Aasem Al-Qadi had been her liaison to the interim government since she'd started this post two months ago. And she had to concentrate to remember who he was, and what he—hell, what *she*—was doing here.

She cleared her throat and mind. "As you know, this affects the whole region and many intertwining international entities, each with their own complexities, interests and ideas about how to handle the situation. A rushed study would only cause more misinformation and complications."

The man raised an elegant hand adorned with an onyx-set silver ring, his refined face taking on an even more genial cast. "The last thing I intend to do is rush you, Ms. Gleeson." And if he did, he knew nothing about her if he thought an in-person nudge would make her step up her efforts. She and her team had been flat out digging in that sea. "I'm merely hoping for a more hands-on role in your investigations, and if it's available, a look at a timeline for your intended work plan."

"I assure you, you'll be the first to know when a realistic timeline can be set." She tried on the smile she'd long practiced, formal and friendly at once, which always gained her cooperation. "And my team could certainly do with the high-level insider's perspective you'd bring to the table."

After much cordiality and what she felt was a reaffirmed faith in her effectiveness, Sheikh Al-Qadi left her office.

She leaned against the door she'd closed behind him, groaned.

What *was* she doing here?

So this post *was* a politico-economic analyst's holy grail. And she *had* been bred for the role. But it had brought her back to where she could stumble upon Haidar.

She'd been certain she wouldn't. She'd kept track of him, and he'd never come back to Azmahar. And then, she was no longer the girl who'd fallen head over heels in love with him. She was one of the most sought-after analyst-strategists in the field now, Azmahar being her third major post. If the "ax lodged in the head," as they said here, and she did meet him, she'd treat him with the neutrality and diplomacy of the professional that she was.

But she wouldn't have risked it if not for her mother.

When all you had in the way of family was your mother, a word from her wielded unfair power. She hadn't stood a chance when her mother had shed tears as she'd insisted that this post, an expanded version of *her* old job, was *her* redemption, the perfect apology for the way *she'd* been driven from Azmahar in shame.

When Roxanne had argued that they should have been reinstating *her,* she'd revealed she had been offered the job but didn't want to come out of retirement. It was Roxanne who was building her career, who was in the unique position of possessing her mother's knowledge along with her own fresh perspective and intrepid methods. She'd been the second on the two-candidate shortlist for this post, and the only one with the skill set to make a difference in it now.

She'd capitulated, signed on and packed up. And she'd been excited. There was so much to fix in Azmahar.

According to Azmaharians, the one thing King Nedal had done right since his *joloos* decades ago was arrange his sister Sondoss's marriage to King Atef Aal Shalaan, winning them Zohayd's alliance. Which had nearly been severed by Sondoss herself, the snake-in-the-grass mother of that premium serpent, Haidar.

Roxanne had no doubt Sondoss's exile-instead-of-imprisonment verdict had been wheedled out of the Aal Shalaans by Haidar, who could seduce the stripes off a tiger.

But when Amjad had become king, everyone had thought the first thing he'd do was deal Azmahar the killing blow of letting go of its proverbial hand. He hadn't owed his ex-stepmother's homeland any mercy. Strangely enough, he hadn't ended the alliance.

Then, one month after she'd arrived, all hell had broken loose.

The arrogant fool of a now ex–crown prince had voted against Zohayd for an armed intervention in a neighboring country in the region's latest defense summit, snapping the tenuous tolerance Amjad had maintained for Azmahar. And the kingdom that had been held together by the glue of its ally's clout had come apart.

Just as Azmahar was gasping from the alienation, catastrophe struck. An explosion in one of its major oil drills caused a massive spill off its shores. Unable to deal with the upheavals, in response to the national and regional outcry, the overwhelmed and disgraced king had abdicated.

His brothers and sons, held as responsible, would no longer succeed him. Azmahar was in chaos, and Roxanne was one of those called upon to contain the situation, internally and internationally, as the most influential clans started fighting among themselves.

Out of the anarchy, consolidations had formed, splitting the kingdom into three fronts. Each backed one man for new king.

One of the candidates was Haidar.

Which meant he would come back. And she *would* stumble upon him.

She wanted that as much as she wanted a hole in the heart.

Then again, he'd already pulverized hers.

She cursed under her breath. This was ancient history, and she was probably blowing it out of proportion, anyway. She'd been a twenty-one-year-old only child who'd been sheltered into having the emotional resilience of a fourteen-year-old.

And *man,* had he been good. *Phenomenal* wouldn't do him justice.

It had only been expected that she'd gotten addicted, physically, emotionally. Then she'd woken up. End of story.

She'd moved on, had eventually engaged in other relationships. One could have worked, too. That it hadn't had had nothing to do with that mega-endowed, sizzling-blooded, frigid-hearted creature.

God. She was being cornered into defending her feelings and failures by a memory. Worse. By an illusion. Beyond pathetic.

She pushed away from the door, strode to her desk, snatched up her briefcase and purse, and headed out of the office.

It took her twenty minutes to drive across the city. One thing this place had was an amazing transportation system. Zohaydan—planned, funded and constructed.

It *would* take a miracle to pull Azmahar's fat out of the fire without Zohayd. No wonder Azmaharians were desperate to get their former ally back in their corner. And a good percentage of them had decided on the only way to do that. Put the embodiment of the Zohayd/Azmahar merger on the throne.

But as people in general were addicted to dispute, and Azmaharians were no different, they couldn't agree on which one. But disunity would serve them well now. Going after the two specimens in existence doubled their odds of having one end up on the throne.

She turned through the remote-controlled gates of the highest-end residential complex in the capital. This job came with so many perks it…unsettled her. Luxury of this level always did.

When she'd asked for more moderate accommodations, she'd been assured the project's occupancy had suffered from so many investors leaving the kingdom. They hoped her presence would stimulate renewed interest in the facility.

Seemed they'd been right. Since she'd moved in, the influx of tenants had tripled. One neighbor had told her her reputation, and her mother's, had preceded her, and her presence had many investors feeling secure enough to trickle back to Azmahar, considering it a sign things would soon be put back on track.

Yeah. Sure. *No* pressure whatsoever.

But the "privilege" she dreaded was being at ground zero with every big shot who would grace the kingdom as the race for the throne began. Word was, none of the candidates had announced a position or plans to show up. That only made stumbling across Haidar a matter of later instead of sooner.

She would give anything for never.

But then, she would give anything for a number of things. Her mother with her. A father. Any family at all.

In minutes, she was entering the interior-decorating triumph of an apartment that spanned one-quarter of the thirty-thousand-foot thirtieth floor. She sighed in appreciation as fragrant coolness and calibrating lights enveloped her.

She headed for the shower, came out grinding her teeth a bit less harshly.

She would have thrived on rebuilding the kingdom's broken political and economic channels. But now the Aal Shalaan "hybrids," as they were called here, would feature heavily in this country's future—and consequently, partly in hers. Contemplating that wasn't conducive to her focus or peace of mind. And she needed both to deal with the barrage of information she had to weave into viable solutions. Even if a new king took the throne tomorrow, and he and Zohayd threw money and resources at Azmahar, it wouldn't be effective unless they had a game plan...

An unfamiliar chime sundered the soundproof silence.

She started. Frowned. Then exhaled heavily.

Cherie was almost making her sorry she'd invited her to stay.

They'd been best friends when they'd gone to university

here, and they'd kept in touch. Roxanne's return had coincided with Cherie's latest stormy split-up with her Azmaharian husband. She'd left everything behind, including credit cards.

After the height of the drama had passed, Roxanne should have rented her a place to stay while she sorted out her affairs.

Though she loved Cherie's gregarious company, her energy and unpredictability, Cherie took her "creative chaos" a bit too far. She went through her environment like a tornado, leaving anything from clothes to laptops to mugs on the floor, dishes rotting in the sink, and she regularly forgot basic order-and-safety measures.

Seemed she'd forgotten her key now, too.

Grumbling, Roxanne stomped to the foyer, snarling when the bell clanged again. She pounced on the door, yanked it open. And everything screeched to a halt.

Her breath. Her heart. Her mind. The whole world.

Across her threshold…

Haidar.

Air clogged in her lungs. Everything blipped, swam, as the man she remembered in distressing detail moved with deadly, tranquil grace, leaned his left arm on her door frame. His gaze slid from her face down her body, making her feel as if he'd scraped every nerve ending raw, before returning to her sizzling eyes, a slow smile spreading across his painstakingly sculpted lips.

"You know, Roxanne, I've been wondering for eight years."

The lazy, lethal melody emanating from his lips swamped her. His smile morphed into what a bored predator must give his prey before he finished it off with one swat.

"How soon after you left me did you find yourself a new regularly available stud? Or three?"

Two

Something finally flickered in Roxanne's mind.

Not an actual thought. Just… *Wow.*

Wow. Over and over.

She didn't know how long it took the loop of *wows* to fade, to allow their translation to filter through her gray matter.

So *this* was what eight years had made of Haidar Aal Shalaan.

Most men looked better in their thirties than they did in their twenties. Damn them. A good percentage improved still in their forties, and even fifties. The loss of the smoothness of youth seemed to define their maleness, infuse them with character.

In Haidar's case, she'd thought there had been no room for improvement. At twenty-six he'd seemed to have already realized his potential for perfection.

But…wow. Had photographic evidence and her projections ever been misleading! He'd matured from the epitome of gorgeousness into force-of-nature-level manifestation of masculinity. Her imagination short-circuited trying to project what he'd look like, *feel* like, in another decade. Or three.

His body had bulked up with a distillation of symmetry and strength. His face had been carved with lines of untrammeled power and ruthlessness. He'd become a god of virility and sensuality, hewn from the essence of both. As harsh as the desert's terrain, as menacing as its nights. And as brutally, searingly, freezingly magnificent.

Whatever softness had once gentled his beauty, warmed the frost she'd always suspected formed his core, had been obliterated.

"Well, Roxanne?" He cocked that perfectly formed head, sending the blue-black silk that rained to his as-dark collar sifting to one side. She would have shivered had her body been capable of even involuntary reactions. She could actually hear the sighing caress of thick, polished layers against as-soft material. Mockery tugged at his lips, enhanced the slant in his eyes. He could see, feel her reaction. Of course. He was triggering it at will. "I've had bets about which of us found a replacement faster."

"Why bet on a sure thing? I had to settle in back home, re-enroll in university before I started recruiting. That took time. All *you* had to do was order a stand-in—or rather a lie-in—from your waiting list that same day."

His eyebrows shot up.

If he was surprised, it wasn't any more than she was.

Where had all that come from?

Seemed she had more resentment bottled up than she'd known. And his appearance had shaken out all the steam. Good to depressurize and get it over with.

"Touché." He inclined his head, his eyes filling with lethal humor. "I was in error. The subject of the bets shouldn't have been how long until you found replacements, but how many you found. I was just being faithful in quoting your parting words when I said a stud or three. But from…intimate knowledge of the magnitude of your...needs, I would bet you've gone through at least thirty."

Her first instinct was to take off his head with one slashing rejoinder. She swallowed the impulse, felt it scald her insides.

No matter how she hated his guts and his nerve in showing up on her doorstep, damn his incomparable eyes, he was important. Vital even. To Azmahar. To the whole damn mess. His influence was far-reaching, in the region and the world. And he had the right mix of genes in the bargain.

And then, she wasn't just a woman who was indignant to find an ex-lover at her door unannounced, but also one of the main agents in smoothing out this crisis. Whether he became king or not, he could be—*should* be—a major component in the solution she would formulate. She should rein in further retorts, drag out the professional she prided herself had tamed her innate wildness and steer this confrontation away from petty one-upmanship.

Then she opened her mouth. "By the rate *you* were going through women when I was around, you must be in the vicinity of three hundred." Before she could give herself a mental kick, the bedevilment in his smile rose, prodded her on instead. "What? I missed a zero? Is it closer to three thousand?"

He threw his head back and laughed.

Her heart constricted on what felt like a burning coal. The sound, the sight, was so merry, so magnificent, so—so... missed, even if she didn't remember him laughing like this...

"You mean 'regularly available'...um, what *is* the feminine counterpart for stud? Nymph? Siren?" He leveled his gaze back at her, dark, rich, intoxicating laughter still revving deep in his expansive chest. "But that number would pose a logistical dilemma. Even the biggest harem would overflow with that many nubile bodies. Or did you mean three thousand in sequence?"

She glared at him. "I'm sure you can handle either a con-current or a sequential scenario."

He let out another laugh. "I *knew* I should have approached you for endorsements. But I also have to burst your bubble. Whatever tales you heard of my…exploits were wildly exaggerated. I had to prioritize, after all, and other lusts took precedence. Success, power, money. The drive to acquire and sustain those doesn't mix well with deflating one's libido in a steady supply of feminine arms. And then, time is not only all of the above, it is finite. You know how time-consuming women can be."

Her lips twisted, with derision, with the twinge that still gripped her heart. "I don't. I'm still playing for the same team."

His eyes turned pseudo-amazed. "You never even…went on loan? I would have thought someone with your…needs wouldn't mind widening her horizons where the pursuit of pleasure was concerned."

"Why? Have you? Widened your horizons?"

He let out another bark of distressingly virile amusement. "How can I, when I'm a caveman who's unable to develop beyond my programming? The only thing I managed was to take your advice—purged myself of any trace of 'creepy territorial crap.'"

She reciprocated his razzing, sweeping his six-foot-five frame with disdain. By the time she came back to his eyes, she was kicking herself. It didn't do a woman's heart or hormones any good, getting a load of how his sculpted perfection filled, pushed, *strained* against his black-on-black clothes. Inviting touch, inciting madness…

She gritted her teeth against the moist heat spreading in her core. "And *that* must be the legendary eidetic memory some of you Aal Shalaans are said to possess. As if you need more blessings."

He slid an imperturbable glance down the foot between

them. "If you feel we've received more than our fair share, you can take up your grievance with the fates." A sarcastic huff accompanied a head shake. "But if you think perfect recall is a blessing, you have evidently never been plagued by anything like it. True blessing lies in the ability to forget."

Her heart squeezed with something that confused her. Regret? Sympathy? Empathy?

No. That would indicate she was responding to something *he* felt. And everyone knew that the ability to feel was not among his abilities or vulnerabilities.

She narrowed her eyes, more exasperated with the chink in her resolve than with him. "Come to think of it, it *must* be terrible to have an infallible memory. There must be so much you would have preferred to forget, or at least blur enough to rationalize and romanticize."

All traces of devilry vanished as he thrust his hands into his pockets. Her gaze dragged from his stunning face down to the silky material stretching across the potency she remembered in omnisensory detail...

"I can certainly do with some blurring to take the edge off at times." The predatory challenge flared again. "But one thing about possessing clarity that time doesn't dull—I make one hell of an unforgiving enemy, if I do say so myself."

She snorted. "Yeah. And I hear so many love you for it."

"Does it look like I'd want or even abide 'love'?"

His mock affront would have been irresistible if it wasn't also overwhelmingly goading. She felt just a second away from venting her unearthed frustration in a gnawing, clawing physical attack on this unfeeling monolith!

She exhaled. "That simpering, useless sentiment, huh? No. From what I hear, you want only obedience, blind, mute and dumb."

His smile was self-satisfaction itself. "And I get it, too. *Very* useful, and blessedly soothing, for someone in my position."

"Your mother's son to the last gene strand, aren't you?"

"I like to think I'm the updated and improved version."

His smirk made her want to drag him to her by the hair to taste those heartlessly sensual lips—and to bite them off.

Had he always been this…inflammatory?

He *had* been exasperating, unyielding in demanding his own way. And getting it. One way or another. Mainly one way. But she'd been so in love—or so in raging, blinding, enslaving lust—that the edge of fury his overriding tactics kept simmering beneath the blissful surface had only made everything she felt for him more explosive.

But now the addiction had been cured. Now that she knew what he was without a trace of the "rationalizing or romanticizing" she'd been guilty of heavily employing, she was reacting to him as she should have all along.

Yeah? With thinly suppressed hostility overlying a barely curbed resurgence of lust?

"Invite me in, Roxanne."

Her heart choked out another salvo of arrhythmia.

The electrifying invocation he made of his demand, her name.

She swallowed, trying to extricate herself from his influence, damning him and herself for how effortless it was for him, what a struggle it was for her. "You…you want to come in?"

"No, I came to conduct a verbal duel on your doorstep."

He moved forward and she surged to abort the step that would have taken him over her threshold. "I couldn't care less what you came to do. But said duel is done. Not so nice of you to drop by, Prince Aal Shalaan. Hope I don't see you again."

He resumed his former position, feet braced farther apart, hands in pockets again. "Tsk. All those reports lauding your ability to deal with the most thorny situations and the most exasperating individuals must have been exaggerated."

"No one factored you in when they were gauging thorny exasperation. Even my super diplomacy powers have a limit."

"Or maybe I'm your kryptonite." His smile was now the essence of patience. A hunter with unlimited time to set up his quarry's downfall. "As much as I enjoyed our opening skirmish out here, I would continue our battle in a more private setting. For your sake, really. You're the one who lives here. Surely you don't want your neighbors to witness our... escalations?"

"Since those won't occur, there's nothing for them to witness. Nothing but your departing back." She started to shut the door.

The polished, maple surface met a palm with two-hundred-pounds-plus of sinew, muscle and maleness behind it.

"You know who I am, right?"

Her eyes widened. "You're pulling rank?"

"You think I use my status to get my way? How boring and juvenile would that be?"

"If you're not referring to being the all-powerful Prince of Two Kingdoms, what the hell was that threat about?"

"No threat. Just statement of fact. Take all the trappings away and who am I?"

The most magnificent male in history.

Out loud she seethed. "A huge pain?"

The look he gave her had all her hairs standing on end. "The son of the queen of bitches."

She stared at him. She couldn't agree more about his mother. But she hadn't thought he had that brutal clarity about her, either, let alone would admit it.

She exhaled. "That you are."

Unperturbed, even satisfied by her agreement, his smile widened, raising the voltage of her distress. "So you realize how far I'll go to gain my objectives. Or do you need a demonstration?"

The seventy-five-hundred-square-foot apartment at her back closed in on her.

"Why is coming in even an objective? If I've aroused your confrontational beast, tell it to go back to sleep. We've used up all the digs we can make at each other. Anything else would be redundant, and neither of us likes to waste time."

His shrug was dismissal itself. "First, we're just getting warmed up. Second, surely you don't think I'll allow another abrupt ending between us? Eight years ago, you took me by surprise. *And* I was young and soft. Third, that was a rhetorical question, right? About why it's an objective to get inside… your personal space? You do look in the mirror on occasion? And you have an idea of how you look now?"

For the first time, she focused on how she must look. How she felt. Tiny and defenseless without her towering heels, business clothes and makeup, with her hair drying in a rioting jungle around her shoulders. With the added vulnerability of being just a bathrobe away from total nakedness.

She could almost feel his gaze slipping beneath the terry cloth to explore, reminisce and appraise the changes eight years had wrought in the flesh he'd once thoroughly possessed and pleasured.

Judging he'd disrupted her to the desired level, he gestured, encompassing her. "Add all *that* to the delights of your tongue of mass destruction, and you're wondering about my motives?"

She wrinkled her nose. "Quote, 'How creepy can you get,' unquote. You think I'll invite a man twice my size, twenty times as strong and two million times as powerful in every other way into my 'personal space,' after he's made his lewd intentions clear?"

His face lost all lightness. "You think you won't be safe with me?"

Haidar might be many things, but to women he would always be master through pleasure, not pain; seduction, not coercion.

Unable to get rid of him that way, she exhaled. "No. But you *are* trying to persist your way in when I don't want you here."

A smile transformed his face back to the supreme male who knew the exact level of estrogen overproduction he commanded in females. "You do. I remember, in unfailing detail, how you want, Roxanne. My knowledge of your mind may be deficient, especially with eight years of maturity and experience, but your body hasn't changed, and I know everything about it. I can sense its every nuance, decipher its every signal."

She wrestled with the overwhelming urge to knee him.

Knowledge glittered in his eyes, threatened to snap her control. "My sudden appearance rattled you. That made you defensive, and *that* made you angry. You want me to go only so you can regroup."

One little kneeing. Surely it wouldn't be too damaging. To her position.

His grin was designed to loosen her restraint another notch. "But you can get yourself together while I'm around. I'll make myself a cup of tea until you do. You can even dress if you must. If you need the fortification of clothes, that is."

"How condescending can you get?"

He inclined his head. "Condescending *is* several steps up from creepy. I must be evolving after all."

"The jury will remain out on that." He leaned more comfortably against her door frame, as if preparing to spend hours hanging around until he achieved his "objective." She looked pointedly at the foot strategically placed across the threshold. "But I still advise you to leave now. You need your beauty sleep to deal with what awaits you here. I heard you were approached for a job. The top job."

His expression remained unchanged, but she could feel

his surprise. And dismay. He had hoped that was still a secret. Why?

He finally jerked one formidable shoulder. "News still travels faster than a speeding bullet around here. As well as rumors, exaggerations and fabrications."

"This isn't any of those. It's why you're here."

His lips quirked. "And if I tell you I'm here for you?"

"I'd say that's bull. I'll also issue you further advice. My neighbors are always coming and going and receiving tons of visitors at all times. You're a famous figure, and I bet if someone sees you standing on the doorstep of a woman in a bathrobe—one who's leaving you standing there, to boot—the footage will be on the internet in minutes and will go viral in hours. Not a prudent way to start your campaign for the throne."

He pretended to worry for a moment before he grinned again. "See? You progressed to giving me strategy advice. You can do that much better when we slip into a more comfortable…environment."

She exhaled. "Very mature. Go away, Haidar."

He folded his arms over his chest. "Why?"

Why? "You want the reasons alphabetized?"

"Just pull out a random one."

"Because I want you to."

"We already established that's a false claim."

"I have no interest in what *you* established, and no intention of arguing its merit."

"Your prerogative. Mine is waiting until you give me a reason I can accept."

"Who says you have to accept anything?"

He cocked his head, his steel-dawn eyes taking on a thoughtful cast. "Still getting back at me for 'summoning you like a lackey' and daring to presume I have a 'claim' to you?"

She balled her fists. "Use that infallible memory of yours

and remember that there was nothing to get back at you for. It just…"

"Put you off. *Aih,* I remember. But you can't have been cringing ever since. And you're not doing so now. This is the very healthy reaction of the hot-blooded spitfire I was afraid had disappeared, from all reports of the imperturbable goddess of analysis and mediation you've become."

This was so unfair. That he could debate as superlatively as he did everything else. But she was no slouch in that department.

Before she could find anything to say to back up that claim, he said, "With that out of the way, repeat after me. 'It's all in the past, and will you please come in, Haidar?'"

"It's all in the past, and will you please go away, Haidar?"

He unfolded his arms, braced his hands on his hips. "You think it's a possibility I will? I'm beginning to lose faith in the clarity of your insight and the accuracy of your projections."

She gritted her teeth. Exchanging barbs was like quicksand. The more she said, the further she sank. She'd say no more.

He gave her one last brooding glance. Then he turned around.

He—he was…leaving?

She watched him walk away, got a more comprehensive view of his…assets as he receded. Just looking at him had longing clamping her chest.

He was messing with her. Haidar didn't give up. He didn't know how.

But he was now at the far end of the hall that led to the elevators. He was really leaving.

Before he made the left that would take him out of sight, he stopped. Her heart revved a jumble of beats. Would he…?

He turned, rang the bell of her farthest neighbor.

What the hell…?

Without stopping, he continued retracing his steps, stopped

by the second-farthest apartment, ringing its bell, too. Without slowing down this time, he did the same at her closest neighbor's.

Then he moved to the middle of the hall, semifacing her, calmly sweeping his gaze across all the doors.

Before his actions could sink in, one door opened. Two seconds later, another did. The last followed.

Then her neighbors—and, just her luck, the female components only—stood staring at Haidar. Their wariness at having their bells rung without a preceding intercom alert turned to amazement as recognition dawned.

Haidar let them marinate in it before he said, "Sorry for disturbing you, ladies. I wasn't sure which apartment I wanted."

Roxanne's jaw dropped. Or dropped farther. Where had that accent come from? He sounded like a redneck!

"Oh, my *God!* You're him!" Susan Gray, the forty-something CEO of the Azmaharian branch of a multinational construction company, babbled like a teenager. "You're Prince Haidar Aal Shalaan!"

Haidar shook his regal head, making his mane undulate in a swish of silk—on purpose, she was sure. "Oh, I'm just his doppelgänger. I was paid five grand online by some lady who wants to act out her fantasy of dominating him. I usually come for less, but I charged extra since she wants to get real kinky. I was given this address, the floor, but not the number of the condo. So which of you has a thing for this Haidar guy?"

Her neighbors gaped at him, at each other, then finally, at her. She was the one in the bathrobe, after all.

Her brain was too zapped to function. But she had to. If she didn't do something, this…this…*madman* would demolish her image. And his own.

She staggered out of her apartment, her perspiring bare feet making her advance on the polished marble precarious.

He watched her with feigned uncertainty. "Oh, it's you?"

His gaze swept her with what looked like earnest assessment. "I somehow thought you wouldn't be a babe. So why can't you find guys to dominate the regular way? Hey...you're not nuts, are you?"

He looked to her neighbors for confirmation as she stumbled the last step to him, grabbed him by the lapel of his jacket.

He pretended to ward her off. "Whoa, lady. The deal is degradation in private. Public displays will cost you extra."

She grimaced at her neighbors, expending all her restraint on not thumping the huge lout. "Sorry, ladies. Haidar is an old friend, regretfully. I left him eight years ago without a sense of humor, but it seems he's contracted some terminal prankster disease. He thinks this is a fun way to say long time no see."

She was dragging him toward her apartment while she talked, for the second time in her life wishing grounds yawned open and swallowed people. The other time had also involved him.

He resisted her, looked back at her neighbors imploringly. "I don't know this dame. Is she dangerous?" She smacked him hard on the arm. "Hey! We agreed on domination, not abuse!"

The son of a literal royal bitch was making the situation worse with every word out of his mouth.

Who was she kidding? It was irretrievable already. *God*.

She could think of nothing to say but "Shut up, Haidar."

He looked down at her, eyes morphing from vapid porn-actor mode to a dozen devils' cunning. "I'm a working dude, lady. Show me some respect. When I'm not on the clock, that is."

Her neighbors' expressions kept yo-yoing from the verge of bursting into laughter to wondering if their neighbor did have a kinky—or worse—side to her.

"You win, okay?" she grumbled for his ears only. "Now stop with the act, take your bows and let the ladies get on with their evening."

He raised his voice for all to hear. "So you'll pay extra if I start pretending I'm this Haidar guy right now?"

"*Ooh!*" She shoved him ahead of her across her threshold.

This time he surrendered to her manhandling, clung to the edge of the door, addressed them over her head. "Do you mind checking up on me in an hour's time?"

She shot her flabbergasted neighbors another dying-of-embarrassment glance, dragged him away from the door, slammed it shut.

Then she rounded on him.

His grin lit up his impossibly gorgeous face. "I did warn you. Next time, give in gracefully."

She stomped her heel over his foot. It felt like ramming rock-enclosed steel. Pain shot through her whole leg, had her hopping on one foot yelping.

He caught her by the arms, steadied her, chuckling. "Go put on your most lethal stilettos and we'll try it again."

Grimacing, she punched his chest, hard. "You reckless jerk."

He groaned, definite pleasure darkening the deep, rich sound.

So the bastard hadn't been lying about his predilections after all. The savage, dominating edge to his desire used to thrill her. But maybe he didn't mind exchanging roles. Something to keep in mind…

The trajectory of her thoughts made her whack him again.

He bit his lip with what looked like intense enjoyment, his eyes sparkling like turbulent seas in a full moon. "Is that the political adviser's indignation? How sweet of you to care."

"I care about *my* effectiveness. As for you, by the time this gets out, and boy will it, you can kiss the throne goodbye."

"Fair enough. As long as I can finally kiss you hello."

He dragged her up until only her toes touched the hardwood floor, swooped his head down to hers and did just that.

At the first touch of his lips, she spiraled like a shot-down plane into the past. All her being was captured into a reenactment of that first kiss that had swept her away on a tide of addiction. He took her mouth with that same lazy savoring laced with coiled ferocity. Her body had learned then what kind of heart-stopping pleasure such deceptively patient coaxing would lead to, had burst into flames at his merest touch, fire raging higher with each exposure.

The conflagration was fiercer now, with the fuel of anger, of eight years of repression. This was wrong, insane. And it only made her want it, want him, more than her next breath.

Gravity loosened its hold on her, relinquished her to the effortless levitation of his arms. The world spun in hurried thuds, then she was sinking into the firmness of a couch as his weight sank over her. Her moans rose, confessions of the arousal that had fractured the shackles of hostility and memory and logic, drowned them and her.

The rough heat of him electrified her as her bathrobe and his shirt came undone. His chiseled, roughened steel flesh crushed her swollen breasts, teasing her turgid nipples into a frenzy. His bulk and power settled between her spread thighs, and he ground against her molten core, plunged into her gasping mouth.

She writhed to accommodate him, enfold him, the decadence of him on her tongue, lacing her every sense.

Suddenly he severed their meld. She cried out as he rose above her. His gaze scalded her, his lips tight with grim sensuality.

"I should have listened to what my body knows about yours and done this the moment you opened the door."

His arrogance should have made her buck him off. But lust gnawed her, ruled her. Hunger for him, as he was now, memorized yet unknown, the same yet changed beyond comprehension, brimming with contradictions, seethed its demand for satisfaction.

He'd come here for this possession, this closure. She'd been aching for it, too. She's only be hurting herself if she denied—

A slam sent the crystal on the mahogany table beside them emitting a harmony of hums, felt like being drenched in ice water.

Cherie.

"You won't believe who I found waiting for me. Ayman in all his glory, wanting to talk. Why now, I ask you…"

Cherie's prattling trailed off. Roxanne met her eyes over Haidar's shoulders, would have giggled at her friend's deer-in-the-headlights expression if she weren't as distressed.

If Cherie had been any later, Haidar would have been buried deep inside her, thrusting her to oblivion.

Even now, with horror at her actions crashing over her, her body still whimpered for his completion.

"Cherie…" was all she could wheeze.

"Uh…I… God, I didn't mean—" Cherie stopped, before spluttering again, "I never thought you'd…you'd…"

She'd never thought she'd find her cerebral friend beneath a lion of a man, naked and wrapped around him, in full view for her to see as soon as she walked in the door.

Haidar began to rise off her. She stared up into his face as it changed from ferocious lust to deprecating resignation.

"A flatmate, Roxanne? Seriously?"

"What am I *doing* still standing here?" Cherie babbled as she ran inside. "Sorry, guys. Please, carry on. I'm not really here!"

By the time they heard Cherie's bedroom door slam, he was on his feet, buttoning his shirt. For one mad moment, she didn't see why they couldn't take Cherie's advice.

Then sanity lodged back into her brain.

She scrambled up, pulled her bathrobe tight around her.

He shook his head at her far-too-late modesty as he turned away.

At the door, he half turned again, his eyes hooded with still-simmering desire. "We'll meet again, *ya naari*."

She lurched. *His fire.*

She'd never thought she'd hear that again. From him. Or ever. She'd long thought her fire had been extinguished.

"But next time, it will be on my turf. And on my terms."

He touched his tongue to the lip she'd bitten, as if tasting her passion. Then, with one last inflaming look, he whispered, "Until then."

Three

"I'd give an arm to know your secret, Roxanne."

Roxanne stared at Kareemah Al Sabahi. Hers was the third and last door she'd knocked on to explain away Haidar's shenanigans.

She hadn't been up to facing another day, let alone those who'd witnessed Haidar's innovative blackmail tactics. But damn him to an as-novel hell, she had to live among them, as he'd said.

Kareemah was the only one who hadn't needed explanations, having watched developments through her intercom camera. Cherie's arrival had had her mind going into hyperdrive. But Haidar had left minutes later, aborting her visions of threesomes. She'd opened her door, hoping for an explanation, when he'd suddenly turned. In his real voice, he'd said he hoped she'd enjoyed the show, had her giggling like a fool as he'd bowed to her before he'd walked away.

"I mean, you're gorgeous and all, but it can't only be that. You have to have a secret. Women everywhere would kill for a tip."

Roxanne shook her head. She wasn't up to deciphering

neighbors' riddles. Now that Haidar had rematerialized in her life with the force of a live warhead and left promising further destruction, her brain was officially fried.

Either that, or Kareemah was talking gibberish. Which was an imminent possibility. The woman *had* been exposed to Haidar, too.

"So what *do* you do to get gods knocking down your door?"

"Uh, Kareemah, if you mean Haidar, I already explained—"

"And I might have bought you explaining one god away. But how do you explain another?"

Suddenly, she realized Kareemah wasn't looking at her. Her eyes were glued to a point in the distance.

Someone was standing behind her.

She whirled around. And her heart hit the base of her throat.

No. Not another Aal Shalaan "hybrid."

Jalal.

He was standing by the door she'd left open, in a charcoal suit with a shirt the color of his golden eyes, hands languidly in his pockets, looking as if he'd teleported off a *GQ* magazine cover.

That might not be far-fetched. She hadn't heard the whir of the elevator or the fall of his footsteps.

For the second time in less than twenty-four hours, one of the two men she never wanted to see again had managed to sneak up on her.

Kareemah tugged on her arm, made her stagger around. "Like we say here, 'the neighbor takes precedence in charity.' I anxiously await a glimpse at your methods."

With that, she cast Jalal another starstruck glance and stepped back into her apartment.

Roxanne stared at the door Kareemah had just closed, her mind in a jumble.

"*Koll hadi's'seneen, kammetman'nait ashoofek menejdeed.*" All these years, how I wished to see you again.

Her heart squeezed so hard she felt it would implode.

Suddenly fury spurted inside it, incinerating all shock and nostalgia. She wasn't letting another Aal Shalaan twin mess her up all over again. She'd hit her limit last night.

She turned, hoping she didn't look as shaky as she felt. "If it isn't one of the region's two most eligible bastards."

The warmth infusing his face didn't waver as he slipped his hands out of his pockets, spread his arms in a gesture that had always had her running into them. "*Ullah yehay'yeeki, ya* Roxanne."

Ullah yehay'yeeki—literally, may God hail you, one of the not-quite-translatable colloquial praises he'd once lavished on her, usually when she'd said something that had resonated with his demanding intellect and wit. Which had been almost every time she'd opened her mouth. They'd been so alike, so in tune, it had been incredible. It had also turned out to be a lie.

For years afterward, she hadn't known which betrayal had hurt more, his or Haidar's.

She stuck her fists at her sides. "Listen, buddy, I had one hell of a night, and I'm expecting a spiral of steady deterioration for the foreseeable future. So why don't you just piss off. Whatever made you pop up here, I don't want to hear it."

"Not even if it's me groveling for forgiveness?"

She walked toward him, each step intensifying her anger. "I've heard that before. Still not in the least interested."

He'd called her out of the blue two years ago, begging her for a face-to-face meeting. She'd hung up on him.

He hadn't called back.

She came to a stop a foot away, had to still look way up, even when boosted by her highest heels.

In response to her glare, he did something that made her heart stagger inside her chest. He cupped her cheek, his touch the essence of gentleness, his face, his voice that of cherishing.

"*Alhamdu'lel'lah*—thank God the years have been as

nurturing as you deserve. You've grown into a phenomenal woman, Roxy."

Only the drowning wave of longing stopping her from scoffing, *Look who's talking.*

Jalal was another case where time had conspired to turn an example of virile perfection into something that was description defying. While the younger man she'd known had been as gorgeous as she'd thought humanly possible, possessing an equal, if totally different, brand of beauty from his twin and a diametrically opposite effect, too, the mature Jalal had become a juggernaut out of an Arabian Nights fable.

"Even if you scratch my eyes out for it, you have to hear it, to know it. *Kamm awhashtini, ya sudeequtti al habibah.*" How I missed you, my beloved friend.

And *God*, how she'd missed him, too.

She grabbed his hand, removed it from her face, tugged him by it. He let her lead him, offering no resistance even when it became clear she was taking him to the elevators.

In seconds, an elevator swished silently open. She gestured for him to enter. With one last pained, resigned look, he complied. And she made up her mind.

She dragged him back out, led him to her apartment.

She let him close the door, walked ahead to her spacious home office, threw herself down on the L-shaped cream leather couch/recliner, looked up at him as he came to stand before her.

She made a hurry-up gesture. "Go ahead. Grovel. Just try to make it interesting."

His expression turned whimsical. "That will be hard. Will you accept pathetic?"

"I'm sure it will be that."

He sighed, nodded. "But I want to make sure of something first. That day—you arrived before you made your presence known, right? You overheard me and Haidar talking about our bet?"

He was only half right about how it had happened. She wasn't about to volunteer more insights. "What do you think?"

"I think it's the only explanation for what you said and did. Even if you were angry with Haidar for his overbearing tactics, even if you'd told the truth about the limit of your involvement with him, you had no reason to cut me off, too. Except if you heard. And misinterpreted what you heard."

Heat rose as she relived the humiliation and heartbreak all over again. "Don't even try the misinterpretation card. What I heard was the truth, and I acted accordingly to get rid of both of you competition-sick bastards. End of story."

Her insults had no effect on him. Just as they hadn't on Haidar.

But while Haidar had been bedeviling and goading, Jalal was accepting and forbearing. He'd let her beat him to a pulp if it would make her feel better.

"You of all people know there are too many sides to any situation for one to be the whole truth."

But she *didn't* want to hear more sides to this mess. Hope was more damaging than resignation. She'd built her stability around accepting the worst, dealing with the pain and moving on.

But…hadn't she spent years wishing there *were* more sides? Ones that might prove that not everything they'd shared had been a means to a "pathetic" end, so she could free a measure of her memories from the pall of bitterness and resentment?

His wolf's eyes felt as if they were probing her mind, following her every thought. Which they probably were. They'd always been on the same wavelength.

Just as the scales teetered toward foolish hope, his gaze grew relieved. He *was* reading her like a hundred-foot billboard.

"Will I get socked if I sit down beside you?"

She flung him an ill-tempered gesture. "Take your chances like the colossal man that you are."

He sat down inches away with controlled strength and poise, cocooning her in warmth and power and a nostalgia so encompassing her throat closed.

She took refuge in sarcasm. "This couch is so low most people flop down on it. Still doing thousands of squats per day?"

"Takes one exercise junkie to know another. You're looking fitter than ever, Roxy." Before she hissed that he'd lost the right to call her that, he silenced her with something totally unexpected. "I need to explain something I should have long ago. My relationship with Haidar."

Her heart blipped in distress at Haidar's name. At the way Jalal said it. At the bleakness in his eyes.

She attempted a nonchalant shrug. "While neither of you ever talked about the other, I gathered the relevant facts myself. You live to compete with each other."

"Aren't you at all curious to know how we got that way?"

"Standard sibling rivalry, how else? As you said, pathetic. But most of all, boring."

"How I wish it was. Maddening, unsolvable, heart-wrenching more like." He wiped a hand down his face in a weary gesture. "You've seen how radically different we are, and we were born that way. But we were inseparable in spite of that. Maybe because of it. Until it all started going wrong. I can trace the beginning of the friction, the rivalry, to one incident. Our tenth birthday party."

Here was her first misconception destroyed. She'd always assumed their rivalry started at birth.

"I almost burned down the palace, and Haidar volunteered to take the blame. Instead of stepping forward, I…let him take the punishment meant for me. Things were never the same afterward."

Their conflict had an origin, one in which Haidar was the wronged party? That *was* surprising. Disturbing.

"He began to treat me with a reserve I wasn't used to, put distance between us. Once I became certain it wasn't a passing thing, I was furious, then anxious, then lost. I needed my twin back. I tried to force the closeness I depended on, dogging his every move, demanding to share everything he did, for him to share everything I did, like we used to. When that only resulted in more distance, I became desperate. I started to do anything that would provoke an emotional reaction from him. He retaliated by demonstrating in ingenious ways that I couldn't get to him. Then he learned a new trick, wielded a new weapon—he started showing me, and everyone else, that he was better than me. In just about everything. And it was so easy for him.

"He got the highest grades without trying, while I had to struggle to keep up. He was a favorite with our elders for being so methodical and achieving. He was a sweeping success with girls for being so good-looking, yet so cool and detached. The only thing I could trounce him in was sports, and he came close to equaling me even in those by mere cunning."

He gave a deprecating laugh. "And of course, all through, our mother was praising the hell out of his every breath. As a boy who then idolized his mother, I grew frantic for equal appreciation, and when I despaired of that, for any at all. She did show me some on occasion, but it always felt like the crumbs that were left over from Haidar's feast. It took me years to outgrow the need for her validation, to be resigned to who she was, and the kind of relationship I had with her. But I could never become resigned to my and Haidar's relationship.

"It was a paradox. I wanted to be with him the most of anyone in the world, yet no one could drive me out of my cool, collected mind but him…at least, no one *then*…" A dark, distracted look settled in his eyes. Before she could ask who else had later done the same to him, he shook his head slightly as if to rid himself of disturbing memories, resumed his focus. "He seemed to want my company as much, in his own contradictory way, showing me moments of emotional closeness before shutting me out again."

You, too? she almost scoffed. Haidar had subjected her to the same dizzying, confusing, addicting pattern.

Jalal sat back, fists braced on his knees, eyes seeming to gaze into his own past. "As we got older, we showed the world a unified front, for the sake of the rest of our family, politics and business. But when we were alone, we butted heads like two stupid rams on steroids. And I think we both were addicted to the conflict. I believed that was who we were, the only relationship we could have, and I had to accept it."

Roxanne gaped at his grim profile. She'd never thought things were that complex and complicated between them. It was fascinating in the most terrible way to learn how these two twins who had everything they needed to forge an unparalleled bond had been driven apart. Needing to reach out to each other yet held back by something inescapable.

And *why* was she including them both in that assessment? She'd bet Haidar felt no equal anguish for the state of affairs with his twin. She'd bet Haidar didn't feel at all.

But where Jalal was concerned, so much now made sense. The wistfulness and guardedness that had come over him when Haidar was mentioned, the snarkiness that took over when his twin was around.

No matter if this snowball had started with an incident in which Jalal was the culprit—that Haidar had set out to punish his twin for it for the rest of their lives proved what a twisted, vindictive bastard he was. He'd even been proud of the fact that he made one hell of an unforgiving enemy.

Jalal threw his head back on the couch. "But accepting it didn't mean I could handle it. Being unreasonable isn't part of my makeup, but I became that with Haidar. And I no longer knew how much of our rivalry was due to what had turned him against me early on, or to my self-defeating tactics in trying to get him back, our mother's divisive influence, or who we are, our choices, actions and reactions. Then we met you at that royal ball."

Her heart did its best to flip over inside her rib cage.

How she remembered that night.

It had been in her first month in Azmahar. She'd thanked the fates for the job that had gotten her mother and herself here. When they were invited to that ball, she'd felt like a Disney heroine entering a world of wonders way beyond her wildest dreams. The impression had grown stronger when she'd met Jalal.

Then she'd seen Haidar.

Just the sight of him, an apparition of aloof, distant grandeur, had kicked to life every contradictory emotion inside her. She'd bristled with defensiveness, burned with challenge and melted with desire.

Jalal turned to her now, taking his account from the profoundly personal to the shared past. "I saw your instant attraction to him, and out of habit, I challenged him for you. We both know how far he took that challenge. But I swear to you, I forgot that silly bet in minutes. Everything you and I shared was real. You were the friend I could share everything with, the sister I never had."

And he'd been her confidant, champion and the brother she'd always longed for.

Still afraid of reopening her heart and letting him seal the hole losing him had blown in it, she narrowed her eyes. "So why did you wait six years to approach me? And even then, give up after just one phone call?"

"Because after you walked out and didn't call me, I assumed you'd overheard us and included me in your hostility. My first impulse was to run to you, tell you what I just told you now. But as I was heading out to your house the next morning, I learned that your mother had been…dishonorably discharged. I held back then because I believed further contact with me might cause you more…damage."

She blinked her surprise. "Why did you think that?"

"Didn't you ever suspect why your mother was fired?"

"Sure I did. I suspected Haidar."

It was his turn to be shocked. "You thought he was punishing you for walking out on him through her?"

"You find that far-fetched?"

He clearly did, found her suspicion very disturbing. "I prefer to think there are some lines he wouldn't cross."

"You think seducing me for a bet was an okay line to cross, but destroying my mother's career to get back at me wasn't?"

"I…" He drove his fingers into his sable mane in agitation. "I guess it's not impossible, considering he must have been enraged at the time, but it just doesn't…feel like him."

"So if it wasn't Haidar you were worried would harm us more if you maintained a relationship with me, who were you afraid of?"

"My mother." He grimaced when her jaw dropped. "I don't have proof, but I felt her hand in this. She employed similar tactics to drive those she didn't approve of away from Haidar and me. Again, I never found proof, but I just *knew* she was behind all those incidents. That's why I ventured to contact you only when she was exiled. Until then, there was no telling how far she'd go if she learned you were still in my life."

She gaped at him. This was a scenario she hadn't considered. Not because she didn't have the worst possible opinion of former queen Sondoss. But she'd thought the queen had already been done with her, had no more reason to go after her or her own.

Then again, knowing that woman, why not?

Could it be? All these years she'd been so busy demonizing Haidar, she'd missed the mother of all demons at work?

Feeling her entrenched convictions being uprooted, leaving her in a free fall of new confusion, she released a tremulous breath. "You've got yourself one effed-up family, Jalal."

"Tell me about it."

She teetered on the verge of throwing herself into his arms and hugging the despondency out of him.

One more thing first. "So why didn't you persist, after your mother was out of the picture and I was no longer in her range?"

His look of self-blame almost made her stop him from answering. "Because I was going through some…heavy stuff, with Haidar, with…other people, and I acutely felt the kind of anger and hurt that could fuel your hanging up on me after six years. I thought I'd be a reminder of your worst memories after you'd moved on. I was also not in any shape to take more emotional upheavals at that time."

Her hands fisted on the urge to reach out. "What's changed?"

"You did." His golden eyes blazed with pride and fondness so powerful and pure, hers started burning. "You came back. It proved to me you're ready to face your demons, to snatch what you deserve from their fangs. I now think having me back in your life won't resurrect painful memories—you're ready to remember the good ones and form new and better ones. And I have also changed. I'm removed enough from my 'effed-up' family that I can be your haven again. *And* the big gun in your camp."

The tears she'd been holding back for eight years cascaded down her cheeks. He reached for her as she did him, took her into his long-missed affection and protection.

He kissed the top of her head. "Does this mean you believe me?"

She raised a face trembling with mirth and emotion. "What else could it mean, you big, wonderful wolf?"

"That you're too softhearted, that you forgive me even if you still believe I befriended you to seduce you away from Haidar."

She smirked, poked her finger into that dimple in his left cheek. "As if you could have seduced me. Or even wanted to."

His smile was relief itself. "*Aih,* I would have found Haidar's accusations hilarious, if I hadn't been so incensed with him. You felt like my real twin from the first time we met, *ya azeezati.*"

A sob escaped her at hearing him call her "my dearest" again. "You don't know how much I missed you...*ya azeezi.*"

"That's it?" he mock reprimanded her. "You're taking me back into your heart? And I'd hoped you'd grown as diamond-hard as the exterior you project. You still have a gooey center."

She knew what he was doing. He was taking this away from acute emotions, even if the positive, wonderful variety. "Takes one mushy core to know another." She jumped to her feet, dragged him up with both hands. "I didn't have breakfast yet. Share it?"

His grin lit up the whole world. "Sure will. I haven't eaten a thing since yesterday, dreading this confrontation."

"Says the man who once went swimming with sharks."

"*Azeezati,* first, that was for a zillion dollars in donations for your list of causes. Second, your possible rejection—and worse, my inability to heal your pain—were far scarier propositions than being gnawed on by sharks."

She kissed him soundly on the cheek for that.

For the next hour, they talked and laughed and shared news and opinions as if they'd never stopped. It felt like being in the past, when she'd raced through her work so she could run to her squash date whenever he was in the kingdom.

They were sipping mint tea when he said, "Apart from being my friend and sister again, I need your professional services."

One eyebrow rose. "Uh-oh. This *was* too good to be true."

"You think all this—" he gestured to their cozy companionship "—was me leading up to this request?"

It took her a moment to make up her mind. "I might be a colossal fool with syrup for blood, but no. I trust you too much."

"You didn't trust me at all till a couple of hours ago."

She shook her head. "That's not true. Even if I didn't hear you defending me to Haidar, I would have believed that however things started, the feelings you developed for me were genuine. It was because I thought you cut me from your life that I developed a grudge against you. I missed your friendship sometimes more than I missed the illusion of my love for Haidar."

He dragged her into his arms for a convulsive hug. "I can't tell you how sorry I am, how angry I am for the heartache my family caused you and forced me to be party to inflicting on you." He set her away, held her by the shoulders. "But I will never let anyone hurt you again." She nodded, a tear slipping down her face. He wiped it away gently. "This means you'll consider my request?"

She mock shoved him. "Without knowing specifics, I have to remind you that friends and business are never a good mix."

"Usually not, but not *never*. When it's the right people, the right friendship, results can be spectacular. And lifelong."

"There *have* been recorded incidents." She faced him, folding her legs on the couch. "Okay. What do you propose?"

He mirrored her position. "With your connections, you must have heard I was approached by four of Azmahar's major clans to be their candidate for the throne."

"I *was* asked to weigh in on candidates. You, Rashid Aal Munsoori and…Haidar are the ones who made it to the final round."

He couldn't have missed her hesitation over Haidar's name, but made no comment. "I want you to be my consultant, my all-round adviser. I am ambivalent about this whole thing, and I need the guidance of someone I trust implicitly, someone neutral, who knows all the goings-on of the political and economic scene. Is there anyone else on the planet you know who fits the bill?"

"With those criteria, no." She chewed her lip. "Though I must qualify your 'neutral' assertion."

His head shake was adamant. "What you lack in neutrality, you'll make up for in professionalism."

"Vote of confidence appreciated and all, but..." She took a deep breath, admitted, "This will put me in contact with... him."

"If that's your objection, then my quest is done. Haidar and I will probably not be in each other's vicinity in this lifetime."

Her heart missed a beat. "It's that bad?"

"I haven't talked to him in two years."

That *was* bad. But... "You were always 'not talking to each other.' Then you'd end up drawn back together like magnets."

"I thought so, too. I left him that day eight years ago with the agreement that we were getting the hell out of each other's lives. But we were drawn back together, over and over. During the crisis in Zohayd, it seemed we were back to being as close as we were as children. Then—" a spasm contorted his noble features "—we clashed again. The last time we met, he renounced our very blood tie."

Her heart quivered, her lungs burned. If their bond had been truly severed this time, Jalal must be bleeding internally.

As for Haidar, his reptilian genes no doubt protected him from injury. The man who'd goaded, manipulated and almost seduced her out of her mind hadn't been suffering from anything.

She drew in a ragged inhalation. "Okay, I'll do it. But I'll make sure that there is no conflict of interest with my job, and I won't divulge anything that would provide you with any unfair advantage, just sort your own findings and add my own insights. And of course I would be helping you on a strictly informal, personal basis, not officially."

She didn't know if he was more relieved that she'd accepted, or that she'd made that stipulation. Seemed he, too, was still considering Haidar and his reactions in everything he did.

That was a reason unto itself to see Jalal to the throne.

She'd be saving a whole kingdom from having Haidar as king.

Four

"How far are you willing to go for her?"

Haidar blinked, unable to turn his gaze from the second most magnificent sight he'd ever seen.

It was downright…magical. The undulating shore hugging pristine, placid aquamarine that in turn tugged at its unique red-gold edge in a tranquil, laced-in-delicate-froth dance. The bay that sent a tendril of land to almost touch the island teeming with palm trees just half a mile away. The canopy of crisp azure adorned in brushstrokes of incandescent white. Every wisp of breeze, every whiff of fragrance, every ray of light… breathtaking.

And he'd thought nothing could take his breath away anymore.

Seemed instead of becoming harder as he grew older, he was getting softer. A tiny, barefoot woman in a bathrobe had done just that last night. Taken it away, and held it at bay with her every move. And this place felt like an echo of…

"Her?"

He repeated the word as his eyes fell on his much smaller, middle-aged companion. He kept forgetting he was there.

The man, overdressed for the time and climate, beamed. "The estate. In the real estate business, everyone refers to it as 'her.' Comes from dozens of men going to lengths to acquire it that are normally reserved for bewitching and out-of-reach women."

He could see how. He'd gone driving last night after he'd left Roxanne, and he'd registered nothing until he'd happened by this place.

He'd parked at the top of the dune that overlooked it, watched it transition through the grandeur of a starlit canvas to the glory of a majestic dawn to that of a sun-drenched morning. That he could appreciate any of it while he wrestled with his need to tear his way back to Roxanne proved this place was phenomenal indeed.

But as he'd sat there suffering, it had become clear to him.

He wanted her. And he would have her. Here.

He'd called Khaleel with his GPS coordinates, told him he would buy this place. In less than an hour the real estate agent had arrived, drooling at the prospect of a record-breaking deal.

They were standing at the ground-level terrace surveying the house that looked like a cross between a huge tent and a sail ship.

"…as you've seen, apart from the unique location and natural assets of this place, the house itself is a miracle of design. All bedrooms suites, sitting areas, upper and lower kitchens, formal and informal dining rooms have a sea view. Everything is arranged in an exquisite amalgam of Ottoman and Andalusian summer courtyard style, with waterways and gardens nestled within the interior—"

"As I have seen." Haidar interrupted the slick Elwan Al-Shami's sales pitch. He'd let him take him through the place, even though he'd already seen it as he'd waited for his arrival. The estate's caretakers had fallen over themselves to show him around as soon as they'd recognized him. "Let's close the deal."

The man's eyes brimmed with eagerness, yet Haidar could see he wasn't ready to do so yet. He was programmed to keep driving a client's acquisition need to fever pitch before he sprang the killing price. Even now that Haidar had made his efforts redundant, he couldn't stop before his program had run through.

"When the owner heard it was you, he named a too-exorbitant figure. That's why I asked how far you're willing to go."

Haidar swept his gaze around the place that answered any visions of heaven he'd ever had. "Shrewd man. He knows it would sell no matter how high he goes."

"And he demands cash. That's why those who bought it before fell behind in paying the installments of the huge loans they took, had to relinquish it to the indebting banks. The owner was always there to buy it back and make a profit."

"He won't be buying it back this time."

"As long as you're sure—"

"*B'Ellahi ya rejjal.* Name your price."

The man blinked at Haidar's growl. Then licking his lips nervously, he did.

Haidar whistled. No wonder many men had been broken by their desire to acquire this place.

Just as the man started to look worried, Haidar gestured to the distance. "Throw in those dunes and the land up to the road and you have a deal. Send me the contract and payment details. I want this finalized by tomorrow morning."

Before the man could express his elation at this once-in-a-lifetime deal, Haidar waved goodbye and headed to his car.

As he drove away, he took one more turn around the area to soak in the sight of the place that would be his in hours. It already felt as if it had always belonged to him.

He could have gotten it at half the asking price.

But this haven of solace and seclusion was worth the expense. It hadn't felt right to haggle for something he appreciated this much.

And then, he had to save bargaining powers for what lay ahead.

The war of reacquiring Roxanne.

Haidar's body now officially hated "Cherie."

If it sustained lasting damage from the blow of deprivation her sudden appearance had dealt it, it would remember her as his worst enemy.

Nothing was working to mitigate the gnawing need for Roxanne. Not even bringing himself to release twice while mentally reenacting their plummet into sensual delirium, this time to an explosive end.

He'd continue to ache until he slaked his hunger in her body. At least three times a day. For a month. To start.

He rested his forehead against the wet marble as he let the barrage of cold, needle-sharp water pelt his flesh, attempt to put out the inferno she'd relit inside him.

And to think he'd sought her out to prove that he'd blown her effect on him out of proportion. That he'd find the older edition of the woman who'd dealt him his life's harshest humiliation and disillusion hard and off-putting. And that gaping hole in his psyche would be sealed once and for all.

Then he'd seen her. Talked to her. Dueled with her. Touched her. Fast-forward to his current agony.

Way to exorcise the memory of her, you idiot.

Instead, he'd only managed to resurrect it to full raging life. Worse. He'd managed to create a new breed of monster. An insatiable one that nothing would appease except total and repeated satisfaction of its every craving.

He had to give it everything it hungered for.

Not that she'd make it easy. Not that he'd want her to.

Sure, she'd melted at his touch, would have let him take everything he wanted, taken everything he gave. But he had no illusions. That surrender wouldn't be repeated. For some reason, she was averse to letting him back into her bed. Perhaps the career woman she was wanted her men safe and convenient, when he was anything but. Or she feared indulging her lust would compromise her career. Whatever it was, the element of surprise had been expended. All he had now was post-almost-sex upheaval.

He had to strike again while the iron was white-hot.

He exited the shower cubicle, didn't bother drying anything but his hands, strode across the hotel suite to his cell phone.

He dialed her number, gritted his teeth as he waited for her to pick up.

She would. Because she wouldn't recognize his number.

"Hello?"

He squeezed his eyes. *Aih*. It hadn't been temporary insanity. If one breathy hello could have him fully hard all over again, she now operated his hormonal controls.

His lips twitched in self-deprecation at his weakness, in satisfaction at intending to give in to it thoroughly.

"Is Cherie gone?"

The silence that greeted his question indicated that it had stopped her breathing. Good. He shouldn't be the only one having trouble breathing over this thing between them.

"I can come over if she is." He marveled at the humorous, sensual goading that came so naturally when he talked to her. "Better still, you come to me. I'm at Burj Al Samaa."

"Your turf is a hotel room?" she finally said. "And what would your terms be? Something from the room-service menu?"

A laugh rumbled from his gut. *Ya Ullah*, but this was new. He'd never enjoyed her wit this much before. But then, he hadn't known she was witty. Now that he thought about it, they'd talked last night more than they'd talked in a month back then. Their limited, stolen times together had been consumed mostly by hot and heavy sex. Back then, all the talking she'd done had been with Jalal. He'd felt left out, and he hadn't even known how much he'd missed.

He wouldn't miss a thing now. He'd have it all. All the fire and friction and fun of her.

"But I'm proposing a continuation of our first round, not a second one. *That* will be on my turf and terms."

"You're…" He could tell she muffled the phone with her hand. He could still decipher what she said. "I'll only be a moment. Sure, I'll take another cup of tea."

His smile froze. She…sounded totally different. Easygoing and eager. She'd never sounded like that with him. Not even when she'd been claiming to love him.

Then he heard the voice that answered her. Distant and muted. But definitely male.

Something hot and harsh spread like an intravenous shot of lava in his veins. Something he'd only ever felt on her account. Jealousy…

Jealousy? Now, *that* was idiotic. There was no application for anything like that in their situation. He shouldn't…*didn't* care what she did or who she did it with.

Even if he was stupid enough to care, she was probably at work, and that was a colleague or an assistant and he was again blowing things out of proportion…

"Listen, you exasperating lout. I spent this morning trying to resolve the mess you left behind, and the only thing I'll do if I come to your temporary turf is kick you where it counts. So it would be potency-preserving for you to get off my case."

Her threats still tickled him. But he couldn't laugh this time. Not after he'd heard her talking to that man. Hearing the difference in her voice now doused his enjoyment.

He still attempted a rejoinder. "Tut-tut, is that any way to talk to your probable new king?"

"First, I'm American if you've forgotten, so at best, the king of Azmahar would be my boss. Second, cows will skate before you become king. So stop wasting everyone's time and fly back to whatever vultures' aerie you swooped down from."

It was no use. Even with the tightness in his chest, which he wouldn't even try to analyze, every word that pelted out of her mouth seemed to find a receptor in his humor centers.

His lips spread. "The only time I'll swoop down will be to carry you away, my luscious lamb."

"Then too late in midair, you'll find out I'm no such thing."

"*Aih*. Thankfully. But the feline you really are is why you found me irresistible."

She used to say he was aptly named, a human lion. He'd called her his wildcat, his lioness, among other things.

"Nowadays, the world doesn't give a fig about your irresistibility, like I don't. But unlike you, who clearly aren't here to take part in resolving the crisis but to indulge in obnoxious score-settling, I have work to do. You had your fun last night, so be a good evil mogul and let me get on with it."

He lay back on the bed, hard as rock again. "How counterproductive can you get? You've just said the magic words that will assure that you won't see the last of me. Not before I make you eat those words, of course. Out of my hand. Again."

She didn't answer for a long moment. His breath shortened, his every muscle quivered with arousal and anticipation. What was that unpredictable storm of fire and femininity up to now?

"Satisfied your last-word syndrome? Just like you did your have-your-way disorder last night?"

And he laughed, deep and delighted. "I knew you had to be brilliant to be where you are today. But that's a truly novel way to have the last word, *ya naari*. I concede. This round goes to you."

"Oh, joy. You mean I can go now?"

"You mean you can't hang up on me?"

She did.

He laughed again, long and loud, as he hadn't done in... probably ever. Certainly never when he'd been alone.

Then he headed to the shower again.

He came out half an hour later, made a few phone calls.

He got the lay of the land, the schedule of relevant events for the next week. The most important function was next evening at the royal palace. A gathering of all political and economic figures engaging in the dance of trying to figure out how not to end up at the bottom of the food chain.

Roxanne was going to mediate the rituals.

Although she'd known because of her sensitive position, he was sure his candidacy wasn't public knowledge yet. Sure, he must have invaded the gossip circles and social media with his stunt at her door by now, but people probably thought he was just passing through, that she was the focus of his visit. He could still resume the secrecy of his purpose in Azmahar.

But she wanted him gone. Better. She'd hurled the gauntlet in his face. That settled it.

To hell with flying under the radar.

Time to prove to her he could get cows to skate.

Time to make an official swoop on Azmahar's vacant court.

The last rays of a blazing sunset were giving way to the dominion of a velvety evening as Haidar arrived at the edifice he'd been recruited to take over.

He pulled his rented Mercedes to a stop in the wide-as-a-four-lane-highway driveway and gazed up at it through the windshield. Twilight conspired with shadow-enhancing, detail-popping lighting to make it look like some colossal creature from a Dungeons & Dragons fantasy.

He exhaled, slammed out of the car. Qusr Al Majd—

literally Palace of Glory—must have seemed like a good idea to Faisal Aal Munsoori, its builder and the founder of Azmahar's now ex–royal family—the regrettable half of his genes. Back in the sixteenth century, overwhelming demonstrations of power, wealth and invulnerability were all the rage, after all.

And though the man's descendants had managed to destroy his legacy, impoverish his kingdom and squander his throne, Al Majd remained one of the world's architectural wonders. Or so it was touted by those who swooned at ostentatious constructions. It certainly gave the overhyped Taj Mahal a run for its money.

But the Taj was doing something useful besides look pretty. He'd certainly have tourists crawling all over *this* place if he ever became king. It should at least earn its keep.

As for him, should the dreaded day come, he'd frequent it only to keep up appearances and conduct power games. But to live, his—as of this morning—house had it beat by light-years.

He handed his keys to a gaping valet, took the hundred and one imperial white granite steps up to the entrance in twos. In moments he was striding through thirty-foot-high, elaborately carved and gilded doors, then crossing the suffocatingly ornate foyer, making a mental note to simplify and modernize the damn place if he ever became its keeper. And to do something about its patrons' sense of style, too.

He swept a coalescing gaze over the loitering crowd, grim humor twisting his lips. Considering that most looked as if they'd stepped out of an Addams-Family-cum-Aladdin masquerade, they had a nerve, gaping at him.

Seemed his presence here really was unexpected. Most probably unwelcome. He might be right, after all, and his recruiters knew nothing about what the people of Azmahar wanted or would accept. That, or the openmouthed gawkers had heard of his escapade at Roxanne's and were trying to imagine him spread-eagle on her bed begging to be used.

Not that either explanation mattered in the least.

He'd taken Roxanne's challenge and would see this game to the end. And if this kingless kingdom needed his leadership, it was damn well getting it.

Without slowing, he headed to his destination. He hadn't been here for over eight years, but he remembered well where all pompous, mostly pointless gatherings took place. In the Qobba ballroom, literally Dome, since it resided under a hundred-foot one at the heart of the palace's main building.

Good thing he also knew the place well enough to have learned its secret shortcuts. He made a set of memorized turns leading to a deserted corridor. Once in its blessed peace and subdued lighting, he breathed in relief to be rid of the bustle and invasive eyes.

Suddenly, footsteps joined his in the muted silence.

They came from behind. Sure, steady. Single. In an alternating rhythm to his footfalls. No attempt to catch up to him, just keeping pace.

A chill crackled through his every nerve.

It wasn't fury that someone was following him. Or even worry at the possibility of an attack.

It was a...presence that had engulfed him.

Immense. Potent. Ominous.

He stopped. So did the steps behind him. He turned slowly, felt the icy menace of that manifestation swirling around, hindering him like a straitjacket of chains. By midturn every instinct was shouting at him, *Don't look back! Just walk away!*

It took all he had to overcome the unreasoning aversion, mostly out of burning curiosity.

Next moment, it was his turn to gape.

Twenty paces away, a man stood so still he might have stopped time in its tracks, so dark he seemed to absorb shadows, snuffing out light. Tall, taller than even him, as broad, in an *abaya* that opened over shirt and pants, falling to the ground like a shroud of night. He projected something far larger than his physical size, emitted a force Haidar had never felt from another human being. His stance was deceptively relaxed, arms passive by his sides, face slightly lowered, dark eyes leveled on him from beneath dense, winged eyebrows, transmitting a message, a knowledge. That it would be at his whim that he walked away from this confrontation. And it looked like...

Rashid?

Every muscle in his body went slack with shock.

But...*no*. It couldn't be. The dimness was playing tricks on his vision, his imagination. He had been thinking of Rashid a lot lately, must be superimposing his memory on this man who resembled him—

"I heard you were pimping yourself out."

A sickening sensation jolted through him. That voice...

It shared elements with the one he'd last heard over the phone. After they'd become enemies. It had been cold and dark then, nothing like the lively, expressive baritone of the man who'd once been his best friend, sometimes closer to him than his own twin. He'd thought the ugly conflict had been coloring it.

It was far worse now. Fathomless with terrible mysteries.

It *was* Rashid. Changed almost beyond recognition, yet undoubtedly him. Then he moved. With every step closer, it became clearer. The orphaned distant cousin who, through what he'd once thought a twist of magnanimous fate, had become the biggest part of his and Jalal's life, had not merely changed.

He'd metamorphosed.

One of the most apparent facets of radical change was his hair. Rashid had always kept it long, to his guardian's distress. It had once reached the middle of his back. Even when he'd joined the army, he hadn't gotten the usual military crop.

It was now almost shaved.

But it was worse than that. As he came to a stop a few feet

away, in the light from a brass sconce, he could see it. A blood-curdling scar slashing its way from the corner of Rashid's left eye down to the corner of his jaw, slithering down his neck, then lower…

"So tell me, Haidar, how long have you been hiding this burning desire to be tied, gagged and abused?"

That new voice, that predatory rumble, revved inside his chest with an oppressive sorrow. For the two-decade friendship that had ended and taken another chunk of his humanity with it.

But regret served no purpose. And his humanity, according to the best of authorities, hadn't existed to start with.

Tilting his head, conceding that there would be no quarter given on either side, his huff was the very sound of bitter amusement. "Dominated. Abused is a whole different sub-category."

"Just goes to show you can never claim to know anyone."

The bile of confusion at how vicious Rashid had become in his enmity rose again. "So true."

Those black-as-an-abyss eyes poured icy goading and burning scorn over him. "Word is you exiled yourself from Zohayd after your mother tried to roast half the region and serve it to you on a platter. I wonder how much effort you put into fabricating that 'fact.'"

Rashid was one of the trio who could ever smash through his defenses, melt the layers of ice at his core. Boil his blood.

But a heated defense was exactly what Rashid wanted.

He'd long been done giving anyone what they wanted from him.

"You know me, Rashid. Such things come to me effort-lessly. I leave it to…lesser men to exert themselves."

Seemingly satisfied he *had* gotten the reaction he'd wanted after all, Rashid said, "So now that Zohayd has wised up and kicked you out on your ear, you've come to blight Azmahar with your presence. But if *you* knew anything about me, you'd know people leave it to me to…deal with discord and its sowers."

Without the tinge of sarcasm in his tone, he would have thought Rashid was deadly serious. Deadly, period. This was the face of someone who would kill without mercy.

As he had before.

Not that it worried him in the least. Two more things he'd been born without were fear and the ability to back down.

He raised Rashid double his provocation. "I just thought I'd come see what I can do to save Azmahar from the dire fate of having to settle for someone with your…fundamental deficiencies. You know how charitable I can be."

Something lethal slithered through the depths of Rashid's eyes—not exactly an emotion, but a reaction. Haidar didn't know why, but it forced his focus back to the scar.

Ya Ullah, how had that happened? When? Not during his army years. He knew that. What he didn't know was why he'd never heard of Rashid having it, or how he'd gotten it. Did anyone know?

He had a feeling no one did. No one but Rashid himself.

"How much did you pay those clans to 'choose' you as their candidate?"

Rashid's voice, harsher now, brought his eyes back to his. He didn't want his scar scrutinized. Especially by him.

Haidar exhaled. "How much did you?"

"I was actually offered whatever I could ask for. A lot of people will do anything to stop you, or your asymmetrical half, from taking the throne."

Suddenly he was fed up. He hated this. Hated that they had to keep stabbing at each other, deepening the wounds, widening the rift. He'd never wanted any of this. Now he wanted it all to stop.

It wouldn't be a concession of defeat if he reached out to

Rashid. It would be an olive branch to an injured adversary. Who should have never become one.

He inhaled. "A throne is something I never thought about or wanted, Rashid."

"That's a famous tactic." Rashid shrugged. "The sour-grapes maneuver. You were the Prince of Two Kingdoms who could never be in line for the throne of, either. What else can you do but pretend you aren't interested?"

"No pretense. After a lifetime of watching what kind of pain in the neck, heart and butt being king is from the woeful example of my father, I wouldn't wish it even on you."

"I'm so touched that you consider me your worst enemy."

Wanting to kick himself for the terribly timed joke, when it was certain Rashid had taken it literally, he started to clarify.

Rashid overrode him. "But don't I now share that status with your pointedly absent semi-demon twin?"

Haidar waited for the mention of Jalal to finish turning the skewer embedded in his gut.

Rashid only stabbed him harder. "I came after you only to tell you how entertaining it will be, watching you two campaign for the throne, adding your arrogance to your uncle's ineptness, your cousins' excesses and your mother's all-round villainy."

Having inflicted all the injuries he'd wanted to, Rashid turned.

He'd walk away, and any chance to heal their severed bond would be lost.

Haidar lunged after him, grabbed his arm.

Rashid's gaze lowered to the fingers digging into his *abaya*-wrapped flesh. Haidar could swear his hand burned.

He didn't care if Rashid possessed heat vision for real and would burn off his hand. He had to know.

"What happened to you, Rashid?"

After a chilling moment, Rashid calmly removed his hand from his arm, stepped away as if Haidar's nearness soiled him.

His gaze was opaque. "You were always a self-involved son of a major bitch, Haidar."

He wasn't up to contesting the accuracy of that summation, wasn't sure how it applied here. "I'm trying to get involved now."

"A bit too late for that. Years too late."

"*B'haggej' jaheem.* Stop being cryptic. How did you get this way?"

"You mean the scar? You should have seen it before the corrective surgery."

Haidar thought his head would burst with frustration. "I mean everything. The visible and…otherwise."

For a long moment it appeared Rashid wouldn't bother answering.

Then he said, "I dropped my guard." His glare could have pulverized a rock. "Trusted the wrong people."

Haidar staggered back a step. "Are you saying I somehow had a hand in this?"

"It's so heartwarming to see how you've mastered self-deception, not to mention self-absolution, Haidar."

Now his brain was threatening to liquefy with incomprehension. "That's insane, Rashid. I know we've had our differences in the past years—"

"You mean we've been trying to destroy each other."

"I've been trying to stop *you* from destroying *me*. And whatever I did in retaliation for your actions, it was only business."

"This…" Rashid tilted his head, giving him an eyeful, slid a lazy finger down the ridge of disfigurement to the base of his neck. Haidar was certain it snaked lower onto his back. It seemed to have forged all the way to the recesses of his soul. "…was only business, too."

Haidar stared at him, helplessness and confusion sinking their claws into his gut. "You're making no sense."

"Neither are you, if you think you can reinstate any personal interaction between us again. And if you think I'd ever be party to making you feel better about yourself in this lifetime, you have me confused with the wrong Rashid Aal Munsoori. One who ceased to exist long ago."

Haidar grabbed his arm again as he started to turn. "Rashid, you at least owe me—"

Rashid rounded on him, snarling. "I don't owe you, or Jalal, or any member of your family a damn thing—"

He stopped, his eyes burning black holes into Haidar's soul.

Then his lips spread in a sinister parody of a smile, his teeth gleaming eerily against his darkened skin.

Haidar barely suppressed a shiver.

What the hell *had* Rashid metamorphosed into?

"I beg your pardon, Haidar." What? "I was inaccurate when I said I don't owe you and your family a thing. I do owe you. A lot of pain and damage. I always pay my debts."

This time when he turned away, Haidar let him go.

Before he exited the corridor, Rashid turned with a serene-as-the-grave glance. "Sit tight, Haidar, and wait for your share of my payback."

Five

I haven't gotten my share of your payback yet?
   What were the past two years all about then?

Haidar struggled not to pursue Rashid, tackle him to the ground in front of everyone and force him to explain.

One thing stopped him. Knowing Rashid wouldn't explain, not even if he beat him to a pulp. Not that he could. Not without being pulped back. Which wasn't a bad idea. They could just rip each other to shreds, get the bitterness exorcised and get it over with. Maybe even get back to the way they'd once been.

According to Rashid, that would require a time machine.

But for the present, the opening round was over. Rashid had pulled back to his corner, expecting Haidar to crush his peace offering underfoot as he stomped to his. Instead, he would get informed. He needed knowledge to convince Rashid to call off the fight. Now that he knew Rashid believed he had some-how been party to whatever had happened to him, he would pay any price to learn the truth.

Until then, he had other struggles to handle.

Roxanne. Jalal. Azmahar and its empty throne. Business conflicts with Rashid at their core...*ya Ullah*, Rashid...

He hadn't thought anything could be worse than what had happened with Roxanne. Or Jalal. Or their mother. This was. This won the category of heart-wrenching developments, hands down.

He found himself entering the ballroom. Seemed he'd continued his path on Auto. The expansive space, decked like an Arabian Nights bazaar, only peripherally registered in his awareness.

Then something sharpened his focus. A decrease in the overlapping voices and clinking utensils, the cessation of melancholy Azmaharian music. He zeroed in on the cause.

Roxanne.

She was walking up the stage. Straight, brisk, no shadow of hesitation or self-consciousness, no hint of a sway or curves to distract from her purpose or undermine her efficiency. She was dressed sedately, the flame of her hair subdued in a twist at her nape, her face made up in neutral colors that downplayed her vivacious coloring and the sensuality of her features. How different from the mass of passionate fire he'd lost his mind over eight years ago. Or the bathrobe-decked firebrand he'd done the same with a couple of days ago. This facet of her still aroused the hell out of him.

Seemed she dialed the password to his libido no matter what.

It was incredible for someone of her youth and looks to be taken this seriously in a patriarchal society where chauvinistic tendencies survived to this day. Here it remained accepted that certain roles were male exclusive or dominated, with women like Roxanne being exceptions.

And what an exceptional rarity she was. He luxuriated in her every nuance as she took the podium, addressed the now pin-dropping-silent crowd, cordial, confident, in control. Something thrilled inside his chest. Admiration, pride...

He gritted his teeth. He didn't have to like or appreciate her to give in to his hunger for her. Those sentiments could actually dampen his lust, hamper his plans to satisfy it. This insidious softening had to be curbed. Starting right this second.

He moved out of the shadows. Instead of keeping to the periphery, he cut right through the tables. Might as well get all the staring and exclamations out of the way en masse.

Sure enough, his passage caused a wildfire of buzzing and bustling to sweep through the ballroom.

His progress was unimpeded until he passed by a table populated by his recruiters. Elation replaced their surprise too soon. They pounced on him, eager to show everyone that he was on their coalition's side. He answered them by insisting he was here to perform *independent* research, impatience rising as opposing brands of passion and compulsion burned into him. Rashid's from the entrance, Roxanne's at the podium.

People rushed to make a place for him at the table closest to her, flipping rabid curiosity between them as if watching an unfolding candid-camera show. She waited in seeming calmness for the disturbance to die down and for him to take his seat. But he sensed her fury.

He would have relished it if he wasn't too raw to enjoy more hostility, even one fueled by a hunger as vast as his.

He had to deal with it. Just as she had to with his presence.

She did, glossed over the disruption he'd caused, resumed her opening address before turning over the mic to the first speaker.

He watched her descend the stage, walk to the end of the ballroom. She took a seat aligned with his view of Rashid, who stood alone at the entrance like a demon guarding the mouth of hell. Very symbolic.

He cast each a look, was hurled back a hail of antipathy.

All he needed now was for Jalal to walk in, and the triad of wrath and rejection would be complete.

He exhaled, tried to focus on the proceedings. Though what he hoped to achieve here, he no longer knew.

The people who had mattered most to him hated his guts. He didn't think his transgressions against each warranted that level of acrimony. Seemed just being himself was enough to earn it.

And he thought a whole nation would want him?

Another major point was they—even Rashid with his scars and transformation—were prospering with him gone from their lives.

Maybe that should tell him something. That there was no escaping his mother's legacy. That all he could ever be was a malignant influence. That redemption was out of the question and the best thing he could do for Azmahar was stay the hell away.

He turned one last time to the two who thought that was a given. At the confirmation in their eyes, a conviction took root.

He turned around, giving them his back, one thing settled.

He'd prove them and everyone, starting with himself, wrong.

Three hours of moderating the self-important, conflicting, anachronistically tribal so-called elite would have been enough. But to do it while being subjected to Haidar's burning focus had shot Roxanne's nerves.

She and her team had worked hard to get all major movers and shakers in the kingdom together, find out their positions and see how they'd mix. She was supposed to come out with a firm idea of who could be part of the solution, and who'd better be sidelined.

Then Rashid Aal Munsoori had walked in.

She'd thought the introduction of that superpower this early would disrupt a balance that hadn't yet been found. The man seemed like such a force of...darkness; he'd swayed people just by showing up. And scared them. She'd thought he was the worst thing that could have happened. Then, enter Haidar.

It had been his presence that had polarized reactions, incited passions and generally disturbed everything.

Seemed his effect on people was universally consistent. And *that* when he'd only sat there silently watching.

She'd barely stopped the situation from devolving into a mess.

Avoiding eye contact with anyone, she strode to get out before people could corner her with questions she couldn't or wouldn't satisfy. Before Rashid could cut his way through his detainers to her. Most important, before...

"So the question is—what *was* the point of all that?"

And she'd almost made it!

She just stopped herself from stomping her foot and screeching a chagrined *no*. From running the hell out of there. Right after taking off her high heels and hurling them at Haidar.

Unable to give their audience any indication of how much she'd like his head on a stick, she slowly turned. And almost toppled over.

He'd looked stunning from afar. It was far worse up close. If possible, he looked better than he had two days ago. In a steel-gray suit the exact color of his eyes that worshipped his every inch and flaunted his proportions, he looked like a sun god. Eyes gleaming in the soft-toned ambience, skin glowing like heated copper, hair shimmering like a black panther's coat.

All in all, a divine masterpiece of masculinity. *And* born to exist in backdrops of such opulence, created to justify their extravagance, which showcased his grandeur.

To make it worse, that voice of darkest wine and velvet cascaded over her again. "Was that a drive for the up-for-grabs court? There *are* enough wannabes to turn the strongest stomach."

Her teeth ground together as he left barely enough distance

between them for public decorum, his scent and virility co-cooning her senses, triggering desire and distress.

Somehow she found enough discipline to pretend an impersonal smile for their now-avid audience. "A king doesn't a royal system make. It was agreed that we have to fill the lower slots in the hierarchy before the top is filled."

"So you want the new king to come to a ready-made government. All I can say is, good luck getting Jalal or Rashid to return your calls once you reveal your figurehead intentions."

If she made him think that was what was on offer, it would send him out of Azmahar within the hour.

Too damn bad she was too professional. "It will be a transitional government until a king sits on the throne."

"Then said king will be free to toss whatever pieces he doesn't approve of back in the box?"

"I don't think such unilateral decisions would be welcome anymore in Azmahar."

"You think any of the candidates will even consider such a deficient position? Such limitation of power? Such an upside-down process? You think *I* would?"

"We're just trying to learn from the mistakes of the past."

"Even in democracies, presidents pick their deputies. You expect a king in our region not to pick his trusted people?"

"As long as they are picked through merit, not nepotism."

"That isn't even an issue in my case, or Jalal's or Rashid's, for that matter. We were headhunted because we proved in the big bad world of business and politics that we know who to pick to help us run our multibillion-dollar enterprises. We're not about to become tribal, blood-blinded throwbacks if we sit on a throne."

His eyes were all *gotcha* when she had no ready answer.

Before she could regain ground, he changed direction. "So I understand why my uncle's slew of successors was bypassed for the king's position. Any reason they are now for all other positions?"

That she had an answer for. "For the same reasons you say you understand. Just as the clans' council that formed after the king's abdication refused to let his sons and brothers succeed him, they wouldn't let them assume any significant roles. It was agreed the sons are too inexperienced and the brothers too same-school, and all are guided by the same entourage that damaged Azmahar."

"And you think the bozos present here today are any better?"

"They're here today so we can weed out the bozos."

His lips spread. "It would be far easier to leave those in, and pick out the non-bozo types. Want my advice on how to do it?"

"No. But you're going to blight me with it, anyway."

His grin grew wider. "Play back the evening's taped hoopla. Eliminate anyone who spoke out of turn or lost his temper. You'll be left with five out of five hundred. I counted. Those are the only people *I'd* have in my cabinet."

That was exactly what she'd thought, too. Damn him.

She wasn't about to tell him that. "You're founding a new kingdom and recruiting ministers for it?"

"Cute. But if you don't heed my advice, just have a raffle. Anyone but those five would be equally disastrous, after all."

"Thanks for the gems of wisdom. But we won't do anything until we're in possession of enough data."

"And what else are 'we' going to do?"

"*We* won't do anything. While *I* have to go."

"Good. I'll tag along."

Yeah. Right. She'd sooner have a lion in tow. One just released after a month of captive starvation.

"Why don't you stay and complete the chaos?"

His eyebrows shot up in what must be simulated surprise. "Chaos?"

Her genial expression didn't waver even as her hiss attempted to disembowel him. "I planned this to be a relaxed event, even a bit festive—"

"*That* explains it. I thought you were trying to start a new tradition—Azmaharian Halloween."

She sharpened her tone. "I wanted to put the attendees in the most cooperative frame of mind, to alleviate the mood of doom and gloom that permeates the kingdom. So thanks so much for spoiling everything."

"Me? What did I do?" Those mile-long lashes swept up and down.

She almost felt their swoosh, certainly felt it fan her fire. "You have the superpower of discord sowing. And you have it on constantly, exercise it at will, actively or passively."

She waited for him to volley back something inflammatory and incontrovertible. Lightness only drained, leaving his face bleak.

Then it got worse. Agony flitted through his eyes as they tore away. She followed their trajectory to the most disturbing presence around. Rashid.

As if feeling his gaze, Rashid half turned. And if looks could dismember, Haidar would have been in pieces.

She shuddered at the force that blasted between the two men. Surprisingly, the viciousness felt one-way. What emanated from Haidar was as intense, but different in texture. Something she'd never thought to feel from him. Despondency.

Haidar returned his gaze to her. "Rejoice, Roxanne. I'm taking my disruptive presence away from inhabited areas."

Then he turned and strode out of the ballroom.

Roxanne stared at Haidar's receding back for the second time in as many days. Then she found herself rushing after him.

She had to pour on speed to catch up with him. In a deserted corridor that seemed to materialize out of nowhere.

It was only when she caught him back that her actions sank in.

What the *hell* was she doing?

He turned to her, something like…hurt filling his eyes, and she blurted out, "What's wrong?"

She almost kicked herself. What did she care if anything— if *everything*—was wrong with Haidar Aal Shalaan?

It seemed he wouldn't answer. Then he exhaled. "A lot, evidently. Probably everything."

She should say something borderline civil, get the hell away.

Instead she asked, "So what did I say that triggered your sudden retreat?" At his surprise, she rushed to add, "I'm asking only so I can replicate my success in the future."

She expected him to slam her with something bedeviling. He didn't.

"You…confirmed something Rashid said to me earlier. It wasn't the only time I've noted your corresponding opinions of me."

"We have more in common where you're concerned. I heard you were friends once. Now you're relentless enemies."

She expected him to say *they* weren't enemies, just no longer lovers. A state of affairs he had no problem reinstating.

Again, he thwarted her expectations, nodded, his eyes returning to the deadness, the defeat, that so disturbed her. "I somehow thought our enmity wasn't such common knowledge."

"Are you kidding? Even if my job didn't revolve around keeping track of the honchos of economy, it would have been kinda hard to miss the two most meteorically rising players in the tech world butting heads. You've been giving *Clash of the Titans* a run for its money for the past two years."

"It might be hard for you to believe, but I didn't start it."

"I believe you."

He frowned. "You do?"

"You never 'start' anything. You drive people to the point where they want to take you apart. When they try, you retaliate, viciously, and to the world it seems it's only legitimate for you to do so."

His laugh was bitter. "Of course, *that's* what you believe. And you might even be right. But not in Rashid's case."

"He *is* too powerful for even you to decimate and assimilate."

"I meant I didn't drive him to it. And since you asked, that's what's wrong—being unsure what did. *And* the…conversation we had."

"It shed light on his motivations?"

"More like caused an avalanche that buried them totally."

She hated feeling dismayed on his behalf, glared at him. "It's not possible you don't know."

"I *thought* I knew. That it was another escalating, self-perpetuating train accident of a mess, which the sweeping majority of my relationships have turned into."

Good thing to be reminded of *that* salient point.

He might be unable to connect his actions to the mess he made of people's lives. Didn't make him innocent of the crime.

Hackles rising, she smirked. "Why wonder if it's your M.O.?"

"Because once I saw him again, it ripped me out of the depersonalized war we've been waging on each other and back to the realm of the personal. And none of it made sense anymore."

A knot formed in her throat at his disconsolate tone. "Did you retrace incidents to what could have started this?"

His gaze clouded, as if he had plunged into his memories, before he said, "We were twenty, he was twenty-one." Her chest tightened more when he said *we,* as if he and Jalal were one indivisible unit. "Rashid and I were taking the same courses, already starting up our tech-development projects. Then his guardian died. He hadn't truly needed a guardian

beyond early childhood—he'd been earning his own living
since his early teens. But his guardian left a mess of debts.
And Rashid took it upon himself to repay them. *That* was
our first fight.

"I was angry that he'd take on the debts of someone who
hadn't taken him in willingly to start with. A man whose sons
were living in the luxury their father's debts had provided them
with. It was they who should repay that money, not Rashid,
whom they'd never treated like family and would have mis-
treated if not for his closeness to us. But Rashid would sit there
and take my anger, and after I exhausted every argument, he
would just say the same thing again. His honor demanded it."

"But what did he think he could do? At twenty-one, without
a college degree or capital, I can understand he could support
himself, but pay off massive debts…?"

He grimaced in remembered exasperation. "He had it all
figured out. An American military base was being erected in
Azmahar, and the Azmaharian army was having a recruitment
drive, promising top recruits incredible financial and educa-
tional advancements. He was confident he'd be among those,
calculated he'd pay off the debts in five years while doing
something he'd always admired and gaining an education he
could have never afforded on his own."

"That does sound like a solid plan."

"Not to us. Not to *me*. It was a shock that he'd chosen his
university not because it was close to his girlfriend but because it was what he could afford. We were determined to help
him, said we'd get the money from our father or older brothers, or make them find a way to get the debts dropped. But
the pride-poisoned idiot refused. *He* would honor his guardian at whatever cost."

"I still don't understand why you so objected to his plans."

"Because the cost might have been his *life*."

"Uh…come again?"

"At the time, due to some major stupidities by my uncle and clan, an armed conflict between Azmahar and Damhoor seemed certain. We took turns telling him what a self-destructive fool he'd be to join the army just in time to be sent to war. *Ya Ullah*…how I never throttled him, I'll never know."

Haidar mimed the violent gesture, his whole body bunching, his face contorting with relived frustration and desperation.

It was fascinating, *shattering,* this glimpse into his past. Another reminder that she hadn't known him at all, more proof of how unimportant she'd been that he hadn't shared this with her, clearly a major incident in his life.

But it was worse than that. She'd believed he'd been born without the capacity for emotional involvement. That had mitigated her heartache and humiliation.

But his emotions did exist. And they could be powerful, pure. Seemed it took something profound to unearth them, such as what he'd shared with Rashid. Nothing so trivial as what he'd had with her.

The discovery had the knife that had long stopped turning in her heart stabbing it all over again.

Which was beyond ridiculous. This was ancient history.

What was important here was the history in the making. This was an unrepeatable opportunity to learn vital information about two of the candidates for the throne. It could be crucial to the critical role she was here to play.

Swallowing the stupid personal pain, she forced out the steady words of the negotiator she was. "It sounds like he should have loved you more for caring so much about his well-being and safety."

"Then you don't know much about how young men can be with each other. Our response to fear, for him, of losing him, wasn't pretty. I especially…got carried away." He wiped a palm over his eyes wearily. "We were drawn to Rashid as children when we recognized that he had big problems, too. We had our share, growing up in Zohayd when our non-Zohaydan half belonged to a family everyone despised and a queen everyone hated. But we had a family. Rashid had only us. And we used that. Jalal pressured him through his loyalty to us. But I knew him better, knew pressuring him wouldn't work, knew how to push his buttons. I played as dirty as I thought I had to."

Another reminder what a prince Haidar could be. How he considered any means justifiable to get his end.

"And you failed?" He nodded dejectedly. "So he still left, only with your creative cruelty as his last memory of you."

"*Aih.*" His eyes let her see into a time of personal hell. "Then war broke out. Zohayd and Judar intervened, but not before thousands died on both sides. Rashid was among the missing. We went insane searching for him for weeks. Then he returned, exhausted but unharmed, leading his platoon across the desert."

Wow. Colorful past that Rashid Aal Munsoori had. And undocumented. Beyond basic data, he seemed to have popped fully formed into the business world two years ago.

Haidar went on. "He was decorated a war hero, paid off his guardian's debts, accumulated graduate degrees and promotions at supersonic speed, and took part in two more armed conflicts by the time he was twenty-eight. We were still speaking then."

Which meant it was around the time she'd left Haidar that his breakup with Rashid had also occurred. "So whatever you did before he joined the army wasn't what caused the rift?"

"It caused *a* rift. He'd answer one call out of five, and when he came back on leave, our relationship was never the same. He wasn't. He rarely went out with us, together or one on one, and when he did, he was subdued, weighing every word. It made me so resentful, so damn worried, I think I…" He gave an exasperated wave.

"Overcompensated?" she put in.

His lips twisted in agreement. "Then one day he told me he'd been offered a major promotion, wouldn't say what it was, but that he'd be traveling all the time and off the grid for most of it. I sensed he was telling me not to expect to hear from him again. And again I…"

"Made it sound as if it wouldn't matter to you either way."

"Will you stop retro-predicting what I did?" He drove his hands into his hair, every move loaded with self-recrimination. "But *aih*. Though it didn't happen quite so…peacefully."

She could fill in the spaces with the worst she could imagine.

"He dropped off the face of the earth. Then three years ago, he suddenly called me. He sounded as if he was drunk or high. I was stunned, since the Rashid I knew was a health and sobriety freak. But what did I know about what he'd become in the years since I last saw him? He said he needed help, gave me an address then hung up. I rushed there, found nothing."

"You didn't find him?"

"I found *literally* nothing. No such place existed. I kept calling him, but the number he'd called from was out of range. Days later, he texted me, saying he'd been drinking, and to please forget it. I texted back, begged to see him. He never answered me. Frustrated with his on-off behavior, I did my best to forget it. And him. A year later, right after the mess in Zohayd was resolved, he came back into my life. As enemy number one.

"I thought he was giving me a hard time to get payback, and to prove that he was 'a year older and a light-year better.' So I called him, offered him a partnership, the one we'd dreamed of as boys. He responded that the only and last time he'd put his hand in mine again would be after I'd signed everything I had over to him, and to never contact him again. I was so frustrated with him and his grudge-holding that I never spoke to him again. Until today."

He was telling her things she already knew—how he couldn't see beyond what *he* wanted and felt. He'd done the same with her. With Jalal. She shouldn't sympathize. But she did.

Maybe because he was explaining the motives behind his actions for the first time…? It changed him from a callous brute to someone who'd never learned how not to appear so. It painted him in grays instead of blacks.

But it still made no difference to those he'd injured.

He looked at her as if he needed her to tell him he wasn't crazy. "But none of that explains his enmity, does it? It was all just…words. And he had to know I didn't mean them."

"So he's a mind reader, too, among his other talents?"

He grimaced. "I mean he *should* have put what I said in context. Even if he bought every word I said, that still wasn't a good enough reason to want to bury me alive."

"Depends on what you said."

Admission blared in his eyes. "Unforgivable things."

Another shock to hear him admit that.

"And at first I felt so guilty, I let him tear into me. But soon his actions made me so mad, I threw myself into what escalated into a war. I was resigned I was responsible for our conflict, deserved his enmity and could do nothing but continue our battles. But seeing him in person again today jolted through me like a thousand volts."

She had to nod. "Quite understandable. He's one scary dude."

"But that's the problem. That's not the 'dude' I knew. And that *scar… Ya Ullah.*"

She frowned. "Scar?"

He looked at her as if *she* was crazy. "How can you miss it? How isn't it common knowledge?"

"I haven't seen him up close. And according to my sources, Rashid's first appearance in Azmahar in the past seven years was today. Seems no one has seen him before to spread the news."

He nodded slowly. "That makes sense."

Not to her. "That's what shook you so much? The change in his appearance?"

"It's not only that. He's become someone totally different."

"Being a soldier can change you. Being in armed conflicts certainly will."

He shook his head. "I thought that, too, but it's more. Something happened to him. Something terrible."

"More terrible than being in a war?"

"Yes. And he believes I had a hand in it."

Her heart kicked her ribs, hard. "Is he right?"

His whole being stiffened, as if she'd kicked him in the gut. "What do you think?"

Haidar was many things. A criminal wasn't one of them. And he would be worse, a monster, if he'd had a hand in his former friend's physical and psychological disfigurement.

She bit her lip. "What will you do to prove him wrong?"

Tension seeped from him—something like…thankfulness?—staining his gaze as he acknowledged her exoneration. "I need to investigate before I can formulate a plan. It'll be harder because I can't have anyone finding out anything I discover when Rashid has gone to such lengths to cover it up."

"Let me know what I can do to help."

This time when his eyes bored into hers, there was no mistaking it. He was grateful. More. Moved.

Tears suddenly stung her eyes. "Haidar…"

Before she could utter another word, she found herself pressed against the wall with two hundred–plus pounds of hard maleness and demand pressing into her every inch. Her gasp of shock was swallowed by his openmouthed possession. His tongue breached her, thrust into her, driving, claiming, conquering.

The taste of him, the heat and feel of him, what he was doing to her, the way his hands sought all her secrets, sparked her ever-simmering insanities. She writhed against him, nothing left inside her but the need for his long-yearned-for assuagement.

He bent, bit her nipples through her blouse, rose to receive her sharp confessions of pleasure. He resumed devouring her as his big, rough hands slid up her thighs, bunching her skirt, pushing beneath her soaked panties, cupping her buttocks with strength and greed, lifting her, spreading her for his domination.

Falling into an abyss of mindlessness, she clung around him, delighting in his bulk and power as he filled the cradle of her thighs, the one thing left to hang on to in her world.

A storm raged through her, rising from the core his hardness thrust and thrust against. Moans spilled from her with his every wrenching kiss as he escalated the rhythm simulating possession into a fever. She opened wider for him, mouth and legs, to do whatever he wanted to her, to give her everything she needed.

"Haidar..."

The coil of tension in her core suddenly snapped. She cried out into his mouth as the pulse of pleasure tore through her. He had no mercy, his every grind against her bucking body continuing to feed it, unwind it, until she was a lax mass of stunned satisfaction in his arms.

He slowed then stopped his thrusts. Then, still hard and pressed against her quivering flesh, his lips relinquishing hers in one last clinging kiss, he raised his head, looked down at her with eyes raging with arousal, heavy with promise.

"I know what you can do to help me, *ya naari*. Let me pleasure you properly, repeatedly, for the rest of the night."

Six

"Come home with me, Roxanne."

Haidar heard his voice, thick, ravenous. Agonized.

His body would implode if she said no now.

But she wouldn't. Every fabulous inch of her voluptuousness was pliant against him with surrender, her eyes stunned with the explosiveness of this encounter, heavy with wanting more.

At least it had been explosive for her. It made him want to thump his chest that he'd made her come, so quickly, so powerfully, without even taking her. It was beyond gratifying to know he could still have her out of her mind with a touch. But his arousal was far past the red zone.

He could have so easily joined her. Her release had almost driven him over the brink. He'd held back with all he had. He would take his pleasure only inside her.

He'd waited too long to have it any other way.

"Say yes, Roxanne." His fingers pressed into the delight of her flesh, his body roaring from the feel of her and the scent of her satisfaction.

Her breasts still shuddered, her chaotic breathing pressing

them against his burning chest. Her full lips, red and swollen with the savagery of his hunger, trembled. Receding pleasure and resurging arousal weighed down her lids, ignited her eyes with an emerald fever.

She would say yes. And he'd spend the rest of the night possessing and pleasuring her in every corner of the house he'd bought just for—

Something tugged at the edge of his clouded awareness. A sound. The unhurried, powerful rhythm of footsteps...

She stiffened. Then she exploded, pushing him away as if she'd found herself wrapped around a slimy monster.

Unable to think, to move, he stood frozen as she struggled to pull down her skirt. Then, without looking back, she ran away.

"I am really curious, Haidar."

Rashid.

He turned, his body clamped in a vise of agony.

Rashid was approaching from the direction of the ballroom this time, his progress slow, steady, his face impassive. Haidar answered his empty stare with a glare reflecting the storm that still raged inside him. Rashid would no doubt add to the havoc.

"Tell me, Haidar, how did you manage to reach any level of success, let alone your admittedly impressive one? Men who can't keep it in their pants aren't known for the discipline and acumen needed to attain, let alone maintain, success."

Haidar gritted his teeth against the urge to blacken Rashid's darker-than-sin eyes even more. "After payback already, Rashid?"

"Actually, I'm doing you a favor. A juvenile demonstration at the door of the kingdom's foremost politico-economic consultant is one thing. Especially since reports confirm you stayed at her place only long enough to get your face slapped. And she made the rounds next day like a mother apologizing for her delinquent teenager's antics. But to...sexually harass her in the middle of a public and vital function she organized, in a corridor, against a wall? I really had to break that up."

"And you're calling this a favor...how? Saving my image? Aren't you supposed to be pulverizing it?"

The scorn in Rashid's eyes could have frozen him, if he wasn't seething. "I'm not using the handicap of your sexual adolescence to beat you, Haidar. Not when there is such an array of far more relevant vices to discredit you with."

"Best of luck with that, Rashid. And just so we're clear, with the way your...favor might have crippled me for life, I think I now hate you as much as you evidently hate me."

"Then my work is done. For today." Rashid gave him a mock bow, slowed down a fraction as he passed him. "And Haidar, this woman—she's good."

Blood shot in his head as he grabbed Rashid's arm. "Don't you ever *dare*—"

Rashid cut his rising fury short, serenely removing his hand. "She is *very* good. I watched her tonight, watched others as they responded to her, questioned them extensively afterward. She's putting together what looks like Azmahar's only chance for stability until our little pissing contest is concluded. Don't sabotage her credibility and effectiveness."

With that, he continued on his way, his *abaya* and that aura of inhumanity billowing around him like a malevolent force field.

He didn't look back.

Haidar was getting used to everyone doing that.

But he had to concede that Rashid was right about one thing.

He was in danger of destroying everything he'd ever achieved. He'd been making uncharacteristic mistakes for the past two years. He'd managed to rectify each so far. But his inability to predict consequences had been coming faster since he'd returned here. Since he'd seen Roxanne again.

He'd come here thinking he'd fulfill his objectives. Nudge Roxanne toward the bed he had prepared for her, and perform a preliminary feasibility study of his candidacy.

But not only had he crashed headfirst into Rashid's unexpected reappearance and uberhostility and disrupted the proceedings he'd intended to learn from, he'd ended up pouring out his bewilderment to Roxanne before losing control and nearly consuming her whole. Against a *wall*.

So, a roundup of the evening? Rashid had had the first and last word. Roxanne had eluded him again. He'd learned zip. And his mind and manhood had been dealt near-crippling blows.

Not waiting for the pain to subside, since it probably wouldn't tonight, he exited the corridor of chaos. He plowed through the masses of people who now tried to swarm him, and for the first time since he'd come to Azmahar, wished his bodyguards were around. He'd ordered Khaleel to keep them away, to Khaleel's anxious chagrin, not wanting them around to witness his encounters with Roxanne. Without them running interference for him, it took him longer to extricate himself from the throngs. It was an endless ten minutes before he was on his way back to his hotel.

He couldn't go to his new house. His fantasies of continuing the night there with Roxanne were so vivid, they might cause him permanent damage if he went alone.

But…maybe he didn't have to go alone.

Fully hard again with anticipation, he dialed her number.

His call was rejected. By the third time, he got the message. The insanity had lifted and her unclouded mind was screaming at her—and probably at him—in outrage for what the gross indiscretion he'd dragged her into might have cost her. She might even think it *had* cost her everything. She hadn't looked back, hadn't seen who'd walked in on them.

He parked in the first off-road shoulder, texted her. It was only Rashid.

It was after he'd resumed driving that it hit him.

Only Rashid? What was wrong with him?

She must now be going ballistic, thinking she'd exposed herself as terminally ditzy and in *his* power to the man whose opinion mattered more than the rest of the kingdom combined.

Swearing at himself, he parked again, texted again. It's purely on me in Rashid's opinion. He thinks you're good. Very good. His words. Absolutely no harm done.

Hoping this was enough to alleviate her anxiety, he resumed his drive. He would give her time to go home, then show up at her door.

No, he couldn't. He never repeated himself.

He needed a new strategy. He'd been going about his pursuit all wrong. He'd been too impatient, too hungry, hadn't been listening to her properly. He now realized the only reason she'd been resisting him was her dread of compromising her position.

In the past, she'd initially held him off to protect her mother's and her own reputation in Azmahar's conservative society. He'd gone to great lengths to arrange for their relationship to remain a secret to free her from that fear. Of course, that had served his purposes, too.

But she was now more serious than ever about her image. So if he stopped his impulsive incursions, assured her of privacy and secrecy, he'd bet she'd beat him to that bed. Just as she had in those months of stolen passion.

Rashid, damn it, had been right about this, too. He couldn't compromise her. For every reason there was.

He needed to locate some restraint. And he'd thought he had nothing but. Seemed that was only because there'd been no temptations.

But seeing this matured Roxanne, discovering this new ability to talk to her, the even more intense sexual affinity... now, *that* was temptation.

It was merciful he posed as overwhelming a temptation to her.

Now to make it safe for her to give in to it, to him, fully.

Absolutely no harm done.

Roxanne stared at Haidar's text message for what must have been the thousandth time in the past week.

There'd been dozens more since. But this was the one she kept scrolling back to. And every time she read it, she wished he were in front of her. So she could break his jaw.

She'd been burning with mortification since that day. She'd seriously considered running out of the royal palace and out of Azmahar. She'd been certain her job had been ruined, that she'd be the laughingstock of the kingdom within hours. Maybe the world, if her viral video prediction to Haidar came to pass.

Haidar had played her like the merciless pro that he was. Softening her with one unexpected reaction after another before slamming her with that sob story, the glimpse into the vulnerability she hadn't believed existed. As his coup de grâce, he'd trained stirred and shaken eyes on her, and she'd melted in his arms. Literally. Anyone could have walked in on them and seen her wrapped around him and in the throes of orgasm.

Rashid Aal Munsoori had.

And Haidar had *dared* to say absolutely no harm done!

It didn't matter that he *had* been trying to reassure her that the incident wouldn't cost her her reputation and position. It didn't matter that she had seen Rashid twice since then, and he'd treated her with utmost respect and decorum, without a trace of knowing in his eyes. It didn't matter that there *did* seem to be no harm done whatsoever.

She still wanted to do Haidar some serious harm.

He'd probably encourage her to. And love every second.

Well, she'd get the chance to oblige him in an hour's time.

She was heading to his house. His turf. And on his terms.

He had managed to make it an official summons, too.

But at least she was one of many. A whole delegation had been summoned to said turf to discuss what she regretfully admitted were relevant and pressing matters.

He *had* been laying much-needed groundwork in the past week, dealing with so much. And to her surprise, he was working, if indirectly, with both Rashid and Jalal to manage the oil spill. The three of them, each with his specific powers and strategies, and with their considerable connections, had surrounded the problem from all sides and were well on the way to resolving it.

She'd joked to her team this morning that the plan to save Azmahar should have three kings playing musical thrones.

He'd summoned the five men that he referred to as his "cabinet" to discuss some of the other serious economic and diplomatic problems. She was to act as analytical statistician of the meeting with Sheikh Al-Qadi. Her job, really.

Not that that made her feel any less...violent toward Haidar. In fact, it inflamed her more that he was having her walk into his lair under a pretext to which she could have no valid objection.

She exhaled, cursed the heavy, liquid throb of arousal that was her perpetual state now. That he managed to keep her in it by remote control was the height of injustice.

Why couldn't she feel this way about someone...human?

Resigned that he had her hormonal number, she turned her eyes to the scenery rushing by the window of the limo he'd insisted on sending her.

Suddenly, the terrain changed, from flat desert to a stunning system of dunes that undulated down to an incredible stretch of red-gold shore. It curved into a bay ending in an arm of land that almost touched an oasis of an island. Between the dunes and the shore lay an estate spread with palm and olive trees. Nestled in its heart was a house.

As the car descended on a winding path from the main road, the house came into clearer and clearer detail. It was… amazing. As pliant as a tent that would billow in the warm, dry winds. As fluid as a ship that would sail down the pier that extended from its enfolding terrace, sail away into the sea. It lay like a graceful hybrid among the sublimely landscaped and the divinely natural, adorned with a mile of emerald and aquamarine liquid.

She sat up, heart hammering, mouth drying.

The sheer beauty of it all, enhanced by the perfection of a golden sunset, soaked into her senses, wrenched at every one with a power that left her gasping with its force, its…futility.

So this was Haidar's home in Azmahar. A home he'd one day share with the woman he'd choose. The family he'd make.

This was also the home he'd asked her to come to last week. In her case, "home" had been only a figure of speech.

She'd always known that. Even when she'd been deluded that he'd felt something genuine for her, *Haidar* and *home* had been two words she'd known would never belong together.

They'd always met on impersonal ground, arrived separately, left the same way. How ironic was it that this time, he'd invited her to a personal place for impersonal business?

She blinked back the pointless disappointments as the car passed through electronic, twenty-foot, wrought-iron gates, wound up a cobblestone driveway and approached the architectural work of art from the back. The grounds were so extensive that it took almost ten minutes to come to a stop by the thirty-foot-wide stone steps that led to the entrance patio.

She thanked the driver, got out of the car before he could open the door for her, stiffened her back and resolve as she climbed the stairs. She wasn't waiting for anyone, starting with Haidar, to receive her or wait on her. She was here for business, would conclude it and leave.

She tried not to notice more about the place. She might have achieved that—had she been carried in unconscious. As it was, she absorbed every detail as she reached a wrap-around terrace from which every aspect of the magnificent property could be seen.

The double doors of the house were open. No one was around. Seemed Haidar still didn't believe in having people around.

She stepped into the house, and air squeezed out of her lungs.

Like the exterior, the interior married the unexpected in a seamless blend, old Arabia concepts with innovative themes, producing something unprecedented. Everything had been chosen with an eye for the comfort of both body and soul, blending sweeping lines and spaces with bold wall colors and honey-colored ceilings. Curved windows and doorways co-alesced with sand-colored marble floors accentuated by vivid mosaic. Furniture both functional and artistic offset wide-open seascapes. A place of contrasts, from the sublimely relaxing to the vibrant and exotic, an oasis of the best nature and man had been able to produce.

And that was just what she could see of the foyer and sitting area. She didn't want to know what...other rooms looked like.

"I named this placed Al Saherah."

His voice hit her dead center in her heart.

Al Saherah. The Bewitching. The Sorceress.

She turned, found him filling an archway leading to an-other part of the house. All in white, a fallen angel masquer-ading as one of the good guys. Big, vital, painfully beautiful.

It was he who was *saher.*

She swallowed the ache the sight of him always struck in her heart. "This place *is* magical."

He walked toward her, as majestic and potentially lethal as the feline he'd been named for. "But I'm thinking of adjusting the name to Al Naar Al Saherah. Or Al Saherah Al Nareyah. To describe its flesh-and-blood personification."

Bewitching Fire. Or the Fiery Sorceress.

Her hand rose involuntarily to her hair. When had he learned to talk like that? Wasn't it enough that he drove anyone with double-X chromosomes insane with lust just by existing? He'd picked up the deadly power of verbal seduction, too? Talk about overkill.

Declining to comment on this salvo of mind-messing flirtation, she cleared her throat. "So where is everyone convened?"

"We met in this awesome inside garden that has the most amazing aqueduct system running through it. Let me show you." He grabbed her hand, tugged her behind him, his grin gleeful like a boy unable to wait to show off a discovery.

She hurried to keep up with him, blinking at his enthusiasm, at the adjectives and intensifiers.

Strange. She'd thought he was too jaded to appreciate material beauty. Or at least that he would be so used to this place, he wouldn't even see its wonders anymore.

As they passed another sitting area, he turned to her. "I fell for this place at first sight."

So. He fell for places. Felt for friends. That made sense. After all, this place *was* unique. And Rashid certainly was one of a kind. But when it came to women, Haidar was indifferent. She'd bet the only reason he wanted her now was the challenge she represented.

She'd better not stimulate his feline tendencies anymore. If she played dead, he'd get bored and go chase some other prey. But—

She stopped so suddenly that she wrenched her hand from the glove of his. He turned to her, eyes questioning.

"You said you *met*." Incomprehension rose in his eyes. She

whacked his arm as hard as she could. "They're no longer here, are they?" His admission was a nonchalant shrug. She hit him harder, her hand stinging from the force of the smack. "You tricked me!"

He rubbed his arm, his eyes flaring, his lips filling. "I didn't. You insisted on coming late."

"There was no need for me to attend lunch, and I wanted you to have time alone with the others. My presence would have only been needed while you wrapped up the meeting."

"And we had to conclude it earlier than expected. Businessmen don't have their time under control. They had to leave."

"You could have told me not to bother coming."

"But I wanted you to come."

His voice, his eyes as he said that…

Images exploded in her mind, sensations in her body. Of every time he'd demanded she come for him, of the last time she had…

She pressed her head between her fists, trying to stop the surge of madness, fury and frustration almost as fierce. "I get that no one walks out on you. Hell, no one is allowed free will around you, and you want to punish me for both transgressions. You headed to my place fresh off the plane with that in mind. So what will it take to satisfy you? Is ruining my career a must?"

"That's the last thing I want, Roxanne."

She staggered back two steps for the one he took closer. "Excuse me as I believe the proof of your actions instead."

His gaze became serious, soothing. "Whatever I did that compromised you, or could have, I didn't plan any of it."

She huffed incredulously. "I wonder how that would hold up in front of a judge. 'I didn't plan to run the lady over, Your Honor.'"

His lips twisted. "*Zain.* I deserve that. And I have no defense. Premeditation isn't better than negligence from the victim's point of view. But I swear to you, I never meant you harm. And I will never compromise you again."

She stared at him. "You mean you'll leave me alone?"

"I mean I'll be the essence of discretion as I do no such thing." He reached for her as he spoke.

This time, she didn't move away. This train *would* hit her. Why pretend outrunning it was an option?

"Roxanne..." He groaned as he enfolded her into his large body.

As if feeling her surrender, he crushed her to his hardness, making no attempt to temper the carnality of his response, of his intentions.

He wanted sex. Raw and raunchy. Dominant and devastating. No pretense of gentleness or emotion. He'd exploit her body and take his pleasure in every way he pleased, plumb her flesh for all the ecstasy she could withstand.

She wanted all that. She was disintegrating with needing it.

She pushed out of his arms.

It took all of Haidar's restraint not to yank Roxanne back and down on any horizontal surface and caress her until he'd aroused her out of resistance.

Not that her reticence was physical. Her arousal cloaked him in echoes of their pleasure-drenched nights, slashed him down to the beast at his core. It had him an inch away from devouring her, riding her hard, shattering her with pleasure, so she'd never again contest his ownership of her flesh, of her every response.

"Roxanne..."

Her raised hand stopped him. What was she...?

Then both hands rose up to her hair, took the pins out. It cascaded in waves of flames down to her shoulders.

Before another neuron could fire a thought, a response in his brain, she was pushing her jacket off her shoulders, then unbuttoning her blouse, revealing the creamy globes of her breasts. *Ya Ullah*, she was…was…

She was stripping for him.

His lungs burned. His hardness passed the point of pain.

He heard himself choking on "While this might be a delight after I've taken you ten times or so, right now it's agony not being the one undressing you."

He reached for her again, expecting her to sweep him away, to continue punishing him with her striptease torture. Again she did something that shocked him into another detonation of arousal.

She grabbed him, climbed onto him, wrapped her legs around his buttocks, digging her high heels into his flesh as she bunched her hands in his hair and brought his lips crashing down on hers.

"Roxanne." His growl was that of a predator at the end of his tether. She pushed against him, making him stagger back and sit down on a couch with her on top. Before he could drag in another breath, she was tearing open his shirt, sinking her teeth into his chest and sucking his flesh.

He bucked beneath her, the pleasure of each nip and suckle acute distress. "Roxanne, let me…"

She slipped from his hold, ended up on her knees between his splayed thighs, her hands as feverish as her lips on the buttons of his jeans.

He watched her, his brain, every inch of him overheating from the sight of her beautiful hands dragging down his pants, dipping into his briefs to greedily surround his erection.

His mind hazed, his body hurtled beyond his control with the first touch of her lips on the oversensitized head.

How he'd missed her touch, her mouth, her breath on him. How he'd hungered for her answering hunger, for her delight in him, in all the liberties he gave her with his body.

But this was spiraling out of control. He had to...needed to slow down, savor it, stop her...

Her hot, moist mouth engulfed almost half of him, the tip hitting the back of her throat.

"Ya Ullah, kaif betsawwi hada?" he raved, mindless now, his hands frenzied in her silken hair. "How do you do that? Make every touch ecstasy?"

She gazed up at him, let him see how she took him, loved it, how her lips and hands milked his hardness. A hot tide surged upward from his loins, outward to his every skin cell. His buttocks and thighs tightened with holding it back. He pulled at her, needing to have this completion within her, *with* her.

She moaned her refusal to let go, the vibration an electrocuting surge of stimulation from every inch she devoured to his every nerve ending.

He collapsed back, surrendered to her demand, liquid fire flooding from the depths of his loins. He froze in the intensity of the moment, trapped in the excruciating pleasure that had him on the verge of splintering into a million pieces.

Just before he exploded, he tried to wrench himself out. She held on, her lips and hands making insistent sweeps, inciting him to madness. And he lost the struggle.

He shouted her name, threw his head back, dug his hands in the depths of her silk fire and spilled his seed on her tongue.

She held his eyes as he bucked again and again into her hold, as she drained him to the last drop.

A long, long moment passed before she let him slip from her reddened, swollen lips. He lay there, gulping air, staring into the depths of her magical eyes and instead of satisfaction, passion roared again, consuming his body in a fiercer fire. Hers. She'd always been what ignited him. What satisfied him.

He tried to pull her up, bring her over him. She pushed his

hands away. Before he could move, she stood up, her eyes smoldering down at him, her voice husky.

"I owed you one. Now we're even."

Then she turned and walked away.

Seven

Haidar's paralysis lasted only seconds. Then he was on his feet, shoving himself back into his pants and bounding after her.

She was buttoning her blouse as she strode away, then finger-combing her tousled hair. He knew she heard him coming. She clearly had no intention of stopping, or letting him stop her.

He did. By taking away her means of walking.

He swept her off her feet, smiled down at her. "Though that was almost literally mind-blowing, who says we're even? You owe me eight years' worth of pleasure."

"Eight minutes' worth is all you get from this gal. Now put me down before I give your perfect nose some crooked character."

He gathered her hands in one of his. "You have to regain the use of your hands first."

He strode to the bedroom suite he'd picked as theirs, expected her to struggle, make good on her threat. She just looked up at him, her normally communicative eyes empty of expression.

How he wanted her. The pleasure she'd just given him had only intensified his need for her. His need to pleasure her in return was also reaching critical levels. He wanted her naked and hot and writhing beneath his hands, his lips, bucking under his body, convulsing around him, her release wrenching his from his depths.

He reached the bed he'd bought just for her, huge and firm and covered in sheets a darker shade of her eyes. He hadn't thought she'd be here this soon. Someone out there must believe he deserved something fantastic for a change.

Laying her down, he descended on top of her, groaning at the feel of her cushioning him, the only flesh he'd ever felt a part of his own. His lips sought hers. She turned her face away.

He trailed his lips down her face, neck, down to the swell of her breasts. "Do you know how many nights I lay awake, craving to feel you like this? Hearing your moans, your sighs and cries, the memory of your body enfolding mine echoing in my cells until I felt they'd burst?"

Her answer was tight-lipped. "How many? Two?"

A spasm twisted inside his chest. "More like two thousand."

"And did you feel that way on those nights, before or after you had sex with another woman? Or three?"

He rose on both arms, frowned down at her. "We're not going there. What we did or didn't do in the past eight years isn't relevant. We're going to enjoy each other now, as we are today." His lips spread again at the sight of her beneath him, ripe and trying not to arch into him. "And from today onward, I am all for any kind of game you want to indulge in."

She pushed at him. "The only game I want to try is hide-and-seek, where you hide, and I don't seek you ever again."

His frown returned. "You're...angry?"

Her eyes spat emerald daggers at him. "Give the man a medal."

"I thought it was part of this sensual game you started. You were always all for those, too."

"Are you high on something? Like insensitivity and arrogance?"

He rolled to his side and watched in confusion as she scrambled away from him. "But I apologized and promised our liaison will never compromise you again."

She rounded on him as she rose from the bed. "And as a first step in assuring this, you had your driver leave me with you in an empty house. The news will be all over Azmahar by now."

"I flew Haleem in from Zohayd. He's fully Zohaydan and wouldn't reveal anything about you at gunpoint. It's why I insisted you come alone. I told my visitors I had informed you they had to leave, so you 'wouldn't bother coming.'"

She tore her gaze away, looked around the spacious room as if noticing it for the first time. He tensed as he waited for her reaction. He'd spent most of last week preparing it.

It was he who felt rewarded. A wave of pleasure washed over him as she stood bathed in the gold-tinged lights he'd carefully installed to showcase her, framed by the color scheme of fire and emerald he'd meant to reflect hers. Gauzy curtains billowed at the balcony doors behind her like swirls of magic, and her hair stirred in the evening sea breeze like tongues of dark flame.

His fiery goddess in all her glory. At least, in her still exasperatingly clothed one. Soon he'd have all that voluptuousness displayed for his pleasure, his worship.

Thankfully, the sensual ambience he'd tailored for her had an as-clear effect on her.

She was more flushed, less steady as she turned to him. "You put a lot of thought and effort into this, didn't you?"

If only she knew how much. Even he was still smarting from parting with that much cash. "Anything to help you relinquish your worries and inhibitions. And after what you just did to me while still suffering from both, I don't know if I'll survive when you let them go completely."

Her face hardened. "This new discretion is for yourself."

He exhaled, perplexed by her continued resistance. "It *is* also for me, since I get to have you. But—"

She cut him off. "You recognized you were being a self-defeating idiot. I bet it took seeing Rashid to make you realize that, and that the throne isn't in your pocket no matter what scandals you cause. You have to clean up your act if you're to have a prayer against him. Now you'll play the committed, conservative contender and shove me back into the dirty-secret slot."

He found himself on his feet, facing her across the bed, memories unraveling with a sick charge along his every nerve.

"What's this? Anyone would think it's you who have a grievance against me, that I'm the one who walked out on you. May I remind you that you are the one who left when I outraged your sense of independence, sinned in believing I was more than an 'exotic fling' to you? And are you pretending that keeping our relationship secret wasn't exactly what you wanted, then and now? I'm giving you what you always wanted. No demands on my side, no obligations on yours, only no-consequences indulgence. What more do you want?"

Why? How?

She'd long known that he felt nothing for her. So why and how did getting confirmation of that tear her apart all over again?

He came around the bed, raven hair raining down his forehead, the shirt she'd torn hanging open to reveal the magnificent sculpture of his torso, which she'd barely had a chance to worship.

He stopped less than a foot away, bearing down on her with

his overwhelming beauty and rising exasperation. "What kind of game are you playing now? What's with the indignant act? According to you, we had only a sexual liaison, and you ended it. Now that it would be feasible and pleasurable for both of us to resurrect it, why are you behaving as if I once betrayed you? As if I'm degrading you and trying to take advantage of you?"

"Because you did. And you are."

He stared at her as if she'd grown a third eye.

And everything she'd spent years holding back came flooding out.

"Being honest about how you'll take what you want and give nothing in return doesn't make you honorable. And it sure as hell doesn't make you the wronged party here. It only makes you an unfeeling bastard who cares only about getting what you want, who would use anyone in the most horrible way for your own purposes, even the trivial one of telling someone 'I told you so.'"

Every word fell on him with the visible effect of a slap. *"B'haggej'jaheem*, what the *hell* are you talking about?"

And she shouted, *"I'm talking about your bet."*

He stumbled back, his face going slack with shock, reactions rioting across his eyes.

Then he finally rasped, "You know."

It was a statement. An admission. At last.

She'd thought it would bring her relief. It didn't.

Feeling hers eyes tearing, she tore her gaze away, looked feverishly around for her sandals.

She shoved her feet into them, tried to regain her shaky balance. "Thank you for not insulting me more by pretending you don't know what I'm talking about."

"You heard me and Jalal that night."

The same conclusion Jalal had come to. She hadn't refined his deduction.

She did Haidar's. "That was only how I made sure."

He blocked her path as she tried to head for the door. "How did you find out in the first place?"

"I don't owe you anything, least of all an explanation. And if you want someone to play sexual games with, I can recommend dozens for you to pick from. I'm sure you have your own waiting list."

He spread his arms, stopping her from circumventing him, his face gripped in urgency and frustration. "*B'Ellahi,* Roxanne, just tell me!"

Her chest heaved with the remembered humiliation, her eyes threatening to pour long-dried tears. "How do you think?"

Realization detonated in his eyes. Certainty. He dropped his arms, staggered away. "My mother."

She let the entrenched fury in her eyes confirm.

"How did *she* know?" he groaned.

She shrugged. "She said she knows everything about you and Jalal. But especially you."

Agitation receded in his eyes, determination filtering into its place. "I need to know everything she said."

"I'll tell you what *my* mother said. When you approached me at that ball expecting me to fall at your feet."

Heated recollection overlapped agitation in his eyes. "Your words were cool but your eyes were incendiary. I could think of nothing but erasing your reluctance, making you admit that your desire was as instant and as powerful as mine."

She backed away as if from the memories. "The jury will remain out on *that* similarity. But my mother saw you for what you are. She also saw that you had me blinded and realized that to stop me from falling for your seduction, she had to tell me a secret."

"What secret could she have told you? I have none."

"Of course you don't. You keep your vices and transgressions proudly out in the open."

That silenced him. His steel eyes, so like his mother's, turned black. As if her opinion hurt.

She ignored the spasm of guilt at what she had to admit was a gross exaggeration. "It was a secret of hers. During her first stint in Azmahar. She was beginning her career, and she fell madly in love with a royal. She discovered his illegal activities, yet still couldn't walk away. But he fabricated evidence against her, preempting her in case she attempted to expose him, forcing her to leave the kingdom in silence or she would have been publicly disgraced and prosecuted."

His eyes narrowed. "Was that man your father?"

It was the first time he had asked her about her parentage. "No. My father was a one-night stand she had when she returned home from Azmahar heartbroken. But years later, that royal found himself in need of her support and got her an even better post in Azmahar. She was in no position to say no. That was when we came here. He tried to weasel himself back into her good opinion and bed, but she told him where he could put his lies and platitudes."

He said nothing, waiting for the punch line.

She delivered it. "Moral of the story—don't get involved with a royal. He will use you for his whims and abuse you for his benefit. And when I didn't listen, worse happened to me."

His frown turned spectacular. "What do you mean, worse?"

"You didn't even notice that my life was being messed up and my future destroyed. The one thing that mattered to you was that I showed up for your scheduled sex sessions."

"Are you talking about the setbacks you had in your studies?"

Her heart lurched. "So you knew. And you didn't ask me about it, or even offer a word of concern or encouragement."

His already black frown darkened. "Jalal informed me you'd started out so far at the top of your class, you were in one of your own. He made it sound as if I was the reason you were falling behind. I…didn't know what to say. Or do."

"You thought our liaison and the hoops you made me jump through to maintain its secrecy were taking their toll on me, but tough for me, right? You had your pleasure and your convenience, and to hell with me and my future."

He grimaced again. "All I saw at the time was that you'd told Jalal, but not me."

"And we're back to the one thing that matters to you. Your rivalry with Jalal."

"It wasn't like that. This was about you."

"Sure. It was so about me you didn't care that my academic progress was in jeopardy, even when you believed you were the reason for the deterioration. You knew me so little you believed I'd let an affair stop me from excelling in my work."

"But…if I wasn't the reason, then…" He stopped, shock blossoming in his gaze all over again.

"And he sees the light. Yep, your mother again. She had more influence in Azmahar than the rest of the royal family put together. Your efforts at secrecy worked on my mother and the rest of the kingdom, but your mother knew everything about us and decided to rectify the situation. I found out how when I was protesting my inexplicable grades to my favorite professor. She confessed she and the rest of the staff had instructions to increase pressure until I had to leave to save what I could of my future. She said I would harm her if I didn't keep it a secret and advised me to stop whatever I was doing to be on your mother's bad side. *You* were the only thing I was…doing."

"And you never told me."

"I didn't know if I could. You always seemed to be…hers." His face became stone, his eyes flint. She didn't care if that affronted him. It was the truth. "But I *was* guilty of romanticizing you, believing I mattered to you, against all proof to the contrary. I ended up deciding to tell you, thought you might intervene, stop her from destroying my education. Uncanny woman that she is, she seemed to smell my intention and preempted me. She had me brought to her. It was quite an eye-opener, meeting her in the flesh. I understood so much about you, then.

"She prefaced her venom by saying she'd tried to be merciful, tried to let me leave with my pride intact. But since I was so foolish as to invite a confrontation, she had to destroy it. She informed me of your bet with Jalal. She was very proud of your talent for manipulation, which you inherited from her and honed with your rivalry with Jalal. I might not have seen it that way then, but I do now. I owe her a ton of gratitude."

His nonexpression, which she'd once thought indicated he felt nothing, cracked, and bewilderment flooded in.

She explained. "Though she was—and no doubt still is—a vile snob, it was her wish to get rid of me sooner rather than later that stopped me from being the unwitting pawn in your power games with Jalal any longer. She read my disbelief, told me to go demand the truth from your own mouth.

"Before I could, you called me and ordered me to drop everything and go to you. I was stupid enough to hope you'd say it wasn't true, or at least have some excuse to mitigate the sheer petty evil of it all. I was so anxious to clear everything up, I arrived at the apartment before you did."

His eyes closed for a moment, opened. "You were there all along. You heard everything Jalal and I said."

Hot needles pushed behind her eyes. "It was only then that I realized the depth of your resemblance to her. And I decided I wouldn't give either of you that last triumph over me. You wouldn't see me humiliated and heartbroken, and she wouldn't see me running off with my tail between my legs. Your mother raised you to use everyone in your power games—mine raised me to never relinquish equal ground."

Time stretched after she'd said her last word.

It seemed an eternity later when he finally spoke. "So everything you said, every word that has been echoing in my mind ever since, was just you maintaining said equal ground."

Her nod was terse. She was giving him validation in retrospect. Any denigrating thing she'd said had just been a desperate attempt to walk out of that battlefield in one piece.

She didn't care. Let him have his triumph.

"What about the things you said before that day, Roxanne?"

He wanted more. A full admission. He might as well have it.

"That I loved you? I meant it, wholeheartedly." She looked away, unable to bear the terrible loss mushrooming inside her all over again. "Not that I ever blamed you for that. You made it clear you had nothing to give me, were true to yourself, to your principles. As you pointed out the first night you came back, love isn't something your species values or tolerates. If I was stupid enough to give it to you, it was unasked for, unwanted, and I had no right to complain when my heart was trodden on."

Another heart-shredding moment of silence passed.

Then he whispered, "I didn't initiate that bet, Roxanne."

"I know. Jalal told me he did."

He stiffened.

Of course. Jalal. The one thing sure to provoke a profound reaction in him. "Don't tell me you forgot about it in minutes, too."

Tension deflated out of him on a heavy exhalation. "I won't tell you that. I can't. I never forgot the bet."

Was there no limit to the hurt this man could inflict on her?

She let out a choppy breath. "Thanks for not wasting either of our time on insincerities."

Something bruised filled his eyes. "I remembered it constantly because I was jealous. Of Jalal. He was coming close to you in ways I was unable to. I didn't know how to get you to talk to me, laugh with me as he did. All I had was your physical hunger. So I took all I could of it, aroused it as fiercely and frequently as I could, hoping it would be enough. It never was."

She hadn't expected him to bother explaining. She didn't want him to explain. She'd long been resigned that she knew all the answers. She didn't want him to threaten that security.

Before she could tell him to let the past lie in its grave, he went on. "At one of the functions you attended with your mother, where you avoided me per our agreement, you were so…at ease with Jalal. You both seemed so delighted with each other. And my mother—*ya Ullah*, my mother again—she commented on how much you had in common. My unease started to turn to dread then." Her heart scrambled its rhythm, her eyes burning as he held them in a vise of bleakness. "One moment, I'd think it was my fault you couldn't be that natural with me, the next I resented you for not granting me the same openness you gave Jalal. All the time I was seething with the need to bring it up. But what would I have said? I want you to *like* me not just love me? I need you to crave my company and companionship, outside of bed? What if all I managed was make you realize I didn't appeal to you in any way but sexually?"

Her heart lurched to another level of agitation. She'd never suspected he could have felt anything like this…

"Then I found out you were faltering in your studies. The fact that I didn't learn about it from you made me so…angry. I considered only what that meant to me, said about us, rather than how the problem itself impacted you."

That's more like it.

Her teeth ground together. "Another example of what made you the icon for self-absorbed sons of bitches everywhere."

He continued to stare at her with that still, searing intensity. "Jalal believed it was due to my…disruptive influence. I didn't know how to stop being disruptive without giving you up, or at least moving back to Zohayd and seeing you sporadically. I thought if he was right, you'd eventually come to the same conclusion. And if you did, you would be forced to make a choice between your progress and me. I feared it wouldn't be me you'd choose. I knew it shouldn't be. That's why I kept putting off bringing it up."

Everything froze inside her as if to stop the influx of new information that threatened to pulverize her long-held beliefs.

"It's also why I remembered the damn bet every single second I was with you. Not because I was afraid of losing to Jalal. Because I was afraid of losing you."

The stillness inside her trembled on the verge of shattering.

But wait—*wait!* Her view of him, of the past, was too well entrenched. It couldn't be changed with a few words…

But were they only words? Or reality? She'd already conceded Haidar hadn't been guilty of feeling nothing in Rashid's case, but feeling too much to be able to show it.

Had he been the same with her?

What if this was his problem across the board? Not that he'd inherited his mother's heartlessness and twisted, obsessive affection for the two people she considered extensions of herself, but only simulated it by his inability to expose his heart?

It would still make any involvement with him impossible, but it *would* rewrite his character, their whole history.

But…he was exposing his heart now, had been *communicating* with her, as she'd never thought he could. What if he'd matured into overcoming his emotional limitations?

As if reading her mind, he said, "Not that never sharing my fears or insecurities with you did any good. I lost you anyway."

If this was the truth, then what she'd said to him, how she'd walked out on him, must have pulverized his pride, his heart. As she'd thought he'd done hers.

Could she— *Dared* she believe?

But what else could she do? There was no reason he'd have said any of that if it weren't true.

Pain crashed over her.

God…what she'd cost them both.

Dejection receded, leaving his face blank. "I had it all planned from that first time I—pardon my presumption— claimed you. I intended us to be together while I worked to establish my success, while you did yours. The logistics of being in Azmahar when my base of operations was ideally Zohayd, of keeping our intimacies secret while being under the microscope of fame and notoriety, drove me to distraction. But I knew we needed to deepen our bond, protect it from intrusions, before we faced what the world would throw at us. With my mother, and your mother's position, with my mixed bag of problems, I knew it would be a lot."

She wanted to scream for him to stop.

He went on. "It was a mess, but I thought the passion we shared made up for the drawbacks. I thought you thought that, too. And though I didn't believe in my ability to make anyone happy, when you claimed to love me, you gave me hope that you saw in me what I didn't. I thought you'd give me the time I needed to trust myself with the new feelings, the unknown needs, the terrible vulnerability. But you didn't."

"Haidar…"

Her plaintive objection faltered. He was right. She hadn't. It suddenly no longer mattered why she hadn't. The fact remained.

The flow of his bitterness continued. "All these years, I rationalized your parting words, excused them. Excused you. I told myself that you lashed out when you saw me out of control emotionally for the first time and feared I'd turn morbidly possessive and controlling. I told myself you had every reason to worry with the gross imbalance of power between us. I kept thinking I must have scared you, made you say what you did to ensure I wouldn't come after you, never stopped imagining how it could have been if I hadn't. I never accepted that the woman I loved considered me a banal adventure. I never believed, not in my heart, that you never loved me at all."

Before she could cry that his heart had seen what had been in hers, he went on, "Now I have to accept that you never did. At the first test, you proved it. What you heard me say could have been interpreted in different ways. You chose the worst one. You'd already condemned me based on the word of your declared enemy. You didn't think me worth the chance to defend myself. All you thought of was how to protect your pride, how to avenge yourself. As if I'd been your enemy all along, not the man you claimed to love."

The urge to say something, anything, mushroomed inside her chest, felt it would rupture it. But anything she said now would be too little, too late.

He wasn't finished. "You have been treating me as your enemy, your only enemy even, since I reappeared in your life. I've been blaming my own actions again and hoping your intense desire proved you felt something real and powerful for me. But it seems you told me the truth only once. I *was* your exotic fling. You dressed it in higher emotions to feel justified in indulging in it, but in truth, you weren't ready to give me anything but stolen hours of pleasure. You didn't even give me what you would have granted any stranger—the right to be considered innocent until proven guilty. Whatever I was guilty of—the reticence and the jealousy and the inability to deal with the weakness my feelings for you engendered in me—I didn't warrant that punishment. But you don't even consider it punishment. You believe it's what I deserve."

She held back tears and self-recriminations. It wasn't time to give in to them. But she had to say something even if it was deficient.

He wouldn't let her. "But I don't accept your verdict, Roxanne. Whatever I was guilty of, I won't take all the blame. I'm sick and tired of being the one everyone demonizes. I will no longer think it okay for the people who once claimed to love me to see my every action in the worst light." His eyes flared with the molten steel of fury. "And I will no longer be held responsible for my mother's actions or accept being considered interchangeable with her character. I am not only her son. I am also my father's. But the thing that matters most is, I am *me*."

Before she could draw another breath, he turned around. Shocked to her core, she watched him cross the room that every brushstroke and article said he'd had done for her, having so accurately read her intensely personal fantasies.

She'd rejected him again in the setting he'd prepared for her with such thought and care.

At the double doors he stopped, turned, buttoning his shirt in deliberate moves. "My mother always told me that no one will love me but her, and to trust no one. Every time I disregarded her wisdom, I lost something vital. You, Jalal, Rashid. But it's clear the loss was always one-sided. You are all far better off without me." His eyes filled with bitter irony. "But I didn't get where I am by clinging to losing propositions. I'll accept that the problem lies within me and deal with it." He finished doing up his shirt, nothing left in his eyes but frozen steel. "So like I told them, I'll tell you. I'm getting the hell out of your life. This time, I'm staying out."

Eight

"Wow. Just…Wow."

Roxanne squeezed her eyes shut. She didn't want to see the incredulity, or the pity, in her companion's eyes.

She was already sorry she'd told Cherie anything.

It had been about four hours since Haidar had walked out of that bedroom. She'd gone after him, but had soon realized he'd left the estate. Haleem, the driver he'd flown in especially for her, had been waiting to take her home.

She'd held on until she'd gotten there. But the moment she'd seen Cherie, it had all come flooding out. The tears, and the whole story.

Cherie's exclamations didn't show signs of stopping any time soon. "I mean, dude…*wow*. And I thought *my* love life was complicated. Roxy, babe, you got the market cornered on complex messes."

Roxanne opened her eyes, exhaled her corroboration. "Yeah."

"And it seems 'tis open season for the destruction of long-held misconceptions. Me with Ayman, you with Prince Haidar. *Man,* you really have a *prince* for a lover!"

Refraining from amending it to *ex*-lover, Roxanne sighed again. "And for eight years I cherished my grudge against him. Then he tears into me with his side of the story, and here I am."

Cherie's eyes filled with seriousness and sympathy. "You must be feeling pretty stupid right now, huh?"

She grimaced in self-deprecation. "Not the description I would have used. Rash, overreacting, insecure, vindictive. But yeah, stupid works, too. Actually sums up all the above."

Cherie gave a bitter snicker. "You and me both. Since I came here, it's been dawning on me daily what an oversensitive moron I was with Ayman. You think it's something we picked up when we were in university together? We both started seeing our men then, and after a period of head-over-heels bliss, you walked out on yours, while I've been on a constant roller coaster with Ayman, mostly my doing. It's a wonder your man even tried to hook up with you again. It's a wonder mine married me and hasn't divorced me." The light blue of her eyes darkened with regret and despondence. "Especially after this last flounce."

"You still love him."

"God, yes. I love him so much it's what screws me up."

"You haven't told me exactly what went wrong between you."

Cherie rolled her eyes. "I'm a messy, outspoken-in-all-wrong-things, emotionally reticent pain in the butt, that's what went wrong."

"And you came here blaming him for being an anal, sanctimonious, overemotional jerk. Now you've switched to shouldering all the blame. I bet there's a middle ground here."

Cherie arched a delicate blond brow at her. "Like it exists in your situation?"

"Touché. But in yours, I can tell you that no matter what, he'd rather have your mess over perfection in a life without you. When I talked to him on the phone, he said, quote, 'Cherie's hell is better than anyone else's heaven,' unquote."

Tears poured down Cherie's cheeks as she collapsed back on the couch. "And of course he tells *you* that!"

"He's been trying to tell you. And he knew I'd transmit his words. So what are you going to do?"

Cherie leaned forward, burying her face in her hands. "I don't want him to put up with me and ruin his life. I want him to have the children he craves. I want him to let me go."

Roxanne scooted over, hugged her. "He doesn't want to let you go. He said he'll do anything to get you back. But have you ever told him what you just told me?"

Cherie raised drenched, smirking eyes. "Which part of emotionally reticent didn't you get?" Roxanne vented a frustrated breath. Cherie echoed it. "One thing we share is, we both pretended to jump because we thought we'd eventually be pushed. But we basically have the opposite of each other's problems. Ayman has always been the one pouring out his heart, and I'm the one who holds back and wisecracks his butt off. While your prince—excuse me again as I boggle over this—you really have a *prince!*" *Had* a prince. Roxanne bit back the correction. "And he was the one who had a glitch in his express-show machine. While you expressed yourself only too well, but only on your terms. So when he needed you to do it on his, tell him you were Team Haidar all the way, you didn't act on your professed love, proving it never existed."

Roxanne plopped back, hands grabbing her head in frustration. "Go ahead. Put it in an even worse light than he did."

Cherie grimaced apologetically. "I'm just sympathizing with someone who shares my inability to gush about my love. At least, *to* the object of my love. I get him."

A spasm pinched her heart. "And I'm only beginning to get him. When it's too late."

It was Cherie's turn to hug her. "Do you have an Azmaharian mother-in-law breathing down your man's neck to discard you and get a model that will provide the required brood? Do you have a terminal disorderliness disorder and live with a neatness freak? Do you have five years of marriage behind you, and you're at the point where you think the only man you'll ever love is better off without your baggage and shortcomings? If you answer no to all the above, you've got it easy, lady."

"Put that way, my problems seem trivial in comparison. Except for one tiny point. Your man wants you back. Mine doesn't."

"Sure he does. He's been holding a torch for you for eight years even after you seemingly pulverized his heart and pride."

"Now he's blown out said torch."

"He's hurt and he's sulking. But one thing for sure. This guy has never run after anything or anyone. He's a high-and-mighty prince-*cum*-god, for Pete's sake. And he's gone against everything in his nature and done all the running in your relationship. He's in dire need for you to go after him this time."

"What if he says to leave him the hell alone?"

Cherie jumped up, and wonder of wonders, started gathering her cups and plates. "Here's what we'll both do. I'll open up to Ayman, and you'll go after Haidar. It *is* a definite danger neither maneuver will work. Are we going to let that stop us from trying?"

Roxanne had started thinking this was a terrible idea. Hours ago. Now she knew it was the worst one she'd ever cooked up.

Even Cherie hadn't thought she'd go this far. She'd thought she'd only go as far as calling Haidar, beg for face time.

She'd texted Haidar instead, *told* him when and where to meet her. She'd thought if she was doing this, she might as well go all out. In a blaze of glorious recklessness.

Not that it was working. She'd been waiting for eight hours.

She'd made allowances for everything that could hold him up. If he meant to come. Every minute after the fifth hour when no more excuses sufficed had felt like sandpaper being dragged over her raw nerves, every one telling her she'd just dialed his outrage higher with her presumption.

Even if she hadn't, why would he want to see her again? He'd made up his mind that he'd heard all he needed to hear from her. She no longer had a right to his indulgence or patience, which he'd been showering her with since he'd showed up in her life again.

Her phone rang.

She fumbled with it as if it were a squirming fish, hit Answer, put it to her ear, heart turned inside out.

"Kaif hallek, ya azeezati?"

At hearing the drawled *How are you, my dearest,* the detonation of disappointment made her cover the mic to groan. *Jalal.*

Why was she so surprised? He'd called her half a dozen times a day ever since that first meeting. They'd made quite the headway in his campaign at first. But since her confrontation with Haidar a week ago, only her word to Jalal had made her work on his case at all. That and the need to get everything out of the way so she could obsess over Haidar with her full focus.

Wanting this over with, she skimmed the niceties. "Have you checked your in-box? I sent you the demographic analysis."

"Aih, I saw them." From the brief pause, Jalal had noticed her haste. As gentlemanly as ever, he glossed over it. "Brilliant work. I don't know what I would have done without you. You have incredible insight."

She almost scoffed. *Selective* insight was more like it. When it came to Haidar, she'd had that in the negative values.

"But this isn't a business call," Jalal said. "You weren't looking as well as usual a couple of days ago."

And you're not doing me any favors worrying.

Out loud she said, "Work is too much sometimes."

"If my side of it is weighing you down..."

She did wish, for so many reasons, she'd never promised to be Jalal's advisor. But she had given her word. She would abide by it. "No, really. Just don't worry, okay?"

"If you're sure." He sounded very unsure himself.

Quit the big-brother probing, already, she almost screamed.

He made it worse. "I heard you've seen a lot of Haidar."

And I want to see a lot more of him, all of him. But I'm not telling you that, or where I am now, or what I'm trying to do.

"You didn't mention our arrangement," he probed.

"No." Even if she wasn't bound to secrecy by her word to Jalal, it had never occurred to her when she was with Haidar. Nothing else existed when he was around.

"I was hoping you wouldn't tell him I'm in Azmahar."

That was strange. "But he must know you're here."

"He doesn't. My appearance at your door evidently wasn't as dramatic as his. I'm not as dramatic in general here as he is. Wearing an Aal Shalaan face comes in very handy in avoiding unwanted attention in Azmahar."

So Jalal was being covert. She could see the merit in that, for the info-gathering stage. But why wouldn't he want Haidar to know of his presence? Did he fear his brother would try to sabotage him? Would Haidar go that far in his rivalry?

"I didn't tell you everything about our last confrontation." When Haidar told Jalal he renounced their very blood tie. "I accused him of being our mother's accomplice in her conspiracy to take Zohayd apart."

Shock screeched through her, made her choke, "B-but Haidar was the one who discovered where she hid the jewels, brought the conspiracy to an end."

"I know. But...there were unexplained activities between him and our mother, extensive amounts of money he'd given her. I asked him about it, and he told me what I could do with my suspicions. I ended up accusing him of only pretending to help us when she was exposed so that he'd appear innocent, that she agreed to play along, since she'd do anything to protect him. I said he manipulated me emotionally until he had me begging with him for her exile instead of imprisonment, and that they were both only biding their time until they came up with another plot to put him on the throne."

She staggered to the nearest flat surface, the ledge of the pier, plopped down on it.

This was...unthinkable. Could it possibly...

No. She wasn't doing this again. She wasn't thinking the worst of Haidar again. Not without giving him every benefit of the doubt first, giving him the chance to explain his side.

But what mattered here was one thing. "You believe this?"

"No." One single word laden with a world full of regret and pain. "But I'm not the collected man you know when it comes to Haidar, not even exactly sane. I was livid, thinking what our mother could have caused, for him. It was impossible, with him being so reticent, to separate my rage with her from him. He was indirectly responsible for everything she'd done, and I wanted to punch him with my accusations until he lashed back, opened up, told me everything, shared with me fully again, if just this once. He didn't. He just walked away."

As he had from her. Seemed he was an expert at that.

But again, what had seemed to be such a callous action had only been an outraged reaction. Haidar had walked away from the twin who, when a real test was forced on him, had behaved as if Haidar had always been his worst enemy. As she had.

It felt weird to change her perspective, see her admired friend as the offender. Seemed Haidar did manage to force out the passionate side in others—their best and worst.

Suddenly, she felt a presence behind her.

Her heart almost fired from her ribs.

"Sorry, gotta go. Talk later," was all she said to Jalal, barely heard his surprised agreement before she ended the call.

She took a shuddering breath before she rose, swung around.

If it was Haleem, she might shove him into the sea.

It wasn't. It was Haidar.

He came.

He was walking toward her from the end of the terrace that extended into a stone passage that traversed the sandy beach. It transformed into a wooden pier that forged into the bay, widened at its end into the circular platform where she was standing.

In seconds he was stepping onto the platform she'd ringed with candles blazing in crimson quartz holders. He glowed like the desert god that he was as he passed between the brass torches she'd lit, their incandescent flames undulating in the calm breeze, accentuating his every feature and line. In all black with the only relief a shirt the color of his eyes, he took her breath away, sent her heart into hyperdrive. Her every nerve quivered at beholding his magnificence, at entering his orbit. Her every sense ignited with no-longer-suppressed responses and emotions.

He transferred his expressionless gaze from her to the candles, to the buffet table at the end of the platform, and finally to the table for two she'd arranged in its center.

He looked back at her. "I see you've invaded and occupied my home."

She shivered as his voice, impassive like his expression, flowed down her nervous pathways like warm molasses.

She'd expected him to comment on her setup. Seemed where he was concerned, the only given was to expect the unexpected.

She licked her dry, tingling lips. "Just your pier."

He came to a stop four steps away, went so still he looked

like a statue of a titan, the only animate things about him his
satin mane sifting around his leonine head, his clothes rustling around his steel-fleshed frame.

Then he shoved his hands into his pockets, the epitome
of tranquillity. "I thought we agreed we were better off staying off each other's properties and out of each other's lives."

She held back from closing the gap between them with all
she had. "We did. Just not at the same time. Or for the same
reasons."

"The sequence or cause of coming to this vital decision
isn't important. As long as we both reached it."

"Problem is, once you did, I unreached it."

His gaze lengthened, the gentle rumble of the sea lapping
the shore deepening his silence. Then without moving, or
changing his expression or tone, he said, "I'm not playing
this game, Roxanne."

"It's not a game. I never played games with you."

"Could have fooled me."

"I actually could and should have known you better." She
took a step closer. "The problem is, we fell into bed too soon.
Once we did, it was impossible for us to have one nonhor-
monally overwrought thought or reaction where the other was
concerned."

One dense, slanting eyebrow rose. "You're saying you chose
to believe the worst about me because passion made you unable to think straight?"

"Why so skeptical? You admitted to about the same. As a
friend pointed out, we suffered from a communication disorder. My verbal-but-not-about-my-issues kind was as bad as
your nonverbal one."

He brooded down at her, clearly unconvinced.

She tried a new angle. "You thought it a possibility I'd
think of Jalal while I was with you. I thought *you* thought of
Jalal while you were with me. We're guilty of the same stu-

pidity, each in our own uniquely stupid way. So how about we call it even?"

That imperious eyebrow rose again. "You really like to say that, don't you?"

Her heart shook at the first ray of change in his expression. "And when I last said that, you said we're not, not by an eight-year-long shot. I believe that now."

He went totally still again. The steel of his eyes seemed to catch the torch fire, singeing her.

"What do you want, Roxanne?"

She shook with the sheer, leashed intensity in that question. He needed her to spell it out. She was only too happy to.

"I want you. I only ever wanted you."

And he moved, away, restored the distance she'd managed to obliterate. "So all you needed to change your mind was me deciding to stop pursuing you? And you realizing I meant it?"

"If you're saying I'm coming after you because you pose a challenge now, *et'tummen*…rest easy. That doesn't even figure into this."

His eyes narrowed to silver lasers. It had once aroused him to near savagery when she'd spoken Arabic to him.

"So what does? My little speech before I walked out?"

Her nod was difficult as her rate of melting quickened, her body readying itself for the onslaught of his passion. "That little speech was sure eye-opening. And heart-wrenching. I spent eight years never once thinking you had a side of the story."

"Are you saying if you faced me then, screamed bloody betrayal, and I'd told you said side, none of this would have happened?"

"No," she had to admit. "I trusted you and what we had too little. And if you, the man who never opened up to me during the year of our involvement, suddenly had, I would have thought you were placating me to carry on your bet."

"So it's because you believe the bet is no longer on, and only because I no longer talk to Jalal, that you believe me now."

"No, again. I believe you because we've grown up and out of our inability to talk to each other. We've been communicating for real during those verbal duels. And you let me see your vulnerability and emotions for the first time. It made me realize I dehumanized you, even when I was claiming to love you. Then I demonized you when I thought you'd never loved me."

Silence stretched until she thought he wouldn't talk again.

Suddenly he moved. "I accept your peace offering. Let's eat."

Her mouth fell open as he passed her.

Once at the table, in perfect grace and control, he took the chair she'd meant for him, his back to the sea. She'd wanted the lights from the house and grounds to join the pier's in illuminating him. He propped one forearm on the table and sat relaxed, majestic, sweeping the buffet table where serving plates simmered on gentle flames that danced in the balmy sea breeze.

He panned his gaze back to her with ultimate serenity as she stopped across the table. "You will serve me, won't you?"

She narrowed her eyes at him, her lips struggling not to spread in delight. "Don't push your luck."

His lips twitched, too. His eyes remained unfathomable.

Turning around, she headed to the buffet table, her heart dancing a jig inside her. He was letting her back in.

As she adorned their plates with an assortment of appetizers, he called out, "Do hurry. The aromas are too mouthwatering."

Her steps back to him were measured, to rein in the urge to plop the plates down, charge him, straddle and devour *him*.

She came behind him, leaned to place his plate before him, let her breasts brush his back, her hair fall over his shoulder. "All delicious things come to he who doesn't rush the chef."

He tilted his head, turning his face partially toward her, his eyes downcast. She felt she might fall over him with the dizziness his scent and heat induced. Which might not be a bad thing...

He reached for his napkin, flapped it open. "Don't tell me you cooked all this."

She straightened like a malfunctioning robot, her body buzzing, her legs rubbery after the contact that had backfired, having no effect on him, but managing to flare her arousal.

"Why so shocked? I can handle myself in a kitchen." She struggled not to fall in a heap in her chair. "But you're right. I didn't. I did a lot of the work, but I was mainly following the directions of the one who designed the meal. Cherie is an incredible artist, in cooking and in many other forms of art."

He only nodded, started to eat with gusto.

After he polished off the appetizers and the two courses of the meal, and she watched him eat while trying to draw him into conversation, he looked up. "Your friend should consider a catering business. I'd be a regular customer."

She grinned, delighted that she'd pleased him, that he appreciated Cherie and her efforts. Even if he didn't include her directly in his praise. "She'll be thrilled you think so. She almost fainted when she saw your kitchen. When she set foot here, really. She still can't believe that she cooked for a prince. That I even know you."

His eyes darkened. "She knows how well you...know me?"

"She knows how well I...knew you. And didn't know you at all. She also knows how much I want to know you, in every way, now."

Another of those silences that engulfed that wide-open night, magnified every ripple of water, every whistle of wind, every beat of her heart, lengthened.

Suddenly he pushed his chair back, stood up. "That was a lovely meal, Roxanne. My most sincere compliments to the chef. I accept your…amends. Best of luck finding the same success in your endeavors to put Azmahar back on track."

She gaped at him as he turned around and strode away.

That was it? He was walking away again? This time on good terms instead of terrible ones?

But she couldn't let him walk away again. She wouldn't.

She scrambled up. "But I haven't *really* made…amends yet."

He stopped. After another endless moment, he looked over his shoulder. "No, you haven't, have you?"

Then with one last look of supreme indifference, he turned and strode away like a lion would from the prey he'd just feasted on.

It took only heartbeats for delight and determination to overcome agitation and hesitation. It was as clear as the star-lit sky he wanted her to run after him some more.

She had no problem with that. She couldn't wait to do it. She would run after him, and she would catch him, if it took the rest of her life.

Nine

Haidar didn't slow down, didn't look back.

The only way to catch up with him would be to sprint. She didn't. He wanted to keep the distance between them.

She let him keep it. All the way to his bedroom.

He strode through the open double doors, disappeared inside.

A smile trembled on her lips as she stopped across the threshold. Why not let him wonder for a bit?

But it was she who couldn't last. She was dying to have him.

She entered the antechamber, swerved into the room...and gaped.

Haidar was reclining at the dark emerald damask couch by the balcony doors, legs stretched out on it, his jacket discarded, his shirt partially undone. And he was reading a book.

He didn't raise his head from his apparent engrossment as she approached him. He let her come within touching distance before he slowly, and without moving a thing, swept his gaze up to her.

"Anything I can do for you?"

His low, dark rumble spread through her, dried her mouth, melted everything else.

In response, she let her shawl slip. "Everything, actually. And not just for me. To me. With me."

His gaze singed down her face, following the autumn leaves–colored silk as it slithered to the ground. On the way, he took note of the sensuality and delicacy of her spaghetti-strap dress. On his way up, his gaze lingered on the breasts now swollen and snug against the top. By the time he came back to her eyes, she was shivering with need, as if he'd caressed her within an inch of sanity.

Instead of reaching for her, he closed his book, relaxed back on the couch, still holding her prisoner to his fathomless scrutiny. So she reached for him.

Bracing a knee on the couch, arousal thundering through her, her hands trembled as they roamed the incredible breadth of his chest. He held her eyes as she moaned at the acuteness of sensations that touching him jolted through her. The intimidating bulge in his pants got impossibly bigger. But the moment she started pulling his shirt out, fumbling with its buttons, her forearms were clamped in inescapable sinew-and-bone manacles.

"You've made those kinds of...amends before." His eyes crackled with what felt like the advance bolts of a devastating storm. He pushed her arms away as he sat up and was off the couch in one of those miraculously effortless moves. "I'm not interested in an encore along the same lines."

She collapsed on the couch, looked up at him as he stood before her, perfect down to his last pore.

He would make a perfect king. Probably the only kind that could save Azmahar now.

He was *her* perfect man. The only one she'd ever want. Or love. Whatever happened, wherever this led, or didn't lead, she belonged to him, heart and soul.

Now if he'd only hurry and claim her body, too.

She rose on precarious legs. "Not that I *was* offering anything along the same lines, but what kind of amends do *you* have in mind?"

Another stormy silence as his probing invaded her recesses.

Then, distinct, slow, annihilating, he drawled, "Surrender. Full, unconditional. And irretrievable."

She almost came right there and then.

This man *was* out to take revenge on her.

Her whole body throbbed like one inflamed nerve. Her core spasmed with the near release he'd driven her to with the force of his intention.

In answer, she pushed her dress straps off her shoulder, reached back to undo its zipper, let the silk sigh to her feet like the shed petals of an alien, emerald flower.

Facing him in only her strapless bra, thong and stilettos, she said a breathless "Done."

His eyes flared with a fierceness that almost knocked her off her feet. His gaze ravaged a path of almost frightening hunger over her, sending her heart flailing with trepidation, almost had her howling with anticipation. He still made no move.

He needed a more definitive demonstration.

She turned on jellified legs toward the bed in the middle of the room that he'd designed in echoes of her complexion. She climbed on top, spread out in its center and held out her arms to him.

He moved then. Before her heart could stumble over a few beats, he was at the foot of the bed, looking down at her spread out before him.

"You will give me everything this time, Roxanne. Everything you have. Everything you are. Everything you didn't think you had to give. If you withhold anything, I will take nothing."

"Everything." Her nod was frantic. "And I want your everything in return."

Something savage blossomed in his gaze. "You know what you're asking for?"

He was demanding more than her body. He'd soon find out he had all of her, through and through.

She struggled to her elbows, meeting his menace with her trust, her vow, her determination. "Oh, yes."

He suddenly clamped her feet, dragged her by them, slid her across the satiny sheets. One hand took one of hers, tugged, bringing her slamming into his flesh.

"I want to invade you, brand you, devour you whole." She gasped her willingness for anything he'd do to her, tried to wrap herself around him. "But you'll have to wait for that."

A flip had her back in the middle of the bed, lying on her stomach. A firm hand at the small of her back kept her down. She resisted him enough to remain propped on her elbows, so she could watch him as he slid up her body, nipping and kneading his way from the soles of her feet to her nape, ridding her of her panties and bra on the way, leaving her with only her sandals on.

He worshipped her with his ferocity, owned her with his voracity. Every dig of his fingers in her flesh had the exact force, each nip of his teeth the exact roughness to extract maximum pleasure from every nerve ending. He layered sensations with each press and bite until she felt devoured and assimilated, until she was overloading.

Something was charring inside her. She undulated back against him in a fever, pressing her clamoring flesh against any part of him in mindless pursuit of assuagement. "*Arjook*, Haidar…"

At her cried-out plea, in Arabic, he growled something and flatted her beneath him. She lay there, naked, her every nerve abraded by the sensation of his flesh through his clothes, quaking at the domination of his heated bulk, at each wholly arousing touch.

"*Maafi raja*...no pleas, *ya naari,* only possession."

His breath burned her cheek, its scent filling her lungs, and everything inside her snapped. She cried out, twisted on her back, surged up to cling around him, to his lips in desperate kisses.

"Eight years, Roxanne," he growled inside her mouth between the tongue thrusts that filled her, conquered her. "Do you know how many times I cursed you for depriving me of this?"

He transferred his lips to her neck and shoulders, tasting every tremor strumming through her as his hands slid down her body, tormented every fiber into a riot of sensation. He dragged a rough, electrocuting hand between her thighs, kneaded and tormented his way to her core. The heel of his thumb ground against her outer lips at the same moment the wet furnace of his mouth clamped over a throbbing nipple. Sensation slashed her nerves.

He dealt her another blow as his deft fingers spread her, probed her readiness, two sliding between her engorged, molten inner lips, stilling at her entrance. She flailed, whimpered, arched up into his hand.

"Do you know what kind of frustration I suffered, wanting to see you like this, to feel you on fire, hunger shaking you apart? How I yearned to do this..."

Those long, sure fingers plunged inside her. Her hips bucked, her squeal morphing into a shriek when he pumped into her in slow in-out glides, filling her, beckoning at her inner trigger. He growled his satisfaction as her slick flesh gripped back at him, tried to wring its release from his torment.

"And do you know how it felt being *unable* to do this? Thinking I'd own your flesh like this again?"

Sensation rocketed, more at the emotion and passion fueling his words than at his expert pleasuring. She keened, opened herself wider for him, needing pleasure any way he gave it, offering her surrender.

"You can have it all now," she gasped. "And always."

"Saherah." His growl singed her, even as his thumb stroked her tight, nerve-filled bud in rhythmic circles, the exact pressure and speed she needed, escalating her need for release with each stroke. He swallowed every tremulous word, every tear until she was on the verge of shuddering apart. Then he let up.

She knew what he was doing. He was punishing her. By building up to an eventual, fiercer reward.

Her body felt it would combust if he didn't push her over the edge. But this was a test of the extent of her surrender. Letting him give her more than she could dream of, his way.

Before she could verbalize her submission, he slid down to lay on his stomach between her thighs, draping her legs over his back.

"And do you know what I suffered, craving the taste of you, knowing I'd never know it again?"

He inhaled her, rumbled like a lion maddened by the scent of his female, blew a gust of acute sensation over her quivering flesh. Her vision disappeared in a haze of crimson lust as he latched his hot lips over her intimate ones, plunging her into a vortex of need. He eased his fingers back into her, his tongue joining in, licked from where they were buried inside her upward, circling until she was sobbing feverishly. No pleas, though. Just confessions of what he was doing to her.

When he'd heard enough, taken her to the edge and dragged her back panting and shuddering enough times, he nipped her, knowing exactly where, how hard.

She convulsed, bucked, smashed her flesh to his mouth, opening herself fully to his double sensual assault, each glide and graze and thrust sending hotter lances skewering through her, pleasure slamming through her in desperate surges. Her climax wrung her out of satisfaction. He growled, drank every drop, kept pushing her, plumbing her flesh for more, until she tumbled from the explosive peak, drained, sated. Stupefied.

Had he ever driven her to such ecstasy?

Sight seeping back, her drugged eyes sought his, as if for answers. They sparkled in the ingeniously placed and calibrated lighting of the room and that of the oil lamps she'd lit, heavy with hunger and gratification.

As if to answer her, he said, "It's merciful, for both of us, time dulled even my memories. Either that or you have matured from a craving into an addiction."

Pride, delight surged, at his confession, at the sight of a long-craved fantasy. Him, clothed, between her legs, her, naked, splayed open over his Herculean shoulders.

Her hands trembled through his lush hair. "Look who's talking."

He chuckled against her inner thighs, cupped her, desensitizing her before he came up, prowled over her prostrate body on all fours like the sexy beast he was.

He straddled her hips, started stripping. That got her mind rebooting, her muscles functioning. She had to be the one to expose him. She raised her hands, only to have them join her thighs in the prison of his. "Your amends are *far* from made."

He licked his lips as if still tasting her, tormenting her with his slow striptease, tightening his knees around her thighs and hands, deepening her helplessness, winding her pounding into a tighter rhythm. She almost relinquished the rules of surrender, to beg to touch and taste him, almost passed out with the pressure of need.

He stood up on the bed, got rid of his pants and boxers in one move. Her senses swam, her mouth watered, the spike of hunger, the pinch of intimidation, the need to feel his daunting manhood, smell it, taste it almost pulling her under.

But she'd had her chance a week ago. He would punish her for that stunt by denying her the pleasure for a period only he would determine. He also had other ways of exacting payment.

He came down over her, pressed his erection to her belly. Feeling the marble smooth and hard column of hot flesh against hers made her writhe, gasp. It awed her that she'd accommodated all that inside her. The remembered sensations as he'd occupied her, stretched her into mindlessness, made her arch up seeking more. He ground harder into her, his knees splaying her thighs, his silk-sprinkled chest teasing her aching nipples.

The moment he crushed her beneath him, she wrapped herself around him, buried her face in his neck, opened her lips over his pulse. Every steel muscle expanded, bunched, buzzed. She whimpered at the relief of his weight on her, the feel of his power, the taste and texture of his flesh beneath her lips, the sheer delight of breathing him in.

"Do you know the depth of longing that preyed on me, needing you beneath me like this? Do you know how much of my sanity I lost wanting to be inside you, yearning to have you around me? Knowing I was destined for starvation?"

His bass groans had regret and agony for the lost years clotting in her heart. *"Haidar, habibi, kamm ana aasfah…"*

At hearing her calling him her love, saying how sorry she was, his hands convulsed in her hair, pinned her for the full vehemence of his passion. His lips crashed on hers, silencing her, wrenching keens from her with scorching, desperate kisses. He lifted her off the bed, one hand supporting her head for his ravaging, the other at her back, holding her for his chest to torment her breasts, driving her into more of a frenzy. Her eyes streamed tears from the emotional and carnal torment. What she'd cost them…

He touched the head of his erection to her entrance, nudged

her, bathing himself in her desire. "*Guleeli, ya naari*—tell me you know, Roxanne. Tell me you suffered the same."

She pressed his biceps convulsively, arched for his completion. "I know. And I did. I suffer worse now…"

His eyes roiled with a dizzying mixture of ferociousness and tenderness. "As you should. Now, *ya naari,* for all the years without your inferno, your solace, now you *pay.*"

He pumped his hips, pushing against her entrance. Though she was melting with readiness, it had always taken a measure of force for him to breach her. His eyes blazed with the need to forge inside her. Her frantic nod begged for the no-holds-barred invasion.

He lunged, was there, where she needed him, penetrating her in one forceful thrust.

The expansion of her tissues around his erection was so sudden, the fullness sharpened into pain that exploded into pleasure so fierce, darkness danced at the periphery of her vision.

She gasped, thrashed. His face clenched with something like agony as he stilled, started to withdraw. She clung to him as she would to a raft as she drowned.

"Eight years' worth," she sobbed. "Take it all now…*now.*"

"*Aih, ya naari,* take it all, give it back to me." He refilled her, his tongue thrusting inside her mouth with the same ferocity.

His growls grew dark as he gave her what she'd been disintegrating for, in the exact force and pace. He invaded her, stretched her more with each plunge, forging deeper, the head of his shaft sliding against her internal flesh, setting off a string of discharges that buried her under layers of sensations.

It all felt maddeningly familiar, yet totally new, a buildup that seemed to originate from her every cell and radiate from his own at once, distilling desperation into a physical symptom.

Then everything compacted into one unendurable moment that detonated outward. She shattered.

She heaved so hard she almost lifted him in the air, her flesh pulsing around his so fiercely she couldn't breathe, not for the first dozen clenches of excruciating pleasure.

"Aih, ya naari, pay for all my suffering with your pleasure."

His rumble snapped something inside her, flooded air into her lungs. She screamed and screamed her ecstasy as he rode her, his hardness pistoning satisfaction into her.

"Roxanne..." He rose above her, muscles bulging, eyes tempestuous, supernatural in beauty. He threw his head back and roared her name as every muscle in his body locked, his erection lodging against her womb, jetting his own release in long, hard surges, setting off her deepest triggers in one more conflagration.

He fed her convulsions, pumping her to the last twitches of fulfillment until the world receded...

Roxanne stirred from the depths of bliss.

She opened her eyes and found herself staring at the breath-taking vista of the sea and the island outside Haidar's balcony. Contentment expanded inside her, had her turning toward him.

He wasn't there.

"Haidar?"

No answer. He must be in the shower. Or the kitchen. Or somewhere. Judging by the setting sun outside, she'd been knocked out for the last twelve hours. Or maybe even thirty-six.

But that was his fault. He'd taken the eight years' worth almost literally, exacted vengeance by ecstasy until she'd lost count. And consciousness.

She got out of bed, waddled to the bathroom, wincing at the soreness from his repeated possession. She needed to soak if she hoped to be ready for more.

She came out of the bath tingling with rejuvenation and anticipation, went in search of him.

She found him nowhere.

She called him. His phone was turned off.

Where was he? What could have made him disappear?

No answer made sense. As hours passed, terrible explanations started to trickle in, expand, take over rationalizations. That he'd taken her up on her offer but had never intended to stay for an encore. That last night had meant only two things to him—vindication, closure.

Was that it? He'd gotten them and just…left?

Unable to accept that verdict, she waited, every sound in the expansive house almost uprooting her heart with hope. But he didn't return.

Night had deepened to utter bleakness when she found herself walking to the pier, to the platform where she'd thought her life had started again.

She looked out to the island that was now an awe-striking shadow under the light of a nascent moon and blazing stars. She'd thought he'd take her there, to explore, to make love, to—

"I thought you'd be gone."

She spun around, saw him approaching through the liquid pain filling her eyes. The conquering lover, the devil-may-care prince, the challenging adversary were all gone.

A frozen man had replaced them all.

His eyes regarded her without a spark of the life or lust that had always filled them. His voice was as lifeless. "But then I thought many things and they all turned out to be wrong. Now I can no longer fool myself into believing what I wish to believe."

God, what did he mean?

He was telling her he couldn't forgive or forget? Worse,

that his injuries remained the same whether she'd meant to inflict them or not?

"So why did you stay? I thought we'd said everything."

Was this his real revenge? Give her miles of hope to wrap around her neck, then push her off her skyscraper of foolish dreams?

But he had to realize this wasn't just retribution. Whatever injury she'd caused him, he'd survived it. Thrived, even. Shattering her heart now wouldn't only be for the second time. It would be for the last. There would be no surviving it.

"If you stayed thinking I'd back down, I won't. I have to end this now, or there'll be no surviving it."

Had she spoken her thoughts out loud?

No. He just knew how much he was damaging her.

Not that she could blame him. He'd walked away, told her to go. She'd pursued him, planned and plotted her own destruction. She'd done this to herself, as she had in the past. No one had forced her to love him, give him more than he'd wanted. The first time she'd been too young, had had the delusion that she could love again, could come to life again with someone else. Now she'd grown up and out of her false hopes. Now she knew. She could only love, and live, if it was him, with him.

And he didn't want her.

Trembling so hard she could barely summon enough coordination to walk, she stumbled back toward him, wishing he would disappear so she wouldn't have to feel him this close one last time.

Then she was passing him, holding her breath so that his scent wouldn't twist the dagger of longing inside her chest. The stretch of the pier into land was ahead of her. The path to escape. To the nothingness that dominated her future...

She came to a jolting halt.

He'd stopped her.

Before she could cry for him to just "sever the artery and let it bleed out," as they said here, he took her by the shoulders.

She struggled to push his hands away. She couldn't *bear* this.

His eyes smoldered down at her as if he was in the grips of a fever. "I can't let you go, Roxanne. I thought I could, but I can't. I will take anything for as long as you will give it. And if you prefer, I won't bring up marriage again."

Ten

Bring up marriage? Again?

Roxanne stared up at Haidar, nothing making sense anymore.

His fingers convulsed on her shoulders. "I was an arrogant bastard, making it sound like a fait accompli. I deserved that 'shut up.' I shouldn't have gotten angry when you said it. I shouldn't have made it an ultimatum, shouldn't have said that it was marriage or nothing."

Every word out of his mouth pushed vague things from the periphery of her mind and into focus. Hazy snippets she might have heard as she'd drifted in and out of oblivion. His voice, hers, the words themselves evaporating like a dream after waking.

He was saying that, during those unremembered fragments, he'd proposed to her? That she'd answered his proposal with... *shut up?*

"If you stayed to tell me I'm an idiot, but that I can stop being one and take what you're willing to give me, I accept."

"Haidar, I don't—"

Suddenly he let her go, turned around to gaze into the star-blazing sky. "Your point-blank refusal reinforced once again that I've never been compatible with human relationships, a classic case of someone 'only a mother can love.' But it was trying to let you go that made me realize what I am guilty of."

"Haidar, you don't need—"

He swung back to her. "I *do* need to say this. In the past I compounded being jealous and suspicious with my uncompromising need to be in total control of myself, and to have every last heartbeat of you. I made it worse by being unable to share anything about myself, yet wanting you to know and accommodate my emotional needs the same way you did my physical ones. When you didn't, dared give appreciation and ease and laughter to Jalal, I got so mad, felt so hurt, that the part of me that is like my mother took over. I demanded more from you physically and withdrew further emotionally, trying to make you come closer to compensate. I made you believe that my feelings where you were concerned were at best not healthy. Believing they were nonexistent was a simple step from that."

She stepped closer, her mind churning. "You're saying you think you deserved my distrust after all?"

"I never said I didn't. I said I didn't deserve all the blame. You were to blame, too, claiming to love me for what I was, when you didn't know what *that* was. You didn't recognize that I was reaching out to you in the only way I knew how, showing you with all the effort and trouble I took to be with you how vital you were to me. I did reach out to you outright that day, begged you to reassure me."

He turned away, shoulders slumping as if all fight had gone out of him. "But you probably did yourself a favor by leaving. Last week, I didn't walk away only because I was feeling sorry for myself, but because I did think you'd be better off without me. I hurt you just by being who I am, even before you found out about that stupid bet, before I exposed you to my mother's abuse."

He turned back to her, his eyes fevered. "But you were right to reject me again. I said I would accept anything you were willing to give, but I won't. I can't. I was all or none in the past, and I haven't changed. When I came back to Azmahar I was in control of my tendencies because I was telling myself I now only wanted you. Then we had our confrontation, *then* last night happened—and that control is gone. I can't and won't be satisfied with less than all of you, forever. It might have sounded exciting to you in the heat of passion, when you thought I was talking about sex. But after you realized I meant everything for real…I don't blame you if that put you off."

"It doesn't," she whispered, the enormity of what he was revealing choking her. "Not if it's a two-way street…?"

His eyes narrowed, his body going still. "It is. You have all of me. If you'll only take it."

Havoc filled her eyes, quivered on her lips with the poignancy of letting go of doubts, seeing her way clear and sure, and permanent back to him. "The bad before the good, huh?"

The hope flaring in his eyes dimmed again. "That scares you?"

And she surged into him, hugged him with all her strength. "Not anymore. I trust you, Haidar. And if it took me a while to get there, it's because you're so full of contradictions, you made it almost impossible to know what you're all about. You also overwhelm me. Which kinda counteracts any attempts at being rational where you're concerned." She looked up at him, her heart in her eyes for him to see. "You were so unreadable I thought there was nothing to read beyond the obvious. You were so confident I thought you had no doubts, no weaknesses. The rest of your assets painted an inhuman paragon with no human failings or emotions. But mainly, you're so devastatingly…potent, I thought you'd never be satisfied with one woman. Hell, I thought you probably couldn't and shouldn't be."

He stiffened in her arms. "Unfaithfulness, let alone promiscuity, is one thing I don't suffer from."

Her smile trembled with all the joy settling in her heart. "I know that, now that I see you for who you really are. I thought you were domineering and controlling, but you're only dominant and in control. You're uncompromising, but you can be flexible where it matters. You seemed cruel, willing to get your way over anyone's dead body, but either you grew out of it, or you never actually walked over anyone who didn't deserve it. You're scarily serious about work, but it turns out you have this supreme ability to be fun and funny, too. And you have insecurities like the rest of us mortals, behind that impenetrable front. To top it all off, the harsh pragmatist in you shares your body with an incredible romantic."

His eyes were widening as she spoke. Now he swallowed. "You see good sides to me?"

"I see *fantastic* sides to you. But most important, they are fantastic to *me*. I would have loved you—I *have* loved you—for far, far less. I love you now for everything you are and aren't."

"But…you told me to shut up!"

She dived into his arms again, groaning. "I don't even remember saying it, but I probably meant the one thing I needed most in the world right then. For you to shut up and let me *sleep*."

He held her away, flabbergasted. "You mean I spent a day in a worse hell than any I have ever imagined because you were sleep-talking? *Ya Ullah*…when I said marriage or nothing, demanded a yes or no, you looked me straight in the eye, said an emphatic no, then turned your back and went to sleep."

"I probably would have said no if you'd asked me if I needed to breathe. You devastated me with your vengeance of ecstasy." She laughed, threw her arms around his neck and clung. "I think we can now say we have one of the most unique proposal tales on record."

His arms convulsed around her, his expression still jittery. "You can laugh. I was considering leaving civilization for good."

She cupped his cheek, reveling in the freedom, in the wonder of being able to show him everything in her heart at last. "Jumping to conclusions where the other is concerned seems to be what we do best."

"Aih." His frown was all dejected regret. Then determination blazed. "But never again. From now on, we never do that. Promise me you will always tell me anything at all."

She dragged him into a fierce kiss, laughing, tears flowing, murmured against his lips, "I promise."

He put her away again. "You *are* saying you want to marry me?"

"If it entails being with you for better or for worse, in sickness and in health, till death parts us and probably not even then, I do."

Haidar shook with the enormity of the averted catastrophe, of witnessing Roxanne's bliss and certainty. He needed to solidify their pact, their claim on each other. Right now.

He swept her up in his arms, didn't feel the ground beneath his feet on his way to their bedroom. His heart thundered as he put her down on the bed, tore at their clothes, unable to bear anything between them. Then he looked down at her, his sorceress, his goddess, in all her naked glory.

Her breasts were a feast, her waist nipped, making the flare of her hips fuller. Her limbs were firm and smooth, her shoulders square and strong. Every curve and line and swell of her was the translation of his every fantasy.

He skimmed her from shoulder to breast, blood roaring in his ears, his loins, as its heavy heat and resilience overflowed in his hand. She thrust her breast into his hold, inviting a harder kneading. He pinched her nipple, bent for a compulsive suckle as he came over her, groaning as her firmness cushioned his hardness.

"Elaahati al nareyah, you're beyond glorious."

Her face flushed with pleasure. "I've graduated from sorceress to goddess?"

"If there was more than goddess, you'd be that to me."

She dragged him down to her, drinking deep of his admiration and desire. Delight expanded through him as he melded their nakedness, fusing their mouths, his hands seeking all her secrets, taking every license, owning every inch. He brought her to orgasm around his fingers, before traveling down her body, draping her legs over his shoulders. She wantonly pressed her back to the mattress, arched her hips at him, opening herself wide for his devouring as he drank her overflowing pleasure.

When he finally slid up her body, she stopped him before he could join them. He rose from suckling her breasts, alarm hammering in his chest.

It dissipated at seeing her eyes, misty with emotion. "Will you stop punishing me and let me have you? Will you surrender to me?"

His own eyes stung with the poignancy of her need for his reciprocation, his need to cede all to her. *"Tulabatek awamer,* your demands are my commands, *ya naari."*

He turned on his back, taking her with him, letting her own every inch of him as he had her.

He threw back his head at the first touch of her lips on his erection. He'd never enjoyed this intimacy except with her. He'd never felt such a purity of desire as she delighted in pleasuring him. The look of blissful voracity that adorned her face as her lips wrapped around his girth, as she pumped and sucked him in abandon, murmuring and moaning her pleasure, soon had him stripped down to his savage male component. Blind with lust, with the need to dominate his female completely.

He still tried to pull away when she took him to the edge. She keened around his flesh, dug her fingers into his buttocks. He climaxed in scalding torrents, the pleasure agonizing as she greedily drank him.

Finally, reluctantly letting him slide out of her mouth, she pressed her flushed, moist face to his thigh. "We *are* even now. You've become an addiction, too."

"I won't concede this. I claim the deeper addiction, and more frequent need of your taste and pleasure as my fix."

She began to protest, but he dragged her beneath him, bore down on her, came between her eagerly splaying thighs and plunged into her flowing depths, the vise of heat and ecstasy she surrendered to him, captured him in. He knew the aggression of his passion sent her insane with lust, that the edge of pain from being barely able to accommodate him made her pleasure more explosive.

With every thrust, his every word detailing his pleasure at being inside her, she writhed beneath him, her hair rippling waves of titian gloss, her breathing fevered, her whole body straining around him.

Her answering confessions came thicker, became more fevered, deeper. "Haidar—I missed you…never felt alive without you, without this…your flesh in mine…do it all to me, give me all of you…"

He obeyed, strengthened his thrusts until she rippled around him and convulsions squeezed soft shrieks out of her, spasmed her inner flesh around his erection.

The force of her release smashed the last of his restraint. He roared, let go, his body all but exploding in ecstasy. He felt his essence flowing into her as he fed her pleasure to the last tremor, until her arms and legs fell off him in satiation.

Shuddering from the aftershocks of the most violent and

profound orgasm he'd ever attained, even with her, he collapsed on top of her, knowing she loved his weight anchoring her after the storm of pleasure had wreaked havoc on them. He felt her lips trembling on his forehead, heard his name in a litany of longing.

Tenderness swamped him. *"Ahebbek, ya naari, kamm ahebbek."*

She went still, her lips freezing on his face.

He rose on both arms, this unreasoning anxiety still so easy to trigger. It spiked to a heart-pummeling level. She was crying.

"That's the first time you've ever said you love me," she whispered.

Blood roared through his head in a riptide of regret. "I more than love you. *Ana aashagek,* I worship you and more, *ya hayat galbi.* And I'll never forgive myself for not telling you sooner."

She tugged him down for a searingly sweet kiss, letting him taste her tears of happiness. "If I forgive you, life of *my* heart, who are you not to? I hereby abolish all self-recriminations."

He could argue that she shouldn't. But her peace of mind depended on turning this page of their past. No one said he couldn't seek redemption in secret for, say, the rest of his life.

He wiped away her tears as he swept her on top of him. "As long as it's a two-way street."

She buried her face in his neck on a sob, nodded.

Soon, her breathing settled into the contented rhythm of deep sleep. He lay beneath her, still joined to her, feeling her blanket him in serenity and joy.

It was merciful that he *had* forgotten just how sublime making love to her was. Or maybe it was different now, with their maturity, their honesty about their emotions.

He encompassed her velvet firmness with caresses, letting awe and thankfulness and then sweet oblivion overtake him.

* * *

"What's *that?*"

From his kneeling position, Haidar grinned up at a stupe-fied Roxanne. "That is a piece from the Pride of Zohayd."

"What?" She snatched the jewelry box from his hands, gaped down at it. "It can't be. It's not possible to get a part of the treasure out of Zohayd without the national guard on its tail."

Now that she had taken the box, his stint at her feet was concluded. He rose, grinning in self-satisfaction. "You're talk-ing to the Prince of Two Kingdoms here."

"You could be the Prince of Two *Planets* and those jewels wouldn't be allowed out of Zohayd for any reason. Certainly not to be my...*shabkah*..."

Gulping as if the word stuck in her throat, she ran trem-bling fingers over the piece he'd picked as her "tying" present, a sublimely worked, twenty-four-carat-gold web ring/bracelet encrusted with priceless diamonds and a one-of-a-kind em-erald centerpiece.

Belief hit her like a bolt, had her stunned eyes jerking up to him. "God, it *is* the real thing, isn't it?"

He smiled at her, enjoying her flustered sequence of denial and realization to no end. "That *is* the whole point."

"B-but how is it possible that you have it?"

Something in her eyes wiped his smile away. "Are you thinking I...took it?" When she only continued to gape at him, bitterness seeped into him. "Or that as an accomplice to my mother's conspiracy, I got to keep some pieces...?"

She pounced on him, one hand covering his mouth. "Stop right there! I am *not* doubting you. I'm never gonna do that again, remember? I'm just...boggling."

He saw it. Her disbelief had nothing to do with him. Her belief in him *was* total.

Hurt evaporated like a dewdrop in a furnace, teasing taking over again. "Want to boggle some more? This is *the* piece."

Her mouth dropped open, remained like that for a whole minute.

Then she cried out, "No *way. The* first piece that Ezzat Aal Shalaan built the whole Pride of Zohayd treasure around? The piece that started the myth-turned-law of the Aal Shalaan's claim to the throne?"

"Nothing less would do what I feel for you justice."

She looked down at the magical beauty and intricacy of the piece. Suddenly she winced. "God, Haidar, no! It's too much of a responsibility. I would be scared to wear it. What if I damage it? What if I *lose* it? What if people realize it's the real deal?"

"The best way to ensure its and your safety is for you to remain no more than two inches away from me at all times."

She whacked the arm reaching for her. *"Haidar!"*

"Just kidding. If not by much." He picked up the hand that had inflicted such delicious pain, kissed its trembling palm. "You can say it's an uncanny imitation, never say it's your *shabkah.* Only we need know the truth and what it signifies as the centerpiece of a legend that has stood the test of time and inspired millions."

Her hand cupped his face, her smile trembling in incipient delight. "You think we have one in the making?"

He took the ring/bracelet out of the box, fitted it on her left hand. "I know we do."

He claimed her in a long kiss until she surfaced with another exclamation. "But *how?* I mean getting *this*—" she raised her hand to gape at the masterpiece of craftsmanship again "—is up there with flying under your own power. And *when?* Your proposal wasn't premeditated. And after I blubbered out my acceptance, there wasn't enough time."

"You underestimate how fast I can get things done." At her warning look he raised his hands. "But your analytical powers are spot on, as usual. I arranged to get it as soon as I received your text informing me of our meeting here. That's why I was so late."

"It wasn't to make me wait an hour for each year I cost us apart?"

He smirked. "That did cross my mind, too."

"But you were waiting for the...*shabkah*..." She fluttered as she examined it again.

He pinched her delightful bottom. "I *could* have arrived at your specified time and had it delivered here."

"So you *were* messing with me." She pushed herself harder into his hand, giving him a better grip. "As you had a right to."

"A right I wouldn't have exercised if I thought I had it. I wanted to run here the second I got your message. But I also wanted to get my hands on your *shabkah,* to be the only one to touch it after Amjad."

"*King* Amjad? *He* brought it to you? As in, *himself?*"

Surprising her was such a joy. He had to keep doing it. "Who else would have such access to the Pride of Zohayd? And who else is mad enough to give me its cornerstone piece, for any reason?"

She nodded. "Yeah. It's said he has evolved from Mad Prince to Crazy King status." A tide of peach spread up her face as she rushed to add, "Which in my opinion is great. His methods are shocking, but their results are amazing. I think he's the most effective king in the region's history since King Kamal Aal Masood of Judar."

He chuckled, soothing her embarrassment. "Never worry about offending my sibling sensibilities. My oldest brother always had a method to his madness, but now it also has a name—Maram. His better ninety-nine percent, as he says."

"So you told him you wanted the Pride of Zohayd's origin piece, and he just gave it to you? How will he justify this—and this *will* come out—to his council, to the people of Zohayd?"

"He's going to tell them to *shut up* or he'll auction off the rest, as he threatened to do before he took the throne from Father."

"Wow." Her head shake was dazed, her lips twitching. "I bet I could fill volumes analyzing him and his methods."

"Just think—when you marry me, you'll have open access to that one-of-a-kind specimen as his sister-in-law."

She scrunched her face. "Yeah, that's the main reason I'm marrying you—so I can get my analytical paws on your big brother."

"How about getting those paws, analytical and every other kind, on me?"

She ran her *shabkah*-clad hand down his chest, gently scraping his flesh. "The problem will be in getting them *off* you."

He took her lips, pressed her hand harder, every abrasion a sledgehammer of arousal. "I only need them off to get work and self-maintenance out of the way. Then they're back on. And on."

She shuddered as he deepened their mouth-mating.

It didn't feel strictly like pleasure. "What is it, *ya naar rohi?*"

"*This*—" her gesture was eloquent with what raged between them "—fire of *my* soul." Her eyes were almost uncertain. "Are humans supposed to attain this kind of happiness?"

He crushed her to him, pledged, "I only know we are."

Eleven

"We are confident you are well ahead of your competitors."

Haidar swept his gaze from the man who'd just spouted such an unsubstantiated claim to his other supporters, who were regarding him as if he were hiding their Christmas presents.

For the past two weeks since he'd proposed to Roxanne, they had left him no waking hour without intrusion, offering strategies, asking about his own, pushing for confirmation that he would go all out to claim the throne. Not to mention constantly pandering to his ego.

He sighed. "Let's not indulge in make-believe, please. Rashid is a formidable contender, an all-Azmaharian war hero—"

The group's spokesman cut in. "He's a fledgling in the world of finance and politics compared to you."

"A fledgling who flew out of the nest a fully grown vulture of the first order, and who might tear me apart if I turn my back on him like...I don't know, like I'm doing now while I pursue this quest? And then there is Jalal, who is the more—'

The man interrupted again. "Jalal is too Zohaydan. You

are the perfect combination we need, if you'll only take this more seriously."

"Like Rashid, you mean?" He huffed. "But aren't you claiming this is all about what's best for Azmahar? If he proves the better—"

"He isn't," another man insisted. "And neither is Jalal. But Rashid is forming alliances beyond his supporters. And Jalal has the kingdom's top politico-economic expert as his consultant."

Everything hit Pause inside Haidar.

There was only one person that could describe. Roxanne.

It was impossible. "You are misinformed about Jalal. Which makes me wonder about all the information you've been feeding me."

"We have proof," a third man said. "Photos of Jalal with Roxanne Gleeson for the past month, phone recordings—"

His heat shot up. "You're monitoring her phone?"

The man shook his head. "His. This is a major fight, and we will do anything to stop our adversary from gaining unfair advantage. And with her on his side, he certainly has that over you and Rashid. Not that we regret breaching her privacy. It's almost unethical to be supplying him with information she has come by from her job here."

Haidar didn't know what he said, or how the meeting came to an end. He found himself alone, paralyzed, in body and mind.

Then in the numb silence inside him, a voice rose. Serene, cajoling, knowing, explaining it all.

Roxanne was playing both of them. Until one became king. Then she'd pick him up like a ripe plum. She thought secrecy would even serve her if Rashid took the throne. She'd remain on his good side, maximize on his good opinion to win an even bigger role. While it would keep her options open with him and Jalal until she decided who would provide the most benefit to her. Probably Jalal. Putting up with a friend-turned-husband was one thing. Dealing with someone as emotionally and physically demanding as *him* was another. She might even dump them both and go for Rashid. And she'd get him. Not only was she irresistible in her own right, she had the insider info she needed to pull Rashid's strings.

He pressed both palms to his ears, shutting out that maddening, *mutilating* voice. The voice he now recognized.

His mother's.

That *was* her talking. She'd passed down to him the seeds of paranoia and mistrust and then fostered them every way she could. Listening to that voice had served him well in the cutthroat world of business. It had decimated his personal life.

He was done listening to her. He was done doubting Roxanne.

He would ask her about Jalal. And whatever she told him, it would be the truth.

End of story.

Haidar dived beneath the turquoise waters, surfaced with Roxanne wrapped around him. He squeezed her satiny flesh, ravaged her lips with smiling kisses that she reciprocated with enough ardor to turn the sea to steam. Though he'd just finished making love to her on the island, that hadn't even begun to satisfy him.

He slid his lips to her ear, gently bit her earlobe. "Race me back to the pier?"

She giggled, nipped his chin. "I have not turned into a dolphin yet. You'd have the fish cooked by the time I catch up."

"But you are a *saherah*. You can just use your magic."

Her eyes blasted him with unadulterated appreciation. "'Look who's talking' seems to comprise most of what I say to you these days."

She did make him feel as if he possessed magic. She made

him feel craved, treasured to his last cell. Just as he craved and treasured her.

He swept her into his arms, swam on his back with leisurely strokes in the still waters that had mercifully been untainted by the oil spill. She nestled into him, the largest part of his soul. His gaze swept what she called their oasis in the declining sun, luxuriated in feeling her through the silk medium of perfect-temperature water, in being with her in such a huge personal space. He had scheduled the estate caretakers to come only when she was at work.

Being here with her had long surpassed any heaven he'd ever heard about.

It would stay their secret heaven until the whole throne business was concluded. He didn't want to beat his opponents through the mass appeal of a fairy-tale wedding and the promise of the best queen the kingdom could hope for. He wanted to either take the throne by personal merit, or not at all. He also wanted to separate *them* from any tinge of business and politics.

They swam to the pier in languid silence, tapping into and feeding each other's energies and emotions in a closed circuit of harmony. Time stretched when they were together. The month since they'd found each other again felt like a year. More. He barely remembered his life before this month.

He certainly didn't want to remember the time after he'd lost her, when the knife kept twisting harder each time his siblings found their soul mates. Aliyah had found Kamal, Shaheen had Johara, Harres had Talia, and most shocking and improbable of all, Amjad had Maram. But he'd found Roxanne again, and at last had her for real, and this time forever. It was nothing short of a miracle.

He sighed, felt enveloped in the contentment and certainty only her embrace imbued him with.

Suddenly she wriggled, broke his hold, kicked away.

She laughed as he gave pursuit. Despite her earlier joke, she was such a strong swimmer, he almost didn't need to slow down for her to beat him to the pier. She pulled herself onto it in one agile move, stood in her flame-colored torture device of a swimsuit grinning down at him.

He took his time following her, to look his fill as she dried herself in brisk movements. Those grew languid as he neared, gathered her, cherished her every inch in caresses and kisses as she stroked him dry.

He lifted her in his arms and she clung around his neck as he walked to the house. "I was thinking of the incredible relationships my siblings have, and it made me think of Maram. I can't wait for you to meet her. You'll hit it off right out of the region."

She nuzzled his neck. "You never told me about her before."

He was realizing more and more how he'd shortchanged her. He never would again. "I adored her growing up. Still do. She's one of those rarities in life, an anomaly who liked me more than Jalal. Turned out my mother was behind throwing us together as part of her long-term plan to put me on the throne of Ossaylan, too. But all it did was create a special bond between us. And boy, did we milk *that* to give Amjad a well-deserved hard time."

"I'm not supposed to be jealous, right?"

"*Never* be, of anything in this world. *B'Ellahi*, I am yours."

His reward for the fervent vow was a kiss that almost had him taking her right there and to hell with showering and eating.

He pulled back, knowing she needed both. "As for Maram, she was my cherished friend, like Jalal was yours. I lost almost all touch with her as she went through the ordeals of her two marriages and temporary defection to the U.S., but once we saw each other again, it was like we never stopped being friends. I hope you can have the happiness of Jalal's friendship back, like I do Maram's."

He waited for her to tell him she *had* been seeing Jalal since he'd come back to Azmahar, that they had resumed their friendship.

She only looked away. "I would love that, too."

Arjooki, ya habibati...please, my love, trust me, tell me.

She didn't.

"You did *what?*"

Cherie's exclamation felt like nails against Roxanne's nerves.

She was again almost sorry she'd run to her friend with this.

But she hadn't been able to share it with her mother. Her mother, who was deliriously happy for the first time in...ever, after she'd told her about Haidar's proposal.

She'd told Cherie and Jalal, too, asked them to keep it a secret until the kingship issue was settled. Her mother had decided to cancel her retirement and come help her settle things faster so that the wedding could happen that much sooner.

Before any of that happened, she had to settle *this* mess.

She'd lied to Haidar point-blank, pretended she hadn't seen or heard from Jalal since the original breakup.

"You call this desert god of yours and tell him the truth right now, Roxanne. The more time you let pass between your...omission to tell him you've been seeing his twin behind his back, and helping him against him... God! What were you *thinking?*"

"It didn't happen that way!" she groaned. "I started this when Haidar was my worst enemy and Jalal my best friend. Suddenly Haidar is my fiancé and I'm helping Jalal, who's now his rival. I'm bound to Jalal by friendship and my word of honor, and to Haidar by love and everything else. But I couldn't tell him when he gave me the opening. It isn't my secret to tell."

"Famous last words." Cherie groaned, too. "You gotta fix this, and fast. Things like this can spiral and spoil everything. And your reconciliation with Haidar is too new and emotions too high."

"But Jalal still hasn't decided how to settle this whole mess between himself and Haidar!"

"Then tell Jalal to get his gorgeous butt settled, and tell your fiancé the truth before it messes up your newly fixed relationship!" Cherie came down beside her, hugged her to her side. "Listen, I took your advice and I'm getting back together with Ayman. We're even moving out of Azmahar so we can adopt. And as you jogged my mind back into the right place, I have to return the favor. Besides, the first time I nudged you to go after your man, you ended up with the biggest catch of the century in your net and the freaking origin piece of the Pride of Zohayd jewels on your hand. So am I good, or am I good?"

Roxanne hugged her. "You're superlative. I owe you far more than I can repay. And oh, I'm so happy about you and Ayman."

Cherie fluttered her lashes at her. "This means you forgive me for the mess I made of your immaculate place?"

A laugh burst out of her tight chest. "I've come to believe immaculate is overrated. And by the way, Haidar is asking if you've thought of his offer to finance your catering project."

"Have I *thought?*" Cherie jumped up in elation. "Apart from Ayman, I haven't thought of anything else. The moment you tell me you cleared things up with him, I'm hitting him with my proposal!"

After more nudges to tell Haidar, Cherie left Roxanne alone In turmoil.

Cherie was right. It wasn't all about Jalal and her promise to keep his secret. She was scared to upset the perfection, the balance. Haidar would be disappointed she hadn't felt confident enough in their relationship to tell him. And after they'd agreed they'd never hide anything from each other again.

But she hadn't been hiding a thing. She just forgot about everything when she was with him. The only time she'd remembered Jalal lately had been when she'd told him, as her friend, about her and Haidar. The conflict of interest hadn't crossed her mind since Haidar's proposal. The only time she'd thought of the kingship issue in the past two weeks had been *with* Haidar, discussing his prospects and plans.

But Cherie was right again about needing to tell Haidar the truth. And Jalal was wrong about Haidar. Beneath the bitterness and alienation, Haidar loved him, or he wouldn't have been so hurt by his accusations. She should be the one to bring them back together, as she'd had an unwitting role in the formation of the fissure that had torn them apart. She'd summon her inner negotiator, go after Jalal—

The bell chime had her jumping.

God, her nerves *were* shot.

Which wasn't strange, with so much at stake.

She rushed to the door, opened it, found Jalal standing there.

"Gebna sert'el ott! Speak of the cat!" she exclaimed, dragged him in and into a hug.

Jalal chuckled, hugged her back. "And he comes bounding. *Konti b'tenteffi farweti ma'a meen*—who were you plucking my fur with?"

"I wasn't talking about you, just thinking of you, really."

"I should hope so, since you texted me to come over."

"But I…"

A key turned in the door. Cherie? She'd come back this soon?

Next second her skin almost pooled to the ground. *Haidar.* Her heart stopped as she watched him walk in. One thing became clear at once. He wasn't surprised to see Jalal. Which meant...

He was the one who'd arranged this. He must have texted Jalal from her phone when she'd been at his house a few hours ago.

He kept his eyes trained on Jalal. Her dazed gaze moved to Jalal, saw her same shock mixed with as powerful dismay, even if it had a different origin.

Silently, Haidar approached them as they stood frozen. He stopped feet away, bent slightly. A sharp smack jolted through her, had her heart stumbling like a horse on ice as her eyes searched out the sound's origin. A dossier on her coffee table.

Haidar straightened, still looking at Jalal. "These are the analysis reports that Roxanne supplied you with, that you were building your campaign around. I thought it only fair to inform you that they no longer constitute an edge, since I have them, too, in case they were the resource you were banking on to get ahead in this race."

Heartbeats blipped inside her chest, none pumping blood.

She didn't have to examine the dossier to know. It contained what he'd said. He knew. About her arrangement with Jalal.

But...he didn't seem angry. Or disappointed. He seemed... nothing. She could feel nothing from him. That opaque wall was up again. Was he hiding his disappointment or...or was this nothingness real?

And if it was...why? And how had he found out? When?

He'd brought up Jalal only yesterday, seemingly in passing, as if he knew nothing. But he couldn't have uncovered all that information during that time. So had he already known when he'd mentioned him? Had he been out to see if she'd come clean, or...?

A suspicion too terrible to contemplate detonated inside her

No. She wasn't suspecting him again. She'd promised Vowed.

But…*God*. He no longer seemed like the man she loved more than life. He was again the unknowable quantity, the inaccessible entity he'd been. The ice in his eyes was obliterating everything, leaving only stone-cold doubts and possibilities.

Could he have known about Jalal from the start? Investigated and put two and two together? He did have an uncanny deductive mind. It wasn't only possible. It was probable.

It appeared to be the truth.

But if he'd known, why had he never broached the subject?

Because you wouldn't have told him anything. Not as things stood between you at first.

So was that why he'd pursued her again? To get her to the point where she would talk? And supply him with better information than she'd given Jalal?

She *had* given him far more info than she had Jalal, thinking she'd been discussing Azmahar's future with her fiancé, discussing his major worries and plans.

Had it all been to beat Jalal at the game, again?

His mother's cold venom came back to her in a scalding rush of memory. Her pride in his long-term manipulative powers, which he'd inherited from her, the woman who'd plotted a region-smashing coup for over thirty years and almost pulled it off.

He'd once said he was her updated and improved version.

Would beating his brother again, for a throne no less, explain everything that had happened between them? Cold logic said that made more sense than what he'd professed. That his emotions had always been so powerful they'd survived the years of humiliation and alienation, that he loved her now above everything, as she loved him.

She had been wondering if it was possible for anyone to have all that, to be so happy. Had she been right to wonder, because no one could? Because none of it had been real?

Her world teetered on the verge of collapse.

Then he looked at her, his eyes empty. And it did.

Haidar looked at Roxanne and knew. Hearts did break.

She'd wept in his arms with pleasure, pledged love and allegiance. And she'd again hidden something of major importance from him. She hadn't trusted him. She hadn't put him first.

She never would.

He now faced the truth at last. What he'd been trying to run from all his life. His mother had been right. No one would ever love him. He inspired nothing but deficient, distorted emotions in those he loved. The proof was his mother's love itself. That monstrously manipulative, obsessively possessive emotion.

But he'd also been right about himself. He hadn't and wouldn't change. He couldn't live with having less than all of her.

That left him with none.

He stood facing the two people who had almost full monopoly of his emotions, formed the major part of his being. They'd again found it right to exclude him, to alienate him, to shut him out. All he could do now was relinquish hope. Accept that no matter what, he'd be forever alone.

"*That's* why you went after Roxanne this time?"

The dreadful growl yanked him out of his numbness.

He blinked, found Jalal in his face, his expression demonic.

"And to think I was agonizing over how to mend the rift between us, over what I accused you of, thinking I was wrong the more I thought about it. I was only wrong in imagining the depth of your depravity. I don't know how I never saw you for the monster you really are all our lives, but you deserve to be alone for the rest of yours. And although I didn't really want to be king, I'll now do anything to take that throne, to stop you from taking it."

Haidar barely registered his twin's abuse, let alone understood it. He saw nothing but the betrayal on Roxanne's face, felt nothing but the agony blasting off her.

But...why would she be the one feeling betrayed, agonized?

Because she was? By what? His choosing to save himself pain by giving up and walking away as she'd once done?

Suddenly, the enormity of his mistake crashed on him.

He'd been *wrong.*

If she chose to exclude him, he shouldn't consider it mistrust, or a deficiency of love. She had a right to help Jalal if she believed he'd make a better king. Even if she didn't, he was her friend, and she had every right to help him, do anything she chose to, his opinion or consent, or even knowledge, not required. And it stood independent from her relationship with him. It didn't affect her love for him, that she maintained parts of herself he had no access to.

He shouldn't ask for all of her. He had no right to it.

He would be happy, *grateful,* with any parts of her she chose to give him.

He reached for her, but something irresistible stopped him. He struggled with it, and something with the force of a sledgehammer struck him. The explosion detonated from the point of impact upward, shooting behind his eyes, jolting his brain.

Roxanne's receding figure buzzed in and out on his retinas, like a movie reel catching, blipping, burning.

Fighting off the disorientation, he tried to run after her. He slammed into something immovable. This time he fought back, moved it, ran after her, caught up with her.

Her hands smacked at him when he reached for her, her voice choked with the tears that ran down her cheeks. "What more do you want? I don't have any more information."

His vision was still warped, and so was his balance. He stumbled a step back when she pushed at him. "Roxanne... I don't..."

"You *didn't* need to go to all that trouble. You will surpass your rivals without any special strategy, just by being who you are. You are the best king Azmahar could hope for. The kingdom needs someone with such convoluted cunning to get it out of the maze of problems it's mired in. Not that I care what happens here anymore. I'm leaving. This time I'm never coming back."

He must still be disoriented. He didn't understand a thing she was saying. She was supposed to be slapping his face for daring to go back on his vow of always telling her everything. He should have told her how he felt, talked it out with her. Where did the throne come into this? What information was she talking about?

He caught her back and suddenly another pair of hands were on him, those he finally realized were Jalal's.

"Get your hands off her, Haidar," Jalal hissed. "This time, you're keeping them off her."

"I can fight my own battles, Jalal," she snapped.

"What battles? What are you two talking about…?" Something warm and wet trickled down his face, distracting him.

He put a hand to it, squinted at what came off. Blood.

He gaped at Jalal. "You hit me!"

"And you have the gall to be surprised?"

Haidar switched his stunned gaze between Jalal and Roxanne. They were in her bedroom. And he suddenly understood. What they were accusing him…worse, what they'd *condemned* him of.

And he did what he'd been seething to do for the past few decades. He smashed both fists into Jalal's shoulders, all his strength and years of fury and frustration behind the blow.

Jalal slammed into the wall with a crack that rattled the whole room. Roxanne gasped, stumbled against another wall Haidar barely noticed, his focus pinned on Jalal who was now gaping at him.

Of course he was shocked. This was the first time in their lives that Haidar had ever shown him physical violence.

Before Jalal could recover, Haidar faced them both, his teeth bared. "Again? You're doing this again? You're passing judgment on me without giving me a chance to defend myself?"

Jalal straightened, returning his glare. "Excuse us as your actions *and* words speak so loudly they drown our attempts to exonerate you."

"So I compile a dossier on your activities and findings since you came here," Haidar hissed. "To prove that I was bound to find out, to show my disappointment that you both excluded me again, and you assume I got it from Roxanne? Worse, that I was with her just to get it? And for what? To foil your bid for the throne?"

Jalal's glare wavered. Haidar heard something distressed squeezing from Roxanne's chest.

He included her in his bitterness. "*Zain,* let's have this out. Air all your grievances and suspicions and accusations, the substantiated and imagined, and get this over with."

Jalal gave a disgusted grunt. "You mean an encore of the lifetime I spent doing just that? When every attempt at closeness or confrontation got me evasions, brush-offs and obstinate refusals to communicate or share anything?"

Haidar countered, "You mean those endless times when you were your pain-in-the-ass, intrusive, invasive, insensitive self?"

Jalal shrugged. "If you choose to see it that way."

"I do choose."

Jalal's gaze wavered. "Bottom line is, you always left me no recourse but to come to my own conclusions."

"And of course they had to be the worst ones. And you know why? Because I'm the walking reminder of what you lived your life afraid of facing, the personification of all your fears. What I spent my life trying not to rub your nose in. But, dearest twin, here it is, dry. You're part demon, too."

Jalal's teeth ground together.

Haidar smirked at the obvious hit. "You may not look it, and you may have convinced everyone you're all Aal Shalaan stock, but you haven't convinced *yourself.* You're as paranoid and suspicious and possessive and unreasonable where it comes to your loved ones as I am. You are my *twin,* Jalal, whether you like it or not."

Jalal's wolf eyes suddenly flared again. "I may be everything you said, Haidar, but *I* didn't finance our mother's conspiracy."

The jagged pain that slashed across Haidar's face yanked Roxanne out of the well of agitation she'd been spiraling in.

She'd misjudged him. Again. Hurt him, again. She was out of excuses this time.

She stepped between the two forces of nature snarling at each other, clung to Haidar's arm, whispered a tremulous "I'm sorry."

He tore his gaze away from his duel with Jalal, looked down at her. "Why? You think none of the things you said to me are true? Would you still be sorry if I tell you what Jalal just accused me of is the truth?"

Suppressing tears with all she had, she shook her head. "It can't be. It isn't."

"Why this sudden and unwavering trust?"

"Because this is my natural state now," she insisted. "I was having a minor breakdown minutes ago."

One eyebrow rose, the rest of his face unyielding. "It didn't look minor to me. And don't be so quick to anoint me with your unconditional belief. I *did* finance my mother's conspiracy."

She shook her head again, her heart bruising against her ribs. "Then you didn't know what the money was for."

"Minutes ago you assumed I screwed you over to get myself a throne. Why assume a couple of years ago I wasn't willing to screw my whole family and kingdom over for an even bigger one?"

"Because you're no traitor." Her declaration was unequivocal.

"You just thought I was," he persisted.

And tears flowed. "That was your mother's long-acting, insidious poison and my own fear that this—" her gesture between them was eloquent with what they had, shared "—is too perfect to be true. The emotions you inspire in me are so overpowering, I'm still having trouble dealing with them, believing they are reciprocated. Mainly—I can't believe my luck."

He regarded her dispassionately, his face impassive. "I still did finance my mother's conspiracy."

He was pushing her. Seeing when her trust would waver, crack.

She wiped away her tears, gave him a serene nod. "And I'm sure you're sorry about it and won't do anything like that again."

And he smiled.

She gasped in the breath she'd been unable to draw, her hand trembling on the terrible bruise spreading across his jaw as she attempted to smile back. "I'm cured. This time, irrevocably."

He dug his fingers into her hair, drew her up for a brief but fierce kiss. She moaned as she tasted his blood, the injury she'd been responsible for.

Seeming to realize this, he withdrew. "No more mistrust?"

"Insecurity," she insisted.

His nod was slow, accepting. Then he smiled again, a teasing sparkle entering his eyes. "And I won't monopolize your emotions and allegiance. You can love other people. Even Jalal here. *If* you must."

"As touching as this is, mind if you don't evade me again?"

Haidar turned to Jalal, that coolness that had once made both her and Jalal believe he was indifferent again coating his face. "You said you were agonizing about how to mend the rift between us, were no doubt loitering because you didn't know how to beg my forgiveness for your accusations."

Jalal took a threatening step closer. "Now, listen here—"

Haidar cut him off smoothly. "You wanted to because you thought they were wrong. What rationalization did you come up with for my actions to think that?"

Glowering at Haidar, Jalal exhaled. "I thought you didn't know why she wanted the money, but being the stupid sap that you are when it comes to her, you gave it to her without question."

Haidar's smile was the essence of concession and self-deprecation. "You think *she's* that stupid? She asked me for money over many years, every time with a reason, saying she couldn't ask our father, and didn't have enough money herself. I realized both were lies, assumed she demanded it as…tribute from me, as a proof of love and loyalty. Once I understood this, I sometimes gifted her with major sums, just because. I never suspected she had an insurrectionist agenda. The worst I suspected was that she'd do nothing philanthropic with it."

Jalal exhaled. "And you still gave it to her."

Haidar echoed his resignation. "It might seem unacceptable to you, and you must think it unbelievable I'd have this inexplicable soft *and* blind spot, but I do love her. I don't think I can stop."

Jalal drove his hands into his hair, wiped them down his face. "I can't stop, either. After all she's done, all she's cost us, I was right there with you, pleading for exile instead of imprisonment. *B'Ellahi,* I even call her regularly and drop by when I can."

* * *

That was a surprise to Haidar. "She didn't tell me. Still plotting, I see."

But then he *was* resigned that she always would be, lived wondering what her next strike would be.

"So…aren't you going to ask me about the other parts of her plans that I seemed involved in? What made you assume I was party to them?" He rubbed his jaw, only now registering the pain. "*Ya Ullah,* how I wanted to break *your* jaw when you intimated that."

"I thought she gave you what must have seemed like unrelated tasks that you couldn't have realized were cogs in the machine of her plan. Except after the fact." Contrition finally appeared in Jalal's eyes. "But I wanted *you* to tell me that."

"I didn't want to tell you anything. I wanted to smash your face in." Haidar smiled as all the remembered pain seeped away. "And you need to get to know me from scratch, like Roxanne needed to, if you don't realize why I didn't share details of my involvement with you or with anyone else. I had suspicion trained on me by the sheer evidence of my existence, by being the one she'd orchestrated all this for. I wasn't about to add my own sonly indiscretions to make a better case against myself. When you discovered them, like the relentless wolf that you are, and faced me, I was so…angry at myself, at you, I refused to defend myself. If you didn't know me enough to know your accusations were ludicrous, I decided *I* didn't want to know *you* at all. Of course I regretted it the moment I walked away. And of course I didn't know how to walk back into your life. I thought you would come to me, as you always did. You didn't."

"I wanted to," Jalal groaned. "Every single second of the past two years. I didn't know how to, either…"

Suddenly Jalal dragged Haidar into a rough hug.

* * *

Roxanne's tears flowed as Haidar stiffened, then groaned and sagged in his twin's hold. Then he hugged him back.

The poignancy of the moment drowned her, her heart battering her insides in delight as she felt the two men who mattered most to her begin to re-form their damaged bond. The man she was born to love, and the brother she'd longed to have, becoming what they should have always been, each other's sanctuary, and hers.

She watched them for as long as she could bear. Then she pounced on them, hugged them both with all her strength, pouring the tears of her relief, love and thankfulness on both their chests.

They at once took her in, at last acknowledging and delighting in the other's love, for one another, and for her.

It was Jalal who pulled back first, smirking at Haidar. "This doesn't mean I'm letting you become king."

Haidar's fist landed in a playful shove against his chin. "And this doesn't mean I don't owe you a broken jaw."

Jalal's gaze narrowed on him ponderously. "You *have* changed. You would have never joked about using your fists."

"I have changed." Haidar hugged her off the ground, gazing at her adoringly. "You're looking at the fuel of my metamorphosis."

Jalal cleared his throat, a bedeviling, knowing look directed at both of them. "*And* this is my cue to leave you two doves to coo to each other and go see if Rashid has already taken over while we indulged in our biannual twinly showdown."

Haidar gave him a considering look. "Maybe we should let him."

Jalal only gaped at him.

Then he directed a stern look at Roxanne. "Whatever softener you're using on him, ease up."

Giving them both a grinning salute, he walked out.

Roxanne hugged Haidar harder, buried smiles and tears into his expansive chest. "Forgive me."

A tender finger below her chin raised her face to his. "As long as you do me." She burst out laughing. He threw his head back and joined her. "That, too. Regularly."

She nestled deeper into his embrace. "And always. Along with everything else."

He squeezed her tight, a tremor passing through his great body at yet another, and this time last, averted heartache. "I'm holding you to that."

She nodded against his heart. "For as long as we both shall live. And beyond."

Epilogue

"Azmahar is and will always be a major part of who I am, and its people are my people. I will always be at its service, will do anything to mend the damage my closest kin have done to it."

Applause spread like thunder in the Qobba ballroom.

Roxanne's heart expanded until she felt it would burst with pride. Haidar had asked her to arrange this event with all the representatives of Azmahar's tribal councils. After his opening words, there was no doubt. They loved him. Believed in him.

The ruler of her heart and life was born to be king.

He was going on. "I am here today to make two announcements. The first is that I have asked for *Al Sayedah* Roxanne Gleeson's hand in marriage, and she has honored me by accepting. Our wedding will be held at her earliest convenience and readiness."

Roxanne's jaw dropped. B-but they'd agreed not...

"And with the pledge of my service and support to Azmahar unchangeable for as long as I live, I make the second announcement. I am withdrawing my candidacy for the throne."

Before anyone could react, before her heart found its next

beat, he was stepping down from the podium, walking toward her.

The moment he reached her, she smacked him.

Murmurs interspersed with laughter buzzed through the ballroom.

"I had to out us." He caught her hand, pressed it to his lips, then to his heart. "I couldn't take having no one cleaning the kitchen after our Cherie-inspired culinary adventures any longer."

She smacked him with her other hand. "Don't even try to joke! When did you reach that monumental decision, and how dare you spring it on me like this?"

"I knew we'd have this argument, and I wanted to have it only once. My mind is made up, *ya naar galbi,* fire of my heart."

"Without telling me?" she seethed. "What about your vow that you'd tell me everything."

"It's right here, where it will always be. But this is not about me. This is for Azmahar's best."

"It's for Azmahar to choose its best, and if it chooses you, you're damn well becoming king whether you like it or not!"

"And do you, without emotions and hormones, think I'm as qualified as Jalal or Rashid for the job, now of all times?"

"Qualified and more, for any throne in the world."

"That's *habibati* talking." His smile was all indulgence as he led her out of the ballroom.

"No, it isn't," she persisted, temperature rising another notch. "Personally, you're everything a king should be, and more."

"But there's more to me than what I am personally. You of all people know how my background—read, my mother—could mess things up. I don't believe I'm the one who can induce the best climate in the kingdom. Not in the top chair. I can do a lot of good from the sidelines, though. As I intend to, with you by my side as my princess. And consultant. I already told Jalal he shouldn't expect your exclusive services in that area."

She opened her mouth to protest and he closed it for her with a kiss. "I thought I would redeem myself by taking the throne and fixing what my mother and her family had destroyed. But I realized I was playing into her hands. The hands I can feel all over my candidacy. She wants me to become king, would do anything to achieve her objective. I believe she's still doing it. Stepping down is the only way to spoil her plans. To outrun her shadow. That will be my true redemption."

After collecting her jaw off the floor, Roxanne rasped, "I don't believe I'm saying this, but I'm on her side on this one. *That* throne you do deserve, and would be perfect for."

Haidar's smile was unperturbed, his determination unwavering. "And you think she'd stop after I'm king? From experience, she'd have more in store, and not anything for the general good. She's my mother, and I'll always be her son, will always serve her and take care of her, but I'm not giving her the chance to use me, or steer my life, *our* lives, anymore. It's as simple as that."

She stopped, realized they were in that corridor at the very spot where he'd once driven her to ecstasy, clung to him. "Haidar, it's not—"

"Can you possibly be that simple?"

Roxanne lurched at hearing the dark drawl, at feeling the presence that made all her hairs stand on end. She felt Haidar stiffen before he turned away. To face Rashid.

Haidar cocked his head at him, his lips twitching. "I'm beginning to think you have a teleportation device, Rashid. Though your materialization is welcome this time. If only to serve as a cue to move on to better topics." He looked back at her, eyes filling with intimacy and indulgence. "Like talking wedding and honeymoon plans."

Roxanne's heart fluttered. With delight at what Haidar was saying, agitation at what he'd just done and anxiety at Rashid's approach.

Rashid stopped a couple of steps away, drawing both her and Haidar's focus back to him.

His eyes bored into Haidar. "Don't tell me you think you can escape my payback by stepping down?"

Haidar shook his head, sighed.

Roxanne put herself between them. "Sheikh Aal Munsoori, I'm convinced there has been a tragic misunderstanding that's led to the current regrettable state of affairs between you and Haidar. But I am confident that we will be able to resolve the situation, and restore your relationship to its former closeness."

Rashid's darker-than-the-night eyes regarded her with nerve-rattling stillness, assessing, contemplating.

Then he gave her a smile that made goose bumps storm over her body. "I told Haidar you were very good. I was wrong. I'm now in possession of enough data to know you're superlative. But it's evident you're blinded by emotions—for now. So marry him, if you currently believe you can't live without him. But also do what will count, in your life and that of others. Join my team." Rashid suddenly picked up her hand, took it to his lips for a brief electrifying peck, his eyes glittering onyxes as he looked down at her. "Just name your terms."

Haidar growled something exasperated at her back. "Don't even think of using Roxanne as part of your payback plans."

Rashid slanted his gaze back to him, one formidable eyebrow arching sardonically. "I think too much of her and too little of you to do that. This is a legitimate offer, and all for her. She will end up wising up and dumping you as she should all on her own."

"Don't hold your breath, or only if you can for the rest of our lives. This is how long Roxanne and me will last. As for you, I'm shoving peace down your throat whether you like it or not."

"And you'll do that while hiding behind your lady?"

Haidar stepped before her and in Rashid's face, his face relaxing in a smile. "Your inflammatory tactics won't get a rise from me again, Rashid. This war is over."

Rasid's summing-up gaze lengthened until Roxanne felt she'd snap with the tension.

Then in ultimate calmness, he said, "I'll grant you only a ceasefire, Haidar, for Ms. Gleeson's sake. Once the honeymoon is over, the war resumes."

Then with a courteous bow to her, he walked away.

Roxanne let out the breath that had been clogged in her lungs on a tremulous exhalation. "We really need to find out what he believes he has against you. Fast."

Haidar exhaled heavily. *"Aih."* He suddenly lifted her off the ground in a fierce hug, smiling full down at her. "After a very, *very* prolonged honeymoon."

Before she could think of a response, he pressed her against the wall, took her lips in a kiss that wiped away anything else but him from her mind.

She surfaced from his kiss struggling to remember the other paramount issue at hand, gasped, "But promise me another thing. If Azmahar demands you on the throne anyway, you won't refuse, for any reason."

"I promise." His solemn expression turned bedeviling as he winked at her. "If I can prove the whole population wasn't mass-manipulated by my mother, that is."

"Haidar!"

He kissed her indignation away, had her objections and arguments blurring before he withdrew to look down at her, grinning teasingly. "So what do you think it is about me that makes the women in my life want to put me on a throne?"

She sighed, dreamily, resignedly. "You'd be gorgeous on one?"

His eyes twinkled. "I thought I was gorgeous on, in and out of anything."

She surrendered, dragged him down for another life-affirming kiss. "You are that, and then awesome."

A long time later, after loving her into the night, he hugged her more securely into his body, whispered against her cooling cheek, "I do promise, *ya naar hayati*. I will answer the call of duty if Azmahar issues it and I'm certain it has made the right decision. But know this. For myself, I crave only your love, aspire only to having you for my lover, my princess, my partner in everything. I want us to work together to bring Azmahar back to its former glory. Whether I become king or not."

She turned to look into his eyes, saw his heart, let him see hers and pledged, "I promise you that, too. And everything else that you yet have to wish for or imagine…"

* * * * *

FALLING FOR THE SHEIKH SHE SHOULDN'T

FIONA McARTHUR

Mother to five sons, **Fiona McArthur** is an Australian midwife who loves to write. Mills & Boon® Medical Romance™ gives Fiona the scope to write about all the wonderful aspects of adventure, romance, medicine and midwifery that she feels so passionate about—as well as an excuse to travel! Now that her boys are older, Fiona and her husband, Ian, are off to meet new people, see new places and have wonderful adventures. Fiona's website is at www.fionamcarthur.com.

To Trishabella—who makes me smile

CHAPTER ONE

THE lift doors opened. Prince Zafar Aasim Al Zamid stepped inside and to his disgust his heart began to pound.

Someone slipped past him into the elevator and he couldn't help the deeper breath he took as the doors shut. A drift of orange soap vividly recalled the memory of fruit-laden trees in the palace grounds as a child, and, by association, the memory soothed him.

Thoughts that calmed were an excellent idea. Life had been much less complicated then. He opened his eyes as the lift shifted under his feet.

Lately he'd been acquiring phobias like new shirts. Since the crash it had been heights, now elevators—worse every ascent—until even a closing door caused symptoms. Perhaps it was a sign the claustrophobia in his life had worsened since he'd been forced to give up his work in favour of royal duty.

He would address his inner calm with the solitude of a retreat as soon as he sorted this latest mess. The vastness of the desert always made his problems seem less significant.

For the moment he was cramped and palpitating in a lift with the painful reminder of all he'd lost. This par-

ticular enclosed space held a fragile-looking new mum
with a baby in one arm, a beaming new father clutching
a balloon, and thankfully the orange-scented woman as
well, dispensing an aura of tranquillity.

The metallic 'It's A Boy' helium balloon bobbed towards him and Zafar leant closer to the wall and regretted his decision to stay at this hotel. A baby hotel. The
last place he needed to be. The image he carried of his
tiny son's body flickered in his mind and he forced it
away. Such happy families were constant reminders he
could have done without but the stakes were high.

He had hoped to find Fadia, his estranged cousin,
prior to the birth but time was against him. He'd discovered she planned to convalesce here instead of hospital
if he arrived too late to find her beforehand.

The lift jerked and his pulse thundered in his ears.

The balloon wielder tugged on the string as the proud
new dad hailed the woman. 'Carmen! We didn't get a
chance to thank you.' He grabbed the woman's hand
and shook it vigorously. 'You were amazing.'

The woman retrieved her hand and smiled at the
young mother. 'Hello, again, Lisa, Jock. Lisa was the
amazing one.'

Her voice soothed like a cool hand to his forehead
and, infinitesimally, a little more of his agitation drained
away as the phobia receded. Thankfully. It would be
useful if his psyche finally accepted the obscenity of
irrational fears.

'It was a beautiful birth.' She cast Zafar a swift apologetic look for their exclusive conversation, and the unexpected impact of her one glance collided with his, as
if that ridiculous balloon had bumped him, before she
turned back to the father.

Medical background, he concluded, and dismissed the stab of frustration the loss of his career left him with. Midwife probably. He'd met women like her before—those natural soothers who could create a rapport with strangers without effort.

He lifted his head and glanced over her. Anything was good to take his mind off the ascent through the lift well.

Thankfully his phobia retreated by the second as he studied her. She had thick black hair coiled on her head like rope. An Irish accent. Carmen seemed more Spanish than Irish yet she suited her name.

He watched her mouth as she said, 'How is young Brody?'

Jock laughed, loudly, and Zafar winced as the noise jarred his ears. 'He's a bruiser.' The father's pride resonated within the four walls as the lift stopped at the fifth floor with an extra jolt. The cage floor fell six inches and bounced before it came back to the level. Everyone laughed nervously, except Zafar. He closed his eyes and swallowed.

There was rustling and movement as the lift emptied and the father's voice, a little further away now. 'We'll see you soon, then.'

'I'll be down as soon as I have handover report from the morning midwife.' So Carmen was still in the lift. He opened his eyes as she waved at the couple.

'That's great. We'll see you then.' Zafar noted the relief in the father's face and his mind clutched at the distraction of wondering about this trend of moving postnatal women from the hospital into hotels to recover from birth.

Not something he was familiar with but it made sense

when he thought about it. A place of quiet comfort, fewer germs, useful for the hospital to have quick turnover and quite appropriate if your health fund covered it.

The lift doors closed silently, though the cage remained stationary, and he returned to contemplate the lights on the panel above the door despite the insidious desire to study the woman called Carmen more closely.

She stepped back and seemed to lean into the wall.

He knew she was tall because her head came above his shoulders and her knot of hair had been near his nose as she'd drifted orange blossom his way. The lift still didn't move. Seconds to go and he would be able to breathe properly again.

He glanced at her from under his lashes and saw her eyes were shut. He frowned. Not a usual occurrence when he shared space with a woman. In fact, he couldn't remember the last time he'd been ignored. In repose she appeared weary. Too weary?

His concern increased. 'Are you unwell?'

Her eyes flew open and she straightened. 'Good grief.' She blinked at him and then focussed. 'A micro-sleep. Sorry. I've been on night shift. It's been a busy week.'

Suddenly he felt empathetic to a perfect stranger because he could remember that weariness from a string of busy days and nights during his internship. Lack of sleep he'd grumbled about, but now the choice was no longer his, he'd love to suffer from that inconvenience again.

That was the problem with returning to Sydney. It reminded him that he wasn't living the life he'd once loved. Made him feel frustration he shouldn't feel towards his duty to Zandorro.

The elevator jerked, ground upwards for a few inches. The sooner the better, he thought, then the lift bounced suddenly as the cable stopped.

His breath caught as he waited. The doors didn't open and the light sat on neither five nor six. Midway between floors. Stopped.

This was not good. He felt his heart rate shift gear, double before his next breath, his chest tightened, and air jammed in his lungs.

'I am so not in the mood for this.' Zafar heard her in the distance as he tried to loosen his throat. He sank down onto his haunches and put one hand on the wall to give himself more blood to his head. With his other he loosened his collar.

The lift was suddenly the cabin of the private jet. His family would plunge in a few spiralling seconds and there was not a thing he could do about it. So now it was his destiny to die. It was almost a relief. And he'd complained about being in line for the throne.

Distantly he realised she'd picked up the phone and spoken to the operator. When he heard her re-seat the instrument she bent down to him. 'You okay?'

He didn't refocus his eyes off the floor until he felt her hand on his arm—warm, firm, comfort personified—and not letting go. He had the bizarre idea he couldn't fall anywhere while she held him. Yet all she did was share touch without moving. He breathed with difficulty through his nose and inhaled drifts of orange. Incredibly steadying, like a shot of Valium through his bloodstream.

He sucked air through clenched teeth and the light-headedness faded a little. This was ridiculous. Irrational. Acutely embarrassing. He forced himself to look into her face. She had dark golden eyes, like burnt twisted treacle, calm and wise and filled with compassion. Mesmerising up close. 'You're a nurse?'

Her eyes crinkled and his chest eased a little more. 'Sort of. I'm a midwife. Do you need some deep breathing?'

'I'm not in labour.' But this was hard work. He shut his eyes again. 'Possibly.'

'Do you have a phobia?' The same gentle conversational voice as if she'd asked if he needed sugar in his tea.

The demons from the past battered against him. He strove to keep his voice level. 'So it seems.'

She sank down. He heard the rustle of fabric and felt the slight brush of her leg as she settled herself beside him on the floor. Her hand rested still on his arm, not moving, as if to transfer energy and calmness from her to him. It seemed to be working. 'What's your name?

He had many. 'Zafar.'

She paused and he felt her appraisal until he opened his eyes again. Her golden interest captured his. 'Well, Zafar. I'm Carmen. I've been stuck in this lift three times this week. Big, deep breaths should help.'

Deep breaths might be difficult. 'It is a battle with small ones.'

Coaxing. 'You can do a couple.'

He wasn't sure but the fact that she'd lived through this three times did help. He was feeling faint again. 'A rule of threes?'

'In through your nose...'

Intolerably bossy woman. 'Out through my mouth. Yes, I know.'

Her voice firmed. Like his mother's from the distant past. The time of orange trees. 'Then do it.'

He humoured her. And felt better. Actually, quite a lot better so he did it again. With her sitting below him he had a delightful view down the valley between her breasts. He glanced away politely but could feel himself improve every second with the picture in his mind. Surely a harmless medicinal remedy.

Imagine if the lift had still been full. He mentally shuddered. There was just her to see this weakness. Thankfully he'd sent his bodyguard and secretary to the suite. In future the stairs would be good for his fitness. Once free, he'd never see this woman again. A good thing, and a shame.

At least it seemed his brain had accepted death was unlikely.

And she had the most incredible breasts but he wasn't going to look again—his gaze travelled back to her face—and a delightful mouth. Those lips... His body stirred. A mouth designed by angels and plump for surrender if he was willing to risk life and limb for it. She may be calm but she looked very capable of protecting herself despite the weariness. His lips twitched.

'Are you feeling better?'

'Much.' Better than she knew. He watched with some amusement as she slowly recognised the direction of his fascination until she stared straight back at him and raised her brows.

She removed her hand from his arm and she shook her head. 'Tsk tsk.'

The lift jerked and resumed its ascent. Zafar shut his eyes briefly but the panic had gone.

It seemed she was good at her job. He straightened

until he stood with his feet firm beneath him, reached down and took her hand to help her up. Such a lovely hand, but workworn. She rose fluidly into his space, as he'd intended.

For that moment as their glances met he forgot the lift, the heights, the strain his life was, all except this unexpected awareness between them that swept away their surroundings, so enmeshed in this unexpected connection that when he said, 'Thank you,' the words hung in the air between them like mist.

An imp of mischief drew his head closer. He expected her to pull away. 'You're very kind...and incredibly beautiful.' He stroked her cheek, his gaze drawn once more to her ripe and luscious mouth.

She did the unpredicted. 'It's okay. I understand.' He heard it in her voice, a note of sympathy that horrified him. Pity?

He recoiled. He needed no one's compassion.

The elevator jolted and the doors opened on seven. They'd missed six altogether. She turned away from him with a frown on her entrancing face.

There was some consolation in the way she compressed her lips together as if to hide the way they'd plumped and reddened in anticipation...of what? The almost brush of his lips on hers? So she had felt something too?

'You certainly look better.' Her comment made him smile again, the dryness hiding undertones he couldn't identify, but there was a subtle flush of colour to her cheeks and her wide eyes searched his face as if seeking a hint of what had passed between them during the last few frozen moments.

Despite his urge to throw himself out of the lift to

safety, Zafar stretched his hand across the doors to allow her to precede him. 'My apologies for my weakness earlier.'

She assessed him with a clinical scrutiny he wasn't used to getting from a woman and strangled back a half-laugh. 'I doubt you're a weak man so I'm sure you've good reason.'

He inclined his head.

She glanced around. 'And I should have got out at level six.' She turned swiftly out to the left of the lift and pulled open the door of the fire escape to go down a flight before he was fully out of the lift himself.

He started to hum. The day was not as bad as it had started out.

Carmen moved quickly to reach the door to the stairwell but she could almost feel the eyes of the man in the lift on her back.

What had just happened? Her lips tingled as if still waiting and she could detect the unusual spicy after-shave from his skin so close to hers. And what a mouth! Sinful was too tame a word. She couldn't pretend she hadn't been tempted.

Not the sort of encounter she'd expected today and she wasn't entirely sure she'd behaved properly. Hopefully she wouldn't see him again.

When the fire-escape door shut with an echoing clang she breathed a sigh of relief as she leant back against it. Cold metal against her back was lovely to counter the heat everywhere else in her body. She glanced around.

Appropriate name. Fire escape.

She definitely felt a bit singed on the edges—like a

ragged sleeve too close to a candle—ragged and breathless. She touched her lips. Burnt and hot without even touching him.

She glanced around again, reassured in a dark stairwell with unpainted concrete stairs and the echo of empty walls, but there was no doubt she was glad of the sanctuary afforded her.

One would have thought she'd learnt her lesson from her ex-husband about smooth-talking men in expensive suits who seduced you and then destroyed your life.

Still. One almost slip didn't make a disaster. She hoped.

Eighteen hours later Carmen O'Shannessy admired the gifts Mother Nature had bestowed on her at five that morning with a soft smile. She knew there was a reason she loved night duty, apart from the fact it allowed her to do two jobs.

Twins. Dark-haired cherubs with skin like dusky rosebuds. Her patient, Fadia Smith, rested back in the armchair like Madonna with her sons poking out under her arms like tiny bundled wings. It had taken a little juggling, a few attempts, and almost an hour of patience, but with both boys feeding well this moment was a very satisfying end to a drama-filled morning.

It had been a long time since Carmen had seen twins born with so little fuss but, then, Fadia hadn't left them with much choice. Her cumbersome arrival alone and a bare five minutes before her first son appeared had left Carmen literally catching the baby. By the time the obstetrician and his entourage had arrived, number two had also decided to greet the outside world and Dr Bennett had waved her on with an incredulous smile.

To continue their no-fuss arrival, both wee boys had cried and then settled on their mother's skin. While they appeared small, there were no signs of prematurity or respiratory distress.

That would be unlike the breathless-from-running neonatal staff, who'd drifted back to their unit unneeded shortly afterwards. Carmen still smiled over their shock when she'd rung for help.

Two hours later Carmen should've been feeling ready to hand Fadia over to the day staff and go home. 'You sure I can't phone someone for you?' Something niggled.

Fadia seemed very sad. On cue with the question, Fadia jumped in the chair and the two babies stopped their sucking with startled eyes before resettling to their feed.

Their mother forced herself to relax. 'No, no. My babies are fine. I really don't have anyone else to call. I'm a widow and there's just a friend of my husband who's been helping me until my relatives arrive.'

Fadia seemed determined nothing was wrong and hurried on. 'We're all safe.' It seemed a strange thing to say.

'Well, your boys weren't waiting for anyone.' She leaned over and stroked a tiny hand that rested on his mother's neck. 'You're amazing, Fadia. Congratulations. Tilly will be looking after you today. I have to go home to my bed, and I'll see you when you move to the baby hotel in a day or two. Have you decided on names?'

'Harrison and Bailey. My husband's names.'

'Lovely. I'm sure he would have loved that.'

'He didn't even know I was pregnant when he was killed.'

Was killed? Not died. How horrible but not the time to ask. 'I'm sorry. But I'm sure, somewhere, he knows. Do try and get some sleep as soon as they do.'

'Thanks, Carmen. You've given me so much strength in all of this. It means so much that you weren't cross with me for leaving it so late.'

'You were always strong, Fadia. So amazing. And we know babies come when they want.' Carmen grinned. 'You must have a guardian angel. And that makes sense. Thank you for a lovely end to my night.' She waved and almost bumped into Tilly, the day midwife, passing the door.

'Finally going home?' Tilly glanced at her watch.

Carmen knew she was nearly an hour late getting away already. 'At last.'

'You working this afternoon as well?'

'Doing the one p.m. at the hotel till seven. I get to sleep in my bed tonight.'

Tilly shook her head. 'Don't know how you do it. I'd be dead doing those hours as well as night duty.'

'I get around four hours' sleep.' Carmen shrugged. 'It's short term. But I'm starting to come down from the night's euphoria. But I am tired now.' She did not want to talk about this or the reason she was almost killing herself. She'd never taken help from anyone and she wasn't going to start now.

Thankfully Tilly wasn't slow on nuances because she changed the subject back to Fadia. 'Well done, you, with this morning. Lucky duck. Catching twins is hard to do without a cast of thousands trying to help these days.'

'And your Marcus didn't push me out of the way.'

Tilly's cheeks went pink and Carmen felt a tug of

wistfulness at her friend's happiness. A fleeting picture of the man in the lift intruded again before she pushed him away.

She hadn't given him a thought for hours. Been far too busy. Which was a good thing. 'It must be great to have everything in your life going well.'

Tilly said, 'I'm fostering Marcus's faith in midwives. I think it's working.' They smiled at each other.

'And Fadia was lucky.' Carmen's smile dropped. 'Her friend's coming in at lunchtime. She's very quiet but, then, she did lose her husband fairly recently. There's no one else listed under "Next of kin" from her booking. Look after her, Till. We need to make sure she has somewhere to go after she's discharged.'

'Yes, Mother Carmen.' Tilly's answer was light but the look they exchanged reassured her that her friend would be extra vigilant. Tilly would be just as determined as Carmen to be there for any mother, let alone one with twins who had twice as many reasons for moments of unusual interest.

After too few hours' sleep it was time for Carmen to dress for work again. This time she would be providing postnatal midwifery in the baby hotel, a pet name the medical profession used for the five-star beach resort that catered for a few privately insured postnatal mothers. It was another warm and fuzzy part of her job and the women she supported often existed on less sleep than she'd had so a few yawns between friends was quite acceptable.

It was even better if she'd been with the women in labour and could follow their progress until they went home.

As she pressed the lift button in the car park she couldn't help thinking of the man on level seven. Zafar. Mysterious name. And what would have happened to him if she hadn't been in the lift that extra floor? The memory of their close encounter burned brightest.

She screwed up her face. 'Go away.' The words hung quietly between her and the closed lift door and she twisted her head uneasily to make sure nobody had heard.

There'd been something incredibly vulnerable about such a virile and powerful-looking man sweating over a stalled lift. Which maybe explained a little why she hadn't backed off more quickly.

There had been nothing vulnerable in the way he'd crowded her after, though. Or the way she'd almost dared him to kiss her. She couldn't help the curve of her lips at the return of that memory and thought ruefully that he'd never want to see her again.

Which was fine. Her husband's underhand conniving had taken her home, undermined her self-respect—though she supposed she should thank him because she was tougher than ever now—and taught her to reserve judgement for a long while yet.

But Zafar's face seemed indelibly stamped in her memory. Dark, tortured eyes under black brows and a firm yet wickedly sexy mouth that captured her attention with such assurance—a mouth that looked used to command. Everywhere. She felt the re-kindling of awareness low and hot in her belly. Outrageous. She shook her head. She wasn't going there.

The guy embodied everything she hated about men. Power and prestige. She knew he had it despite his aversion to a stalled lift, and she had no doubt he could be as cynically ruthless as he looked.

He had to have extreme wealth, of course. The very expensive watch and the suit that shrieked of a tailor her ex would have killed to find were dead giveaways. Though why he was out in the beach fringes of eastern Sydney was a mystery.

She really needed to stop thinking about him, but once inside the lift she could picture him across from her easily, too easily, in fact, for someone she'd met for five minutes twenty-four hours ago.

The lift stopped on six and she stepped out onto the main baby floor and made her way to the midwives' room. To work, woman!

As she discussed her patients with the morning shift midwife she was surprised to hear that Fadia had already been moved to the hotel. Occasionally a very well woman with her second or subsequent baby would move across after four hours but for a first-time mum with twins it was very unusual.

'And the paediatrician said it was okay? And Tilly's Dr Bennett as well?'

'They'll both be visiting daily here and a mothercraft nurse transferred across with her.'

Special considerations, then. Not the first time wealthy clients had brought their own nurse but she hadn't envisaged Fadia being like that. 'That will help.'

'Not any more. Fadia sent her away as soon as she was settled. Apparently didn't like her.'

Carmen raised her eyebrows. 'Curiouser and curiouser.'

Fifteen minutes later when Carmen knocked on

Fadia's door, the last person she expected to open it was
the man from the elevator.

Zafar.

Her pulse jumped and he captured her gaze easily
and held it, just as he held the small smile on his lips.
Heat flooded her cheeks.

CHAPTER TWO

'Ah. The midwife. Come in.' As if she was always turning up on his doorstep.

She hoped her mouth was closed because he looked jaw-droppingly handsome when he wasn't terrified. He seemed ten times taller and broader than before but she guessed her first real impression must have been coloured by his distress.

'It seems I must thank you for your magnificent skills at the delivery of Fadia's twins.'

'Being there was a privilege. Fadia did all the hard work. I was just catching.'

He smiled sardonically. 'Yet some skill is required with multiple birth.'

He leaned casually against the door. Funny how she had the idea he was as relaxed as a tiger about to spring.

Fadia, perched on the edge of the chair with one of her sons, looked anything but calm and Carmen's fluttery surprise turned to bristling protection of her patient.

Was the lift almost-kisser the person Fadia was scared of? 'Is this your husband's friend?'

Fadia shot a startled glance at Zafar and then back at Carmen's face. 'No. Goodness, no.' Carmen couldn't help the relief. That saved a bad lack of professionalism and would be a sorry pickle.

'No, this is my cousin. From Zandorro.' Fadia sent another glance his way—this time slightly less anxious. 'He's come in response to a letter I sent to my grandfather and to see if I need help.'

Zafar inclined his head. 'Ensuring you and your babies are well. So I can pass the good news onto your relatives, yes.' He turned to Carmen and raised one sardonic eyebrow. 'So you haven't met the elusive friend of our newest family members either, then?'

'No.' Carmen had no plan to elaborate. She shrugged to let him know that family dynamics were none of her business. 'But perhaps you could excuse us while I spend a short time privately with Fadia?'

'Is that totally necessary?' Such surprise when she'd said it and obviously a request uncommon in his experience. Carmen bit back her smile at his shock. So, we don't like being asked to leave, she thought. How interesting.

Just who was he? But it didn't really matter. She'd had four hours' sleep, she was worried about Fadia, and wasn't in the mood for tantrums. 'Yes. Afraid so.' Tough. Out you go, though she didn't say it out loud.

He frowned down his haughty nose and thinned those sexy lips until they almost disappeared, which was a shame, but proclaimed this man expected obedience, not orders.

Welcome to my back yard, buddy. Carmen squared her shoulders and fixed the smile on her face. She could be as tough as he was. Or tougher, if needed.

His eyes clashed with hers. It seemed he was going to cross his arms and flatly refuse.

What would she do then? She had no idea. Figure something out. Mentally she crossed her own arms. Bring it on. Never hassle a woman off night duty.

He didn't. On the brink of refusal he hesitated, gave her a mocking smile that actually made her feel more uncomfortable than a flat refusal—almost a promise of retribution—and annoyingly her satisfaction at the win dimmed.

She didn't like that look. Or the feeling it left her with. Who was this guy?

'I shall return,' he said to his cousin with a stern glance in Carmen's direction, 'when your midwife is finished with you, Fadia.'

Fadia nodded, twisted her hands, and Carmen inclined her head politely. She couldn't wait to ask Fadia what the problem was.

'We won't be long,' she said sweetly as she opened the door for him. The lock shut with the heavily finality hotel doors had and thankfully the room returned to a spacious suite.

Amazing how much breathing space one man could take up. Carmen looked at her patient. 'You okay?'

'Yes.' The young woman hunched her shoulders and tightened the grip on the baby in her arms. Fadia didn't look okay. She looked shattered, on the brink of tears, and Carmen just wanted to hug her.

'And your babies?'

'Fine.' Fadia glanced across at her other baby asleep in the cot and visibly shook. 'I can't believe he actually left. You told him to go!'

'Of course.' She wasn't wasting time on him, she was worried about her patient. Something was badly wrong here.

'Zafar wasn't listed as next of kin?'

'I didn't know if the family recognised me.'

'So his arrival was unexpected?'

'Yes. No.' She lowered her voice. 'I wrote to my grandfather last week but Tom said I would be sorry when the family took over my life. But I'm glad Zafar is here while I decide what I wish to do.'

'Well you have a few days to think about it before you have to go anywhere.' She took Fadia's pulse. It was faster than normal, she hoped just down to agitation and not a postnatal problem. 'I'm surprised to see they allowed you out of hospital so soon after birth.'

'They said I could come across to the hotel today as long as I brought the mothercraft nurse. My cousin visited me soon after you left this morning and arranged one when I asked.'

Carmen glanced around the otherwise empty room but didn't comment on the fact the mothercraft nurse was nowhere to be seen.

Fadia shrugged. 'We did not get on. So she left.'

'Oh.' Not a lot she could gather from that. 'That's very quick transfer for twins. Because of your over-extended uterus you're at risk of bleeding. We need to watch for that. And you'd get much more help if you stayed on the ward. I could have you readmitted back there.' Especially if your cousin helped you leave, she thought.

Fadia shook her head. 'Now that he's found me, I'd prefer to be here. Apparently the paediatrician will visit me as well. I hate hospitals, which is why I was so late coming in. Zafar wants me to have private nurses. I said I knew you and was comfortable without.' She looked up and pleaded, 'That is my biggest concern. I want to care for my babies myself, not with some nurse taking control as soon as they cry. Which is why I am unsure if I wish to return to Zandorro.'

Carmen could understand that but she wasn't so sure Fadia knew how much work two small babies could be. 'Well good for you, but it will be exhausting, even if it's a great way for a mother to feel.'

Fadia nodded with relief. 'Access to the baby hotel is why I chose your hospital. Tilly said you were working here today so I wanted to come across now.'

'Okay, I can understand preferring to be here than hospital.' But that didn't explain her cousin's agreement when most people would realise the twins needed more observation too.

'I do feel a little less alone now Prince Zafar has arrived.'

'Prince Zafar.' Carmen blinked. Prince of what? 'Like Prince Charles?'

'From the desert. Zafar is fourth in line to the throne of Zandorro.'

'A sheik?' That explained a lot. 'So you're from this Zandorro, too?'

'My family were from a small but powerful country in the desert. My father is dead, my mother left five years ago and brought me to Australia with her, but she sadly passed away not long after we arrived.'

So much drama and tragedy for one woman to cope with. But why was Fadia so unsure it was a good thing her cousin had found her?

She'd known Zafar was someone out of the ordinary, but it wasn't an everyday occurrence to run into a prince. Or be trapped in a lift with one. Or be almost kissed by one.

No wonder he expected to be obeyed. And she'd coolly told him to leave. She struggled not to smile. Too funny.

She needed to think about this. 'So if he's your cousin,' Which made Fadia...? 'Does that make you a princess?'

'Yes.'

She pointed to her sons. 'I'm guessing they're princes too, then?' She looked at the babies. 'And you walked into the hospital at the last minute alone to deliver twins?'

A cloud passed over Fadia's face and her voice lowered until Carmen strained to hear her. 'Unfortunately, when my husband died, I was alone and pregnant and the only help I've had has been from friends of my husband, but I'm starting to think I don't really trust them.'

'Tom told me I was being followed and I moved out of my flat close to the hospital into a hotel for what turned out to be the last day of my pregnancy. The poor driver was beside himself that I would have my babies in his taxi.'

Carmen could imagine it. She'd bet he was terrified. 'You were lucky they weren't.' Crikey.

Fadia's eyes filled. 'I think Tom didn't want Zafar to find me. Zafar is here to take me back to his country, and I am starting to think that is a good thing, but it will separate me from the memories of my husband and mother. Yet my sons need their heritage. Tom said he will help me stay in Australia.' Her voice became a whisper. 'But I'm not sure that is what I want.'

'So when is your husband's friend—Tom, is it?—coming?'

'Today. And I'm scared for my sons.' Fadia began

to shake and Carmen frowned as the woman struggled to pull herself together. 'I hate being weak. But I seem to have lost my strength since my husband died.'

Poor Fadia. And, boy, she was really in the middle of something here, Carmen thought. Then the twin in his cot screwed up his face and let out a blood-curdling wail as if aware of the tragedy of his mother. At least she could do something while her brain raced.

She unwrapped the little boy and checked his nappy before she re-wrapped and lifted him out of the crib. 'Don't be cross, little prince.' Then she tucked him into her neck and gently patted his bottom. The unconscious rhythm soothed them both.

She needed to understand how she could help Fadia. 'So do you want me to keep this Tom away?'

Fadia's eyes widened. 'Can you do that?'

'Midwives are very good at screening people without upsetting them.' Carmen shrugged. 'Lots of times a mother's labour is going slowly because of an inappropriate person in the birthing room.' She grinned. 'Like a scary mother-in-law or a friend she couldn't say no to.' She smiled. 'We suggest they have some time out and they don't get them back in until the mother asks us to.' She spread her hands. 'I could hold Tom off for you. But isn't your cousin better for that?'

Fadia stroked the bed sheet with her fingers. 'No. The situation could escalate more than I want'

A strange thing to say but Fadia's fingers twisted and turned and Carmen held her tongue. 'Or Zafar might do something to him.'

Carmen barely stopped herself from rolling her eyes. Oh, come on. This isn't the Middle Ages.'

'You don't understand.'

'Okay. So, this Tom? Have you got a photo of him?'

Fadia thought for a moment and then nodded. She reached for her purse and removed a photo of a smiling couple, the woman Fadia.

'Your husband?' Fadia nodded. Carmen looked at the third person in the photo and there was something about him that reminded her of her ex. Carl. A hardness around his eyes, a sleaziness in his smile. She was good at picking that up now.

Fadia was shaking and Carmen felt for her. That was enough emotional drama for this exhausted mum. 'Fadia. Can I borrow this? I'll copy it and give my friend downstairs a copy. We'll keep an eye out and and nobody will be hurt. But for now...' she held the baby towards his mother '...we could get these boys fed because this little one is going to bring the roof down if he really gets going. And you're not going to have time to worry about annoying Toms, or frowning Zafars, because these boys will keep you on your toes without them. And after that you get to rest.'

Fadia nodded and some of the strain left her face. 'You're right. Thank you.'

An hour later, when Carmen opened the door of Fadia's room, a tall man in a flowing robe stood up from the chair at the end of the corridor and stared at her as she hesitated in the doorway. What was going on here?

Good grief. This was getting worse. She was guessing Zafar had put a guard on Fadia so maybe there was more she needed to know.

They were infecting her with their dramas but the last thing the new mum needed was more tension and Carmen needed to know what she was up against.

Carmen stiffened her shoulders, let the room door shut behind her and marched up to the guard. 'I'm assuming you're Prince Zafar's man?'

He bowed his head, though his expression remained anything but subservient. 'Yes, madame. I am Yusuf.'

'Then, Yusuf, perhaps you could take me to your prince, please.'

'No.'

'No?'

'I think not.' The guard raised his eyebrows, looked her up and down, as if to say she was only a woman and a servant at that, and Carmen's usually dormant temper flickered. She glared at him. This was really beyond a joke.

Any minute now Fadia could poke her head out and see she was under guard.

Her voice firmed. 'I think so. Right now, thank you. I'm quite happy to use the stairs.' She smiled sweetly. 'The prince and I do know each other.' A white lie. Serve Zafar right for flirting with her.

She and Yusuf, her new best friend—not—stared at each other for a moment and she could see a faint scar running the full length of the man's face. He was probably extremely used to defending his prince.

There was stalemate as the silence went on and she threw caution to the winds. 'I'd hate to have to pass on my displeasure.'

The man's face tightened and he shrugged fatalistically. 'As you wish. This way.' He opened the door to the stairwell and allowed her to precede him. Carmen could hear the swish of his robes behind her, even though his footsteps were silent.

'Please wait.'

She glanced back and Yusuf held up his hand.

She paused at the top of the stairs and the guard leaned forward and opened the heavy door for her. That second of waiting gave her time to realise she had no clear agenda for her visit with the prince when she arrived. Was it enough of her business to barge in? What on earth was she doing here?

On the seventh floor Carmen could see another guard standing outside the door to the presidential suite and the reality sank in a little further about how different this man's life was from hers. And how out of her depth she really was.

She paused to say she'd changed her mind but one glance at the cynical face beside her told her dear Yusuf had picked up on her discomfort. Great to know she was providing him with amusement.

That decided her.

Yusuf glanced once more at her determined chin, nodded at the man standing guard, then knocked on the large wooden door.

A few seconds later a tiny robed woman appeared and they spoke a language Carmen didn't understand but it wasn't hard to guess what was said—something along the lines of stupid woman annoying our prince, no doubt.

The woman glanced over Carmen, shrugged and stepped back to allow them to enter.

The room opened into a window lined terrace and the magnificent blue vista of Coogee Bay curved like a sickle seven floors below. The scent of sandalwood was strong and quiet discordant music played discreetly in the background.

Several low armchairs were grouped together and

there were heaped cushions on colour-rich carpets, all facing the entertainment centre on one side of the room, and a boardroom table with a dozen comfortable chairs took up space on the other.

She'd been in this room before and the furnishing had changed dramatically. It seemed Prince Zafar travelled with his own furniture. A tad different from her bedsit with a rickety bed.

A door leading off into another room opened and Zafar came out—no, she thought, he made an entrance. Dressed in white traditional robes of an Arab, with his head covered, she couldn't help a little more gaping.

His brows drew together when he saw her but he came forward until he stood in front of her. He looked even bigger and more formidable surrounded by his servants but this time it was not only his physical presence, more the scent of distinct power.

'You wished to see me.'

She felt the pressure from interested eyes, and he too glanced around. He spoke three short, sharp words that cleared the room like magic.

Despite herself, she was impressed and to her irritation couldn't deny a little nervous thrill now that they were alone.

'Please…' he gestured to the lounge chairs '…be seated.' He gestured to the tiny kitchen. 'Would you like a juice or water?'

'No, thank you.' Despite her dry mouth. Maybe she should have had one to give herself time to think of something to say.

He sat when she did. 'In that case, what can I do for you?'

She had no idea. 'I wish to discuss your cousin.'

He inclined his head and she suspected a fleeting crinkle of amusement before he assumed a serious face again. 'I had guessed that was the case.'

Now she felt silly. Of course he did. She wasn't here because he'd almost kissed her. Was she? The thought brought a tide of pink to her cheeks and she felt like sliding under the gorgeous carpet or pulling one of those cushions over her face. How did she get herself into these situations?

Another flash of humour. 'Let me help you.'

She blinked. It wasn't where she expected help to come from but she'd take it.

'You're wondering if I am an ogre, or some medieval lord who drags around unwilling women and their babies...' he caught her eye and she was sure he could read her agreement in her face, but he went on, '...back to being imprisoned in their homeland.'

Just making sure it's not something like that. 'Not quite so dramatic but yes.'

'Thank you for your honesty. Let me explain. Apart from things you cannot be aware of, I think to clear the air between us could save us both some time.'

He smiled at her and she could feel herself soften. Even lean slightly towards him until she realised what she was doing. He seemed so reasonable and she was starting to believe she'd done the right thing to come here in the first place. This guy had serious charisma when he turned it on. She needed to remember that.

A random worry niggled and jostled with her hormones for attention. Please, don't let me fall again. Carl had been this smooth. This 'open' and friendly at first. Before she'd agreed to marry him and discovered how dark his soul really was. She was too easily sucked in by smooth guys. Guys she almost allowed to kiss her in elevators. She felt her shoulders stiffen with the thought. Good.

'By now you have discovered who I am, although I imagine my title would mean little to you?' The inflexion made it a question and she answered like the puppet she was trying not to turn into.

'You're right. No idea.'

'So...' He smiled at her and there was no way she couldn't smile back, damn him. 'I am from the small Arabic state of Zandorro that has, by the blessing of Allah, found itself abundantly supplied with oil and precious gems.'

There seemed to be a lot of those around, Carmen thought cynically, but she nodded to show she was paying attention.

'Our grandfather, King Fahed Al Zamid, is ruler, though his health is not good. Fadia's father, my uncle, was second in line to the throne until he died.' He looked at her. 'Unnatural causes.'

Unnatural causes. She fought to keep her eyebrows level. He went on when she nodded. 'It was thought Fadia had passed away with her mother several years ago, and as the succession passes only to a male child her wellbeing unfortunately slipped beneath the family's radar.'

He didn't explain that but went on. 'My eldest brother is next in line and I too have become closer to the throne because of these misfortunes.'

He paused, a short one, to see if she understood, and she was glad of the respite while she filed the succession order away in her brain.

She nodded and he continued. 'But now, with Fadia's

children being male and healthy, they are automatically next in the line of succession.'

She thought about that. Next in line? Major succession. Then he carried on. 'Unfortunately, this also increases their risk from certain elements once their birth is known, and that is something I have tragic personal experience of. Naturally I am concerned that my cousin and her sons remain safe. And she did ask for help.'

'Safe. Physical danger? Do you mean kidnapping?' This was a little more complicated than Fadia had led her to believe. If she believed him, that was, a calm inner voice suggested.

Zafar went on in that reasonable tone that seemed to flow hypnotically. 'At best. Hence my urgency to find Fadia once we knew she was alive and return her to our country before the babies' birth in case all of them were in danger away from the palace. At least until we can settle the dangers once and for all. A goal I have been working on.'

'Do you think there really is a risk of danger?' She couldn't help thinking about Fadia's concerns about Tom.

'Certainly. Her eldest son is next in line to rule when he comes of age and the younger brother is the next in line after that. Fadia's sons could provide leverage over the monarchy, which unfortunately is not an uncommon occurrence with our hostile neighbours.'

She was starting to get that.

He shrugged philosophically. 'Fadia needs to come home, at least for the time being, for her and her sons' safety, now she is a widow.'

'I don't suppose it's easy for her. I think she has some friends and a life in Australia.'

His lip curled. 'The friendship of a man who has plans to control a royal widow? A man who pretended to be a friend of her husband, who has helped her remain cut off from her family now she has no husband to protect her?' She could see the implacable intent in his expression. 'What sort of man preys on a young woman like that?'

So he knew a little about this Tom. Okay. But wasn't it Fadia's final decision they needed to wait for? She stamped down her initial unease over saying something. 'She seems to have relied on him in the past.'

His gaze sharpened and she could almost smell the briny scent of storm to come. 'So she has mentioned him?'

She looked away. 'No.' She really didn't think she'd get away with her pitifully thin denial but he wasn't looking at her.

He'd focussed across the room at the windows. 'But has he already found where she is?'

She wasn't touching that assumption. 'Is that why you have a guard in her corridor?'

His gaze returned to her but he declined to answer that question. 'Her marriage and the birth of her sons has been an unexpected development for our family.'

His eyes bored into hers. 'She must come home. But even I would not whisk a new mother with twins away until she has had a chance to recover.'

'And is that your intention?' She could see it was.

His look measured her. 'Yes.' There was no doubt in his mind anyway.

Now they were down to the real thing. Was he the type of man, like her ex-husband, who saw only his own wants and needs? Did he even care about Fadia the person or just her sons? 'Even if she's not a hundred per cent sure she wants to go?'

'I believe it is in her best interests, and the best interests of her babies to return to Zandorro.'

Controlling creep, then. It seemed Fadia's wishes were not in the equation at all. 'You didn't answer my question.'

'Again, you do not understand. It is my prerogative to not answer any question.'

Well, that was straight out. She was on Fadia's side until the young mum definitely decided what she wanted to do. She stood up and he did also. 'I see. Thank you.' Her voice was dry. 'And thank you for seeing me.'

He studied her. Intently. And she felt he could see not just her but right through her. Into her brain. Hopefully not through her clothes. It wasn't a comfortable feeling. 'I found our conversation to have been most illuminating.'

'Yes.' Well, she had learned a little. 'Some of it was.'

'Good day, Miss Carmen.' He bowed and a small smile teased at the side of his mouth. The air in the room seemed suddenly more heavily scented, the music dimmed, and his eyes burned into hers. She knew he was thinking of that moment in the lift. She was too. She could feel the flush in her skin, her neck warmed, and yet she couldn't look away. His perusal drifted down and swept the full length of her. And it was as if he'd trailed a feather down her skin. She shivered and his eyes darkened even more.

She needed to get away. 'Good day, Prince Zafar.'

'My word, it is, Miss Carmen.'

CHAPTER THREE

ZAFAR accompanied her to the door and watched her walk away up the corridor. Actually, he couldn't take his eyes off her, even toyed with the idea of calling her back until he realised what he was doing.

Her shapely legs would show to advantage in traditional dress and her formless tunic still did not disguise the lushness of her body. He could quite clearly remember his view from yesterday and had even recognised the scent of her skin next to his today.

Unexpected recognition when he barely remembered any woman since his wife had been killed.

The memory saddened him and pulled his mind away from Fadia's midwife.

Poor, sweet Adele. Theirs had been an arranged marriage, she younger than him, eager to please and expecting her husband to keep her safe. Her broken-hearted family had entrusted him with their precious daughter and he'd failed. The burden of that guilt still weighed heavily on him, the picture of her frightened eyes before the plane crashed haunted him in his sleep.

He hadn't looked at another woman since. Had lost himself in his work until recalled to royal duty.

Now his task was to ensure Fadia and her sons were

safe. Nothing else. But he feared it would not be easy. That was his real problem. He feared. Feared he would not be able to stop something terrible happening. Feared he'd be unable to save Fadia and her sons like he had been unable to save his own family.

Prior to two years ago he's been afraid of nothing. Evil had arrived and until it was conquered he would not be distracted.

His eyes strayed to the empty corridor. Perhaps the midwife could help, though. And so his concentration returned to Carmen as he turned thoughtfully back into his suite. She had braved the lion in his own den. He admired her courage. And she amused him with her determination not to be cowed by his prestige. But she'd lied about Tom.

So the dog might be here in the hotel. He would have Yusuf investigate. And delve into the delightful Miss Carmen's past too. Perhaps she could help his cousin more than they knew, and such information would be useful.

He needed Fadia and the twins well enough to travel as soon as possible. He would feel better when he had them back in Zandorro.

Zafar strode across the room and out the doors onto the balcony, punished himself with the rise of gall in his throat from that height, forced himself to grip the rail and glance down. His gut rolled and he stepped back as he drew breath.

His mind roamed while he stared out over the rolling sea. If he cut off the bustling town below, the ocean seemed not dissimilar to the rolling dunes of his desert, and he could feel a lightening of his mood that normally only came when he retreated to solitude.

A whimsical thought intruded where none normally went. He wondered what Miss Carmen would think of the desert or the ways of a desert prince. It was an unexpected but intriguing scenario.

Carmen clanged the door behind her. Her favourite place. The fire escape. He'd burnt her again. It was criminal to be that handsome and mesmerising. But at least she'd found out Fadia was just a pawn on his gold-embossed chess set and she, Carmen O'Shannessy, didn't like the idea. Or him. If Fadia needed an ally, Carmen was her girl.

It brought back too many unpleasant memories. The way Carl had turned, as early as their honeymoon, swearing at her, keeping her awake with tirades when she'd needed to sleep, wearing her down, demeaning her after a year of desolation until she'd finally accepted the enormity of her mistake and run away. Had moved jobs, states, lost friends until finally she rebuilt her life.

Domineering men did not have a place in her life. She straightened off the door and began her descent. Unfortunately, she could picture this man's wicked smile so easily and the warmth she'd felt.

No. No trust, especially for men who could cool and heat her body with just a glance. So why did she want to run back and relive the sensation? How did that work?

When Carmen opened the door on the sixth floor, of course her friend the guard was still there. He rose from his chair when she appeared and nodded coldly as she walked past him towards her own room at the end of the corridor.

Made a good little enemy there, she thought as she stared past him to the rooms of mums and babies that looked out over the beach. When she reached the end of the corridor the midwife's room welcomed her with a sanctuary, which she couldn't help embracing, from his beady eyes.

So what if her room only held spare supplies? At least she could shut the door—which she did firmly—and lean back against it.

Unfortunately, the barrier didn't stop the thoughts of Zafar that followed. She couldn't remember ever being this unsettled over a man and that loss of control brought unpleasant reminders of her marriage.

Carmen pushed herself off the door and straightened the empty baby cots before energetically restocking the linen from the trolley into her shelves. Still needing distraction, she wiped over the bath equipment and scales she used to weigh the babies.

'Done. Hmm.' She rested her hand on the computer at the desk, but she didn't see any of it. She could see Prince Zafar, though, in her mind's eye, and recalled the way he made her feel.

On Tuesday, refreshed after a full night's sleep, Carmen welcomed the new mothers recently arrived from their birth at the nearby hospital. When she'd finally made it to her room the phone shrilled with neglect.

'Midwife. Can I help you?'

'Carmen? It's Fadia. I've been trying to reach you for ages. There's a new pink rash on Harrison that's a bit pimply. Can you come to my room when you get a minute, please?'

'Sure. Everything else okay?' No word from Tom, she hoped.

'The boys and I are fine otherwise, if that's what you mean.'

Carmen relaxed. 'Is it okay if I check on one of my other mothers first?'

'Oh?'

Carmen smiled into the phone. 'I'll be as quick as I can but might be ten minutes, unless it's urgent.' A little of the privilege she was used to had crept into Fadia's voice. Interesting family. 'That way I can spend longer with you when I get there.'

'Of course. No problem. I'll see you soon.'

The time Carmen spent with the other young mum seemed to fly and she glanced at her watch as she waved goodbye. She needed to arrange times for weights for those who were going home that day but she'd better check the princess first. She made her way to Fadia. With two babies to care for, she needed the most help.

Carmen knocked, then opened the door with her key, and almost walked into Zafar who again was with his cousin.

His black brows rose in disbelief. 'You have a key?'

Carmen shared her own frown. That tone. That arrogance. She wasn't sure why it goaded her so much but thankfully she wasn't one of his underlings. 'Yes. To all the mothers' rooms so they don't have to get up to let me in.'

She tilted her head at him. 'Of course I always knock first.'

Now inscrutable, his 'I'm sure you do' left Carmen seething again. What was it about this man that pressed her buttons? Normally the easiest-going person, just a glance from him was enough to raise her blood pressure, and yet his actions were almost reasonable in the circumstances. So why wasn't her response more tranquil?

She narrowed her eyes at him. Did he think she was in collusion with Tom? 'I hope Fadia is able to rest between feeds. Having you come so often, that is.'

'My cousin would be able to rest if the midwife came immediately when she was asked.'

So now we get to his Excellency's displeasure. Tsk, tsk. Real world. 'Unfortunately, your cousin is not my only patient.'

His lips tightened and he glanced at his watch. 'Then I will arrange it to be so.' There it was, his red rag to her bull.

It's not all about you, buster. 'You will do no such thing, Your Highness.' She stressed the title, more to calm her own urge to throttle him than out of respect. Was this guy for real? The most annoying part was that she couldn't let it show because drama was the last thing Fadia needed. She smiled at her patient before she turned back to the royal pain.

'Perhaps this topic is best saved for a time that isn't taking up your cousin's.' She moved past him. 'Now, Fadia, would you like to show me your baby's rash?'

Zafar's voice floated over her shoulder, blandly. 'I have already told her it is erythema toxicarum, a rash very common in the first three days in newborns.'

Carmen blinked but didn't turn to look at him. Obviously he had a medical advantage he hadn't mentioned. Typical.

'My cousin is a paediatrician and established the new children's hospital in Zandorro before he was recalled to his duty to the monarchy,' Fadia explained.

That would explain his knowledge and also a little

more about why they'd let the twins out so early. She looked at the red pimply rash on Harrison's neck and arms. So he knew what he was talking about.

'He's right. And mums are naturally concerned.' She smiled at Fadia. 'You might find that the rash moves with heat. So if you were to hold Harrison's leg while you changed a nappy you might find the rash had suddenly become more prominent there and less prominent from where it showed a minute ago.'

Zafar was over harmless rashes. 'I agree that my cousin looks tired. Is there a nursery where the babies can go while she sleeps?'

And who had made it easier for her to leave the hospital ward too quickly? Carmen thought. Hmm. 'I'm afraid we don't have that option here. This facility is for transition to home. If Fadia wanted to have the babies minded she could return to the hospital or have a relative stay in the room while she rests.'

She spread her hands. Her look said she doubted Fadia would relax while he was watching over her.

'Or I could hire a mothercraft nurse for you again. Surely that would be easier?' Zafar queried his cousin, but Fadia's eyes pleaded as she shook her head. 'No. Please.'

'For the moment we will do as you wish.' Zafar frowned and Carmen wondered if he was regretting he'd hurried her here.

She watched his face but he gave nothing away. 'I will discuss this with your midwife later today.' It seemed Zafar was choosing to leave this time or was he wary of her asking him to go. Either way, Carmen was pleased she didn't have to fight about it.

Left to their own devices, the women had the babies

fed and settled within the hour. Despite a tantrum from Harry that rattled the windows and an inclination from Bailey to sleep through the feed, finally the curtains closed so Fadia could have a rest.

'You can ring me if they wake and I'll help you get sorted for the feed.'

Fadia nodded sleepily.

'Ring the midwife's room if you get stuck. If I get tied up, the other midwife will be here and I'll see you tomorrow.'

The day seemed to stretch for ever, not unusual after Carmen's run of night duty was finished, but tonight was the second of the four in her week when she could fall into bed and sleep the night through.

As seven o'clock drew closer, she found herself looking forward to a break. Handover took longer than normal for the night midwife because the intricacies of Fadia's case involved so many layers. Finally she was riding down in the lift to the basement on her way home.

'You look exhausted.' Zafar was leaning against her car.

Was that a coincidence or did he really know it was her vehicle? Tiredness suddenly took a back seat to nervous energy. 'I'm feeling a little wired after today. Strange men who recognise my car make me even more cross.'

He smiled, unperturbed, but offered no explanation as he watched her.

She tapped her foot with irritability—not nervous energy. She wished he'd go away. Almost. 'Did you want something, Prince Zafar? Apart from to tell me that I look tired, which was very kind. Thank you.'

Zafar pushed himself off her bonnet and loomed in

front of her. 'I wish to invite you to walk with me. Even tired, you are lovely.'

Yeah, right. Lovely with little sleep. She resisted the urge to step back. A walk? 'Now? It's almost dark.' She narrowed her eyes. Kidnapping had been mentioned. 'Why?'

He shrugged. 'Because it would be good to get out of the hotel. Walk along the cliff top. What is it you say? Blow away the cobwebs? That is one of the things I miss most about Australia. The graphic expressions.'

So he'd lived here before. It had been an endless twenty-four hours but his background and history couldn't but intrigue some part of her. Had he lived here before he was a prince perhaps? A young doctor? That made him more normal. She met those every day.

The idea of walking in the fresh air before driving to her solitary flat was tempting. Let the stresses of the day be whisked into the salty breeze that blew a mere hundred metres away. It held some attraction, as did the idea of hearing a little about this enigmatic man in front of her.

'Perhaps a short one. I sleep better with exercise.'

'So obliging,' he mocked gently.

Carmen glanced at her car, shrugged her shoulders, and added, 'Or I could go home now.'

He smiled. And what a smile. The most spontaneous grin she'd seen. 'I am walking. Would you care to accompany me?' Still optional, and it seemed she did want to go because her legs made their own decision and followed him up the ramp like she was on a string.

It was still light, towards the last before sunset, but the salty tang of ocean breeze made her glad she'd ventured out.

She didn't know what made her look back—in truth, she'd forgotten about his bodyguard—but Yusuf was there in the lee of the building, watching them. His eyes met hers coldly.

Zafar saw her frown and with a flick of his wrist banished the man from sight.

He wasn't sure why it had been so important to spend time with this woman. His brain had suggested a discussion about Fadia but his mood had lifted as soon as she'd stepped out of the lift. How did she do that? And did he want her to?

They waited at the traffic lights and strangely the silence was not heavy between them. His interest in the companionship of a woman had been absent for the last two years and yet her company made him feel light and free.

They chatted about his homeland and his love of the desert until the 'Walk' sign propelled them across the road and down to the cobbled path that ran around the headland.

'I've never been to the desert.'

'It is very beautiful and harsh.' He smiled down at her. 'Like some Australian women.'

What was it about her that captured his interest? He glanced at her. Perhaps it was the genuine empathy she could feel for his cousin. Perhaps her obvious lack of ulterior motive. Or her transparent emotions that enticed him to savour her moods, even when he annoyed her. He felt his mouth curve until he realised what he was doing. He was not here for this.

Carmen ignored the teasing inherent in that remark and stamped down the excitement she could feel growing at his company. This was not good. They were worlds apart and she didn't need to fall for another domineering man. But she could enjoy her walk and satisfy her curiosity. No strings attached. 'So, if you are a prince, do you have a palace?' A little tongue in cheek. He probably lived in a nice house in the city.

'My brother and I each have our own palace in the mountains, and share service to our grandfather at his palace in Zene, the capital of Zandorro.'

Oh. She hadn't actually thought he was that grand. It was all too fairy-tale but it made her feel safer that he wouldn't be interested in an ordinary midwife. 'What about an oasis in the desert with tents?'

It was as if he'd read her mind. 'Absolutely. You would not believe it.'

'Lawrence of Arabia?' They smiled at each other. 'Tell me.'

He shrugged, amused. 'A true Bedouin camp is a little earthier than mine. My oasis belonged to a tourist company that went bankrupt. I bought them out when I could have just waited for them to leave but the karma is good. I use it for business negotiations when Western wives accompany their husbands. Their fantasies are always good business. Bathing in oils, traditional dress for the meal. I think you might enjoy it.'

It could be fun. 'Are you saying Westerners are easily swayed by that fantasy?' She was having a few pretty pictures of her own. She smiled at him. 'I'm all for fantasies as long as I can get off when I want to.'

Zafar watched her face. Saw the dreamy expression in her eyes change as she thought of something unpleasant. He felt his own mood lower in response.

He realised he'd like to see this kind woman pampered, cosseted, cared for. The worries of the world removed from her lovely shoulders. Perhaps one day, when he was not called to royal duty and all this was over, he might come back and search her out. See if she still wanted to see the desert.

It was an intriguing idea he shouldn't consider and it seemed her curiosity was greater about his time in her own country. 'So you've lived here before?'

He looked across at her as they walked past the old baths. 'My mother was buried in Sydney.'

'Did she leave Zandorro late in life?'

He put his hand on her elbow to steer her safely aside as a pushbike rider pedalled past. Her skin was like silk yet taut with youth and vibrancy. He could feel the impact of her arm on his fingers.

Touching her skin was too distracting. Zafar let his hand drop. Too soft yet supple, too enticing, and he had no right to touch her. Guilt swamped him. How could he forget his wife so easily? Just two years and for the first time he was burdened with the beginnings of lust. For a woman so different from his beloved.

So why did he want to capture this woman's hand and bump his hip against hers as they walked? Why now, suddenly, did he see Carmen as attractive when for ages he'd barely acknowledged other women existed? What was it about her? He glanced at her animated face as she waited for an answer. What had she'd asked? Ah, yes. His mother.

'Yes, my mother left Zandorro when my father died. She married an Australia diplomat a few years later.'

He didn't want to think about how she'd left him and his brother behind in their grandfather's care. How much they'd missed the brief chances to feel her gentle love and support, which they'd taken for granted in their busy lives. It hadn't been until he'd demanded he come to university here that he'd learned the truth. She'd had no choice if she'd wanted a life for herself and the hour or two each day she saw her sons hadn't filled the gap his father had left.

Her face was turned to him. Not passive attention but real empathy in her gaze. 'So where did you live when you were here?'

And he was allowing her truths he shared with no one. 'With my mother and her husband all through university. Then I bought a house near theirs until I completed my time as registrar three years ago.'

'So you worked here as well?'

'I studied under Dr Ting at Bay Hospital.' They had been good years and he'd taken innovative ideas back to Zandorro and set up a state-of-the-art paediatric hospital in Zene. He'd been bitten by passion, obsessed with creating a better place for sick children, research for hope, and he had achieved a lot of that dream.

He had the sudden urge to tell her but that had all been before he'd had to hand it on and take over his royal duties.

Dr Ting? Carmen was stunned. 'So you're a consultant?' If he'd been under the eminent paediatrician, he was no slouch. No amount of money would have secured the radical but brilliant Dr Ting's agreement unless Zafar was worthy. She looked at him with new respect. 'I'm impressed.'

He frowned. 'Don't be. I'm unable to practise as much as I wish.' Such was the despair in his voice she backed away from the topic. This guy could create tension with just a word and she wasn't used to that. More layers she didn't understand and more reasons for her to be careful.

The silence had a bite to it now. Something had happened to stop his work. She wondered but shied away from digging. 'The view is spectacular along this path.'

The darkness in his tone made the water in front lose its sparkle. Such was his presence that the idea didn't even seem too fanciful. Maybe night was just coming on more swiftly than she'd anticipated?

They walked quite briskly along the cliff past the steps to the ladies' baths and onto the wide grassed area near the playground. Suddenly she noticed the families gathering blankets and children under their arms. She turned curiously to survey the way they'd come. A summer storm threatened, and she lifted her hand to point it out when she was distracted by a young woman in a pretty sarong, kneeling on the grass. At first Carmen thought she was praying.

As she drew level the woman moaned and they both stopped. The woman's glittering, pain-filled eyes made Carmen draw breath and they both crossed over to her.

Carmen rested her hand gently on her shoulder. 'You okay?'

The woman moistened her lips. 'No. My baby.'

Must be the month for pregnant women to be out and about alone in labour, Carmen thought as she glanced around. In fact, the busy park lay almost deserted as the cooler breeze sprang up. 'Are you in pain or have your waters broken?'

The young woman laughed, a little hysterically. 'Both.' She turned her head and she, too, realised they were the only people left. Her eyes sought Carmen's. 'I'm so scared. The pains are coming like a freight train.

You won't leave me?' The woman stopped and moaned as she tried to catch her breath.

'Ambulance, please, Zafar?' Carmen glanced at her companion, who nodded and raised his phone to make the call, and Carmen knelt down beside her. 'What's your name?'

'Jenny.'

'I'm Carmen, Jenny. And this is Zafar. Is this your first baby?'

The woman nodded. Carmen's shoulders relaxed a little so hopefully they'd have time to transport. 'Can you stand? We've called an ambulance. Would you like to move to the bench?'

Jenny looked at the short distance to the bench. 'No. I'm too scared to move. I need to stay like this.'

Carmen's eyebrows rose. She glanced at the roomy sarong. It was one of those tube ones held up by elastic, and she decided the woman was probably as comfortable kneeling as she'd be anywhere and at least she was covered for privacy.

Carmen smiled to herself. They could probably have a baby under that sarong and nobody would notice.

At work most of her births were in the semi-dark and by feel anyway, but surely it wouldn't come to that.

'That's fine. Your comfort's the most important thing while we wait for the ambulance.'

She exchanged glances with Zafar and he nodded. She had support. All was good.

'So I'm guessing the contractions are pretty powerful?' The girl nodded. 'Well, you're breathing really well. It's so important not to get scared.'

'I'm freaking here,' Jenny ground out. 'It should not be this quick.'

Carmen pressed her hand into Jenny's shoulder. 'You're doing great. They say fear's your worst enemy. I try to remember that when things happen that scare the socks off me. Birth isn't an enemy—it's nature's way. Everything will be okay if a little unusual in setting.'

Jenny shook her head. Emphatically. 'It still shouldn't be this quick.'

'Sometimes that happens,' Zafar said reassuringly. 'Carmen's a midwife and I'm a paediatrician. We know babies.'

'So someone up there's looking after you.' Carmen sent Zafar an ironic glance that she hoped she was ready. 'And babies are spontaneous and pretty tough. Do you want to slip off your underwear in case? Might be tricky otherwise.'

Zafar compressed his lips to hide his smile. The woman was clearly terrified but Carmen had it all well in hand. He could only observe, uselessly. There wasn't a lot he could do without interfering and he was afraid he couldn't achieve the same degree of calm she had with so little time. But he was more than willing if there were complications with the newborn.

Jenny shook her head. 'I don't want to move from here.'

'And we can work with that if we have to.' Carmen tilted her head down lower so the woman could see her face. 'If your baby is born, I'll catch and pop him or her through your legs to you at the front. Do you understand?'

The woman moaned and then a look of surprise and horror crossed her face. 'This can't be happening.' Her eyes darted around as if the ambulance would suddenly appear.

'It's about to happen.' Carmen looked at Zafar to back her up if needed. She knew an imminent birth when she heard one. Her voice was serene as she repeated, 'Afterwards, just lift your baby and put it against your skin under your dress and pop your baby's head out the neckline. The length of the umbilical cord will tell you how high to lift it. Okay?'

'Oh, no-o-o-o,' Jenny wailed, then groaned as she suddenly she eased her panties off.

Carmen rolled the woman's underwear up neatly as it appeared under the dress and Zafar decided that no doubt she had a use for that too.

He was reminded of her calmness in the lift and it was the same here. As if she was saying that having a baby in the park was no big deal. She was very focussed and even the woman looked as though things might be fine after all.

A mindset that had seemed a pretty big ask two minutes ago. Why wasn't he surprised?

He should really say something more but he was only a spectator at the moment, an appreciative one, unless his skills were required. He hadn't used them enough lately. 'We'll be here for you and your baby until the ambulance comes.' He copied the same calm tone Carmen used then stripped off his jacket and bundled it up like a pillow to keep the warmth inside for the baby when born. He had no doubt Carmen would manage most of the impending birth.

It had been several years since he'd worked on a neonate and a nice natural birth was not something he'd expected along a cliff path. He hoped this baby was well because he didn't fancy resuscitation out here in the freshening breeze, but they would manage what they had to. The ambulance wouldn't be too far away.

The woman groaned and he focussed back on the present. Carmen had shifted around behind Jenny, shielding her from the path and lifting her dress slightly. 'Head-on view,' she murmured, and held her hands either side of the baby's head. He wished he'd had gloves he could have given her but doubted she'd give it a thought at this moment.

The sound of the ambulance in the distance overlaid the sound of Jenny's breathing. All the while in the background the crash of the surf on the cliffs melded with the moment of expectation and added to the surreal, amazing, incredible moment he hadn't anticipated.

'Here it comes,' Carmen said calmly. 'You're doing beautifully.'

Jenny moaned, the baby's head appeared, and then slowly the little face swivelled to face the mother's thigh. Seconds later a shoulder and then two arms eased into Carmen's hands in a tangle of limbs and cord and water and the baby gasped at the cold air on wet skin and cried loudly as his legs and feet slid out.

Zafar smiled at the swollen scrotum. Definitely a boy. 'Hello there, young man.' Then the memories rushed in. His own son. Limp and lifeless.

Zafar quickly wiped the little boy over with the warm inner lining of his jacket to dry him a little so he wouldn't be chilled and then Carmen fed him between his mother's legs into her waiting hands.

Zafar listened to her voice from a distance as he shook his head to shut out the clarity of the past. His own joy at Samir's birth. The look between he and

Adele at the moment of birth. The summit of their expectations. His family.

Then family lost. Both dead and buried. The bleakness of loss washed over him until the newborn cried
again and he shook himself. This was not his son. This
baby was vigorous and healthy and beginning life on a
windswept headland.

'Oh, well done, Jenny.' Carmen's voice. It was over.
Incredible.

He heard Carmen mumble, 'Nice long cord, that's
handy.'

Handy, he thought. Such a handy length of cord, and
suddenly his mouth tilted, the painful memories receded
and the miracle of new life made his lips curve into a
smile he wouldn't have believed possible a moment ago.

Women amazed him, these two in particular, and the
memory of the last ten minutes would no doubt make
him smile for years.

Carmen glanced across at him and his smile broad-
ened. 'Very handy,' he said.

She frowned and then remembered what she said.
He mouthed, 'Handy cord,' and she grinned at him then
back at the mother.

Within fifteen minutes the ambulance had arrived,
the officers took over, and he and Carmen stepped
back. Zafar was glad to see the officers offer towels
and hand steriliser to Carmen, who blithely washed
herself down. His jacket had been bagged for cleaning
because Carmen wouldn't let him put it in the bin.

'You could reminisce when you put that on,' she'd
said. He doubted he'd wear it but she had a point. His
mouth curved again.

Soon mother and baby were tucked into the back

of the vehicle with blankets, everyone was happy with their condition, and with the air-conditioner set on warm they were ready to go.

Zafar dropped his arm around Carmen's shoulder and pulled her body in next to his as they watched the flashing lights disappear. She fitted into the side of his body too well and he fought to keep the moment platonic because for him something had changed. Not just in the way he felt about this amazing woman but about the colour of the world.

The idea of new life in unexpected places, perhaps even the easing of the pain he'd carried since that fateful hijacking two years ago when he'd lost so much, and now for the first time he felt hopeful.

He frowned. Because of Jenny's birth? An unknown woman's son? Or because of the midwife? Perhaps he did owe some of this amazing feeling to this woman. And again, outside his usual experience, she genuinely didn't want anything in return for the blessings she'd given him.

CHAPTER FOUR

'It's almost dark,' she said.

Zafar, too, had noticed. 'Indeed, I fear we're in for a storm.'

'Good grief, look at that.' While they'd been busy a new weather front had rolled towards them and looked worlds nastier than a summer storm.

He glanced up at the wall of cloud that rolled like dark oil off a cliff, grey and black clouds with angry faces shape-shifted as they lit.

Zafar gestured her to precede him. 'I think we should return more quickly.'

'You think?' she muttered, and scooted along in front of him, but it was too late.

He pulled her into the lee of a bull-nosed iron picnic shed just as a sheet of rain blew across the path. They were instantly splattered with pea-sized drops followed by a deafening crack as a bolt of lighting exploded into the ground on the cliff edge. Carmen jumped and he tightened his arms around her. Felt her shudder beneath his hands.

Zafar loved storms but it seemed Carmen had her own phobias. At least he wasn't the only one with irrational fears. 'Shh. We'll be fine here.' It seemed so long since he'd held a woman to comfort her, felt his chest expand with the need to protect, set his feet more firmly as if to ward off anything that would threaten her.

The briny scent of ozone seared his nostrils and two seconds later thunder directly overhead rattled the roof of their shed like a giant hand had slammed their pitiful shelter with a baseball bat.

Carmen shuddered. Zafar's arms felt so safe around her and instinctively she tucked her forehead into his chest. His shirt was fine but thin and she could feel the corded muscle rock solid beneath her cheek, warm and welcoming, and the steady thud of his heartbeat in her ear.

The spice of an exotic aftershave, one that made her think of souks and incense, made her bury her nose and banished the smell of rain and ozone with a big shuddering inhalation. It was just that she hated storms. She'd always been afraid of storms.

'I'm not enjoying this thunder,' she mumbled shakily into his shirt when finally the ringing in her ears made talking possible. She ignored the tiny voice inside her that wondered if this time she told the whole truth.

He leant down and even the warmth of his breath calmed her as he spoke into her hair, 'We will stay until the lightning has passed.'

There was no sign he would loosen his embrace and she was quietly pleased about that. There was something primal about the extreme force of nature around them and she knew about the danger of reckless exposure.

She should distract herself from the storm and think about Jenny and her new baby but, come to think of it,

Zafar's arms kept the outside world at bay like a force field, a zone she was very happy to be within.

To her disgust she snuggled deeper into the haven he afforded. It was so darned reassuring to be wrapped firmly in strong arms against this amazing wall of masculine strength and, to be honest, that first bolt of lightning had given her the willies. 'Just let me know when you're ready to move,' she mumbled into his chest.

He shifted his mouth until his breath was warm in her ear again. 'I was thinking of making a move now.' And squeezed her arms with teasing pressure. His voice was low and with a distinct thread of humour she couldn't miss, along with overtones of seduction. She felt the tug of her own smile.

The guy knew how to make the most of situations. She unearthed her nose from his shirt and looked up at him, but she had to lean back in his arms to gain some distance. 'No cheating.'

'Third time lucky?' Dark and dangerous eyes were brimful of wicked intent. 'I won't ask for anything you're unwilling to give,' he murmured as his head descended. 'But I will ask...'

The heat. That was her first thought as her traitorous mouth accepted and then returned his kiss with precocious enthusiasm. What was this recognition, as if she'd been joined to this mouth many times before? How could that be?

He bent again, less gently, and the kiss deepened, became more sensual than she'd imagined, more insidiously addictive than she'd bargained for.

Carmen merged into the burning pressure of his lips against hers, the drugging assault as their bodies melded, and the rising heat between that mocked the puny storm around them. Then the coolness of his leaving as he skimmed her neck with hot lips, leaving his own trail of electrical activity where before there'd been the chill of sleeting rain.

When he bent to brush his mouth between her breasts she felt her nipples jump like bobbing corks in a sudden sea of arousal. She had to hang on or she'd fall down. Her fingers slid up to bury themselves in hair like strands of silk beneath her fingertips, until she forgot that sensation in a host of new ones as he tipped her backwards over his arm like the marauder he was and suddenly she felt like ripping open the buttons of her shirt to give him access.

Then he was back at her mouth and she was drowning.

A scatter of drips from the leaking roof splashed her hair and annoyingly penetrated the fog of arousal. Good grief. She'd kissed him back as wildly as he'd kissed her, for heaven's sake.

If she wasn't careful, he'd take her on the picnic table behind them and she'd blithely wrap her legs around him with delight. She pushed her hand against his chest and eased at least her chest out of his embrace. What was she turning into?

'Whoa there, cowboy.'

He stopped, looked down at her, stared for a moment and then to her surprise he threw back his head and laughed. Really laughed. And if she'd thought him a handsome man before, this laughing god was a million light years ahead of any man she'd seen before.

He eased her away slowly, almost unpeeling her from where they were plastered together at the hip, and with both hands he straightened her shirt. 'I'm sorry.' He raised his brows with amusement still vivid in his face. 'Cowgirl…' He put her from him. 'You are without doubt the most original woman. It is fortunate one of us has their wits about them.'

'You're pretty special yourself,' she muttered as she increased the distance between them. Where had that sensual onslaught come from? And no little peck. Good grief. She couldn't remember a kiss like that, ever. A year of marriage hadn't prepared her for that. That mother of all kisses and she'd let him. Encouraged him. But what else was a girl to do when snuggled into a man such as Zafar in a picnic shelter during an electrical storm? Not that!

She needed to get clear of this guy because already she was like one of those puddles the storm had just dumped. Wet, formless, muddied with lust.

She glanced around and the inky front was noticeably lighter above them as it rolled out to sea. 'It seems to be passing. Let's get out of here.'

He'd distanced himself from her too. She could feel it. Good. Maybe he regretted their ignition as well. He removed the phone from his pocket, dialled, spoke, and then tucked it away. 'Yusuf will pick us up from across the grass.'

'We can walk.' As she finished speaking a long black car pulled up opposite the park. So the henchman had been out there waiting in the storm anyway. She shivered. So now she was cold without Zafar holding her? What the heck was she doing when she got close to this guy? Apparently whatever he wanted.

She needed to remember he was from his own world, with his own rules. Rules that differed from hers no matter that he'd worked here for a while.

Zafar pondered Carmen's silence and staunch independence as he slid into the car after her but he pondered his own response more. What had happened? The heat they'd created between them, the shock of unexpected connection had rocked him. But perhaps it had just been his body requiring sex. Either way, it was not something to rush. As was the change he could sense in himself. Very unsettling. He filed away the fire between them in the storm for future thought.

For the moment he had decided he needed to secure her services for his cousin. And he did not want her caring for other women, only available for them. This was certainly a new direction for his usually solitary thoughts.

'I believe we were going to discuss the possibility of you caring for Fadia as your only client.'

She shifted beside him and avoided his eyes. 'There is no discussion.' Her words were clipped as if her mind was elsewhere and did not want to be disturbed.

Almost in panic? Why did that amuse him? So she could sense the strangeness of the shift too. 'That is not an answer. More a knee-jerk reaction, I believe they call it.'

'I have a knee if you want one,' she muttered, and he wondered if he had been supposed to hear that. Such a physical woman. More clearly, she said, 'I'm afraid I can't help you.'

Why was she so sure of herself? She did not know him. Still, this woman could be most annoying.

He restrained himself from correcting her. 'Because…?'

What was so absorbing outside the car that she must look past him out the window?

'Because I have two jobs already.'

Of course. She worked at the hospital. Fadia had said Carmen had been her midwife at the birth. No doubt that's why she looked so tired. The money answer would be the simplest one. 'And why have you two jobs?'

'That's none of your business.'

He caught Yusuf's eye in the mirror and his driver nodded. Not yet but it soon would be. Perhaps Yusuf already had gleaned some information.

She went on, militantly, so he had annoyed her with his questions. He suppressed his smile. 'If you wish Fadia to have a personal mothercraft nurse, of course you can arrange that, but it won't be me.'

'I was thinking a professional midwife to act as flight assistant for Fadia for the trip to Zandorro and to help her settle in.' Such a prickly woman.

'No. Thank you.'

'A week or two only?' The look she gave him suggested a change of topic. 'Let's leave that for the moment. Tell me how this baby hotel works. Do all the midwives work at both here and the labour wards at the hospital?'

She frowned as if collecting her thoughts. 'How did you know I worked at both places?'

'My cousin told me, remember?' He liked her off balance.

She narrowed her eyes at him but then looked away past him again before she said, 'I do the occasional night shift at the hospital as well as this. Yes.'

She was lying again and he wondered why. Fadia had said she worked nights every Friday, Saturday, Sunday, and worked day shifts on the five weekdays. That meant two double shifts a week. She had to be exhausted.

Every time she did not tell the truth she looked away. A hopeless liar. Then again, that was not a bad thing.

She answered a question he'd moved on from in his head and it took a moment for him to refocus.

'We have eight beds on floors five and six that are kept in the hotel for the private patients who transfer from the hospital. Most new mothers stay two to four days before they go home.'

Ah. His question about the baby hotel. He was interested in the concept. It could work in Zandorro. Perhaps even for the children's hospital. 'So after the birth, when they wish, mothers transfer here?'

'That's right. As Fadia did. If their birth was uncomplicated. And their doctors will visit. The beauty of the hotel as opposed to the hospital is the mother's support people can stay. Friends can visit less rigidly than in a hospital.'

She hurried on as if to avoid the topic and he had no difficulty understanding why. She looked away again. He fought back a smile. Her complicity with Fadia was not something he wished to bring up now.

'In fact,' she said, 'up to two other children could also stay with the parents in their rooms, and the access of the midwife means the transition period to home is less stressful than a busy ward in the hospital or the return to full household duties at home.'

'And the midwife provides what?'

'Help with feeding problems, settling techniques and to talk about postnatal needs out of the hospital environment. The hotel provides food and housekeeping.'

She shrugged. 'The lovely part here is the view. Mums can gaze over the beach from their balcony. It's

a great place to regather their resources before they
go home.'

His attention was caught. Regather their resources.
He liked that. Just looking at Carmen regathered his
resources. He hadn't realised just how low his reserves
had fallen until the lift incident and the more he saw of
this woman, the more alive he felt.

It seemed some time with the delectable Carmen
could even be as beneficial as the solitary sojourn in
the desert he'd prescribed himself. He would see what
Yusuf turned up.

'That is all very interesting.' He glanced ahead to
where they would pull in as the car glided to a stop.
'We are back. Thank you for accompanying me and
my apologies for your exposure to the weather.'

'I doubt even you have control over the weather.' She
gave him a little mocking smile he did not appreciate
then raised her hand to open her own door.

He was pleased to see her start of surprise when it
opened from the outside. She would learn a woman
should be cared for and protected.

Carmen didn't like this henchman of Zafar's. This
man with a scar who did his master's bidding unsettled
her. Judging by the cold expression on Yusuf's face, the
feeling was mutual.

Still, another two or three days and the lot of them
would be gone. She hoped Fadia decided sensibly but
it was none of her business.

She glanced back inside the car but Zafar had exited
and moved to her side. 'Oh. Here you are. Goodnight.'

He reached, took her hand, bowed over it briefly and
then deliberately turned her fingers to expose her wrist
before he lifted it to his mouth.

The kiss lingered, with subtle eroticism, and her response to the intimate caress was totally unexpected. Still not fully recovered from the passion in the storm, his mouth sent shock waves surging back through her that weakened her knees. She hoped that explained the absolute melting of every bone in her body as soon as his lips touched her skin. Good grief.

She turned away shakily, ignored the expressionless face of Yusuf, and passed through the doors into the lobby to use the lift to the car park. She doubted her suddenly wobbly legs would be able to traverse the steep driveway down to her car without her falling over.

Her wrist burned like a brand and she rode down the lift with it covered with her other hand. Get a grip, she warned herself fiercely. He's just a man. You're just out of practice and your hormones pulled the rug out from under you.

The drive home passed in a blur, automatic pilot obedient, as her brain whirled and her eyes strayed to her wrist near the steering-wheel. What was she doing? What was he doing? Did he have intentions of seduction and if so, why? Did he want his cousin watched so badly he thought she might be useful?

Was she tempted?

When she arrived at the door of her block of flats a group of youths called out and weaved towards her. A bottle smashed into the gutter across the road and, not surprisingly, she fumbled with the lock. The outside light had broken and she dropped her keys in the dark. She hated it when that happened.

Someone approached the youths and spoke to them. Whatever was said worked because they turned and walked hurriedly back the other way. Her neck prickled and she resisted the urge to peer into the gloom at her good Samaritan across the road. Which was ridiculous, wasn't it?

She glanced uneasily over her shoulder before bending down and scooping the keys from the cold tiles. Her eyes were scratchy with tiredness and she just hoped that blasted Zafar hadn't interfered with her ability to sleep.

Managing the next four days depended on this good night's sleep before she started work at lunchtime tomorrow and Thursday, then after work on Friday night duty would begin again.

She felt frustration gather as she contemplated the unrelenting schedule. As Tilly had said, working seven days a week was crazy but it was only for another six months until she'd paid all the debts her husband had left her with and she'd be free. She wanted her credit rating back.

That was when she'd been offered the baby hotel job, which paid well, and for the moment she had her head above water. If she needed to work seven days a week for another few months, at least she loved both her jobs.

Carmen stripped off her clothes, hurriedly showered and fell into bed.

Lord, she was tired.

Carmen slept despite being seduced by her dreams, wonderful, stretch-like-a-cat-and-purr dreams, and the wisps of memories remained when the sun rose and left her with a small kink in her lips that peeped out while she brushed her teeth.

'You need a swim,' she admonished the sultry-eyed woman in the mirror. 'In fact, you need a freezing cold shower.' But her skin belonged to a womanly her and not the machine-like work person she'd turned into, even if her 'admirer' was some nebulous dream man with a magical mouth. She rubbed her arms. Scrummy dreams, whatever they'd been.

Life seemed a lot more interesting than it had two days ago and she couldn't pretend it had nothing to do with a certain dark-eyed sheikh.

She glanced out the cramped window of her room to see the sun shining onto the road, enticing her to play. She hadn't done much of that for a while either; more work and worry than play. The morning stretched ahead before her baby hotel shift at one p.m. and she decided to pack a small lunch and head to the beach.

Coogee glittered with tourists. Sun-loving mums toted babies to play in the waves and reminded her why she'd preferred to live in a bedsit here than a unit some-where else.

Carmen dropped her towel and bag on the white sand and shed her sarong, along with the cares of the last few months. Life was too short and the waves beckoned with their walls of cheeky fish daring her to join them. The fish scattered into white wash as she splashed through the tingling freshness of the surf with a grin on her face.

Zafar watched her run in his direction. She hadn't seen him because her smile was carefree, oblivious, and outshone even the brightness of the sparkling bay.

So this visceral response was not from the emotions of an unexpected birth or a wild storm.

His body quickened with the promise of her bare skin close to his. There was no doubt this woman drew him like mythical mermaids drew sailors to rocks, attrac-tion destined for disaster if he wasn't careful, but still he pushed through the wash towards her. Why he felt so alive posed a threat to his peace of mind. But that was for later.

She surfaced and wiped the sea water out of her beautiful eyes, squeezing and shaking her hair like a boisterous puppy, but it was the jiggle of her body that deepened his voice as he hailed her.

'I had forgotten the delights of an Australian beach.' He watched her face change from carefree to careful and the sight saddened him. He didn't know why, just that in the last two years he would never have noticed such a thing.

Obviously he'd startled her. 'Prince Zafar?' But she recovered quickly. He was beginning to think this woman would recover in any circumstances.

'We are not in a formal situation. Please, Zafar.'

He saw the crinkle of amusement in her eyes as she glanced around at the water and the frolicking children. 'No. Not formal at all.' She might even be laughing at him and he didn't mind if she was because it was worth it to see her expression become more relaxed. How strange.

'Is this what you do before work?'

'Not enough. But I'm going to make concerted effort to do it more often.' She looked away from him and spread her arms. 'Isn't it glorious?'

His blood thrummed despite his intent to retain his self-respect. 'The view is indeed spectacular.'

He needed to direct his energies elsewhere or he would pull that delicious body against him and who knew where that would lead? 'Do you swim well?'

'Better than you,' she tossed over her shoulder as she dived into the next wave and struck out for the centre of the bay.

A challenge. We will see, he thought with satisfaction as he followed her with a powerful overarm stroke that soon had them level out past the breakers. They stopped and floated. 'You were saying?'

She grinned across at him and a wave slapped her in the cheek. She choked and coughed. He laughed back at her and she trod water until she had her breath again.

She tossed her head. 'You might have speed but I could swim all day.'

He raised his brows and his voice lowered. 'In my youth I was famous for my stamina.'

To his delight she blushed. So she had been thinking of him. A delectable warning of danger for both of them. 'A race to the beach, then.'

She didn't answer. Just turned and swam, and this time he outpaced her so that when she arrived, breathless, he was waiting for her. She swam well. As well as any woman he'd seen, but she'd pushed herself hard to catch him. A hint of competitiveness he admired. He couldn't help teasing her.

'Such rapid breathing.' And a delightful sight he enjoyed as her breasts rose and fell. 'Perhaps you would like me to carry you up to your towel?'

She stood up and rested her hands on her knees to catch her breath. 'Never. I would rather crawl before then.'

'I believe you.' He inclined his head. Then words came unexpectedly. 'Perhaps we could share lunch before you go to work?'

She shook her head. 'I don't think it's a good idea to have lunch with one of my patient's relatives.'

Or for him to give in to the temptation to know this

woman more. Yet… Ridiculous. Who would presume to judge? 'I see nothing wrong with it.'

She tilted her head at him as if he were some object from outer space. 'Of course you don't.'

Truly, other people's opinions of him were the last of his worries. 'You are afraid?'

She narrowed her eyes at him and he withheld his satisfied smile. She didn't like that. Baiting this woman warmed his cold soul when it shouldn't.

'Then only if I pay my share.' Capitulation, though not complete, was sweet. It had been a long time since he'd tasted sweet.

But he did not charge women for food. He shrugged. 'Not possible.'

'Then you eat on your own.' She began to wade through the water towards the beach, not looking to see if he followed. He wondered if she knew she drew him like magnet as he watched the swing of her hips. It was indeed an unexpectedly glorious day.

'Perhaps you would wish to pay for my meal.'

She stopped and looked back at him and a small throaty chuckle delighted him. 'You're on.'

Fanciful thought.

CHAPTER FIVE

AT THE baby hotel later that afternoon in midwife hand-over, Carmen heard that Fadia and her babies were managing splendidly.

They went on to discuss the other mothers and their plans for discharge. As she took over the care Carmen left Fadia until last, because no doubt that'd be the longest visit. That way the other families would know where she was if they needed her urgently. One mention of twins and the mums were instantly sympathetic.

Yusuf was not at his usual post and outside Fadia's door she knocked and waited a moment for Fadia's call to come in before she used her key. A tall, swarthy man approached her and Carmen instantly recognised him from the photograph.

'Excuse me? You are the midwife?' He smiled, eyed her up and down, and she didn't feel flattered.

'Yes?' She withdrew her hand from the door lock.

'I wish to visit my friend, Fadia Smith. Can you tell me which room she is in?'

'I'm sorry.' She smiled at him. 'Or I could, but then I'd have to kill you.' Not the time for levity. As soon as the words left her mouth she regretted them. His face darkened and he looked even more like her ex-husband. She could feel the menace. Ironically appropriate?

Before anything else could be said, Zafar appeared from the fire escape and the man took one look at him and turned to disappear down the corridor in the direction of the other lifts.

Fadia's voice floated through the door. 'Come in. Is that you, Carmen?' Carmen looked at Zafar and his frown as he came towards her and decided discretion was the better part of valour.

She swiped the card and opened the door. 'Yes.' She stepped inside and held the door for Zafar as if nothing had happened.

His eyes held hers. 'Did he threaten you?'

'No. But he might have. I think your timing was good.'

'I hope it continues to be so.'

He opened his mouth to say more but she shook her head as she mouthed, 'Later'. He walked past her into the room and nodded at his cousin. 'You look rested.'

'Thank you.' Fadia smiled at them both and looked much happier. 'They've been perfect. They're sleeping now.'

'I will return shortly.' Zafar nodded and swept out again and Fadia raised her brows.

'Zafar was coming down the corridor just as you called for me to come in. Maybe he thought I was going to throw him out again.' They both tried not to smile. 'So tell me. They've both been sleeping?'

'Since just before lunch. I managed by myself. I can't believe it.'

'They'll wake up soon and maybe even for the next twenty-four hours will want lots of feeds. Be prepared.

Then it will settle down. You're doing amazingly well. It'll soon be easier.' She was talking to Fadia but her mind was elsewhere. Judging by the expression on Zafar's face, he'd taken off after Fadia's thwarted visitor.

It was all unsettling but as long as Fadia was not unsettled then useless speculation wouldn't help anyone and it was her job to help.

Carmen went through the bath routine and by the time they'd finished it was almost time for tea.

'I'll be off to see the other ladies. Just give me a ring if you need me. Maybe you could sit out on the veranda afterwards. That way you can enjoy the view over the beach.'

Fadia nodded. 'One day my boys will be big enough to run on the sand.' They both smiled at the distant future.

The whole shift passed without Zafar since that brief sighting in the corridor, which she would have liked to discuss, but the opportunity didn't arise.

She noticed Yusuf in the limo as she drove out of the car park on the way home. What went on in the henchman's head? she wondered, and then decided she didn't want to know. Whatever it was, his master had ordered it.

The next day, as Carmen approached Fadia's room, she could hear distressed babies and their mother's sobs through the door.

'Fadia?' She used the keycard that hung around her neck to get in. The noise dumped on her like a wall of sand from a collapsed sandcastle and hastily she shut the door.

'Fadia? You okay?' She could see she wasn't.

The young mother lay face down on the bed, shuddering into the mattress, the twins bellowed, red-faced and in unison as they waved tight little fists in their cots. Locked in with them for a moment, Carmen felt every minute of lost of sleep from the last two months. Then her brain kicked into gear.

Babies first to lower the noise level seemed a good place to start. She unwrapped Harrison, deftly changed his sodden nappy, which slowed the high-pitched roar to a hiccough, and re-wrapped him in a new bunny rug, before placing him back in his cot.

Then she did the same for Bailey and popped him in with his brother so the two tiny wrapped bundles lay facing each other with little frowns.

'Fadia. Sit up, honey. What's happened?' The young woman sobbed more dramatically into her sodden pillow and Carmen glanced around. 'What's happened?'

'The boys have fed every two hours since yesterday evening, I had little sleep, and Tom sent a note this morning to say he wouldn't come back.' She sniffed. 'I'm just so tired and I was going back to Zandorro anyway, but he was my last link to my husband and it makes me so sad.'

Carmen wondered if Zafar had had anything to do with Tom's blessed absence but the lack of sleep was definitely taking its toll. 'Of course I understand.'

Fadia wasn't listening. 'It will be good when I get to Zandorro. I'm not managing as well as I thought I would.'

Poor Fadia. And it was day three after two babies. 'You're being hard on yourself. Yesterday was too good and it's payback today. You've had a very tragic start to your family. On top of all that you have two babies that need you twenty-four seven. I think you've been amazing.'

Fadia sniffed tragically. 'But yesterday everything was going so well.'

'And today is a difficult day for you, plus after birth day three is a notorious time for getting the blues. We talked about that. With twins, the boys are hungry and feeding more often to bring your milk in. There's twice as many hormones floating around and with so little sleep of course you're going to feel fragile. You need help.'

'I thought I could manage.'

'And you are. But perhaps help from family is a good answer for now. Try not worry. I'm sure the last thing Tom wants is for you to lose sleep over him.' Though if Tom was as like her ex-husband as he looked, she doubted he thought of anyone but himself.

There was a knock on the door and Carmen's heart sank. Visitors were the last thing they needed now. When she opened the door it was Prince Zafar.

He narrowed his eyes at his cousin's red face and puffy eyes. 'Yusuf says there is a problem?'

'Good old Yusuf,' Carmen muttered under her breath.

As if to support his comment, both babies began to cry again and Carmen sighed. She wasn't even going to go near the Tom fiasco. 'Babies need feeding, mothers need sleep. It's a day for feeling blue.'

She looked at Fadia, who teetered on the verge of casting herself into her bed again. 'Fadia, perhaps you could wash your face while we mind your sons?'

Reluctantly, she heaved herself off her bed. Carmen picked up Harrison and handed him to Zafar. 'Here. See how you are with princes. I'll go you halves.' Then she picked up Bailey, tucked him into her shoulder and patted the little bottom.

She shouldn't have been surprised when Zafar did the same, calmly and confidently, and even cross little Harry seemed to understand the command to settle. He even twitched his mouth in a windy smile. 'You're very good at that.'

His look mocked her. 'Should I not be?'

She shrugged. Actually, she was surprised but the guy had to love kids if he'd studied paediatrics. She had the feeling this man could do anything. And do it well. 'I'd forgotten you specialised in paediatrics.'

'And will again, one day.' When my duties allow and I can stand the pain, he thought. Zafir stroked Bailey's bunny-wrapped back in slow, steady waves and stared down at the baby's soft dark hair. 'I had personal experience with children. I had a son. Samir.'

He could feel her eyes on him but he didn't look. He did not want her sympathy. So he kept stroking Bailey and speaking to the little downy head.

Still he didn't look at her. 'My wife and small son died in the same hijacking that almost killed me.'

He glanced out the window and added flatly, 'Of course I wish I too had died. You can imagine my horror when I actually woke up.'

Zafar felt the tightness of grief again in his chest. He wished he'd never come here to be reminded so forcibly. Why on earth was he telling her? His hands tightened as he looked down at the baby. 'I remember his weight in my arms.'

Carmen suddenly understood the bleakness she often saw in his face. 'That's terrible. I'm sorry.' She moistened her suddenly dry mouth. How much tragedy did this family hold?

He looked her way but he wasn't seeing her. His voice remained devoid of anything she could offer sympathy to, but the depth of his suffering reached out to her. 'Two years ago now, but I remember how to care for a baby.'

Fadia returned from the bathroom and Zafar ended the conversation as he spoke to her. 'You are exhausted. Now will you have a mothercraft nurse?'

Fadia looked at him, turned and ran back, sobbing, into the bathroom and shut the door.

Carmen didn't say anything. She patted her baby's back once more and laid him back in his cot before she turned to Fadia's bed and straightened it. She needed to do something with her hands or she'd strangle him.

'What? Nothing to say?'

She glared at him. Oohhh. She counted to three and at least her voice came out calm. 'Nothing you don't already know. You may have skills with babies but you're not that hot with new mums.'

He frowned. 'I do not understand her wish to be without help when she has had such difficulties.' His next comment she didn't expect. 'Or yours. I wish to speak of something else…'

His voice changed, heralding something she knew she wasn't going to like. Her instinct proved correct. 'Forgive me, but I have been told your husband proved a poor choice? This is correct?'

He looked anything but apologetic.

How did he know that? She felt sick. She didn't even want to think about how. 'Not something I wish to discuss.' Just what had he been doing poking into her affairs?

His gaze didn't waver. Mr Arrogance was back and of course he didn't stop there. 'And swindled you out of your home and left you with debts.'

This wasn't happening. 'Who told you that?'

Again he ignored her comment. 'You live in a slum area. Live alone, unprotected? Yusuf spoke to men who accosted you the other night.'

Carmen shook her head in disbelief and incredulous anger at his intrusion into her private life simmered up from her stomach and into her throat. The men in the alley. The smashed bottle. She did remember that incident. But it didn't matter. She would have managed. He'd had her followed? Carl had done that after she'd left him.

'How dare you? Neither of you have the right to intrude on my privacy.'

The wet washer of reality. Another horror of a man. And she'd be attracted. He didn't think like normal people. Never would. She wasn't sure who she was angrier with, him or herself, for being drawn to him.

He shrugged. 'Privacy can be bought.'

'Not my privacy, buster.' And to think she'd kissed him with abandon in a shed.

The arrogant sheik stood very much in evidence and she reminded herself he was just as high-handed about Fadia. No wonder she had misgivings about returning with him. No wonder she wanted Carmen to come and stand up for her. She lifted her head and glared. 'What an attractive person you are.'

His eyes narrowed. 'Sarcasm does not become you, Carmen.'

'Funny.' She couldn't remember being this angry. She sucked in air, trying to calm herself so that her words came out low and biting. 'Yet bullying suits you very well.'

Despite her low tone, anger vibrated in her voice and she wasn't sure she could contain it. She still wasn't sure if she was more wild with him or herself. A bitter exchange carried on in quiet voices. The air quivered with tension.

He brushed that off. 'I am not ashamed of my actions.'

She almost laughed in his face. 'Why am I not surprised?' She rolled her eyes.

He didn't like that. 'You would be wise to hold your tongue.'

So, she'd pushed him too far. Carmen stamped down the cowardly urge to do what she was told. Tough biscuits.

'Hold your own tongue, buster. I've met men like you before. I married an arrogant, self-important bully. And I won't be bullied again. Ever!'

She spun around and walked to the door before he could comprehend she'd actually walk out on him. 'I'm no woman in your harem. And I'm not in your employ.'

She called through the bathroom door, 'I'll be back later, Fadia,' and let herself out before he could stop her.

As she walked down the corridor to her room, anger bubbled and popped like a little lava pool from sudden volcanic eruption. She didn't do loss of control. Someone had to remain rational. She rarely did anger because she liked to be level-headed. That was how she'd escaped her marriage. Level head. Planning. What was it about this man that pushed all the buttons of high emotion?

Her eyes narrowed as she concentrated on any sound behind her of pursuit. Listened for the sound of the door opening again, but it didn't. She could feel Yusuf's frown follow her as she increased the distance between them, could admit she was ridiculously glad his chair was near the lifts and not positioned at her end of the corridor.

She should have shut the door to the midwife's room but she refused to have them think she was scared. She really did like the mums to feel they could poke their heads in any time. It wasn't quite the same when Yusuf appeared. She couldn't help the jump in her pulse rate.

Yusuf folded his arms. 'Prince Zafar wishes to see you in his suite.'

She didn't stand from her chair. 'Tell him I'm busy.'

His eyes narrowed and he took a step towards her. 'You will come now.'

And you are dreaming, Carmen thought. She stood up, casually reached for her handbag and rummaged around inside. 'Should I comb my hair?' She removed the small can of attacker spray a friend had given her when she'd first divorced.

'Do you know what this is? Paint. It won't hurt you but they say it takes a week to wash off.' Her voice remained pleasant. 'Please tell Prince Zafar I'm busy.'

Five minutes later her phone rang. Zafar sounded amused. She doubted Yusuf was.

'So I must come to you?'

'Or not. I really am busy.'

'I apologise. I did not intend to bully you.'

'Well, you tried!' An apology? She hadn't expected

that. She may have overreacted a tad. But the pain was still there from her shattered illusions in the past and perhaps a few from the present. 'I'm touchy on the subject of pushy men.' But she did feel less tense that he didn't seem angry at her defiance. And an apology was something her ex had never mastered.

Zafar went on. 'I wish to apologise more fully. And I still need to discuss Fadia with you. Perhaps we could find a time that you are not busy. Dinner? If I were to arrange a table in my suite for seven-thirty? That would be half an hour after you finish your shift tonight.'

Didn't he realise he was being arrogant and pushy again? Perhaps it was a failing with royalty as well as creeps. Shame he couldn't see her sarcastic salute.

'That would give you time to change.'

Unbelievable. Like she had a cocktail dress in her handbag? 'Change? From my uniform into my sarong and swimmers, you mean?'

There was silence. 'Whatever you wear will be acceptable.'

'Gee, thanks. But no thanks.'

He sighed. 'You are tiresome with your objections.'

'Heaven forbid.' She swallowed the hysterical laugh that wanted to escape. She needed to shut the lid on the box of memories he'd opened and a cosy dinner wouldn't help.

There was silence on the end of the phone. It went on until she was the one who felt like a petulant child. Not fair. To her own disgust she thought of poor Fadia, how much she needed her support, and relented. 'Oh, very well. I'll see what I can find.'

She put the phone down gently but her heart pounded

in a way that wasn't gentle at all. She should not have agreed.

But she had.

She could just picture herself sitting in the suite in her uniform, or her sarong, and she couldn't deny the fact that she didn't like the picture.

The last thing she needed to feel was at a disadvantage dressed like an employee or a beach bum.

She picked up the phone again and spoke to the best concierge in Sydney, Donna, her friend from downstairs, always good value and someone guaranteed to know the quickest place to buy anything.

'A cheap dress that looks good? There's a great specials bin in the boutique at the moment. I'll send something up in your size. No worries. Do it all the time for guests.'

The clock seemed to be going twice as fast as normal as the afternoon sped by in a blur of breastfeeding issues, baby weights and newborn bathing demonstrations.

When she visited Fadia the young woman seemed to have recovered her composure and Carmen wondered if, now that Tom was absent, Fadia would come into her own. Carmen had no doubt that Fadia had strength that would astound her cousin.

Perhaps Tom had played up to Fadia's emotions to keep the girl dependent. She hoped Prince Zafar didn't intend to continue the trend. Again she thought of her own marriage.

Her mind twisted and turned as she prepared to take blood from the twins for their newborn screening tests. Fadia grimaced for their discomfort and breastfed them one at a time to help distract them from the sting of the lancet prick.

When it was over they tucked the boys back into bed and Fadia shook her head in disbelief. 'But they didn't cry.'

'Because you fed them at the same time.'

'I'm glad it helped.' Then another worried frown creased her brows. 'When I go to Zandorro, if the results come back bad, how will they find me?'

So she'd decided. It would be hard here with her babies on her own and she couldn't help her instinct that Zafar was a much safer bet than a man like Tom. 'The results go to your doctor. We would find you and follow up.'

Fadia put her hand out. 'Are you sure there's no chance you could come with me? Just for a while?' Her dark eyes pleaded. 'You help without fuss. I would not be as nervous if you were with me. Once I'm back I know the older women will try to take over.'

Had Zafar told her to ask? 'I'm sorry, Fadia. I can't. I have my job here. But you will be strong.' Carmen gestured to the sleeping babies. 'For your boys. You're amazing and nobody can ever take that from you.'

She hugged Fadia. 'Maybe a mothercraft nurse from here isn't such a bad idea. Someone whose loyalties lie with you? I'm sure Zafar would agree.'

She shook her head. 'I want you. Just for a few weeks?'

Such imploring eyes and Carmen could feel herself weaken. Then she thought of Zafar. Of her response to him. Of being under his 'rule'. A disturbing thought.

But then so was Fadia without a champion if she needed one. 'I don't think I can. It's a long way to go for something a lot of people could do. I'll think about it but it's unlikely. I'm sorry. I'll see you in the morning. Make sure you ask the night midwife if you need help.'

By the time she'd written up her notes and handed over to her colleague, it was seven-fifteen.

Carmen used the midwife's bathroom to wash and pulled the new dress from the bag to check out the tag. Slashed price, non-iron and machine washable. She loved Donna.

Carmen shivered with the silky slide of fabric down her body and she hoped it wasn't an omen. Maybe she should wear her uniform. What was she doing anyway, trying to impress a prince with her bargain-bin clothes?

She shook her head at herself. No. She was dressing for herself and it looked good. Maybe the maroon fabric did plunge a little into her cleavage but that was fixed with the cream silk scarf Donna had added. The pair of slip-on half-heels were perfect and she'd even thrown in costume jewellery. God bless her favourite concierge.

At least she didn't feel like the poor relation any more.

Mascara and lipstick would do if she didn't want to be late. Carmen paused with lipstick in hand in front of the mirror. Did she want to be late?

She smiled at herself. She'd probably pulled enough tails today. In fact, she'd take her attacker dye.

'Evening, Yusuf.' The man's eyes glittered at her as he stood up to accompany her. 'I can find my own way.'

He bowed impassively. 'But I will accompany you.'

He didn't have to ask her to wait while he opened the heavy door at the top of the stairwell. It was funny how they all opted for the stairs now. She guessed she'd learned some of the rules at least.

While she waited she remembered the first time she'd stood here like this. Had it been only three days ago? So much had happened.

So much that her world might prove a little flat when all these unusual people moved on from her life.

In the hallway the other guard, still standing like before, watched them approach. She doubted he even leant against the wall when he was tired.

Yusuf knocked and the same woman opened it. *Déjà vu*. Except this time Carmen wondered if the woman was Zafar's concubine. She banished that thought because for some reason it spoiled her evening.

As she walked past the woman inclined her head in deference. Carmen frowned. She was pretty sure she hadn't done that last time.

She was still pondering when Zafar's door opened and he came through—in tailored slacks and a silk shirt. A very poor attempt at not looking like a million bucks.

'*As asaalum al aikum*. Peace be with you.' He smiled. Nice of him to translate for her. 'Good evening.'

'Now, why did I think you would be late?'

Carmen shrugged. 'Because you don't know me?'

'But I will,' he said quietly. He gestured to the cushions spread on the carpet beside a low table or a table and chairs on the balcony, then said more conversationally, 'Would you prefer to sit inside or out? Fatima will lay the table.'

She glanced out the door to the balcony, screened from other guests by a metal lattice and with a northern view over Coogee it would be criminal to waste.

Lots of air space around them if not physical distance. And she'd rather be at eyelevel with him on a chair.

'Outside.'

He nodded to Fatima, who picked up a wicker basket and moved outside, where she proceeded to produce everything needed, like Mary Poppins or, more appropriately, an Arabic genie, out of the bag. When the table was set she disappeared into the tiny kitchen and wheeled out a trolley with dishes of food.

Zafar picked up a bottle from a stand of ice. 'Perhaps I could pour you a drink while we wait. Champagne?'

Something to settle the butterflies that had landed in her stomach perhaps. It seemed he wasn't a strict Muslim, thank goodness, for the way she felt at the moment... 'Champagne would be lovely.'

He held the glass and she reached for it carefully, ridiculously anxious not to touch his fingers, until his eyes met hers. He knew. And with that one glance she knew he knew. She frowned, decided not to play the game and took it firmly. His fingers tingled against her own.

'Thank you.'

He turned away, but not before she could see his amusement.

Carmen looked at Fatima and took a couple of calming breaths. The servant had arranged dishes of food and napkins beside a huge flat dish of white rice, another with sliced lamb roast. She recognised the bowls of stuffed tomatoes, a dark and aromatic stew with lime-green beans wafted an amazing aroma her way, along with several dishes she didn't recognise. Surely far too much for just the two of them. Carmen looked away.

'Ah. Fatima is finished.' He tilted his head at his servant. 'Leave.' The woman bowed and left the room.

'Now, I find that offensive.' She'd thought she was talking to herself as she moved out to the balcony but apparently not under her breath enough.

'And you think I should care what you think?'

Carmen threw her head up but his eyes were crinkled with amusement. It seemed she was hilarious, Carmen thought mutinously.

She must have looked murderous because he held out is hands. 'I'm sorry. Couldn't resist. I can almost see you with your can of Mace pointed at Yusuf.'

She narrowed her eyes at him. 'Mace is illegal. This is dye for self-defence.'

This impossibly handsome man, ridiculously wealthy, accustomed to his servants obeying his every command and probably accustomed to women falling at his feet. He must find it strange to be less revered in another culture. It must be strange when he was with her.

He was watching her. Still with amusement in his eyes. 'Did you bring it?'

Now what was he talking about? 'I'm sorry?'

'Your pressure-pack protection.'

She smiled. 'You'll never know.'

For a moment she thought he was going to ask to see her purse. He didn't and it felt as though she'd won a small victory.

It made her wonder why he didn't become more impatient with her lack of amenability. 'How can you be normal at times and so arrogant at others?'

'With you?' So he had read her mind again. 'I'm still working that out. It is novel for me. I was born into privilege, which I assure you comes with responsibility, but I studied in England and latterly Australia. You have very good schools, a school system that levels a young man so he understands your abhorrence of our feudal system.'

He shrugged. 'I understand a little of the differences between you and the women in my culture.' He pulled out her chair and waited for her to sit.

'But I am first of all a prince of my country and second a travelled man. I was angry today and not without power. Perhaps it would be wise for you to remember that.'

He sat opposite and she took a sip of her drink to fill the silence between them. When she put her drink down she did have something to say. 'I don't like it that you had me investigated.'

He nodded. 'I noticed.' Well, at least she'd got that point across. He went on. 'It is as well we discuss this now.'

He leaned across to top up her glass but she covered it with her hand. 'I need my wits with you.'

He put the bottle back and she noticed he wasn't drinking. 'I'm flattered.' He didn't look it.

'Don't be.' She thought he was going to follow up on her comment but in the end he changed tack.

He hitched the sleeve of his right hand and gestured to the food. 'Eat.'

Carmen carefully transferred some rice and a tomato to her plate with her knife and fork. She couldn't bring herself to use her fingers.

There was something erotically earthy about a man eating slowly with his fingers. Zafar watched her. 'Try this.' He picked up a sliver of something that turned out to be aromatic lamb, which she obediently tasted, but the taste was nothing to the feel of his fingers against her lips and her stomach kicked at that sensation.

'Please don't feed me.'

Zafar could not take his eyes off her. He savoured the play of light across her skin as her expression changed like the ocean in front of them. Her sense of humour amused him—she made him smile more than he'd smiled for a long time—and her anger was transparent because she made no attempt to disguise it when he had annoyed her. A new experience for a woman to show her displeasure and probably good for his soul. No doubt a concept that would have amused his departed mother.

The change in his thinking had continued since he'd witnessed Carmen help that woman give birth in the park. He was touched by the way she had cared for the frightened young woman. He wasn't sure why it had made such an impact on him. Then she spoke of it. 'I rang the hospital today to see how our mother and baby are doing.'

Had she read his mind? If she had, she would have read more than she'd bargained for. He bit back a smile. 'And are they well?'

She smiled at him and he took the gift of that and stored it away in a corner of his cold heart.

'You know they are. You checked as well. I understand they haven't seen a flower arrangement so exotically expensive for years. Jenny feels very special.'

He watched her taste the rice and an expression of unexpected pleasure crossed her face at the subtle tang she would not be used to. 'I'm glad she liked it. I am not just the arrogant bully you think me.' He held up his hand. 'And I do beg your forgiveness for that. Holding my nephew brought back the reality of my loss and I behaved badly towards you. I apologise.'

She looked less than convinced but inclined her head. 'I accept your apology. So what else do you do when you're not being an ogre or having people investigated?'

'Tsk. So hard on me.'

She shrugged, unrepentant, and to his horror he wanted to pull her into his arms and seduce her bravado away. How could he forget the pain from the past? The time was not right for that, could never be, while his role lay in the royal household.

Where were his barriers? His safeguards from creating a relationship?

He should be thinking of more important things. 'My investigation of you was carried out because I wish to offer you a short tenure as Fadia's assistant.'

CHAPTER SIX

SOMETHING was going on in his mind that was outside the conversation. Carmen could sense it. Physically feel it. Even discern his slight withdrawal. She opened her mouth to refuse but he held up his hand and to her utter disgust she waited obediently.

'And I need to be sure she and her sons would be safe with you.' Now he paused to wait for her comment.

'So I can talk now?'

He nodded good-naturedly and she realised she was in danger of sounding ill-tempered. How did he put her in the wrong when he was the chauvinist?

Carmen straightened the scarf around her shoulders as if to gather her control closer to her chest then counted to three. She spoke in her usual calm voice. 'I see her need. But I'm a midwife, not a mothercraft nurse. I'm afraid you've wasted your money on investigations.'

'You are good at your job. Fadia likes you and needs a friend.' He shrugged. 'So that is enough for me. I wish to secure your services.'

'It seems she lost a friend today.' She tilted her head at him.

'Did she?'

'I gather Tom is not in the picture any more?'

Zafar questioned her blandly. 'Is he not?'

She decided he looked lazily ruthless. And disgustingly attractive with it. So now she was attracted to dangerous men? What was happening to her? 'I'm asking you. He is conspicuous by his non-appearance since the one time outside Fadia's door.'

No answer to her question. Just one of his own. 'So you assume I have done something?'

She just raised her eyebrows. 'Don't look so surprised.' As if. He didn't look surprised at all.

He shrugged. 'It is my intention to be aware of things that are my concern.' He added some lamb to her plate.

Now they were down to the nitty-gritty. 'Then be concerned for your cousin's state of mind. With Tom off the scene she will be alone again and she has already lost her husband. Safeguards need to be in place. She's frightened she'll lose control to the palace servants and maybe even access to her sons.'

He leaned forward and pinned her with his full attention. 'I thank you for sharing that.' He shook his head, obviously pained. 'I would not do that. I have learned the difficult choice my mother had to make. I've lost my own son and know that feeling of emptiness.' His sincerity made her throat tighten.

He went on. 'I will champion Fadia and only want what is best for her in this difficult time. Hence the real need for you to consider my request that you accompany her.'

And Fadia had pleaded as well. Carmen pushed temptation behind her and looked away. There were too many variables for that course. Too many dangers, and one of the most dangerous sat opposite. 'I've already told you I have two jobs.'

He brushed that aside. 'And you're almost too tired to do either. You work at least seventy hours a week on mixed shifts. Why? For money. Ridiculous.'

See, she admonished herself. He'd been checking up again. 'That's none of your business.'

He ignored that. Perhaps he ignored everything people said that he didn't agree with. 'I believe you have holiday leave owing?'

Yes, but none she could take without a big drop in pay. Why was she discussing this? 'I suppose you have that in writing from my employers?'

'I have verbal confirmation, which is sufficient.' He shrugged that inconvenience away. 'What if I offered to clear all your debts for the sake of two weeks work in Zandorro with Fadia?'

She'd forgotten he'd known about the debts. It was obscene to have that much money to tempt people with. He was forcing her hand.

Or was she a fool to throw away the chance of a new life for two weeks work with a woman she wanted to help?

Could she leave Australia? Go to a country where she couldn't even speak the language or understand the customs? Could she trust him? Her nerve endings stood up and waved in distress.

'Well, what would you say?

'I'd say I sold my soul to the devil.'

He tossed his head. 'You are being dramatic.' His eyes no longer smiled. 'But would you say yes?'

She stared back at him. Could feel herself weakening

under his gaze. Bowing before his will when she didn't want or mean to. She knew how this could end. 'No.'

'Why not.'

She knew the answer to that one too. 'You're arrogant enough while you have no power over me. I imagine you'd be intolerable as my employer.'

His gaze bored into hers. The food lay forgotten between them. 'You don't know that.'

'I'm not stupid.'

He smiled at her and she almost smiled back. 'No, you're not, but what is it most that worries you?'

Everything, nothing, nothing she could pin down. 'I could find myself adrift in a strange country without any job.'

He didn't deny her fears. Just rang a bell and Fatima reappeared and began to clear the table.

Carmen was left in limbo. Confused at the sudden halt in the conversation.

No doubt it was all a part of the Eastern customs of taking one's time with negotiations. She was more of the thrash-it-out-and-finish-it kinda gal but there wasn't much she could do.

Time passed as options kaleidoscoped in her head in confusing patterns. She was no nearer to a decision when Fatima had finished and poured small gold cups of thick coffee, which she placed beside them. At Zafar's command she left a jewelled coffee pot in the centre alongside a tray of tiny baklava.

'Coffee?'

She nodded and he poured. 'Please, finish the conversation.'

He took a sip and held his cup. 'If I promised that wouldn't happen? If I paid what I promised into your bank account here, now, and you would keep that even if the job didn't work out? Plus a return air fare you could use at any time.'

Stop tempting me. Ridiculous offer. Carmen bit her lip. Surely he was joking. 'Nobody would pay that.'

'You say I am a nobody?' The cup went down and his chin went up. Oops. Insulted him again. Every inch the prince. Too easy to offend. She watched him regather his patience and go on.

'Supplying money is not hard. Finding people to trust is.'

She could see his point. But that was the crunch. She didn't trust him. Or perhaps herself. 'You may have decided to trust me but it's not mutual.'

He brushed that side. 'That is not necessary. I have given my word.'

She didn't laugh. Could see he meant it. Just wondered if his interpretation differed from hers. What was she thinking, even considering this? She wouldn't fit in. Then again, what did she have to fit in with? 'And what of your henchman? Yusuf hates me.'

That perplexed him. 'This worries you because…?'

She guessed it was unlikely Yusuf would do anything his master wouldn't like. But she didn't need any more pressure. Doing it for money was bad enough. 'Let's not talk about it any more. I'll think about your offer.'

To her relief, he agreed to leave the subject for the moment.

Night had fallen. She wasn't sure when that had happened. A ship with lights blazing passed across the horizon out to sea. Heading off to who knew where. Did she want to do that? Even contemplate leaving everything she knew to accompany these people she didn't really understand?

They carried their coffee inside and talked desultorily about where they'd both travelled, and of course the things he'd seen were different no matter if the destinations were the same.

Time passed insidiously. She grew more comfortable with him, though she seemed to do most of the talking. He made her laugh with stories about his internship in Sydney, and she with her midwifery escapades returned the favour, until it was unexpectedly late.

She glanced at her watch. He saw her eyes widen, and she jumped to her feet. 'I must go.' As if suddenly woken from a dream, she needed distance from.

Zafar, too, glanced at his watch. He'd savoured her company, understood her a little, wondered about the destructive power of her bad marriage, could admit to himself there was danger in knowing too much and that it was not just a culmination of abstinence. The moral issues of being attracted to a new woman, someone other than the woman he had vowed to stay faithful to, and where it led—that was what worried him.

He needed to think this through. Maintain distance. Especially if she agreed to join them. 'I apologise for keeping you late.'

He believed she would come. Probably not for him but because she would worry about Fadia. And that was where he would apply the pressure. 'One question.'

She paused and turned on her way to the door as he caught up with her. 'Do you have a valid passport?'

'I haven't agreed to go but, yes, I renewed it last year. I used to travel a lot with my parents when I was young.'

'Very well. You have less than a day to decide. We leave for Zandorro tomorrow afternoon at four. If you do decide to help Fadia, there are things we must arrange.'

'Don't count on it.'

'We will see.' He lifted her hand and she realised what he was going to do before it happened. Tried to pull her hand back but he held her firmly and she didn't tug—actually, couldn't tug because her arm wasn't listening. Her mouth dried and she tried not to lean towards him. Head down, still watching her face with his dark eyes, he turned her wrist and brushed her skin with those wicked lips. Goose-bumps scattered like drops from a fountain until her body overloaded and she shivered.

He smiled as he straightened. '*Fi aman illah.* Go in God's keeping.'

'Goodnight.'

Carmen didn't know who to turn to. She never asked for advice, something her mother had quizzed her on all through her childhood and later in her teens, but this was too big a risk without some insurance and someone knowing where she was. And she was running out of time.

As soon as she left the presidential suite she rang Tilly. Her friend lived within walking distance of the hotel and they agreed to meet in the bar for a nightcap to discuss the job.

Tilly arrived with her fiancé, Marcus Bennett, head of Obstetrics and the man who had been there for Fadia's second son's birth. Carmen decided it was a good thing having friends in high places.

Marcus dived straight in. 'Tilly says you've had a job offer you're not sure of. With Zafar.'

'Yes.' She hadn't expected this. 'Do you know him?'

'As well as someone can know him. Sure. We did uni together, he worked at the Royal when I was there, then specialised in paediatrics. He may be a prince but we usually meet for a meal when he's in Australia.'

Tilly's jaw dropped. 'You didn't say he was a prince.'

Carmen brushed that aside. 'He's a sheikh. There are lots of desert kingdoms and he's not directly in line for the throne.'

Marcus smiled. 'I think he is but not in the first instance. So he's our twin lady's cousin?'

'Estranged. Apparently the twins are too close to succession to be unmonitored. He's here to help Fadia get back to her country.'

'She's a widow, isn't she?' Marcus looked at Tilly, who nodded.

Carmen's chair faced Reception, unlike the others', who had their backs to it, and she saw Zafar walk in through the front door with his henchman. So he'd gone out after she'd left. To do what? She let the conversation flow around her as she tried to halt the colour in her cheeks.

She put her head down but he'd seen her and even from this distance she could tell he was studying who she was with. She glanced at Tilly.

Marcus's voice drifted back in. 'Wasn't there a friend involved, helping Fadia?'

'Umm.' Carmen concentrated on the conversation. 'The friendship cooled, I think. Either not a good friend or I did wonder if Zafar may have bought him off.'

Tilly, oblivious to Carmen's discomfort, was relishing the idea. She hunched her shoulders and lowered her voice theatrically. 'Or he could have threatened him.'

'No.' Carmen shook her head. 'I think there was more to it than that. Zafar has power.'

Marcus laughed. 'You girls watch too much TV. Zafar's a bit stiff but he's an honourable man. One who's had his share of tragedy.'

Carmen listened to the absolute belief in Marcus's voice and let her breath out. That was lucky because he was coming that way.

She'd just needed to hear the words before the topic of their conversation came within hearing. 'So you're saying his job offer would be genuine and reliable.'

'I would say so. Yes.' Marcus nodded emphatically.

Carmen wanted it spelt out. 'And if I don't come back, you'll ask him where I am and he'd tell the truth?'

He nodded again. 'I believe so.'

That was it, then. She couldn't not take the offer because it would solve all her money problems in a couple of weeks. She'd just hope she didn't inherit other dilemmas worse than money issues. 'Thank you. I really appreciate your advice.'

Tilly rubbed her hands. 'So when do I get to meet this prince?' Just in time for Zafar to hear. Carmen winced and looked up.

'Perhaps you could introduce me to your friends?' Zafar stood above them, quite splendid in black. Yusuf, three steps behind, watched Carmen impassively.

Marcus stood and turned and Zafar smiled with delight. He held out his hand. 'Well met, Marcus.'

'Zafar.' Marcus gestured proudly. 'Allow me to present my fiancée, Matilda. Tilly's a friend of Carmen's.'

Tilly was blinking and Carmen smiled sourly to

herself. She knew how that felt. Zafar lifted her hand
and kissed Tilly's fingers. Not her wrist, a little voice
gloated, and Carmen frowned at herself.

'Congratulations on your engagement. You are both
fortunate people. Of course any friend of Carmen's is
a friend of mine.'

Yeah, right. Carmen watched Tilly's eyes glaze over
and felt slightly better that even a woman deeply in love
could be knocked askew by Zafar's charisma.

Marcus filled the awkward silence. 'Carmen says
you've offered her a position for a couple of weeks in
Zandorro until Fadia's babies are settled.'

Zafar glanced at Carmen. 'I am glad she is considering my offer.'

She met his enquiring look with a bland face. 'I'm
setting up a safety net.'

Zafar raised his brows and spoke to Marcus as if
the girls weren't there. 'These Australian midwives are
feisty, are they not?'

Marcus smiled down at Tilly. 'I'm living dangerously
and loving it.'

The conversation moved on between the men and
Zafar and Marcus became immersed in the topic of
hospitals. Tilly caught Carmen's eye as they both sat
down. She winked and Carmen had to smile.

'So?' Tilly whispered. 'You going?'

'I guess so.' She shrugged. 'I feel better that he
knows Marcus and there's a big bonus that will clear
my feet and then some.'

'I'm glad. You're killing yourself here and you've
always enjoyed travel.'

'Not in the royal entourage.'

Tilly grinned. 'Why not?'

Carmen had to laugh. Maybe it was exciting to think about being whisked somewhere without effort.

Suddenly it was easier to let go of a little of the responsibility to work everything out for herself, something she hadn't done for a long time, and when she glanced across at the men Zafar was watching her.

She wondered what he was thinking.

So these were her friends. Zafar wanted to drop his arm around her shoulders like Marcus was doing with his woman. He wanted to take her wrist and savour the feel of her skin, the scent of orange on his lips, and pull her back into his body.

These thoughts shouldn't intrude when the information he'd found out tonight was of such national importance and here he was fantasising about a woman.

Such poor timing to feel alive again.

A time of great danger approached and he had failed to keep those he cared about safe before.

CHAPTER SEVEN

THE next day proved hectic after a whirlwind of formalities made more intricate with Carmen joining the party at the last minute. Carmen only had time to glimpse Coogee beach recede in the distance as they drove away she was too busy checking her handbag to make sure she had everything. Her leave from work had been smoothed by the fact she hadn't taken any holiday for so long. She'd been waved away with little censure of the short notice. Carmen couldn't help but wonder if Zafar had spoken to them.

The baby hotel had said to return when she could. All too easy. Or maybe nobody would miss her?

Even Donna had said, 'Enjoy, lucky thing'.

Carmen couldn't help feeling she'd been manipulated by a force that was stronger than she'd realised. Zafar.

They'd left the hotel in two cars, which shouldn't have surprised Carmen, and maybe added that tiny hint of needed reality, being relegated to the secondary car with the twins and Fadia. What did she expect? To ride with Zafar? Of course she was a glorified nanny.

Thankfully the babies were remarkably settled and Fadia seemed mostly relieved with her decision.

Now the decision had been made, Carmen was glad

she'd come to support the young mother and help her as
she became reacquainted with her homeland. Despite
Zafar's assertion that he would not force the widow into
anything she didn't want, Carmen knew Fadia was worried.

They both knew, though, that he would have other
matters to distract him.

Carmen tried to put herself in the young mum's
shoes. 'Are you worried about returning to Zandorro?'

Fadia nodded. 'A little. It's been six years. And I'm
nervous about meeting my grandfather again. He is a
powerful man. But Zandarro is becoming a more pro-
gressive country, not as traditional as our neighbours,
which causes friction between the two countries. I hope
it continues that way.'

They both pondered the differences between a
monarchy-ruled Arabic state and the relaxed vibe of
Coogee.

Carmen smiled. 'Might be a little removed from what
we've been used to.'

The short trip to the airport passed silently and once
they arrived in Zafar, or more likely his staff, had arranged for them to slip through diplomatic transfer to
their private jet.

'Would you like something to drink before take-off?'
The exquisitely dressed hostess appeared from nowhere
and Carmen looked at Fadia.

'No, thank you, we're fine.'

The woman inclined her head. 'We'll be taking off
in ten minutes.'

Not too long to ponder her decision, then. Surely
she was doing the right thing. Carmen shivered as last
regrets surfaced. It was momentous to allow herself to

be whisked off to an unfamiliar country with people who played by their own rules.

Fadia seemed disinclined to talk and Carmen let her be. All she could do for the moment was check the babies and later through the flight ensure they were fed, changed and settled.

Carmen glanced across at the boys in their capsules strapped to the opposite seats. Two little heads tilted towards each other, matching frowns as if they were squinting to see through the hard plastic sides of their beds to see each other. Maybe reassure each other during their first trip in a plane.

She smiled at flights of fancy and gradually she realised she was actually relieved to be there, and even excited by the prospect of visiting a new country and finding out more about these fascinating people. Just so long as she wasn't focussed on a particular fascinating man.

Zafar had fulfilled his obligations and now it was for Carmen to fulfil her own. And she would, diligently, and she was certain Fadia would be better away from the horrible Tom.

'So why did your mother leave Zandorro?'

'When I was fifteen she divorced my father. She never wanted to go back and here I am doing just that. I hope it's the right thing to do.'

'Did you never want to go back at all before this?'

'Perhaps but it is a big thing to lose my new identity in a country I loved. I see the advantage for my sons in Zandorro, but wonder what is there for me. I am constrained by my station. When I left last time I was betrothed to a man I never saw. Thankfully my mother paid back the bride price from Australia so he has no hold on me.'

Carmen struggled to understand the concept of arranged marriage, something well outside her experience. Everything Fadia spoke of was new and interesting. She encouraged Fadia to talk. 'So where did you meet your husband?'

The girl smiled sadly. 'At university in Sydney. We were both studying pharmacy and he was three years older than me.' She shrugged tragic shoulders. 'We fell in love but now he has gone without even seeing his babies. Killed by a hit-and-run driver. Without even knowing I was pregnant. All I have left of him are my sons.

'I think I will try to sleep.' Fadia rolled over in the pod the hostess had prepared for her and Carmen gazed thoughtfully at her back. Good idea.

Zafar was in for an interesting time with his cousin and she just hoped he had some plan for long-term support.

They arrived in Dubai twelve hours after take-off for refuelling and the high temperature shimmered off the tarmac outside the window. Robed figures seemed to float around their plane, maybe on flying carpets of heat, Carmen thought fancifully as the engines and fuel tanks were tended too.

Zafar had alighted without glancing at her and she stifled disappointment, not for his company, honestly, but for not having a chance to at least see the airport. She consoled herself that she would see that on her way back in a couple of short weeks.

Both women had slept well between feeds. Fadia

and the boys' routine had become swift and efficient at feeding time with Carmen's help, so despite the distance travelled Carmen at least felt rested, pampered and ready for her first sight of the desert.

Mid-afternoon Dubai time they prepared to leave for Zandorro, and Zafar boarded the plane just before they took off.

Fadia followed her gaze. 'He does not even see us now that he has achieved what he came for.'

Carmen glanced at her. 'Wasn't that the only reason he was in Australia? To find you?'

Still she watched her cousin. 'And bring my sons home. He is a man who gets what he wants.' Now she looked at Carmen with warning in her eyes. 'My mother used to say a Zandorran man uses any means needed.'

Carmen glanced away from the concern in Fadia's eyes. 'Do you really think that?' She didn't share Fadia's concern. She was fine and not afraid of Zafar. She stared out the window but all she could see was the reflection of her own face. She knew Zafar's will was strong, but so was hers.

They'd left the azure blue of the ocean and soared over mountains craggy with rock and then the golden desert stretched as far as the eye could see, undulating like a sleeping monster, shimmering with stored sunlight that would cool quickly.

'It's stark yet beautiful.' Carmen began a new topic, shelving her own unease in the relief that at least she and Fadia had each other.

'The desert has great majesty. But it is a furnace by day and freezing at night. I think I prefer the sand of Coogee Beach.'

Fadia's comment revealed her ambivalence about

her return. Then she winced uncomfortably because her bodice was bulging at the front of her dress and Carmen just wanted to hug her—carefully. No problems about the boys going hungry but it looked very tight and painful in Fadia's body at the moment.

'Another twenty-four hours and you'll be much more comfortable again. I'll ask for another cold pack.' She raised her hand and the hostess appeared within seconds.

They'd been sliding cold sports packs down the front of Fadia's dress and Carmen had even managed to draw a smile at least once at the relief against poor Fadia's hot and aching breasts.

'Is it nearly time to feed them again?'

'Not quite. Both boys have their eyes closed. Probably another half an hour before they wake.' Fadia nodded and closed her eyes as well.

Carmen glanced at the boys tucked into their travel capsules sound asleep, and looked out the window again. She'd travelled a little with her parents but those happy days seemed from another century. Everything had changed when she'd married and her parents had died. She just wished she'd chosen more wisely or at least chosen a man of honour.

Did Zafar have honour? Marcus had seemed to think so and Carmen doubted she would be there if her gut feeling hadn't reassured her. Why did she feel reassured by a man she didn't know well? Was that how she'd made her last mistake? She winced. No. It wasn't like that because she wasn't getting involved with Zafar. She knew better now.

There was no doubt Zafar had changed since they'd left the hotel and not only into flowing white robes. He'd

distanced himself from her, created a barrier through
which he didn't see or hear little people like her.

She wondered if there'd been more to the Tom saga
than she'd been told. Big surprise there she hadn't been
included. She was really having difficulty with this servant attitude she needed to get. Since they'd left it was
more obvious she had slid down the totem pole.

His persona of Prince who travelled with entourage,
immersed in business documents at the front of the
plane, was daunting even for her. It seemed obvious
his plan was that she'd take the whole problem of Fadia
and her sons off his hands until the girl settled into
Zandorron life.

Then again, who was she to complain of that because
he'd paid handsomely for just such a purpose? And she'd
sold her soul to clear her debts and start a new life. As
long as she didn't throw her body—or her heart—into
the bargain, it was worth it.

Carmen wished she didn't feel so unsettled by the
man underneath the trappings yet that attraction seemed
to grow insidiously despite her reluctance. Those wild
unplanned moments in the storm were hard to banish,
especially when she could see him up at the front of the
plane.

Her gaze strayed to the back of his head, the glimpse
of his aristocratic profile as he turned to speak to the
stewardess, the distant deep timbre of his voice. She
felt herself warm at the memory of the way he'd kissed
her, held her in his arms. Was she mad? What possessed
her to have followed him to a land where his power was
absolute? She breathed in and out slowly, three times,
and reminded herself to relax. Calm. She was still in

control and would just have to be careful. She was just feeling a little overwhelmed.

It was all such a surreal experience, travelling with Zafar. Her father had been worldly but Zafar was princely and there was a huge difference. She suspected that clothed even in rags he would still be commanding, and she couldn't deny she felt drawn to the man regardless of his station. She dragged her eyes away from him again. Drawn but immune.

She'd be totally professional, cool and collected. And she was not going to think about the way he had kissed her or why.

Zafar put down the papers he'd been battling to concentrate on and tried not to think about kissing Carmen. Or summoning the midwife to his on-board bedroom and seeing just what could happen. As if stepping onto the plane meant the time of pretending he was not fiercely attracted to her was past.

While most of his attendants had dozed during the long flight he'd prowled the cabin, had looked down at her as she'd slept in her pod, realised it was the first time he was privy to that view and vowed to himself he would have at least one night where he could drink his fill of the sight.

He could picture her now, her thick lashes curled on her cheek, that beautiful mouth soft in repose instead of militant the way he often saw it. The blanket, fallen to her waist, had left her vulnerable, but that strangely only made him lift it to cover her. Not like him at all.

He smiled at the memory and then other memories flickered like an old-fashioned movie. That first drift of orange blossom from her skin in the lift. They said that scent was the only true memory. He could very easily remember that first glance of hers, a basic recognition he hadn't been able to deny, and that wild kiss in the storm had rocked him. He remembered that with clarity.

Then the cameo moment she'd hugged the woman in the park—imparting her strength to her like she had to him during his weakness in the elevator, a moment he still didn't understand.

Interesting, phobia-wise, this morning when he'd unconsciously pressed the button and descended to check out of his suite. It seemed that his aversion to lifts had been put to rest. Because of her? Or because he was moving on and creating new moments of life instead of dwelling on death? Even his fear of heights had receded a little.

Not huge events but remarkable and requiring thought.

Still, there remained a lot on his mind. Fadia's ability to settle in Zandorro, the kidnap attempt Yusuf had discovered with Fadia's 'friend' just a weakling pawn in a larger plan. He'd quashed that risk but information had been gained that put his grandfather—in fact, his entire family—at risk as well.

Yet a corner of his mind had been building with anticipation for the moment he had Carmen in his country, his palace, the chance to show her the sights and sounds and scents of Zandorro. To see her smile.

Normally he worked right through these flights.

'Can I get you anything, Excellency?' Yusuf hovered.

'No. Rest yourself.' Yusuf nodded and subsided but

when Zafar glanced once more at Carmen he noticed his manservant's eyes follow his.

Another memory clicked. She was right. She was not a favourite with his man. He would need to watch that. He fixed his gaze on Yusuf's face and spoke softly and clearly. 'But I will hold you personally responsible if she is not happy in the palace.'

Inscrutable, Yusuf nodded. His man had allies in the palace but Zafar had many more.

They landed not long before the sun set above the surrounding mountains outside the main city. The waiting limousines, complete with baby capsules, whisked them through several miles of desert hills to the massive gates and into the turreted city tucked behind a towering stone wall.

Dark faces peered at them from doorways as the vehicles climbed curved alleys and Carmen acknowledged with a sinking heart it would be difficult to find the way out again. She turned away from the window. That was okay. Really it was. She would be fine. She'd be able to leave any time she wanted. Zafar had promised.

Thankfully she was distracted as they rounded a bend and there ahead of them shone the palace as if positioned to receive the final light in the country through a break in the mountains. She couldn't help her indrawn breath.

Rooftops shimmered in a blanket of precious metal vying for space in the skyline with domes, towers and minarets reflecting the sun. Golden turrets glistened and one soaring tower in the middle with arched windows and a spire that reached for the sky watched over all.

'It's beautiful. Look at that tower.'

Fadia actually smiled at her enthusiasm. 'Yes, it is lovely.' They both glanced again at the magnificent building.

Harrison stirred and yawned and Bailey opened his eyes and blinked. Even Fadia's tiny sons seemed touched by the moment.

'Your babies sense something's happening.' Carmen leant over and patted their blankets but it was unnecessary. The boys didn't cry. Just lay in their capsules awake and alert as their car pulled up behind Prince Zafar's and a solemn manservant, accompanied by two older men, opened their door.

Two older women stood behind the men and Carmen could only guess they were there to help with the babies. The castle steps loomed away to the huge front door at the top and a long line of servants stood waiting to catch a glimpse of the royal heirs.

'You take Bailey, I'm taking Harrison.' Fadia had decided no stranger would carry her boys and Carmen was glad to see her eyes brighten with intent. 'They can take the bags.'

Carmen obligingly leaned across and extricated Harrison from his capsule and handed him to his mother then lifted Bailey for herself. 'No problem.'

'How did my cousins and their mother travel?' More softly. 'And you?' Zafar stood outside the car, waiting for them to alight. He was looking at her, not the others, and she could feel her cheeks warm.

Had he grown taller again or was it just the backdrop of the palace that made him seem larger than life? He was waiting.

'We travelled well.' He didn't look convinced. 'We were very comfortable.

'I am sorry I did not speak to you.' His cynical smile lifted the hair on her arms. 'I had things on my mind.'

His scrutiny pinked her cheeks more. Maybe she was wrong and she wasn't invisible. She felt herself blush and frowned at him.

He nodded. 'We will discuss this later. Rest today. We visit the King tomorrow.' He moved away to be greeted by the dignitaries lined above them.

Carmen looked across at Fadia, who was only now alighting, and the young mum's wary mood seemed improved by the excitement of their arrival. Perhaps she'd have a chance to talk to Zafar about that later. For the moment it seemed they had to run the gauntlet of the stares.

To Carmen's relief they were whisked in a huddle past the greeting party and into the palace while Zafar remained behind. Carmen wondered just how powerful this man was.

Carmen, Fadia and the boys were shown to a whole wing of the palace that had been turned over to them. Carmen's room was sumptuously decorated, pleasantly cool, and looked out over a tiled courtyard graced by a tinkling fountain. It was much grander than she had anticipated and with a sinking feeling she realised how small her voice would be amongst these people who didn't have to speak in her language if they didn't want to. Just what had she got herself into?

Then she straightened her shoulders. Not the right attitude if she wanted to help Fadia keep control of her boys and her life. And that was why she was there.

She thought wryly that she'd never had a room so

huge or opulent. The boys' room took up almost a quarter of their floor, nestled as it was between those of the two women.

A maidservant dressed in flowing chiffon pants and overshirt bowed and offered to put away her clothes. Carmen glanced down at the one small case she'd brought and shook her head with a smile. 'I think I'll manage, thank you.'

She knew her few toiletries would be lost in the marble bathroom and her clothes would hang pitifully in the cavernous walk-in closet. She needed to remember they'd all fit back perfectly into her one-bedroom flat when she went home. A much-needed dose of reality.

When she crossed the expanse of the room to peer into the closet there were half a dozen silk camisoles in varying lengths, sleeveless, short-sleeved and long-, all loose with matching trousers in soft shades of blue and green and lemon, and even a longer black version.

'His Excellency said you may wish for more comfortable clothes. Until the palace seamstress has your measurements she has sent up these.' The girl cast an expert eye over Carmen. 'I'm sure they will look very pretty.'

'I'll probably wear my own clothes.'

The young girl smiled and bowed her head. 'As madam wishes. Excellency said it is the young nursemaids who will help so it is I and my sister who will be your assistants whenever you wish for the young princes.'

'Thank you. I will tell Princess Fadia.'

When the girl left Carmen peered through the open door to the boys' room where Harrison was yawning and Bailey lay wide awake in his huge cot. Her feet sank into the luxurious carpets that overlaid each other like pools of shimmering colour. It seemed sacrilegious to walk on them.

'At least you boys can spend a bit of time lying next to each other. Your beds are huge.'

Deftly she undid Bailey's nappy and popped him in Harry's bed unwrapped and legs kicking while she did the same for his brother. Then she laid them side by side and watched them turn their heads towards each other. Harry touched Bailey's face and Bailey seemed to smile as Harry kicked him.

Fadia's room door opened and the new mum came in. She looked tired but a small smile lit her face as she saw her boys together.

Carmen gently drew her over to the boys. 'Look. I swear your sons are more handsome every day. And there's only us here and two young girls who will do as you wish. Everything will work out perfectly.'

'I hope so. I'm glad you're here but when you go I will be alone. I hope they won't marry me off like a parcel.' She clutched Carmen's sleeve. 'I miss my husband. I miss my life.'

So Fadia was feeling the weight of the palace too. 'Of course you do. But perhaps for now this is better than being alone on the other side of the world. Anything could happen to you there.'

The girl nodded. 'My boys are safe. That is good.'

'Zafar promised you would have choice in your future. I believe him.' He hugged her. 'You're a wonderful mother. Your husband must be smiling at your beautiful boys.'

'I agree.'

They both turned at the unexpected empathy from

Zafar as he entered the boys' room and crossed to Fadia. Kiri, the maid, followed him with a tray of light refreshments. 'I am sorry for your loss, Fadia, and know it is hard for you to come back here.'

Fadia turned tear-filled eyes towards him and nodded. 'We will see how good your word is.'

Carmen winced and glanced at him, not sure what he would do. She couldn't help feeling uneasy. It was blatant disrespect for his authority—in public—and the maid's gasp ensured that more than those in the room would hear of it.

Since her arrival she'd become more aware by the hour of the difference in power in the palace. From what the maid had said, Zafar's authority seemed almost as great as his grandfather's and at this moment his face seemed chiselled from the same stone as the mountains she'd seen on the way in. His eyes narrowed as he watched his cousin escape.

Unable to stop herself, Carmen dived into the breach of protocol. 'She's been away from Zandorro a long time. Of course she is upset about being here.'

He raised haughty eyebrows then clapped his hands and the maid ran from the room. He turned back to Carmen. 'She does not need your championing. She is as royal as I.' His brows dropped lower. 'Why look at me like that? As if I would throw her in irons?'

She couldn't help being a little relieved that had been said out loud. 'You should see your own face in the mirror. Pretty scary.'

To her surprise he smiled, though grimly. 'First I am a cowboy and now I have a scary face? You are the strangest woman.'

'No. Just different.'

'No doubt of that.' Zafar strode to the window and then turned back to her, exasperated. 'You of all people should realise I am a civilised man.'

'I'm sorry.' She smiled. It had been a silly thought. 'Thank you. It's reassuring. But this place can be a little overpowering...' she glanced around and then back at him ruefully '...and I don't like the feeling of being overpowered.'

He shook his head and the last of his anger faded from his face as he crossed the room until he stood a few feet in front of her. 'I do not fully understand you, Carmen, but I doubt the strength of an empire could overpower you if you felt strongly enough.'

Did this man really think that about her? It was a hefty compliment out of nowhere and she couldn't help the glow it left her with.

'Once I was overpowered, and I vowed I would not let that happen again.'

He nodded and she felt he really did understand. 'That has made you strong. I respect that.' He went on. 'Tomorrow, when we return from my grandfather's audience, and after the boys are fed, Kiri can mind them for an hour or two while I take you both for a tour. It will be good to remind Fadia how beautiful Zandarro can be. Help her to settle in.'

'That sounds sensible.'

He didn't look pleased at her response. 'I had hoped it would be less sensible and more enjoyable?'

Despite his flippant comment, he still seemed to be worried about something and she hoped it was nothing Fadia should know. 'And when she has settled, you promise not to arrange a marriage for her.'

He looked past her and his voice dropped. 'You may

not think so but I do feel her pain. The loss of loved ones.'

He lifted his head and stared at her as if determined to say the words to her face. 'I buried my son. Prepared his body and laid him on his side with my own hands, facing Mecca in the warm earth. I knew then I could never face the fear of that loss again. Could not face the failure of keeping those I love safe. Who am I to ask another to do the same?' His voice dropped. 'Of course I understand.'

She believed him. But it hurt, when it shouldn't matter to her at all, to see him still so badly wounded by his past. 'I'm glad.'

'I will do what I can. But she should know I do not have the final say.'

She let her breath out with relief. 'She's no girl now. She's a widow with children. And a princess. Life has been hard on her but she is strong. She just needs time.'

He sighed. 'Again it is not I who has to give her time. Already there has been some talk of an alliance for her. Our grandfather believes the sooner she has a man to care for the better she will be. I have disagreed and believe I will prevail. He is not an unreasonable man. We are to discuss it again tomorrow morning before the audience.'

Ouch, but still, Carmen thought, with Zafar on her side Fadia would have a strong champion. She had faith in him, unsure where such faith had come from, but didn't doubt his intent to protect his cousin.

She shook her head and crossed to the boys. 'She says she feels safe here. I hope that's true.'

'As she should. We discovered her Tom had hoped to hide Fadia away while he bargained with me for her whereabouts. He was part of a cell that seeks to bring down our government.'

She couldn't say she was surprised but it gave her the shivers to hear it out loud. 'He's not my Tom. I barely met him.'

He raised his brows at her. 'But you would have hidden their plans from me.'

'Not hidden.' But perhaps she would not have tried to prevent Fadia if she had wanted to run away.

He shook his head at her foolishness. 'You do not understand. It is different here. Risks are greater. I believe Fadia's husband's death was no accident. What if she was expected to die with him?'

And Tom had been in on that? Who were these people they could discuss death and murder so easily? 'So you didn't pay him off?'

'It was suggested he leave my cousin alone. But I believe we have not seen the last of his family. They are eager for a chance at the kingdom.'

She was coming to understand that. 'But what if Fadia decides to return to Australia?'

He dragged an exasperated hand through his hair. 'For the moment she needs to stay here.'

'You can't make her stay if she's unhappy.'

'A woman's view.' He looked away and again she felt there was something he was keeping from her. 'Now, I do not know why I am discussing this with you.'

She straightened. 'Because I'll tell you the truth when everyone else is too scared to.'

'That's right, Carmen.' The way he said her name lifted the hairs on her neck. His words were gentle but his eyes darkened as he closed the gap between them. 'You are not afraid of me.'

Just a tinge of danger and perhaps she should choose her next words a little more carefully. It was different here. Marcus had suggested she tread carefully until she understood the culture more. She should have listened. Zafar wasn't finished.

'Not afraid from the first moment we met, were you?'

And suddenly it was back. That tension between them, like the glow from a hundred candles slowly lighting a room, like a storm overhead in a picnic shed, a moment in a lift, the brush of his lips on the inside of her wrist. 'But, then, you have not been in Zandorro long enough to learn our ways.'

CHAPTER EIGHT

HE'D made her uneasy. Zafar understood her more than she realised, had learnt a lot while he'd attended university in Sydney about Western women, had enjoyed the company of many before he'd married. But this woman was different.

He could see her zeal for her work, her integrity, and most of all he could see the fire within her. Perhaps a fire she had no idea she held or the passionate woman she could become for the right man. A fire that matched his in a way he had not expected.

He watched her search for words to lessen this pressure between them and it amused him that she who lived by defusing tension had momentarily lost her touch. Bravado was all she had left.

'No. I'm not afraid of you.' She only just held eye contact and they both knew it a lie. 'You were the one who said the strength of an empire would not overpower me if I felt strongly enough. I do feel strongly about protecting Fadia. That's why I'm here.' Her voice remained firm—on the outside anyway.

He stepped closer. 'Perhaps you should be. Afraid of me.' A slow, leisurely perusal of her—head to foot—her posture taut with defiance, and he wondered just how angry he could make her, and what would happen if he did. 'Are you not here for the money?'

Her eyes flashed. 'Apparently money was the only way you could get me here!' There it was. So she had given up holding her tongue.

He watched her regret the words as soon as they left her mouth. What had happened to the usually placid Carmen? It seemed he did something to her too. Incited her. Well, she incited him, and he could barely keep his hands by his sides with the need to pull her against him and quieten that mouth of hers with his.

She hurried into speech. Aware of more peril now. Happy to clutch at any straw to avert a difficult situation. 'Your friend, Marcus, said you were a man of honour.'

'That was in Australia.' His eyes travelled over her again with deliberate scrutiny, watched the pink rise in her neck, watched her lick her lips for the taste of danger. 'We are not in your country now. Here honour and law interchange. Here my word is law.'

He closed the last space between them, captured her gaze with his and held it with the easy power of generations of royalty.

Carmen could feel her heart pound. He'd stopped a hairsbreadth away, just short of the fabric of her shirt, fabric she could suddenly feel caress her breasts as she breathed in and out more quickly to calm the agitation caused by his invasion of her space.

'Your law is not my law.' Some foolish pride, some devil inside, refused to allow her to step back.

His voice hardened. Became emphatic. 'You are in Zandorro now. It is my law.' Then softly, 'Come here.'

She blinked. Was he kidding? 'I doubt I could get

much closer without bumping into you.' And some evil
twin inside urged her into his arms. She wasn't sure
who was the more dangerous to her safety—him or her
inner temptress.

He raised his brows. 'Indeed.'

She could feel the aura between them. The air shimmered, thick with vibration that wasn't all words and
power struggle, more at stake here than pride and stub-
bornness. Her brain screamed of danger and her body
dared her to walk into him. Give in. Submit.

She unstuck her tongue from the roof of her mouth.
'You might be living under ancient rule but I am not.'
She stepped back. She met his eyes unflinchingly and
then, to her eternal gratitude, Harrison cried. Actually,
almost lifted the roof of the palace with his demands.
Thank you, dear, dear baby Harry.

She took the few steps to the ornate cradle, picked
up the baby and lifted him like a shield. 'If you'll excuse me, Prince Zafar—' her voice was very dry '—I
will take Prince Harrison to his mother.'

He watched her, even with a glimmer of a smile, and
nodded once. 'We will return to this subject another
time.'

'I don't think so.' She said it as she walked away but
she had no doubt he had heard her and she could feel
his eyes on her back until the swish of his robes told
her he was gone.

She looked back and the room was empty. She leant
heavily against the doorframe with a sigh of relief and
clutched the baby. What had she fallen into? Just how
reliable was his honour? And how reliable would hers
be if he took her into his arms again?

* * *

Zafar walked away. He was annoyed with Carmen, annoyed with himself for playing cat and mouse and having a ridiculous argument when what he wanted to do was feel again the rapport they'd had in the park in Australia. All he'd succeeded in doing was alienating her. Of course she was there to stand up for Fadia if she thought her badly done by. What did he expect?

But he was doing the best he could. Had used all his persuasive powers with his grandfather. He would just have to try harder for Fadia. And be more patient with Carmen—and with himself.

Fadia went to bed early. Carmen decided bed was a safe place, a haven, and a good option for herself as well. She didn't sleep well.

The next morning after breakfast she received a message via Yusuf that Prince Zafar wished to see her. The manservant and the midwife eyed each other and she thought of her little can of dye. Yusuf smiled grimly.

She was taken to the library off the huge tiled entry and through a massive studded door. The room had long, arched windows that opened onto a terrace and inner courtyard with the largest fountain she'd seen yet. The tinkling of falling drops filled the room with a background symphony as she crossed more carpets that shimmered and glowed like pools of coloured light, each more beautiful than the last. At the back of the room ceiling-high bookshelves circled the wall.

It could have been an overpowering room with murals and giant urns, except none seemed to have the magnificence of the man standing front of her in full traditional robes. He suited the room too well.

'How did you sleep?'

How did he think? After the first two hours it had taken her to banish their last encounter. 'Fine, thank you.'

'And the boys?' So he was to be solicitous this morning?

She answered calmly. 'We have a routine. Necessary with twins that are breastfed. They sleep longer at night.'

Still he watched her. Did she have a smut on her nose? 'And they are growing well.'

She glanced around the room, looking for clues to this conversation. 'They certainly seem to be. I don't have scales but as long as they're giving us plenty of wet nappies a day, they're fine.

He nodded decisively. 'I will have scales sent to the nursery.'

'As you wish.'

He allowed himself a small smile. 'Now, was that so hard to say?'

She glared at him. 'Am I allowed to ask what happened with your communication with the King this morning?'

'The king has agreed to leave Fadia in my hands for the moment. Which is why I have summoned you.'

She let him get away with summoned because this was much more serious. 'Does she know?'

'I will inform her this afternoon before our audience.' He walked to the window and looked out. 'We meet to postpone our tour tomorrow. Of necessity our time away from the boys will be short. I wish to know if you have a preference for the souks or a drive around the city to see a broader example of the sights?'

'Perhaps the sights, and at least then I may understand the city better.'

'As you wish. The city, then. Taqu, my friend, wishes to accompany us. Do you mind?'

'Why should I mind? But I'm not sure about Fadia. Does she know him?'

'No. Though he was originally betrothed to Fadia before her mother left. He is a good man and wishes to see her.'

'So at least she knows him?'

'They have never formally met and since then he did marry but is now a widower like myself.'

'So he's the one her mother returned the bride price for? Is this a trick to have them meet?'

'What little faith you have in me.' She did have yesterday. Before their discussion.

Then he calmly said, 'No. This allows my grandfather some face and to take pressure off Fadia.'

'What's he like? What makes you think she'd even talk to him?'

'He is not old or unsavoury.' He smiled as he turned back to face her. 'Though, in fact, as a friend of mine, perhaps he is a little old in my cousin's eyes.'

She had to smile back. 'Not too old, then.'

'My thanks. Prince Taqu lost his wife in childbirth, which for someone in our profession is perhaps just as horrific as a hijack.'

Her breath sighed out. She wondered where Zafar's tragic hijack had happened but she should be thinking of Taqu and his loss. 'I'm sorry to hear that.' She watched his face. 'When you say "our profession", is Prince Taqu a doctor too?'

'He is. But I was referring to your midwifery as well.

Taqu has taken over the running of my children's hospital. He also has a young daughter who needs a mother and he knows Fadia is a kind woman.'

Carmen's brain connected to the next thought. 'Should the unlikely happen, and Fadia and this Taqu fall in love and marry, then have children, doesn't that mean you will be further from the throne? Fadia's new husband would act as guardian of her sons, and your brother Prince Regent until Harry comes of age?'

'That is correct.'

'And you don't mind?'

'Not at all. It places me another step further from the throne. A step closer to return to my work. Zandorro has already lost a future king. Now, when the time comes, if Fadia does not remarry, my brother will act as regent until Harrison is fit to be king in his twentieth year. When Harrison has children then I am further removed.'

'Don't you want to be ruler?'

He shook his head. 'It was never my place. If my country needs me I will be there, of course, but I long to return to my work.' She watched his face change.

His eyes brightened and she felt a kinship towards him for a passion shared. 'One day soon I would like to show you. I have great plans for my oncology research. Sick children can never have enough chances of cure. If it is my destiny I will be able to return to the world I love.'

Then he became a prince again and the light died. He pinned her with his gaze. 'So tell me how you think Fadia will take this?'

'Unimpressed.'

He smiled cynically at her. 'Succinct.' And paced some more.

Carmen sighed. 'She's brilliant with the boys but she is worried about how much control she will have over her life.'

He stopped and considered her words and tried to see what she was seeing. He remembered Fadia as a quiet but cheerful girl, watching him from afar, with shy smiles and even shyer laughter. There had been a time when they had been close.

Before he'd had to learn to be a man. Before his mother had left. 'She was always a happy little thing.' His cousin had suffered the same pain he had and he didn't want her to suffer more. He just wished he knew the right thing to do.

Carmen rubbed her forehead. 'This could really upset her.'

He knew that and he needed Carmen to watch over her more than ever. 'Then it is for you to be vigilant.'

He sighed and as if in slow motion his hand came up and he tucked a strand of thick black hair behind her ear. 'Between us we will see if we can return the smile Fadia's face. But for today my grandfather wishes to see his heirs. I will send ceremonial robes for them to be dressed in before lunch. The audience is at one o'clock.'

She'd bet that wouldn't be fun. 'Of course. I will see they are dressed.'

'I would like you to come.'

Carmen smiled and he felt the day improve with just one lift of her mouth. 'If you wish,' she said, tongue in cheek.

'As you appear to be compliant this morning, is there any chance you would wear the clothes in your room?'

She glanced down at her tailored slacks. 'Not appropriate for a royal audience?'

'I'm sure my grandfather would understand if necessary. Of course that is your choice. The palace seamstress was glad of the extra income. If you do not wish to accept clothing from me, you could always wear them while you are here and leave them behind when your tenure is complete. We would donate them to the needy. I will have her informed you do not wish the rest that I ordered.'

'So if I don't wear them I ruin a poor working woman's wage with my pride.' She looked at Zafar and he wasn't smiling so why did she think he was amused? 'Of course, if I may leave the clothes here, I'm happy to fit in with everyone else.'

He didn't look at her as he replied, 'You may even find our style of apparel is better suited to our climate than yours. Everything has a reason in Zandorro.'

Dryly. 'I'll remember that.'

'Tonight you are both expected to dine with the women, who are all anxious to meet you. They are very happy to dress well for the event.'

The women. The harem? Or the female relatives? Either way, she was the hired help. Oh, goody. 'And you?'

'I?'

She raised her brows. 'Who will you be dining with?'

He smiled as if he knew she wouldn't like it. 'Of course I will be dining with the men.' He inclined his head.

She kept her face bland and saw he was even more amused. 'After the meal tonight, I will bid goodnight to my nephews and I expect you to be there. There are things we need to discuss.'

And she was expected to wait around for that? 'Perhaps it could wait until tomorrow?'

'Tomorrow we will see the sights we discuss tonight.'

The King sat on a gilded throne at the end of a long hall. From the breadth of his shoulders Carmen gathered he must have once been a warrior like Zafar but his hands and wrists were twisted and thin with the passage of years beneath his flowing black robe.

To her surprise, his face, though lined, looked wise and compassionate. She hadn't expected that.

Two guards, surely Yusuf's twin brothers, stood on either side of him, wearing the curved swords she'd always thought Yusuf lacked.

Zafar headed their party. Fadia stood proud and tall beside him. Zafar carried Harrison and Fadia carried Bailey.

'Show me the heirs!'

The king gestured for them to approach and much of what followed Carmen didn't understand.

Zafar took Bailey from Fadia so that he held both. He stood tall and imposing, with a tiny baby in flowing gold robes in the crook of each arm. The twins blinked and gazed about as if searching for each other. Fadia watched her sons. Carmen watched Zafar. She saw the fleeting shadow of pain as he held the boys up.

Of course he would feel his own loss, his own investment in the future gone with his family, and she almost took a step forward to comfort him before she remembered where she was. That would not have gone over well.

Carmen closed her eyes. So much pain in this family. It seemed she didn't hold the franchise on that one.

After a few minutes of discussion with Zafar and Fadia in their native language the King waved his hand at the boys.

'Hmph.' The old man sighed. 'I congratulate you on your fine sons, granddaughter. They look healthy but must be renamed. In respect of your wishes and in honour of their father I name the future king Hariz, meaning strong, a ruler's name, and for the second born Ba Leegh, meaning eloquent and level thinking, to support his brother.'

He waved his hand at Zafar. 'They may go.' Zafar signalled to Carmen to approach and between them she and Fadia carried the boys from the throne room.

'I will see you later,' he murmured before he returned to the King's side.

So it was over, great-grandsons checked and accepted, and she and Fadia could just toddle off while the big boys talked. How her life had changed since she'd met these people.

So how much input had their mother had into her son's names? Perhaps Fadia did wield some power. An effort had been made to compromise. Hariz for Harrison and Ba Leegh for Bailey. She wondered whose idea that had been and hoped secretly it had been Zafar's.

She followed the royals back to their quarters. Every hour she realised more how insignificant she was here and became more determined not to be overwhelmed. Her sympathy lay even more strongly with Fadia. In a moment of trivial thought she wondered what Zafar's name meant. Probably big of chest or something.

She chuckled to herself and Yusuf turned and glanced at her. She smiled at him and he stared stonily back.

'Please to come this way. I will return for his Excellency this afternoon.'

They followed Yusuf obediently back to their wing of the palace. She couldn't help wondering what she'd do if Zafar went away. Apart from Fadia, she had no other allies in the palace.

Fadia fed the boys and they removed their robes then Carmen went for a walk to the palace garden to gather some fruit for her and Fadia's afternoon tea. The sticky almond cakes didn't hit the spot as much as a freshly picked orange did.

Soon it would be time to prepare for dinner with the women and then be ready for her audience with Zafar. She would do as she had been bidden on the small things—it was the large issues she wanted to win.

Like making sure Fadia was happy, and that she, Carmen, made it safely home when all this was over. With her debts paid and her heart intact.

That night after the meal, a learning experience she actually enjoyed with the women, Fadia stood nervously twisting her hands as they awaited Zafar, upset at the idea of seeing the man she was once betrothed to during tomorrow's excursion.

To Carmen's relief, when Zafar came to bid the boys goodnight he was quick to see his cousin's distress. She watched as he soothed her, his voice calm and gentle against her pain. 'You need a friend as well and he is a good man to keep others at bay. You can deal well together without pressure. I give you my promise I will protect you.'

Fadia nodded before she pulled away and looked with distress at them both. 'I'm sorry. I'm so emotional lately. My poor babies will think their mother is always crying.'

'It is early days. Less than a week. You have been through much. Be gentle with yourself.'

She turned and walked quickly from the room and Carmen moved to follow.

'Wait.' Zafar put his hand on her arm and motioned for Kiri to follow his cousin.

She sighed. 'I'm still so worried about her.'

He shifted until he could look into her face. 'As am I. But Yusuf will stand guard for the time being and Kiri will help with my nephews. Do you not need a moment to think of yourself?'

'I'm fine.'

He shook his head. Lifted his hand as if to move that strand of hair again but didn't complete the action.

'It will all be as it should. Trust me. One day she will be happy again. Tonight I will discuss with Taqu tomorrow's excursion. He is my friend and a good man, and knows we are keeping the King happy. I will ask him to come just for company. I must go away for a few days soon and you will both be alone until I return. At least ask her not to worry and try not to think about reading anything into his presence. Then we will talk again.'

Carmen nodded and Zafar went on quietly, 'Will you walk with me?'

'Now?' She tried not to guess his purpose but she could feel the nerves building as she waited.

'Why do you always say "Now?" when I ask you that?'

'Because you ask at the strangest times.' And I don't trust myself not to follow you into a deserted bedroom somewhere, she thought. She said, 'I'd hate to compromise myself.'

He smiled. ''Now is not the time. When it comes there would be no compromise.' No matter how hard she tried, there was no doubt about his meaning.

So there was to be a time? Did she have no say? She looked down at the sleeping babies and pretended to herself she was affronted by his assumption yet inside the temptress stirred and smirked. 'Their mother is still unsettled. I need to be here.'

'Kiri is here. As is her sister. They will watch over them. And Yusuf will stay so he can find us if we are needed. I wish to show you something. I won't have a chance tomorrow and after that I will be busy until I leave.'

So he really was going. 'Very well.' She dropped her pretence and glanced down at her palace clothes, worn for dining with the women, filmy swathes of fabric that made her aware of her own curves and left her with little armour to shield herself with against this man. 'I'll get my coat.'

He saw her glance and held out his hand. 'Your clothes are perfect. It is too warm for a coat.'

He took her through the palace, through a dozen different turns she would never remember until they came to a courtyard, the tinkling of the fountains the only sound as they stepped out into the moonlit night.

'Where are we?'

'At the south wall. The vehicles enter by the north gates and climb the hill.' He strode to a gate and selected a large brass key from a ring of many such keys. 'This is the other side of the palace and there is no descent to the desert from here.'

He gestured for her to precede him and they came out onto a walled ledge that hung over the cliff. The shimmering moon-bathed desert lay before them hundreds of feet below.

In front lay miles of undulating dunes, expanses of sand and rocky outcrops, all ghostly silver in the night so that she felt they were the only living beings as far as the eye could see. As if they themselves were on the moon.

She slowly turned her head and sighed. 'It's incredible.'

'When I can't get away, this is where I come. In the past it was the place I could find some peace, even if just for a short time.'

He lifted his arm and she followed the direction in the silvery light. 'Can you see that small hill under the moon to your right?'

It was surprisingly easy to distinguish. 'Yes.'

His voice lowered. 'There my family lies. I tell you not for your sympathy but because I am more at peace than I have been since the day I awoke. It began that day in the park, with new life unexpected yet beautiful, and you have helped me to heal.'

'Thank you for sharing this with me.'

'I know our ways are different, and I know you try hard to understand. But I want you to know that I see you. If it seems I am ignoring you, or have forgotten you, that is not true. I owe you much. When I am gone for a few days, you may like to come here and find peace for yourself.'

It was as if finally he was allowing her to see a tiny part of his mind. And his heart. She wondered how hard it had been for him and how much the darkness out here had helped.

She took his hand and laced her fingers through his, and when he bent his head she lifted her lips and kissed his cheek. She wanted to do more than that but it was time to go before she did something she regretted.

'Please take me back to Fadia.'

For a moment she thought he would protest but he didn't. Just nodded. 'As you wish.'

CHAPTER NINE

When Carmen woke to the sound of Harry in the morning, it wasn't his usual royal demand. It was fear. A primal bellow that made her throw the covers and slip from the bed more swiftly than normal.

'What's wrong, little man?' She picked him up and glanced across at Bailey just as Fadia arrived. Harry's twin brother lay pale and still in the bed and Carmen's heart thudded with fear as she thrust Harry into his mother's arms, scooped little Bailey from his bed and tipped him over her arm to tap his back.

'Lights,' she called, and Fadia hurriedly switched them on. 'Get help. Tell them to get Zafar!'

Fadia ran from the room, her other son clutched to her chest, and Carmen laid Bailey down on top of the padded dresser and tilted his chin up a little to open his airway.

There was no chest movement but his pale skin felt warm as she searched swiftly for a pulse in his neck. Faint and slow, less than sixty, so obviously not her heart rate, she felt, but such a relief to have something.

She puffed three quick breaths over his mouth and nose and began to compress his little sternum with her first two fingers. One, two, three, breath, one two three, breath, all the while the pounding of her own heart threatening to drown out the world as her fear rose.

Zafar swung through the door, Yusuf and Kiri on his heels, and he moved in smoothly beside her and took over the cardiac massage.

Fadia arrived with Harry just as Bailey's little body twitched and he coughed and began to cry weakly. Carmen bit back her own tears as she stepped away, her hand covering her mouth as the restrained fear rose in her throat like bile.

She opened her arms for the distraught mother and hugged the shuddering Fadia as they stood clutching hands and watched Zafar. Yusuf handed Zafar a stethoscope and Carmen bit her shaking lip as she waited. Zafar bent and examined the little chest front and back and both sides.

Carmen chewed her lip as Bailey's cries grew louder and she hugged Fadia, her own need for comfort almost as great as hers.

Then she saw Zafar's face. Saw his cheeks suck in and his mouth work before sound came out. 'Good air entry now. Probably a choking episode.' He paused and blinked and inhaled. It was much harder to be calm now that it was over. 'We'll take him for an X-ray, though.' His eyes sought Carmen's. 'Tell me what you found.'

She ordered her thoughts in her head, strangely more focussed now she knew Zafar needed her control. 'Pale, blue face, not breathing. But skin warm and heart rate around sixty.'

'Too close.' Their glances met. Zafar shuddered, it was subtle but she saw it. She didn't think anyone else did but this had rocked him. Both of them knew how close it had been. 'Well done.' He took another deep breath. 'So fortunate you were here.'

Carmen looked up at him and he drew strength from her support. No doubt his own face was as white and strained as hers. His own eyes just as wide with shock. He knew later he had to hold her close, alone, so that he could banish the fear that would live, like the pain from the past, but for now he needed to reassure his cousin.

Carmen was saying something. 'Harry's cry was frantic. That's why I jumped up.'

'I, too.' Fadia sniffed and wiped her eyes and hugged her eldest son and kissed him before she handed him to Carmen, who hugged him into her chest with her own need for comfort. 'Harry saved him. I've never heard him cry like that.'

The two women looked at each other and Zafar placed Bailey gently in Fadia's arms and gripped his cousin's shoulder. 'It seems he is fine. Obviously your sons are designed to give us all grey hair.'

'Thank you, Zafar.' She turned to Carmen. 'And you, my dear Carmen.' She squeezed Carmen's hand in gratitude.

Carmen just nodded and stepped back further, bumping into Kiri, who was shaking like a leaf. The little maid slipped her hand into hers and Carmen, juggling Harry, hugged her to stop the shudders. She felt frozen on a treadmill of mental pictures. Couldn't help imagining if she'd been too late. If they'd been unable to save Bailey.

She squeezed Kiri's hand and turned away, and Zafar had no doubt she wanted to hide the tears he had seen spring to her beautiful eyes. They were so fortunate she had been here, had been so quick thinking, and he closed his eyes for a moment at the horror that could have been.

Zafar followed her and turned her gently to face him, saw the streaks of tears across her skin and the trembling of her mouth. He took Harry and handed him to Kiri and then drew Carmen in until she was against his chest. 'Let me hold you.'

Zafar searched her face, could see that shock had set in and needed to feel her against him and show her how much her quick thinking had saved them all. How bravely she tried to control the shudders that rolled through her body in the aftermath of horror. His brave Carmen. 'Thank you,' he whispered against her hair. 'Again. For caring for my cousin and my nephews.' He closed his eyes as the scent of her stirred memories of another time, of other comfort, and the strange way this woman felt so right in his arms. 'And for me.'

He spoke into her hair. 'We will take Bailey to the hospital and check his lungs more thoroughly. Would you like to come?'

Of course she would. She nodded under his mouth and he couldn't help the kiss he brushed against her hair.

'Then go. Dress. We wait for you and Fadia. We can bring Harrison.' He smiled. 'No doubt he too has concerns for his brother.'

The next hour proved reassuring as Bailey was X-rayed and examined again, this time by the head of Neonatal Intensive Care, and Carmen was surprised when Zafar suggested they leave Fadia and the doctor to talk while they minded Harry.

'Distressing episodes like this need discussion, and

she needs to ask everything she can. I think she will listen more if it is not I who tells her that all will be well.'

So Carmen walked around the children's cancer ward with Zafar, and tried not to think of those few moments in Zafar's arms. To feel him around her when death had been so close made her realise how precious life was. How easily lost. She shuddered as Harrison slept on Zafar's shoulder as they watched the children have their breakfast.

Inquisitive little faces peered at them from beds and highchairs. 'It's a lovely ward.'

'We tried to make it more like a pre-school than a hospital. And also so the mothers can sleep comfortably in their children's rooms.'

'And you designed this?'

'With the help of Dr Ting in Sydney. We had many discussions but it is a first for Zandorro and our staff are very dedicated.'

'And you gave this up when Fadia's father died?'

'It was my duty.'

She could tell he missed it. 'Perhaps one day you will be able to return.'

'Perhaps.' He slanted a glance at her. 'I'm hoping soon now. Another time, perhaps we could discuss the baby hotel concept and if it would work for sick children. If the whole family could come, and the sick child could visit the hospital instead of being admitted.'

'Of course. I'll look forward to that. For children on cancer treatment I think it would work well. I'm sure it would be less daunting for them without the separation of siblings.'

'Good.' He smiled down at her and she could see how passionate he was about this. 'We will discuss this again.' He looked up as a nurse approached and spoke to him. 'They are ready for us to return.

It seemed Bailey's all-clear had come through and she had an idea Zafar had been trying to distract her from the stress of the morning. Or perhaps distract himself. She couldn't rid herself of the idea he was still in shock and no doubt either of them would ever forget the image of that moment.

The ride back to the palace was quiet but there was a feeling of unity and support for each other that had previously been missing. Fadia kept her eyes glued to her sons and every now and then tears would well and then her glance would sweep between Zafar and Carmen and she would sigh and relax back in her seat.

Zafar and Carmen spoke quietly about the idea of building a child-friendly hotel next to the hospital for families and soon they were back at their rooms in the palace.

But always at the back of his mind Zafar could not lose the memory of Carmen's support in his moment of need, her quick thinking in Bailey's crisis, and as quickly as possible he finished the multitude of tasks he could not put off before he could return to check on them.

The female servants hovered around Fadia and her boys, and Carmen vibrated with a restlessness that was probably due to the stress of the morning, but it made his brows draw together as his glance lingered on her face.

'Would you like to walk with me?'

His heart warmed as he watched her struggle not to give away her relief at his request. She did need to lose the edginess that possessed her. 'I shouldn't leave Fadia.'

'Go.' Fadia waved her away. 'We are fine here and perhaps a walk will help you settle. You have stood and sat a dozen times these last few minutes.' She smiled at Carmen. 'No doubt your nerves are as bad as mine. The girls are here.'

Zafar nodded. 'Come. I will leave Yusuf here and he will phone me if we are needed. We will return in a while.' He smiled. 'Or maybe longer.'

Carmen followed him through the palace until they came to a part she hadn't seen before. The furnishings were more ornate, grander in the hallways, until finally they came to an entrance with a carved wooden door flanked by giant pots, then he stopped.

She knew. 'Your rooms?'

'We will have peace and privacy here.'

She nodded and he drew her through the doors and closed them behind his back. 'I need to hold you.'

She couldn't say no because her body still felt frozen in limbo and somehow she knew that Zafar could make her feel again. And she could help him. When she moved into his embrace he pulled her in against his chest and the strength of him made her close her eyes with the wash of comfort and relief.

'Thank you,' he whispered against her hair. 'Again. For saving Fadia, for saving me from another tragedy.'

She closed her eyes as his warm breath stirred memories that lingered of her times in this man's arms.

She sighed. 'It was such a shock.'

He shifted until he could look into her face. 'Yes. Yet you managed. But Yusuf will watch them all for the moment. I too need time to soak in the fact that all are safe. You need to let yourself be comforted for once.'

'And perhaps you do too.'

'I know you saw that. But for you we would just be at the beginning of more pain.'

'No. Anyone would have done the same.'

'Perhaps, but not as magnificently.'

He shook his head. Stroked her face. 'We were blessed the day Fadia met you.'

'Fate.'

'Perhaps. My brave Carmen, I just wish I knew what fate had planned for both of us.'

His hand rose and cupped her cheek then he leant down and kissed her. Firm lips tightly leashed with control yet full of dark emotion as he took her mouth and showed her he had been truly rocked by the morning's events. In return she couldn't help share her own horror and both grasped the lifeline, and a promise that they could forget how close they'd been to disaster.

For a moment sanity surfaced and she pulled back reluctantly. 'Can you let the pain go? Please. From now—and from the past?'

His eyes burned into hers. 'At this moment I need you held against my heart.' If only she could, and as if she'd spoken out loud he drew her back against him. 'The horror if you had not been there...'

'Let it go, Zafar.' She didn't want to think of horror in this moment. She saw his need. Answered it. 'You were there too. You made it happen.'

He tightened his grip. 'For once. Take the comfort I offer.'

But what if she lost herself? 'And will you take mine?'

That was all she wanted to do. Feel every glorious

inch of him against her; be crushed by his power and reborn with his possession. Stop fighting, for once, against the magnetism of this man who drew her like no other. Put away her fears of the ramifications she knew would follow.

His mouth came down and she sighed into him, let herself go, savoured the defeat of her fears, absorbed his pain and ached to heal it. Her shirt buttons fell away, as did his; she tasted his skin, dug her fingers into his corded muscles, soaked his strength into hers and gave freely and openly of her own. He lifted her and she wrapped her legs around him as she held his face against hers.

The world shifted under her as they turned as one, skin against skin, his eyes adoring as they skimmed her body. Then a shift, a shrugging off of more clothes, and she could do nothing but glory in his possession as she opened herself to him, her back against the wall, the rhythm of their need pounding in her heart until both were lost in the maelstrom. Soaring into the light. Suffused with heat like the desert that stretched away on the other side of the drapes.

Lost in a sandstorm of sensation she'd never imagined. Clinging to the centre of her world. Until slowly they returned to earth like the blown grains of sand outside.

They rested, panting against the wall, eyes wide and stunned at each other and the storm they had created between them, until Zafar carried her across and lay down with her still cradled in his arms.

When Zafar lifted his head the world had changed, along with his acceptance of the inevitable. He needed her. Loved her. Was endangered by her in his very soul, for how would he let her go? Staring into the shadows of his room with Carmen's cheek resting on his chest, Zafar inhaled the scent of her. He stroked the thick silken strands of her hair and a part of him died inside to think of her gone. What had he done?

A magical connection that had smashed into a million brightly jagged shards his foolish idea of perhaps loving her once and banishing her hold from his heart.

The most glorious foolishness of it all was he could not regret his heart's decision. He'd had no idea this was how it was meant to be. Or what price he would pay. All he knew was that if he did not return tomorrow, he could not regret this knowledge.

When they woke she shifted against him. 'I must go.'

Her forehead leant into him as his hand touched her cheek. She turned her head and with her own hand she stroked his fingers. With such tenderness she held his heart.

'Go to Fadia.' Yet even as he said it his hand tightened to keep her in his arms 'And later I will come to you.'

He sighed, captured her hand, and drew it to his mouth. 'We are going to regret this.'

'Perhaps.' So she realised that, too. 'But thank you.'

So he was already regretting it. Carmen understood because her mind had already accepted that this man was no ordinary man. Zafar the prince made her feel like a queen, more woman than in her whole year of marriage, more girl than a decade of flirtation, and, no matter what, she would always remember this time of mutual need as part of her destiny, even if their future could not lie together.

Later that night he did come to her but he didn't stay.

He pressed a key into her hand. 'I leave tomorrow. If I am detained…' he glanced away at the windows and then back at her, and she couldn't deny the flicker of unease his words caused '…perhaps unavoidably, then I would like you to remember there is magic in Zandorro as well as the things you don't understand.'

He sighed. 'I tell you that if I do not return shortly I have arranged for you to fly back to your own country as soon as possible. But in the meantime you may use the east courtyard as your private sanctuary.'

'I don't understand.'

'To have you here is a gift but difficult times lie ahead and I wish you back in the safety of your own country. As it stands now, there is no future for what we have.'

'Are you in danger?'

'I have safeguards arranged but I will be safer if I do not have to worry about you.' Unable to argue with that, she nodded reluctantly.

The next morning the sun was shining in through the windows when Kiri opened Carmen's blinds. 'Good morning, Miss Carmen.'

No. It wasn't. Zafir had gone. Probably into danger.

Carmen felt cold. Which was ridiculous. She was in the middle of a desert city. Eggs could fry on car bonnets. It seemed her heart lay packed on ice for its own protection.

She hated that here, as a woman, she had no power; she was not allowed to help Zafir. But, then, would Zafir even want her help? He'd hinted that they had no future. The uncertainty was stretching her heart to breaking point. She couldn't live like this. To be here was to be helpless.

She needed to believe that for her own safety. The safety of her heart. She was just a pawn like Fadia and the twins and even Zafar himself. As soon as Fadia was settled she would go home. The sooner she went home to the world she understood, the better.

Zafar was away for days and Carmen told herself she was glad. The distancing effect of time allowed her to see how powerless she was. How ridiculous her attraction to Zafar was in the royal scheme of things. How little future they had, no matter how she felt.

Thankfully every day Fadia seemed to recover a little more of her self-confidence and enjoyment of the simple pleasures in her life grew as she became more comfortable that Bailey would be fine in the long term.

Contrary to her fear, the older ladies in the palace were kind and helpful and doted on her babies and her. But the biggest change in Fadia was that from victim to advocate against Tom, against people who could so coldly plot the death of her husband, perhaps her babies. And Carmen began to see the fighting spirit of Zafar's family.

When the babies' feeding had settled into a routine and Fadia became more confident and her boys began to develop personalities that made them all laugh.

Hariz truly was the leader. Along with his demanding roar his little clenched fists waved impatiently when he wanted to be fed, while Ba Leegh would lie quietly, watching the world, observing, secure in the knowledge his needs would be met.

Carmen grew fonder of the young maid, Kiri, and her sister and the way they cared for Fadia and the twins.

And so the days passed but Carmen began to fret at being stuck in the castle. She never did get that tour.

Often she was superfluous in the boys' care now and took to spending an hour at the hidden eyrie Zafar had shown her as she prepared herself to return to her old life.

On the third day after Zafar left, word came to their wing that Prince Taqu, who had arrived in the palace the day Zafar had left, wished to take Fadia and Carmen for an outing to the souks.

'I do not want to go,' Fadia said as she wrung her hands and Carmen tried to calm her.

'Of course you don't have to go. We can say that.' Carmen peered out the window but she couldn't see the forecourt. 'Is that what you want?'

'Yes.'

'Aren't you a little curious?'

'No.'

'Fine.' She walked to the door. 'I'll go down to apologise and say you're too tired today.'

Fadia twisted her hands. 'Do you want to go, Carmen?'

'I'd like to get out, yes. But I can see the souks when Zafar comes back.'

'You could go.'

Carmen laughed. 'I'm sure the prince would love that. A strange foreign woman instead of you.'

'Let me think. Perhaps he could come back tomorrow and if Zafar is not back we could go out for a short time. I do not like leaving the babies.'

'Of course. But I won't promise anything in case you change your mind.'

Carmen's first sight of Prince Taqu reminded her

how much she missed Zafar. The man was tall, not as broad across the chest as Zafar, but a truly impressive specimen, and with a smile that promised kindness, not greed. She wished Fadia could see that she didn't need to be afraid of this man.

He came towards her. 'You must be Miss Carmen. Zafar has told me about you.'

'Prince Taqu. I bring apologies from Princess Fadia.'

He didn't look surprised. 'And they are?'

'That today she is tired. And her sons need her.'

'I am here for a few more days. Perhaps tomorrow.'

Carmen couldn't help her smile. It was too early to be sure that Fadia would but she liked this man. 'Perhaps. But the princess thanks you for your kind offer.'

'Does she?' Too polite to disagree with her. He shrugged. 'Or perhaps you do out of kindness. It does not matter. I will return this time tomorrow and ask again.' He glanced at his watch. 'Please tell Princess Fadia I await her pleasure. Assure her we will go out for a short time only and perhaps a change of scenery will assist in her recovery. And for your entertainment too, of course.'

'Of course. Thank you.'

On the fourth day, despite Fadia's misgivings, she and Carmen visited the souks, accompanied by Prince Taqu. Vendors bowed respectfully as they showed their wares, much less vociferous than Carmen had expected. No doubt their escort helped with that. Although the first day proved very formal, by the time the two-hour visit was over Fadia looked less strained and had agreed to another foray.

The next day, the fifth Zafar was away, saw them examine all the mosques in the city, along with a leisurely lunch at a city restaurant. Prince Taqu had studied at the same university as Zafar and his stories of their escapades had Fadia giggling in a way Carmen had never seen.

On the sixth day, the day Prince Taqu was to leave, they went back to the souks to search for more treasures for Carmen to take back to Australia. This time the prince brought his daughter and afterwards they all returned to the palace to show the young princess the twins.

It proved to be a delightful day and by the end of it Carmen's presence was barely necessary. Unobtrusively she drifted further away from them.

She was glad to see Fadia more relaxed and there was no doubt that Taqu had planned a concentrated assault on the princess's defences. His promise to return the following week seemed to be greeted with pleasure by Fadia and already there was rapport between his daughter and Fadia.

Carmen realised her need to be in Zandorro was drawing to a close, which was a good thing. Carmen just wished watching them didn't make her feel so alone.

On the seventh day Zafar returned, and even the sight of Yusuf coming towards her made her smile in anticipation.

'Prince Zafar wishes to see you.'

'Where is he?'

'The library.'

Zafar waited. Pacing back and forth over the carpets. Unseeing as he strode from side to side. Every morning and every night of the last six he'd looked forward to this day. The day he would return to Carmen. But now the day filled him with dread. Taqu had discov-

ered a spy in the palace and unearthed plans to kidnap
Carmen and Fadia.

Imagine if he had not asked his friend to come and
watch over the women while he had searched for the
rebel stronghold. He needed to have Carmen safely back
in her own country before the final coup attempt. If he'd
realised how dangerous the situation would become so
quickly, he would never have brought her here.

The door opened and she was there. Her face shining, her eyes alight, looking at him as he'd dreamed she
would look at him. How had all this happened without
his knowledge? To give his heart to a woman from the
other side of the earth when his world balanced on the
edge of danger.

To fall for a woman who did not understand the dangers. Who unwittingly exposed his own throat and hers.
Who could prove his next failure to keep those he loved
safe. A failure he could not bear to repeat. She was so
fragile. So unprepared. So precious.

When she entered the library she didn't know what to
expect but the distance between them came as a shock.
Zafar nodded in greeting but there was no smile in his
eyes, no move towards her, and she halted inside the
door. Yusuf let himself out and closed the door.

'Is everything all right?'

'It is time for you to leave.'

CHAPTER TEN

THE words flew like darts from an unexpected ambush and punctured her euphoria. Destroyed her dream of him opening his arms to her. Mocked her anticipation until it fell in tatters around her slippered feet.

'Fadia's fine now and the boys are settled. It's time for you to return to Sydney.'

She heard the words, glanced around at the opulence of his office and unconsciously rubbed her arms. 'Today?' Go home. It would be soon but…leave them all right away? 'Why the hurry?'

Zafar's dark brows drew together as he looked past her shoulder. 'Your job is done. Your time here is over.'

Carmen looked away herself. To hide the shine of tears she could feel. She was such a fool. So she'd slept with him and that was that. And she'd been like a damsel in the tower, waiting for her prince to return. More fool her. Huge fool her. 'As you say, you want me gone. There is no reason for me to stay.' Still she wouldn't look at him. Couldn't.

She heard him move and her heart leapt. She turned her head and he was pacing, but not towards her.

Fool again. What did she think? That he hadn't really meant it and she could stay? That the royal family would greet her with open arms because she'd kissed him a few times? Slept with him once.

She lifted her chin. Well, damn him. That was that. And she felt remarkably, frozenly calm. It proved he wasn't to be trusted. She had reason to hate him now, which was so much safer than that other emotion. Why was that?

It all happened very fast after that. Her clothes were packed when she arrived back at the children's wing, Fadia was stunned and white-faced, Kiri sniffed and hid red eyes as she gathered all Carmen's things. In the background, waiting, Yusuf stood, arms crossed, impatient for her to say goodbye.

She was bundled down to the car, and when Yusuf opened the door he seemed surprised Zafar was already seated. 'I will accompany you to the airport.'

Yusuf stared at his master for a moment and then inclined his head before shutting the door. Carmen became more confused. The car started and within minutes they were leaving the palace behind. 'What is going on here?'

'I need you out of the country. For both our sakes.'

She thought about that and couldn't help a glimmer of foolish hope that he didn't really want her to go.

As he sat beside her in the limousine the darkened windows kept the interior dim and intimate. He didn't speak so she looked out the window as they drove through the winding streets. She never had got to explore on her own. She should have.

'I understand you saw the souks with Prince Taqu and Fadia?'

'Yes. I enjoyed it.' How could he carry on a normal conversation after the last half an hour?

She looked away again and a woman dressed in black with all but her eyes covered disappeared into a doorway as they drove through the big gates out into the desert. 'It's very difficult for a woman like me to understand your culture and customs.'

'But not impossible?'

'No. I should thank you that I had the chance to set out on an adventure to an exotic land in the company of exotic people.' Once started, she couldn't stop. 'Just as long as I remembered this was a job that would end…' she glanced away from him to the sand that stretched into the distance and her mouth hardened '…suddenly. But, of course, I am only the hired help.'

'Have you finished?'

She inclined her head mockingly. 'Of course, Excellency.'

He ran his hand through his hair and she smiled grimly. At least he wasn't immune to how he was treating her. 'Listen to me. You are at risk and I need to have you safe. I will not be responsible for harm befalling you.'

'I can look after myself.'

His eyes burned into hers. 'You will leave now and be safe.'

She narrowed her own, sifting through the mixed messages, reading between the lines. 'You said I could never be bowed.'

'Listen to me, Carmen. At this moment—'

A sentence he never had the chance to finish as gunshots rang out. Disjointed cracks like stones hitting the side of the car. She'd never heard them for real before but she'd watched enough movies to get the gist of what was happening.

Yusuf swerved the car onto a side road and suddenly they were airborne as they crashed through the scrub beside the road and into the desert along a barely discernable track.

The window between Yusuf and them wound down as Zafar pushed her onto the floor and he slid lower in seat with his phone out. His eyes held hers as he spoke rapidly into it and for some crazy reason she was too angry to be frightened.

'Three vehicles. They will catch us.' He nodded to Yusuf. 'Support is coming. They will meet us at the valley pass.' Then he turned back to her.

'I have arranged for us to be picked up in an armoured vehicle in fifteen minutes. We wait by the rocks in the crevice. We must quickly hide ourselves. It is too late to get you away. We must return to the palace until it is safe.' She shook her head. She didn't understand.

'If anything happens, and we get separated, keep quiet and unobtrusive and I will find you.'

'Why is this happening?'

'It is almost done but I feared this last assault. The last of the rebels have nothing left to lose. They wish to capture me but do not worry. Safeguards are in place.'

Now she was scared. 'I'm not letting you out of my sight.'

'Nor I you.' He grasped her arm and eased her up beside him. 'This is my world and when this is done it will be done.' He dropped a swift, hard kiss on her lips. 'Do as I command and you will be safe.'

For the moment the other vehicles were out of sight as they passed a large outcrop of rock and before she realised what was happening the car slowed. Zafar reached in front of her and pushed open the door on her side. She could see the sand rushing by.

'Go,' he said urgently, and pushed her so that she slid across the seat and out of the door onto the sand in an ungainly heap. He followed her and Yusuf in the car accelerated away from them in a spray of sand and dust, and suddenly the car was gone. She was in the middle of the desert, at midday, and Zafar was pulling her towards a crevice.

Zafar cursed his own stupidity as he crawled across the sand towards her. He'd known trouble was brewing but he'd thought they'd had another twenty-four hours before it escalated enough to pose a threat. And he'd dragged his woman into danger because he'd wanted to have her safe on a plane.

He froze. His woman.

It would be best when the fog that weakened him flew out from Dubai until all this was settled. His Carmen was a resourceful woman but the worry gnawed at him like a rat in the palace dungeons. All she had to do was lie low and wait to be picked up. Why did he worry she wouldn't?

The hurt he'd seen in her eyes would pursue him. She didn't trust him and he couldn't blame her. He had missed her like a limb for the last seven days until the communication they had captured had outlined the revolt. And the plan of kidnapping Carmen to force Zafar's hand had driven him back to the palace.

But the plan of shifting her to safety had backfired so now there was no time for thinking. Only surviving.

Carmen heard the growl of approaching vehicles and her heart thumped in her chest in time to the revs of the engines.

'Go.' Zafar's voice was urgent behind her. Spurred into action, she crawled inelegantly across to the out-crop and there was a crevice, sand crusted and pushed a couple of feet back into the rock, just as Zafar had said, which afforded some protection from the road. When she pulled herself in, it was deeper than she'd thought and she fell several feet down into a heaped pile of sand. It was dim, and something scuttled away from her hand as she tried to steady herself. Carmen shuddered and pulled her hands in close to her chest. Zafar fell in beside her.

The roar of the approaching vehicles seemed to vi-brate through her body and she blocked out the animals or reptiles she'd disturbed to worry about later as she jammed her head down into his chest and squeezed her eyes shut as if she could squeeze the whole crazy ten minutes away. This was not happening.

That thought at least brought her some sanity. And Zafar's arms around her helped.

'Fear's your worst enemy.' His voice in her ear. She'd heard those words before, the woman on the headland, a test by solitary birth that Jenny had had to go through, and she'd said that to Jenny. Well, fear was in this dark and dismal hole right alongside them both, and she wasn't happy.

'Who are they?'

'Friends of Tom's.'

The cars roared past and the sound bombarded her more than the sand that flew into their crevice and coated their hair and cheeks. Her heart thumped in her ears, staccato thumps, and then she realised it was not her heart but the sound of a battle not too far away. An explosion. Then the whoosh of heavy fire and the rattle of machine guns. Then the distinctive sound of vehicles driving off.

Now beneath her own dread was her fear of what had happened. And even a little for the annoying Yusuf. Who was attacking them and why? And just how out of her depth was she?

Zafar stood and pulled himself up. 'Stay here. You are safe here.'

And then he was gone. The previous tenants scuttled against her hand and she shuddered. Zafar's footsteps faded.

She shifted onto her knees and peered over the ledge. He'd told her to wait there but she'd never been good with orders. The sound of fighting over the rise had been quiet for ten minutes now and she had a bad feeling about it.

The tenant brushed past her hand again and that decided her. She was out of there. If need be, she could come back to get out of the sun but she had to know that Zafar wasn't in danger.

It had been easier to fall into the crevice than climbing out, but with a skinned knee and three broken nails she finally crouched on the outside of the opening. She shuddered as she glanced back into the dark interior. It would take a fair incentive to get her back in there.

The hot breeze dried the perspiration on her face and she licked her lips. Sand grated against her tongue and she could smell the smoke that was rising from ahead. Thirst was an issue already but not one she could worry about just yet. Keeping low, she scurried to the next outcrop and stayed crouched as she listened. No sound from over the hill and no vehicles that she could hear.

When she made it to the top of the sandy ridge she

could see the remains of the battle. She gasped when she saw Zafar's car teetered on its side next to another burnt-out wreck of a Jeep. A collision with consequences, and then she saw Zafar edging towards the car. Yusuf!

She scanned constantly for movement as she skidded down the hill from outcrop to outcrop until she was ten yards from where Zafar crouched. He turned and looked at her; his eyes flared briefly then he sighed and shrugged. 'Of course you came.'

The low groan made her jump and she flattened herself against the rock and twisted her head from one piece of wreckage to another. It came again, guttural, weak and definitely masculine.

They crawled across the open ground to Zafar's car and peered through the smashed rear window. Yusuf. The man seemed trapped. Crumpled against the steering-wheel. The smell of fuel reeked. The burning Jeep smouldered too close for comfort. They slid around the chassis of the car until Zafar could stretch up and peer through the driver's window. 'Yusuf?'

With a struggle he opened his eyes. 'Leave here. It is too dangerous.' He closed his eyes and whispered, 'It is the will of Allah.'

Typical. She was getting so sick of men giving orders. 'Not until we get you out.'

Zafar was concentrating on the task ahead. 'Let us see if Allah wants you out first.'

He turned to Carmen. 'I cannot budge it alone. If we put weight on this side that teeters, maybe the whole car will fall back on its wheels.'

Away from the flaming wreck beside it. Neither mentioned that. 'Not easy to do that without getting closer to the flames.'

As they circled the car the tyres began to smoke as the building heat encouraged the fire to cross the distance between cars.

'We need a wedge, something to give leverage. We're running out of time.'

'Yusuf.' Zafar's command snapped the man awake. 'Reach the lever for the boot.'

'Leave, Excellency. Take the woman.'

'Not without you. Do it.'

She heard keys rattle and then the boot latch clicked. Zafar scooped out a large coil of rope and a tyre lever. And her suitcase, which she thought strangely thoughtful.

'We can do this.' He glanced around. 'That rock. Can you tie it there?'

She estimated the length of the rope and the nearest outcrop, and Zafar took his own end of the rope and tied it quickly around the doorframe next to Yusuf.

She ran and circled it until she had tied the car to the rock with as much tension as she could. She'd always been lousy with knots but the granny would have to do. The rear tyre burst into flames and smoke grew acrid in her throat until she coughed. They weren't going to make it.

She could feel the thunder of her pulse as the sweat ran down her face. They were going to be too late and Yusuf would burn. She'd really grown used to having him around.

'Fear is your worst enemy,' she muttered, and gritted her teeth as Zafar caught the rope and twisted it with the tyre lever to tighten it slowly. The rope creaked, the car creaked she watched him strain against it to shorten the rope. She ran back to him and heaved as well. Between them it finally shifted.

In the end it didn't need much, just enough to change the centre of gravity, and when it happened she wasn't prepared for it and the car swayed and then fell with a whoomph.

Yusuf cried out as he was bounced around like a cork in a bottle. Zafar wrenched open the door. A now unconscious Yusuf half fell out onto the road and she ran to help Zafar as the rear of the car filled with smoke. Flames began to lick along the interior roof lining as they dragged him free.

It was going to blow. She could hear the words in her head and she kept pulling, yanking, cursing this heavy lump of a man who had uselessly fainted on them, until he was partially sheltered behind a rock.

That was when she heard the sound of an approaching vehicle. The outcrop that almost protected them was too small to hide behind. Zafar pulled her behind him. Would this day never end?

The low throbbing rumble distracted them just as the vehicle erupted into a fire ball and she ducked her head into Zafar's back. A blast of heat singed the hands she held over her head and then it settled to a steady roar of heat.

The rumble became a throb from an armoured car, which slowed and then stopped beside their outcrop. Good guys, she hoped. Please let it be Zafar's back-up.

Two young men with machine guns jumped out of the armoured truck. One ran to the front of the vehicle and the other to the back as they guarded the road. A third climbed down and approached her with obvious relief. 'Excellency. Are you well?'

He turned a blackened face to Carmen and no doubt she looked just as much a disaster. He grinned and she realised he'd almost enjoyed himself. Men! 'It seems so.' He raised his singed eyebrows. 'Carmen?'

She nodded and after one searching look at her he stood up. Then he pulled her into his arms and kissed her. Thoroughly. 'I must go.'

Strange thing to say. She wasn't planning on staying either. 'Me, too.' A few minutes earlier for the cavalry would have been nice, she thought sourly as she peered through the smoke. Carmen sat up beside the unconscious Yusuf, bedraggled, singed and over it all.

'Miss O'Shannessy?'

'Yes.'

'His Excellency said we were to transport you to the airport.'

Now? Like this? A vehicle drove off. Of course he did. 'Yes. But what of your prince?'

'He has already left.' He reached down and helped her up. 'Our orders are clear. We have matters in hand and you must catch the flight.'

He gestured to the front soldier, who'd run in a crouching position towards the rise and after a brief surveillance had returned. 'His Excellency wishes you a safe journey.'

Carmen flew back to Australia first class from Dubai. After she'd been given fresh clothes. The strangeness of being greeted by name and with deference was both unexpected and uncomfortable. Yet all was overshadowed by the desolation she felt as the distance widened between her and the man she should hate. Even the engines seemed quieter up here, which didn't help drown out the ache in her heart.

On arrival Coogee was filled with memories of Zafar, and everywhere she turned made her want to run. And hide. She needed to get away. Maybe one day, when it didn't hurt any more, she would return here. She almost wished she could return to her double-shift working life so she could fall exhausted into bed and sleep, instead of gazing out the window and thinking of Zandorro.

Instead, the next week dragged by as she tidied up the loose ends of her life, paid the last of her husband's debts, attended exit interviews, finalised the lease on her flat, applied for and accepted a job in the new birth centre in Yalara, the access town beside Ayers Rock in Central Australia.

She had to go somewhere remote, unfamiliar, safe from memories, for the next few months.

When some time had passed then she'd see where she ended up. For the moment she told herself she needed to meet her need for escape. She'd arranged for the few sentimental possessions she had left to be stored in a box at Tilly's and she spent the last night here before she flew out.

Donna, the concierge, had arranged with Tilly a farewell morning tea at the baby hotel with a few friends from both workplaces. It was the last thing Carmen wanted but she smiled and nodded her way through the morning until her head ached as she waited for the time she could pick up her bags from her room and head for the airport.

When she could finally escape towards her suite,

compliments of the management and ironically on the seventh floor, her head throbbed with memories of another time as the lift doors opened. At least the lift hadn't jammed.

Her room lay only a few doors down from so many memories and the corridor seemed strangely empty without a man standing guard outside the tiled entrance to the presidential suite.

Carmen's door lock clicked behind her and she crossed the room to drag open the heavy sliding door to let the stiff breeze from the ocean beat against her. The wind was up and she staggered a little as it whipped the curtain from beside her and flapped it against her head. The sting of salt lifted her face and she asked herself again why on earth she'd chosen the furthest place in Australia from any beach for her new job. But she knew why. She hated the weakness she hadn't realised she would be a party to. Her hands gripped the cold metal as if to soak in as much of the sea as she could before she left.

Zafar let out his breath. She was here. She hadn't left. He'd been to her flat, peered through the windows into the empty room until he'd driven to the hotel to hear she had resigned.

He'd managed to wrangle her room number from the staff, but not access. He'd also known she was checking out today.

He'd seen her downstairs, but talking to her there was impossible. How could he get privite time with her.

'If you take a room on the same floor, you're almost neighbors,' the receptionist had purred, giving way to his charm. 'And you can see each other on the balcony.'

It made sense. He'd known she couldn't leave without her baggage; couldn't leave without saying goodbye to the sea.

So here he was, and here she was.

'I'd prefer you to move back a little. I've had bad experiences with heights.'

She didn't turn her head but he knew she'd heard him. Felt her stillness. Prayed she would forgive him for taking so long to claim her. But he'd needed to finish it. Once they'd threatened Carmen he hadn't been able to rest until it was done. For the future, they would face it together, but for the past he had needed to finish alone.

Carmen felt his presence. Memories fluttered around her like butterflies in the sunlight. His eyes on hers, his wicked mouth curved and coming closer, his angled cheeks beneath her hand. She could see it all without turning her head. So he'd come back to haunt her.

She turned to see Zafar leaning uncomfortably around the privacy screen two rooms up. If he hated heights…'Then why are you out here?'

He moved back a little to safety now that he had her attention. 'I need to see you. You won't answer the phone in your room.'

'I haven't been in the room. What do you want, Zafar?'

One word. 'You.' One command.

'Still giving orders? Another quick romp?' She had to finish this. 'Go away.'

He crossed his arms. 'Not until I have had the chance to explain.'

Of course he wouldn't go away. 'No.'

'The flight was long.'

Tough. 'I'm sure there were other business affairs of state you need to do here.'

He'd had enough. 'Your room or mine?'

Impossible man. She needed to get this right. 'Give me a moment to think.' She turned and stared at him and his smile glinted.

'As you wish.'

See, that was the problem. She ducked into her room again. She had to bite back a smile. It had to be his room. Hers was so much smaller and he would be too close no matter where he stood. When the phone rang, still she hesitated. Was she agreeing to more disillusion or should she just get it over with? She let it ring again. But he would come if she didn't, she knew that, and she hated being a coward.

She picked it up, said, 'I'll come, but must leave for my flight in twenty minutes,' and put it down again.

It seemed strange to know he was there and no guard stood outside in the corridor. Zafar opened the door himself and stood back to allow her to enter.

She slipped past carefully and he didn't try to touch her.

She positioned herself in the middle of the lounge area, creating as much space as she could from anything that could hem her in. She saw by his face that he knew what she was doing.

The silence wasn't comfortable. 'Where's your staff?'

'I came on my own.' He smiled and the warmth in his eyes almost blinded her. 'Except for Yusuf, who is downstairs in the car. He does not dislike you any more.'

'Should you be here without protection? Are you safe?'

He shrugged. 'Yes, we are all safe. At last my country will have peace.' His eyes bored into hers. 'Alone is best for this goal I seek.'

She frowned. 'And what is your personal goal?'

He took a step closer. 'I believe you know.'

'No idea.' She crossed her arms protectively across her stomach and he stopped. 'But I do have a plane to catch.'

He spread his hands. 'Your flat was empty. Moved from. I was too late.'

'For what?' She was so distant. Yet incredibly beautiful. How could he have forgotten the way she twisted his chest until it hurt? He wanted to pull her into his arms and bury his face in her hair. Breathe her in. Tell her that his fears had overcome him, so afraid he could not save her. Yet she had been the one to risk all by his side so they could all be safe.

He smiled at her. 'I'm sorry I bundled you out of Zandorro.'

'You bundled me out of a speeding car.'

His chest shook with silent laughter at her indignation. 'Because I discovered a plan to use you against me. I thought you were not safe.'

'And would their plan have worked?'

He took a step closer. 'Because of that? Like a shot.'

'Don't talk about shooting.' She shuddered. 'Why are you here? It's a long way to come to say you're sorry.'

Just what was he asking? For her to make a bigger fool of herself? 'I need to leave here and decide on my future.'

'I have no quarrel with that.'

She blinked. Then he came closer until he was right beside her. Until his warmth seeped across the tiny gap of air between them. If she wasn't careful, he'd thaw her protection. 'I would like you to leave here and come back to my country. Then decide on your future.'

'I'm not going back to Zandorro.'

'You must. I wish to show you my desert.' He took her hand, and she tried very hard not to shake. 'Most especially the desert. We spoke once before about the desert but still we haven't slept there.'

The desert. 'I tasted the desert. When the sand flew into my mouth after...'

'Yes, I know. I threw you out of the car. Tsk tsk. So unforgiving. Where is that famous sense of humour?'

He was rubbing her neck. Smiling into her eyes, and the warmth was melting her heart. She stepped back.

'You're doing it again.'

'What?'

'Playing me.'

'Come play in the desert with me.'

'You come to the desert with me. I'm due in Central Australia this afternoon.' Sure now that he wouldn't.

She'd love to see his desert. Properly. With him. But she wasn't that much of a fool. 'Better yet. Don't.' She needed to get away. Just standing here talking to him was killing her.

'Is it too much to ask that I at least try to leave you with good memories of my country? Of me?'

She had to get away. Even if she had to lie. 'I have no wish to see the desert with you. I just want you to go.'

He stared at her, narrowed-eyed, and she remembered how he'd measured her when they'd first met. In the hotel. As if he was looking under her skin, into her brain. She tried not to fidget as she forced herself to hold his gaze.

Then he nodded. 'I see.' He glanced at the window and the brightness outside. 'Then at least let me drive you to the airport. I will place my jet at your disposal to fly you to your central Australia.'

'I have my own ticket. Thank you.' So he wasn't going to fight for her.

It was over. Her shoulders dropped. It was relief. Honest. She blinked away sudden dampness in her eyes and chewed on her lip. She wasn't sure why she'd thought he would stop her, and she certainly hadn't wanted him to. Had she? He'd only come to apologise.

'I insist. Change the ticket you have for another day. Cash it in. I don't care.'

'Thank you.' She wouldn't but he could think what he liked.

Zafar watched her. This was not what she wanted. This woman who had walked unaided from an ambush. Who had helped him save his man. Had he discovered his amazing Carmen's only fear—that he might not love her enough?

Ungrounded fear. He would give up his life for her.

He did not know why she had decided she wasn't going to give him time to woo her. Then, perhaps, she would have to do without the wooing. He wanted her. Badly. More desperately than he could remember wanting any woman. And he knew she wanted him. He prayed she did.

Ridiculous to be so obsessed with her, with the dream, Carmen with him always. The life he wanted, return to his real work, for the rest of his life. But life would be nothing without his Carmen. He needed her by his side.

'Or you could come back with me.'

'Why? So you can send me away again when you've satisfied yourself? Or when you decide it's too dangerous for me?'

'I would not send you away again. This time I will go where you go.' His fear had almost cost him that. She needed less protection than he'd anticipated. He would always protect her. His lips twitched, and he supposed if needed she could protect him. He did not like the thought but she was no fragile flower. His brave Carmen.

'I know it is different for you in Zandorro. As it was for me when I lived in Australia. There are good facets of all cultures and the world will be a better place when we learn to meld and bring the best out of both worlds.'

She looked back at him. 'Do you think that will ever happen?'

'Slowly, but surely.' He smiled and it wasn't fair. He melted her with those smiles. The chameleon. 'When people work together, miracles happen.'

The more he talked the more he wore the persona of the man who had attracted her so much here at Coogee beach.

The smiling god in the water.

The man after the storm with his head thrown back and his eyes filled with laughter.

Seeing him today had been worth it to leave her with these memories because those glimpses were lost in the prince. They were the dream man, not the reality. The reality had driven away from her in an armoured car. Sent her home. Gave her no choice.

'I did not have a voice,' she said. 'I can never live like that.'

'I know. I understand more than you can guess. I'm sorry you felt excluded. Forgive me?'

'No.'

He sighed but wasn't as downhearted as she'd thought he'd be. Typical. It was all probably a ruse to seduce her anyway.

'If that is your last word then I will drive you to the airport.'

She frowned. He was up to something.

CHAPTER ELEVEN

Yusuf held the car door open for her, and this time he bowed low to her. His face was still inscrutable but his body language was different. She touched his shoulder as she passed. 'Good to see you are well, Yusuf.'

'Madam.'

She slid in and Zafar slid in behind her. The leather smelt familiar, the tinted windows reminded her of another limousine, and how she'd thought Yusuf would die. How Zafar could have. Her pride was nothing to that fear.

He took her hand and kissed the inside of her wrist. Her skin remembered. It felt ridiculously right to feel her hand covered by his. She was hopeless. With his other he gestured to the space around them. 'Now we are alone.'

'Really? Must be a remote-controlled car.' She raised her brows and glanced at their driver.

'But that is Yusuf. He is with me always.'

'I noticed.'

He shrugged. 'I have decided to accompany you on your flight.'

She struggled to keep the shock from her face. Now

more than ever he mustn't know her thoughts. 'When did you decide that?'

'When I said I would accompany you to the airport.'

It had seemed too easy. 'Why am I not surprised? It seems my instincts to run from you are better than I believed.'

He was amused. Nice. 'Then why did you get in the car with me?'

Stoke up that anger. It was a good defence against the urge to put her head on his shoulder. 'What choice did I have?'

Now he was openly smiling. 'True. None.'

Too handsome. Too charismatic. Too close to her heart. 'So where are we going?'

He lifted his head and though he wasn't smiling she could sense his deep love of the destination. 'I had planned to propose to you in the desert but cannot force you to leave the country with me. So we go to your oasis. Your desert camp instead of mine. I believe they have luxury tents in the desert that watch over the ancient rock of yours. There I will woo you until you have agreed to be with me for ever.'

'As what?' She raised her brows. Fighting back the excitement as she drummed up some form of defence. 'Am I to be your concubine? Your midwife for nieces and nephews?' His bride? She was fighting a losing battle and she wasn't losing it with him but with herself. She loved him, had from the first, and she suspected she always would, even if she never saw him again.

She tried again. 'I have to work.'

He shook his head. 'Not for a few days yet. I wish to share the desert with you. At night. To show you the stars.'

She raised her brows. 'Is that all you want to show me?'

His strong hand stroked her wrist. 'What can you possibly mean?'

The conversation like foreplay. Like a teasing breathe on her cheek. Like the squeeze of his fingers against hers. 'Are you sure you're not going to try to seduce me again?'

He leaned closer. 'I certainly hope so. But you would still have the option of refusal. Or you will have agreed to be my bride.'

His bride?

The word hung. Loaded with meaning. Loaded with promise.

So belovedly arrogant. 'You have tickets on yourself.'

'Ah. Colloquialisms. We must teach our children.'

She laughed. Gave up. Leant across and kissed him, and he drew her into his arms. She was home. 'Let's not go to the desert here. I will see your desert first and another day I can show you mine.'

He leaned forward and pressed the button to lower the window between them and Yusuf.

'Stop the car.'

The limousine glided to a stop beside a children's playground. A little like the park where their unexpected baby was born all those weeks ago. Swings, a slippery slide, two little girls and their mother on a park bench.

The door opened and he stepped past Yusaf and held his hand in to her. 'Come. This is what I wish to show you.'

His hand closed over hers and she gave it and herself into his keeping. She had no idea what he was doing but she would follow this man anywhere. Anytime. And that was the measure of it.

He crossed the little park to the play pit. A small boxed area with white sand and a fogotten plastic spade. He drew her into the square and she glanced around, saw the bemused interest on the mother and the two little girls until she turned back to him and fogot everything else.

He went down on one knee. Her mouth opened to tell him to get up but she shut it again. The love that shone from his face, the way he held her gaze, the unwavering strength as his hand held hers ordered her to listen, ignore distraction, and hear his need.

'In this bed of sand, that symbolises my heartland in some tiny way, I, Zafar Aasim Al Zamid request your answer.'

He paused and the sun beat down up on her hair, his eyes smiled, though his mouth was firm and solemn, and she could feel the trickle of sand as it filled her shoes, and crazily, never had there been anywhere as romantic as this.

'Will you, Carmen O'Shannessy, be my soulmate, my lover and my wife, be by my side, bear my children, and love me until the day we close our eyes together for the last time?'

Her eyes stung and she blinked away anything that could spoil this moment. What miracle had brought them to this? Him to this? This arrogant, generous, tender, tyrannical, amazing man she'd been destined to meet.

'Of course.' It came out less definite than she intended.

He deserved more than that. And more strongly so

that it carried across the sand in a wave of truth like an arrow to his heart—like he had pierced hers. 'I will. Of course I will.'

She loved him. He knew it. Zafar watched her breathe in and moisten her lips.

'I love you, Zafar, have done for weeks now, and offer you all of my heart, all of my soul, and if we are blessed, my dearest wish is to hold your babies in my arms.'

His heart surged in his chest and he rose, brushing the sand from his knees. 'My love.' He needed her in his arms.

His lips met hers as they stood in a square box of sand and the giggle of children drifted in the breeze until they both pulled back with smiles.

'Come.' He grinned down at her with the giggles of children warm between them. 'Now let us begin our life together.' They strolled arm in arm back to the car where Yosuf held the door open.

'Return to the hotel.'

Zafar handed her in and slid in after her. The car started and she caught Yusaf's smile in the rear vision mirror.

CHAPTER TWELVE

THEY married quietly in the presidential suite of the baby hotel. Tilly and Marcus acted as witnesses and then they flew back to Zandorro with barely two hours to celebrate.

They stopped overnight for the formal part of the Zandorran wedding, a civil ceremony attended by dignitaries and the King, but finally Zaraf could carry his bride into the desert. It took an hour to reach the oasis in his helicopter.

Late afternoon saw them come upon a circle of tents on the sand beside a stand of tall palm trees, ridiculously like a movie set with shaded pool and tethered camels. An outsized tent sprawled in the centre of the oasis as large as a six-room house, and Carmen couldn't keep the smile from her face.

'You did tell me?

He frowned. 'When?'

'In Coogee.'

He smiled as he remembered. 'Before the birth in the park.' He nodded. 'That is when I fell in love with you.'

He stroked her cheek. 'Tonight I hoped we could share a traditional wedding night Bedouin style. Our official Zandorron wedding will take place in a month, when I can introduce you as a married woman. This night is just for us.'

A woman approached, vaguely familiar, bowed to Carmen and more deeply to Zafar. 'I am Kiri's mother. And Yusuf's wife. My allegiance is yours.'

Zafar smiled at Carmen's shock. 'See, others love you as I do.'

He took Carmen's hand, turned her wrist and kissed her as if the caress belonged only to them. 'We will meet again an hour before sunset. Sheba will help prepare your bath.'

Bath? She shivered. More delay. Rituals and traditions that she must now learn. Lessons for the future. She nodded, glad that she had spent some time with the Zandorran women and had an idea of what was ahead, but inside she held a little trepidation. She wasn't good at being pampered and by the smile in Zafar's eyes he knew it.

She gazed at her husband, a man she had already wed twice, and still he hadn't taken her to bed.

'Patience,' he said.

Patience would kill them both. But she had to smile. She loved him, would always do so, and she knew, without the shadow of a doubt, he would always love her. But after tonight they would live, wonderfully, she hoped prolifically, between their two countries, and his strong face framed that light in his eyes as he watched her go. Dark eyes that promised the wait would be worth it.

In the two hours that followed she discovered she could learn to cope with the hardship of luxury but the slowness of it would take some getting used to.

Kiri's mother, Sheba, took her robe and helped her

settle into a claw-footed bath strewn with rose petals
and scented with oils that seemed to shimmer in the
water. When she left there she was gently massaged
with more aromatic oils and her toes and fingernails
painted with colourless shimmer. Her ankles and wrists
were traced with henna-coloured flowers and her hair
dried and dressed in a coil on top of her head.

Then came the veils. Layer after layer, promise after
promise to lie waiting for her husband to remove. Even
the one that covered her face and left just her kohled
eyes to stare back at herself, this stranger, this Eastern
princess she had never planned to be but could never
regret. Enough. She just wanted Zafar.

Memories of the caresses from their one time together, the promise of a night in his arms with nowhere
to rush off to. She could feel awareness gathering in her
belly and finally it was time to go through to Zafar's
rooms. The impatience grew until it consumed her and
she tried to slow her steps, but too long she'd been a
doer, used to being busy. This had all taken so long
when she knew where she wanted to be.

Zafar's heart squeezed. Finally she was here! He'd
been ready to tear down the tent to get to her. But the
wait had been worth it.

The veils, her eyes, her shapely body. How he loved
this woman. He could see her impatience, she made him
smile. He too had been impatient and he would leave her
in no doubt about that but seeing her like this...loving
her like this, loving her as a midwife, loving her naked,
loving her any wat she'd accept, as long as it was forever.

'You are so beautiful, my wife. Like a vision!'

The relief was there in Zafar's voice and she smiled at him. So he felt it too.

'Thank goodness you are, too.'

'My impatient wife.'

'My frustrating husband.'

He laughed out loud. 'Now I will introduce you to our traditional wedding feast.'

She rolled her eyes and he laughed again. 'Come, eat with me on cushions, drink from my cup and I will drink from yours. We will climb to the top of the dune and you will see the stars from the safety of my arms.'

Now that she had Zafar by her side, time passed swiftly. The wine they sipped tasted incredibly sweet, almonds and honey and no doubt secret ingredients she'd never discover, but its nectar left a trail of heat that coiled in her belly and spread back up over her breasts until time slowed to a second-by-second beat of the distant drum.

Tiny bells tinkled in the tent, discordant yet mesmerising music played softly in the background, and Zafar offered her morsels of flavoursome meat, tiny slivers of candied fruit and spoonfuls of rice so aromatic she closed her eyes. Each touch of his fingers to her mouth fired the flame that grew inside her.

When she returned the favour, he sipped from her fingertips, his eyes burning into hers, but his physical restraint was a more powerful aphrodisiac than if he had taken her finger into his mouth.

Never had she felt so aware of a man, so eager to feel his arms around her, so needing to be crushed against him, to be as one...

Zafar rose and held out his hand. His heart was bursting with wonder at this woman who had saved him from a darkness he had never thought would lift. Together they would achieve whatever goal was set before them.

'Come, wife. It is time we begin our life together.' She followed him to a platform of cushions set with candles, and outside a shadow guarded silently as they began a new dynasty that promised health and happiness to their kingdom.

* * * * *

CHAPTER ONE

'JUST because some bloke with more money than sense has bought the place, we don't need to go into a full-scale meltdown. He's bought the hospital, not our bodies and souls. We have to—'

Dr Elizabeth Jones was addressing her slightly panicked night shift staff outside the special care neonatal unit of Giles Hospital when a deep, slightly accented voice interrupted her.

'This word "bloke"? It means?'

She turned to face the source of the voice and her heart thudded to a halt, flopped around a bit and then went into a gallop rhythm she couldn't recall ever having felt before.

He wasn't drop-dead gorgeous, or even astoundingly good looking—he was just so, well, very *male*!

Arrogantly male!

His bearing, the slight tilt of his head, the imperious look in his near-black eyes, all shouted *leader of the pack*.

'Oh! Um—it's actually nothing. Aussie slang, you know—means a man…'

The words faltered out in dribs and drabs, her brain too busy cataloguing the stranger's attributes to construct sensible sentences.

Smooth olive skin, the slightest, neatest of clipped beards and moustache emphasising a straight nose and a strong jaw, not to mention framing lips like—well, she couldn't think how to describe the lips, although the words 'eminently kissable' had sneaked into her head.

He wore a dark suit, though the way he wore it—or maybe it was the suit itself—made her wonder if she'd ever really seen a man in a suit before.

'I see!' the lips she'd noticed before the suit mused. 'So the "bloke" who bought the hospital has more money than sense?'

It was the accent making her toes curl in her strappy sandals and sending feathery touches up and down her spine.

It *had* to be!

'It was a stupid thing to say,' Liz added, back in control. Almost. 'It's just that this particular hospital is hardly a money-making concern because part of the original trust that set it up ensures we treat a percentage of non-paying patients, although—'

She stopped before she insulted the man further—if this *was* the man with more money than sense—by assuming he'd change that rule. In fact, from the day the staff had learned the hospital was on the market they had all assumed it *would* be changed. After all, who in their right mind would invest in a business that ran at a loss?

Who would invest in a business that ran at a loss? Khalifa could see the words she didn't say flashing across her face.

An interesting face—arresting. Though maybe it was nothing more than the black-framed glasses that made it that way. What woman wore glasses with heavy black plastic frames these days? They did emphasise her clear creamy complexion but certainly didn't match her hair, ruthlessly restrained in a tidy knot behind her head, yet still revealing more than a hint of deep red in the darkness of it.

Intriguing, but he was here on business.

'I am the bloke you speak of, but I do not intend to make money from the hospital,' he assured her and the small group of staff who'd been her audience when he'd approached. 'I will continue to run it according to the original charter, but I hope to be able to bring some of the equipment up to date, and perhaps employ more staff.'

He paused. He'd intended outlining his plan to a meeting of the heads of the different departments, and had walked down to look again at the special care unit because it was his main interest. But now he was here, perhaps a less formal approach would be better.

Or did he want to spend more time studying the woman with the black glasses?

'My name is Sheikh Khalifa bin Saif al Zahn. Just Khalifa will suffice. I have bought the hospital in the hope that you, the staff, can help me and that I can, perhaps, offer those of you who wish to take part an interesting and hopefully enjoyable experience.'

The blank looks on the faces of the small group told him his explanation hadn't worked.

'I have built a new hospital in my homeland—an island state called Al Tinine—and it is operating well. My next wish is to set up a special care neonatal unit like this one. I am hoping to bring staff from my hospital to work here to gain an insight into how *you* work, and I would like to think some of the staff at this hospital would enjoy working for short periods in my country.'

He was certain this further explanation had been perfectly clear—perhaps the blank looks were caused by surprise.

Then the woman—he knew from photos she was Dr

Elizabeth Jones, the one he wanted most of all—although in the photos she hadn't had the ghastly glasses and hadn't looked quite so—attractive?—stepped forward, knocking a pile of papers from the top of a filing cabinet and muttering under her breath before holding out her hand. One of the other women began gathering the papers, tapping them into a neat pile.

'How do you do, Dr Khalifa?' Dr Jones said formally, adding her name. 'Forgive us for reacting like dumbstruck idiots, but it isn't often anyone takes notice of our small hospital, let alone wanders in and offers us a chance to visit other countries. As for new equipment, we should be dancing with glee and cheering wildly. We make do with what we have and our success rate here in the special care unit in particular is first class, but the money from the trust that set up the hospital has been running out for some years.'

Khalifa heard the words but his brain had stopped working.

The woman he wanted, now she'd stepped out from behind the filing cabinet on which she'd been leaning, was undoubtedly pregnant. Not a huge bump, but pregnant enough to notice.

The shadow of pain, the fiercer thrust of guilt that chased him through each day had registered the bump immediately.

Dr Elizabeth Jones was as pregnant as Zara had been the last time he'd seen her...

Realising he'd dropped the conversational ball, Dr Jones spoke again.

'It sounds a wonderful opportunity for our staff to travel to your country and I'm sure we'd be very happy to welcome staff from your hospital, to learn from them as well as show them how we do things.'

There was a slight frown creasing the creamy skin, as

if she wasn't absolutely certain of the truth of her words, but before he could decide, or even thank her for her kindness, a faint bell sounded and the group of women broke away immediately.

'Excuse me,' the doctor said. 'That was an end-of-shift meeting we were having. The new shift is on duty and I'm needed.'

She whisked away from the makeshift office—was one small desk and the filing cabinet in this alcove off the hall all they had?—and entered the glass-walled room where two lines of cribs held tiny babies. Two women—nurses, he assumed—in black and white patterned smocks leant over one of the cribs, straightening as Dr Jones joined them. Uncertain as to the isolation status of the ward, he remained outside, watching through the glass as she bent over the crib, touching the infant's cheek with one finger while reading the monitor beside it.

One of the nurses had wheeled a small trolley laden with drugs and equipment to the side of the crib but in the end Dr Jones straightened and shook her head, writing something on the chart at the end of the crib and stroking the baby's cheek, smiling down at the tiny being, before leaving the unit.

'You're still here!'

She spoke abruptly, obviously distracted by whatever it was that had summoned her to the baby's crib, then she proved his guess correct by adding, 'She has a little periodic apnoea but I don't want to put her back on CPAP.'

'Has she just come off it?' he asked, and the woman frowned at him.

'You understood that? I was really thinking out loud. Very rude, but I suppose if you've built one hospital and bought another, you probably do know a few things about medicine.'

'I know a few,' he said. 'Enough to get me through my medical degree and a follow-up in surgery.'

'I'm sorry,' she said, flashing a smile that almost hid a flush of embarrassment in her cheeks. 'It's just that health care seems to have become big business these days and the business owners don't necessarily know anything about medicine. But I'm holding you up. You'll want to see the rest of the place, and talk to staff in other departments, won't you?'

'Not right now,' he began, uncertain now that the woman's pregnancy had thrown his plans into disarray. 'You see, I'm particularly interested in this special care unit because I *had* hoped to persuade you to come to Al Tinine to set one up. I have heard and read so many good things about the work you do here, running a small unit that offers premature babies surprisingly successful outcomes on a limited budget.'

She studied him, her head tilted slightly to one side, and he wondered what she was seeing.

A foreigner in an expensive suit?

A bloke with more money than sense?

Guilty on both counts!

'So are you looking for something similar in size? Will there be limitations on the budget of the unit you wish to set up?'

Shocked by the assumption, he rushed into speech.

'Of course not—that wasn't what I meant at all. Naturally, we won't be looking at gold-plated cribs, but I would want you to have the very best equipment, and appropriate staffing levels, whatever you deemed necessary for the best possible outcomes for premature infants born in the southern part of my country.'

She smiled again—not much of a smile but enough

to light a spark in the wide blue eyes she hid behind the chunky glasses.

'Gold plate would probably be toxic anyway,' she said, then the smile slid away and the little crease of a frown returned. 'My next question would be, are you setting it up as a working, effective unit that will give preemie babies the very best chance of leading normal lives later on, or are you putting it in because you think hospitals should have one?'

The question shocked him even more than the previous assumption had, although would he have considered it if not for Zara's and the baby's deaths?

That thought angered him.

'Are you always this blunt?' he demanded, scowling at her now. 'I expect you to set up a properly organised special care neonatal unit with some facilities for infants who would, in a larger hospital, go into a neonatal intensive care unit. I understand you have such facilities in your unit here at Giles, which is one of the reasons I chose this hospital.'

No need to tell her that the other reason was because he'd heard and read such impressive reports of *her* work with neonates.

'Fair enough,' she said easily, apparently unperturbed by his scowl and growling reply. 'But when you said "you", did you mean "you" as in someone from the unit or me personally?'

Direct, this woman!

'I did mean you personally,' he told her, equally direct. 'It is you I wanted—or was you.'

'And having seen me, you've changed your mind?' The words were a challenge, one he could see repeated in the blue eyes for all she hid them behind those revolting glasses. 'Too tall? Too thin? Wrong sex, although the

Elizabeth part of my name must have been something of a clue?'

'You're pregnant.'

He spoke before he could consider the implication of his statement, and as her face flushed slightly and her eyes darkened with some emotion he couldn't read, he knew he'd made a mistake.

A big mistake!

'So?'

The word was as steely as the thrust of a well-honed sword, but as he struggled to parry the thrust she spoke again.

'Pregnancy is a condition, not an illness, as I'm sure you know. I have worked through the first thirty-two weeks and I intend to continue working until the baby is born, returning to work…'

The fire died out of her and she reached out to support herself on the filing cabinet behind which her 'condition' had originally been hidden. The air in the alcove had thickened somehow, and though he knew you couldn't inhale things like despair and sadness, that was how it tasted.

'Actually—' the word, her voice strong again, brought him back to the present '—a trip away right now might be just what the doctor ordered. I presume if you're setting up a neonatal unit you already have obstetricians and a labour ward so my having the baby there wouldn't be a problem. As far as this unit is concerned, we have visiting paediatricians who are rostered on call, plus there's a new young paediatrician just dying to take over my job, so it would all fit in.'

The steel was back in her voice and he wondered if it came from armour she'd built around herself for some reason. She'd shown no emotion at all when she'd talked about her pregnancy, no softening of her voice, just a statement of facts and enquiries about obstetric services.

Neither did she wear a wedding ring, although handling tiny babies she probably wouldn't...

'Well?'

Liz knew she'd sounded far too abrupt, flinging the word at him like that, but the idea of getting away from the turmoil in her life had come like a lifeline thrown to a drowning sailor. She was slowly learning to live with the grief of Bill's death, but Oliver's continued existence in a coma in this very hospital was a weight too heavy to carry, especially as his parents had banned her from seeing him.

Oliver's state of limbo put her into limbo as well—her and the baby—while the unanswerable questions just kept mounting and mounting.

Would Oliver come out of the coma? Would his brain be functioning if he did? And would he want the baby?

She sighed, then realised that the man had been speaking while she was lost in her misery.

'I'm sorry,' she said, and this time heard him asking about passports and how soon she could leave the country.

'Right now, today!' she responded, then regretted sounding so over-eager. 'To be fair, I'd need a week or so to bring my replacement up to date. She's worked here before, which is why she wanted to come back, so it won't take much. And it's not as if I won't be coming back— you're talking about my setting up the unit and getting it running, not offering a permanent placement, aren't you?'

The man looked bemused, but finally he nodded, though it seemed to her that his face had hardened and the arrogance she'd sensed within him when he'd first spoken had returned.

He didn't like her—not one bit.

'There is no one with whom you should discuss this first?' he asked.

Liz shrugged.

'Not really. Providing I leave the unit in good hands, the hospital hierarchy won't complain, and as you've probably already discussed your idea of staff swapping with them, they won't be surprised. And this first trip shouldn't take long, anyway. It will be a matter of organising space, equipment and staff. It's not as if you'll be taking in babies until those are all in place.'

Now he was frowning. It had to be the pregnancy. He obviously wasn't used to pregnant women working. Well, it was time he got used to it.

The silence stretched, so awkward she was wondering if she should break it, but what could she say to this stranger that wasn't just more chat? And though she certainly hadn't given that impression earlier, she really didn't do chat.

Relief flooded her as he spoke again.

'Very well. I will be in touch later today with a date and time for our departure. I have your details from the HR office. In the meantime, you might make a list of equipment you will require. My hospital is the same size as Giles, and I would anticipate the unit would be similar in size to this one.'

The words were so coldly formal Liz had to resist an impulse to drop a curtsey, but as the man wheeled away from her, she gave in to bad behaviour, poked out her tongue and put her thumbs to her ears, waggling her fingers at him.

'He'd have caught you if he'd turned around,' her friend Gillian said, before taking up what was really worrying her. 'And what on earth are you thinking? Agreeing to traipse off to a place you've never heard of, with a strange man, and pregnant, and with Oliver the way he is, not to mention leaving all of us in the lurch?'

Liz smiled. The sentiments may have been badly expressed but Gillian's concern for her was genuine. Could she explain?

'You know Oliver's family won't let me near him,' she began, 'and Carol is the perfect replacement, and she's available so no one's being left in the lurch. That said, what is it you're most worried about—the pregnancy, the strange man, or that I've never heard of this Al Tinine?'

'It's the decision,' Gilliam told her. 'Making it like that. It's totally out of character for you. You took months mulling over doing the surrogacy thing—could you do it, should you do it, would you get too attached to the baby? You asked yourself a thousand questions. And while I know you've been through hell these last few months, do you really think running away will help?'

Liz shook her head.

'Nothing will help,' she muttered, acknowledging the dark cloud that had enshrouded her since Bill's death, 'but if I'm going to be miserable, I might as well be miserable somewhere new. Besides, setting up a unit from scratch might be the distraction I need. I love this place, would bleed for it, but you know full well the staff could run it without much help from me, so it's hardly a challenge any more.'

'But the baby?'

Gillian's voice was hesitant, and Liz knew why. It was the question everyone had been wanting to ask since the accident that had killed her brother and put his partner in hospital, but the one subject they hadn't dared broach.

Liz shrugged her shoulders, the helplessness she felt about the situation flooding through her.

'I've no idea,' she admitted slowly. 'The accident wasn't

exactly part of the plan when I agreed to carry a baby for Bill and Oliver, and with Oliver the way he is and me not being able to even see him, who knows what happens next? Certainly not me! All I can do is keep going.'

She suspected she sounded hard and uncaring, but from the moment she'd agreed to carry a child for her brother and his partner, an agreement made, as Gillian had reminded her, after much soul-searching, she'd steeled herself not to get emotionally involved with a baby that would never be hers. She'd played it music Bill and Oliver loved, told it long stories about its parents, cautious always to remember it was their baby, not hers.

It would never be hers.

Now its future was as uncertain as her own, and she had no idea which way to turn. No wonder the challenge the man had offered had seemed like a lifeline—a tiny chink of light shining through the dark, enveloping cloud.

Then another thought struck her. Had the man said 'our' departure? Did he intend to hang around?

She felt a shiver travel down her spine, and her toes curled again…

Khalifa sat in the hospital's boardroom, listening to his lawyers speaking to their counterparts from the hospital, but his mind was on a woman with heavy-framed glasses, a pregnant woman who seemed totally uninvolved in her own pregnancy. Zara had been transformed by hers, overjoyed by the confirmation, then delighting in every little detail, so wrapped up in the changes happening in her body that any interest she might ever have had in her husband—not much, he had to admit—had disappeared.

To be fair to her, the arranged marriage had suited him as he'd been building the hospital at the time, busy with the thousand details that had always seemed to need his attention, far too busy to be dealing with wooing a woman. Later, Zara's involvement in her pregnancy had freed him from guilt that he spent so little time with her, though in retrospect…

He passed a hand across his face, wiping away any trace of emotion that might have slipped through his guard. Emotion weakened a man and the history of his tribe, stretching back thousands of years, proved it had survived because of the strength of its leaders. Now, in particular, with El Tinine taking its place among its oil-rich neighbours and moving into a modern world, he, the leader, had to be particularly strong.

'Of course we will do all we can to assist you in selecting the equipment you need for the new unit in your hospital,' the chief medical officer was saying. 'Dr Jones has updated our unit as and when funds became available. She knows what works best, particularly in a small unit where you are combining different levels of patient need. I'll get my secretary to put together a list of equipment we've bought recently and the suppliers' brochures. Dr Jones will be able to tell you why she made the choices she did.'

He hurried out of the room.

Dr Jones… The name echoed in Khalifa's head.

Something about the woman was bothering him, something that went beyond her apparent disregard for her pregnancy. Was it because she'd challenged him?

Not something Zara had ever done.

But Zara had been his wife, not his colleague, so it couldn't be that…

Was it because Dr Jones running from something—the father of her baby?—that she'd leapt at his offer to come to Al Tinine? There had been no consultation with anyone, no consideration of family or friends, just how soon could she get away.

Yes, she was running from something, it had to be that, but did it matter? And why was he thinking about her when he had so much else he hoped to achieve in this short visit?

It had to be her pregnancy and the memories it had stirred.

The guilt…

He, too, left the room, making his way back to the neo-natal ward, telling himself he wanted to inspect it more closely, telling himself it had nothing to do with Dr Jones.

She was bent over the crib she'd been called to earlier and as she straightened he could read the concern on her face. She left the unit, sliding open the door and almost knocking him over in her haste to get to the little alcove.

'Sorry,' she said automatically, then stopped as she re-alised whom she'd bumped into. 'Oh, it's you! I *am* sorry— I'm a klutz, always knocking things over or running into people. My family said it was because I live in my head, and I suppose that's right at the moment. The baby in that crib was abandoned—found wrapped in newspaper in a park—and the police haven't been able to trace the mother. We call her Alexandra, after the park.'

Liz heard her rush of words and wondered what it was about this man that turned her into a blithering idiot, ad-mitting to her clumsiness, thrusting ancient family his-tory at a total stranger.

'The baby was found in a park?'

Despite the level of disbelief in the man's voice, her toes curled *again*. This was ridiculous. It had to stop. Probably it was hormonal…

'Last week,' she told him, 'and, really, there's nothing much wrong with her—she was a little hypothermic, oc-casional apnoea, but now…'

'Who will take her?'

Liz sighed.

'That's what's worrying me,' she admitted. 'She'll be taken into care. And while I know the people who care for babies and children are excellent, she won't get a permanent placement because she obviously has a mother somewhere. And right now when she desperately needs to bond with someone, she'll be going somewhere on a temporary basis.'

Why was she telling this stranger her worries? Liz wondered, frowning at the man as if he'd somehow drawn the words from her by...

Osmosis?

Magic?

She had no idea by what. Perhaps it was because he was here that she'd rattled on, because worrying about Alexandra was preferable to worrying about her own problems.

'You think the mother might return to claim her? Is that why the placement is temporary?'

Liz shook her head.

'I doubt she'll return to claim her. If she'd wanted her, why leave her in the first place? But if the authorities find the mother, they will do what they can to help her should she decide to keep the baby. It's a delicate situation but, whatever happens, until little Alexandra is officially given up for adoption, she'll be in limbo.'

Like me, Liz thought, and almost patted her burgeoning belly.

The man was frowning at her.

'You are concerned?' he asked.

'Of course I'm concerned,' Liz told him. 'This is a baby we're talking about. She's already had a rough start, so she deserves the very best.'

It didn't add up, Khalifa decided. This woman's attitude to a stranger's child, and her apparent disregard for her own pregnancy, although perhaps he was reading her wrongly. Perhaps this was her work face, and at home she talked and sang to her unborn child as much as Zara had to hers.

She *and* her partner talked and sang—

'Will the authorities also look for the baby's father?' he asked, and surprised a smile out of her.

'Harder to do, especially without the mother, although Alexandra's plight has been well publicised in local and interstate papers. The father may not have known the mother was pregnant. A man spends the night with a woman, and these days probably takes precautions, but there's no sign that flashes up in the morning, reminding him to check back in a few weeks to see if she's pregnant.'

There was no bitterness in the words and he doubted very much that her pregnancy had resulted from a chance encounter. Klutz she might be, but everything he'd read about her suggested she was very intelligent.

Though klutz?

'What's a klutz?'

Now she laughed, and something shifted in his chest.

Was it because the laughter changed her from a reasonably attractive woman to a beautiful one, lit from within by whatever delight the question had inspired?

Because the blue eyes he was drawn to behind the glasses were sparkling with humour?

He didn't think so. No, it was more the laughter itself—so free and wholesome—so good to hear. Did people laugh out loud less these days or was it just around him they were serious?

'It's a word we use for a clumsy person. I'm forever dropping things—not babies, of course—or knocking stuff over, or running into people. Hence the really, really horrible glasses. Rimless ones, thin gold frames, fancy plastic—I kill them all. Bumping into a door, or dropping them, or sitting on them, I've broken glasses in ways not yet invented. I tried contact lenses for a while but kept losing them—usually just one, but always the same one. So I had five right eyes and no left, which would have been okay for a five-eyed monster, of course. Anyway, now I go for the heaviest, strongest, thickest frames available. I'm a typical klutz!'

She hesitated, as if waiting for his comment on klutzdom, but he was still considering his reaction to her laughter and before he could murmur some polite assurance that she probably wasn't that bad, she was speaking again.

'Not that you need to worry about my work abilities, I'm always totally focussed when I'm on the job. In fact, that's probably my problem outside it—in my head I'm still in the unit, worrying about one or other of our small charges.'

Yes, he could understand that, but what he couldn't understand was how freely this woman chatted with a virtual stranger. Every instinct told him she wasn't a chatterer, yet here she was, rattling on about her clumsiness and monsters and an abandoned baby.

Was she using words to hide something?

Talking to prevent him asking questions?

He had no idea, but he'd come to see the unit, not concern himself with this particular employee.

Which was why he was surprised to hear himself asking if there was somewhere other than this alcove off the passageway where they could sit down and talk.

'Of course! We've got a canteen in the courtyard, really lovely, but I suppose you've seen it already. I'll just let someone know where I'll be.'

She stepped, carefully, around him and entered the unit, stopping to speak to one of the nurses then peering behind a screen and speaking to someone before joining him outside.

'How much space do you have at this new hospital of yours?' she asked, the little frown back between blue eyes that were now sombre.

He glanced back at the unit, measuring it in his mind.

'I've set aside an area, maybe twice the size of what you have here,' he told her, and was absurdly pleased when the frown disappeared.

'That's great,' she declared, clearly delighted. 'We can have decent, reclining armchairs for the visiting parents and a separate room where mothers can express milk or breastfeed instead of being stuck behind a tatty screen. Beginning breastfeeding is particularly hard for our mothers. The babies have been getting full tummies with absolutely no effort on their part because the milk comes down a tube. Then suddenly they're expected to work for it, and it's frustrating for both parties.'

She was leading him along a corridor, striding along and talking at the same time, her high-heeled strappy sandals making her nearly as tall as he was.

A pregnant woman in high-heeled strappy sandals?

A doctor at work in high-heeled strappy sandals?

Not that her legs didn't look fantastic in them...

What *was* he thinking!

It was the pregnancy thing that had thrown him. Too close to home—too many memories surfacing. If only he'd been more involved with Zara and the pregnancy, if only he'd been home more often, if only...

'Here,' his guide declared, walking into the leafy courtyard hung with glorious flowering orchids. 'This, as you can see, is a special place. Mr Giles, who left the bequest for the hospital, was a passionate orchid grower and these orchids are either survivors from his collection or have been bred from his plants.'

Khalifa looked around, then shook his head.

'I did notice the courtyard on one of my tours of the hospital, but didn't come into it. It's like an oasis of peace and beauty in a place that is very busy and often, I imagine, very sombre. I should have thought of something similar. I have been considering practicality too much.'

His companion smiled at him.

'Just don't take space out of my unit to arrange a courtyard,' she warned. 'Now, would you like tea or coffee, or perhaps a cold drink?'

'Let me get it, Dr Jones,' he said, reaching into his pocket for his wallet. 'You'll have…?'

'I'm limiting myself to one coffee a day so I make it a good one. Coffee, black and strong and two sugars, and it's Liz,' she replied, confusing him once again.

'Liz?' he repeated.

'Short for Elizabeth—Liz, not Dr Jones.'

He turned away to buy the coffees, his mind repeating the short name, while some primitive instinct sprang to life inside him, warning him of something…

But what?

'Two coffees, please. Strong, black and two sugars in both of them.'

He gave his order, and paid the money, but his mind was trying to grasp at the fleeting sensation that had tapped him on the shoulder.

Because of their nomadic lifestyle in an often hostile country, an instinct for danger was bred into him and all his tribal people, but this woman couldn't represent a danger, so that couldn't be it.

But as he took the coffees from the barista, the sensation came again.

It couldn't be because they drank their coffee the same way! Superstition might be alive and well in his homeland, but he'd never believed in any of the tales his people told of mischievous djinns interfering in people's lives, or of a conflagration of events foretelling disaster. Well, not entirely! And a lot of people probably drank their coffee strong and black with two sugars.

Besides, he only drank it this way when he was away from home. At home, the coffee was already sweet and he'd drink three tiny cups of the thick brew in place of one of these...

CHAPTER TWO

COULD ten days really have flown so quickly?

Of course, deciding on what clothes she should take had consumed a lot of Liz's spare time. Khalifa...could she really call him that? So far she'd avoided using his name directly, but if she was going to be working with him she'd have to use it some time.

Not that she didn't use it in her head, sounding it out, but only in rare moments of weakness, for even saying it started the toe curling—and she had to stretch them as hard as she could to prevent it happening.

Anyway, Khalifa had given her a pile of wonderful information brochures about his country, explaining that the capital, Al Jabaya, was in the north, and that his eldest brother, while he had been the leader, had, over twenty years, built a modern city there. The southern part of Al 'inine, however, was known as the Endless Desert, and the area, although well populated, had been neglected. It was in the south, in the oasis town of Najme, that Khalifa had built his hospital.

For clothes Liz had settled on loose trousers and long shift-like shirts for work, and long loose dresses for casual occasions or lolling around at home, wherever home turned out to be. Wanting to respect the local customs, she'd made sure all the garments were modest, with sleeves and high necklines.

Now here she was, in a long, shapeless black dress—black so it wouldn't show the things she was sure to spill on herself on a flight—waiting outside her apartment block just as the sun was coming up. Gillian, who would house—and cat-sit, waited beside her.

'Your coach approaches, Cinderella,' Gillian said, as a sleek black limousine turned into the street.

'Wrong fairy-tale, Gill,' Liz retorted. 'Mine's the one with Scheherazade telling the Sultan story after story so she didn't get her head chopped off next morning.'

Had she sounded panicked that Gill looked at her with alarm?

'You're not worrying *now* about this trip, are you? Haven't you left it a bit late? What's happened? You've been so, well, not excited but alive again.'

The vehicle pulled up in front of them before Liz could explain that sheer adrenalin had carried her this far, but now she was about to depart, she wasn't having second thoughts but third and fourth and fifth right down to a thousandth.

Better not to worry Gill with that!

'I'm fine,' she said, then felt her toes curl and, yes, he was there, stepping smoothly out of the rear of the monstrous car just as she tripped on the gutter and all but flung herself into his arms.

He was quick, she had to give him that—catching her elbow first then looping an arm around her waist to steady her.

She'd have been better off falling, she decided as her body went into some kind of riotous reaction that was very hard to put down to relief that she *hadn't* fallen!

'You must look where you are going,' he said, but a

though the words came out as an order, his voice was gruff with what sounded like concern.

For her?

How could she know?

And did it really matter?

The driver, meanwhile, had picked up her small case and deposited it in the cavernous trunk so there was nothing else for Liz to do but give Gill a quick kiss goodbye and step into the vehicle.

In the back.

With Khalifa.

'Wow, look at the space in here. I've never been in a limo!' she said, while her head reminded her that it had been years since she'd talked like a very young teenager. Perhaps she was better saying nothing.

'Would you like a drink? A cold soda of some kind?'

Khalifa had opened a small cabinet, revealing an array of beverages. The sight of them, and the bottles of wine and champagne—this at six-thirty in the morning—delighted Liz so much she relaxed and even found a laugh.

'You're talking to a klutz, remember. I can just imagine the damage a fizzy orange drink could do to this upholstery. Besides, I've just had my coffee fix so I should manage an hour's drive to the airport without needing further refreshment.'

It was the laugh that surprised him every time, Khalifa realised. He hadn't heard it often in the last ten days but every time it caught his attention and he had to stop himself from staring at his new employee, her face transformed to a radiant kind of beauty by her delight in something. Usually something absurd.

'So tell me about Najme,' she said, a smile still lingering on her lips and what sounded like genuine interest in her voice.

He seized the opportunity with both hands. Talking about Najme, his favourite place on earth, was easy.

And it would prevent him thinking about his companion and the way she affected him—especially the way she'd affected him when he'd caught her in his arms...

'Najme means star. It has always been considered the star of the south because of the beauty of the oasis on which it is built. Date palms flourish there, and grass and ferns, while reeds thrive by the water's edge. When oil was discovered, because Al Jabaya was a port from ancient times, used for trading vessels and the pearling fleet, it seemed right that the capital should be built there. So my brother and his advisors laid out plans and the city grew, but it virtually consumed all his time, and the south was not exactly neglected but left behind. Now it is up to me to bring this area into the twenty-first century, but I must do it with caution and sensitivity.'

He looked out the window as the sleek vehicle glided along a motorway, seeing houses, streets, shops and factories flash by. It was the sensitivity that worried him, bringing change without changing the values and heritage of his people.

It was because of the sensitivity he'd married Zara, a young woman of the south, hoping her presence by his side would make his changes more acceptable.

And then he'd let her down...

'Is the hospital your first project there?' his colleague asked. Pleased to be diverted, he explained how his brother had seen to the building of better housing, and schools right across the country, and had provided free medical care at clinics for the people in the south, but he had deemed the hospital in Al Jabaya to be sufficient for the country, even providing medical helicopters to fly people there.

'But the people of Najme, all the people of the south, have always been wary of the northerners. The southern regions were home to tribes of nomads who guarded trade routes and traded with the travellers, providing fresh food and water, while Al Jabaya has always been settled. The Al Jabayans were sailors, pearl divers and also traders, but their trade has been by sea, so they have always been in contact with people of other lands. They are more... worldly, I suppose you would say.'

'And you?'

The question was gentle, as if she sensed the emotion he felt when talking of his people.

'My mother was from the south. My brother's mother was from the north, so when she grew old, my father took a second wife—actually, I think she was the third but that's not talked of often. Anyway, for political reasons he took a wife from a southern tribe, so my ties are to the south. My wife, too, was a southerner...'

He stopped, aware he'd spoken to no one about Zara since her death, and none of his friends had used her name—aware, no doubt, that it was a subject he wouldn't discuss.

'Your wife,' Liz Jones prompted, even gentler now.

'She died in childbirth. The baby was premature, and she, too, died.'

Liz heard the agony in his voice, and nothing on this earth could have prevented her resting her hand on his.

'So of course you want the unit. It will be the very best we can achieve.' She squeezed his fingers, just a comforting pressure. 'I know it won't bring back your wife or child, but I promise you it will be a fitting memorial to them and be something you'll be proud of.'

Then, feeling utterly stupid, she removed her hand and tucked it in her lap lest it be tempted to touch him again.

This time the silence between them went beyond awkward and, aware she'd overstepped a boundary of some kind, Liz had no idea how to ease the tension. She leaned forward, intending to take a drink from the cabinet—but as she'd already pointed out, spilling fizzy orange soda all over the seat and undoubtedly splashing her new boss probably wasn't the answer.

Instead, she pulled one of the information leaflets he'd given her from her capacious handbag and settled back into the corner to read it. If he wanted the silence broken, let him break it.

He didn't, and, determined not to start blithering again, she refused to comment when the car sailed past the wide road that led to the international air terminal. Sailed past the road to the domestic one as well, then turned into another road that led to high wire fences and a gate guarded by a man in a security uniform.

To Liz's surprise, the man at the gate saluted as the gates swung open, and the limo took them out across wide tarmac to stop beside a very large plane, its sleek lines emphasised by the streaks and swirls of black and gold paint on its side. It took her a moment to recognise the decoration as Arabic script and she could be silent no longer.

'What does it say?' she asked, totally enthralled by the flowing lines, the curves and squiggles.

'Najme,' her host replied, and before she could ask more, he was out of the limo and speaking to some kind of official who waited at the bottom of the steps.

The driver opened the door on Liz's side and she slid out, not as elegantly as her companion had but, thankfully without falling flat on her face.

'This gentleman will stamp your passport and one of my pilots will check your luggage,' Khalifa told her, al business now. 'It is a precaution he has to take, I'm sure you understand.'

Totally out of her depth, Liz just nodded, grateful really that she had no decisions to make. She handed over her passport, then hovered near the bottom of the steps until a young man came down and invited her inside.

'Khalifa will bring your passport and the pilot will put your luggage on board,' he told her. 'I am Saif, Khalifa's assistant. On flights I act as steward. He prefers not to have strangers around.'

Liz smiled to herself, certain the young man had no idea just how much he'd told her about his master. But there was no time to dwell on these little details for she'd reached the top of the steps, and entered what seemed like another world.

There was nothing flashy about the interior of the plane, just opulent comfort, with wide, well-padded armchairs in off-white leather, colourful cushions stacked on them, and more, larger, flat cushions on the floor near the walls of the aircraft. A faint perfume hung in the air, something she couldn't place—too delicate to be musk, more roses with a hint of citrus.

'Sit here,' Saif said, then he waited until she sank obediently into one of the armchairs before showing her where the seat belt was and how a small table swung out from beside the chair and a monitor screen opened up on it.

'You will find a list of the movies and other programmes in the book in the pocket on the other side of the chair, and you can use your laptop once we're in the air. Press this button if there's anything you require and I will do my best to help you.'

Saif turned away, and Liz realised Khalifa had entered the plane. He came towards her, enquired politely about her comfort, handed back her passport then took the chair on the other side of the plane.

'All this space to carry two people?' she asked, unable to stop herself revealing her wonder in the experience.

'It can be transformed into many configurations,' Khalifa replied. 'The flight time is fifteen hours, and I thought you might be more comfortable in a bed, so the back of the cabin is set up for your convenience.'

'With a bed?'

It went beyond Scheherazade's fantastic stories, and now Liz forgot about hiding her wonder.

'I've read about executive jets, but never thought I'd experience anything like this. May I have a look?'

Was it the excitement in her voice that stirred the man? She had no idea, but at least he'd smiled, and as she felt a slight hitch in her breathing, she told herself it was better that he remained remote and unreachable—far better that he didn't smile.

'Wait until we're in the air. The aircraft door is closed and I assume the pilot is preparing for take-off. Because we have to compete with both the international and the domestic flights for take-off slots, we can't delay. But while we're on the ground, Saif could get you a drink. Perhaps champagne to celebrate your first flight in an executive jet?'

'I can celebrate with orange juice,' Liz said, and although Khalifa was sure he saw her right hand move towards her stomach, she drew back before she touched it. The mystery of her pregnancy—or her attitude to it—deepened. He'd seen a lot of Liz Jones in the last ten days and not by even the slightest sign had she acknowledged the baby she carried.

Neither had she ever mentioned the baby's father, an